THE ALCHEMIST THE SIREN & THE THIEF

THE ALCHEMIST THE SIREN & THE THIEF
Mia Dorsch

Paperback ISBN: 979-8-9916886-0-4
Hardcover ISBN: 979-8-9916886-1-1

*For Mairin, Gavin, and Caleb, my real-life Alouette, Atlas, and Edwin.
And Eric, and Owen, and Bella, the rest of our crew.*

To no scurvy!

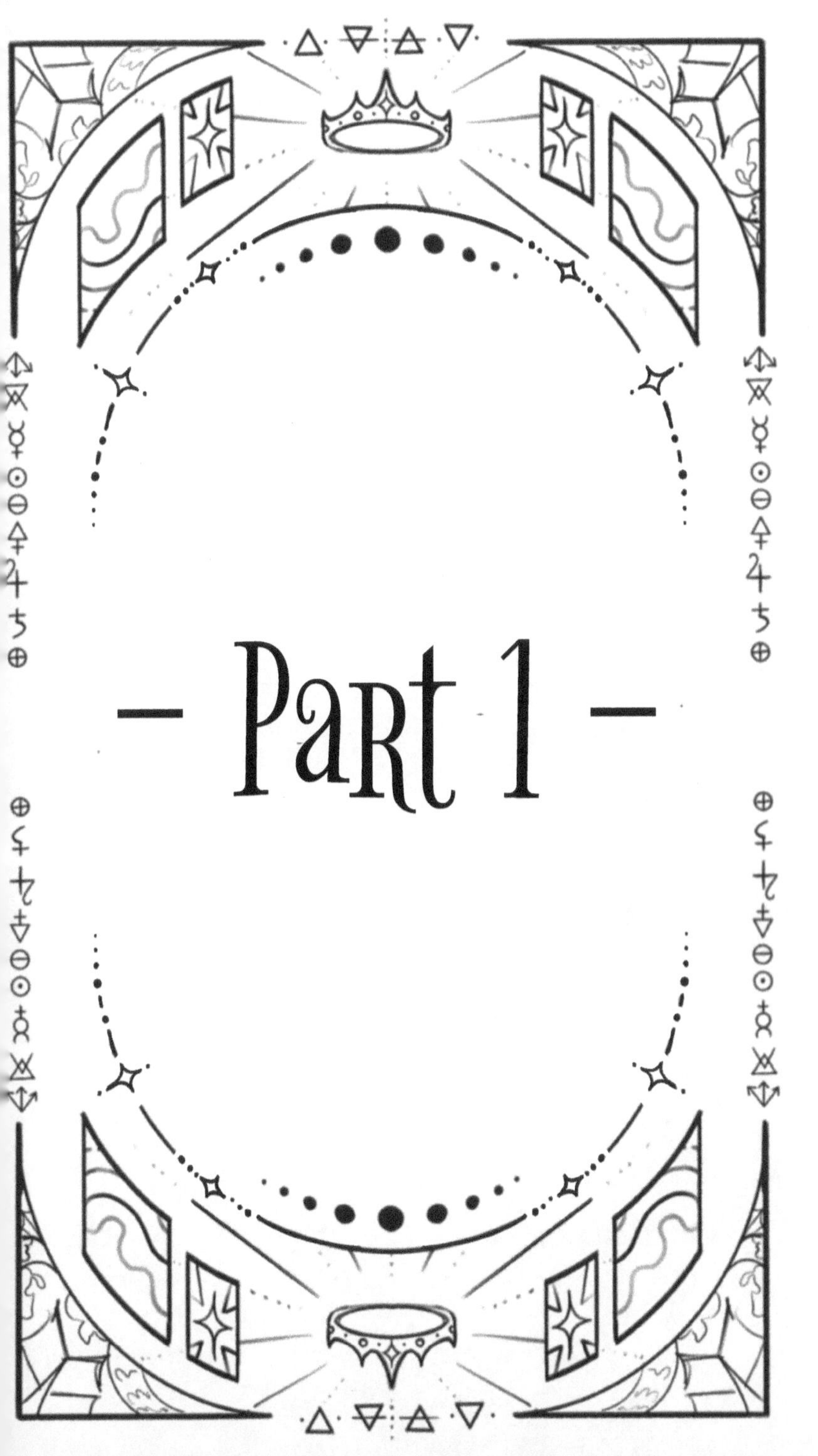

– Part 1 –

PROLOGUE

— The Alchemist —

"Walk the plank," they shout.

I'm jabbed with the tips of swords and backs of brooms from behind. The gulls above screech and call. I look up. They're only small white specs in the endless blue sky. I'll only be a drop in the vast sea below. Hands tied behind my back, I stumble forward. I told them they didn't need to do that. After all, I can't swim. The rickety board beneath me sways. Somewhere between the sea and the sky, land nowhere to be seen, the wind whips my curls against my sunburned cheeks.

"Is this really necessary?" I lean over the edge. The blue waves churn like the acid brewing in my stomach. "I'm not a witch, you know."

Roars, restless and resentful, ring out.

Those aboard know that well.

Because, in their eyes, I am something far, far worse.

Chapter 1

— The Alchemist —

I thought I'd die in a cool way, like in battle. My sword held high as I took a fatal blow. My comrades rushing around me. Remembered as a hero. My story isn't like that. Pirates are nasty fellows. With silver teeth and draped in fool's gold, unsuspecting victims perish at their hooked hands every day. My death wasn't anything special. No one would have spoken of my valiant sacrifice.

Luckily, I didn't actually die.

I'm wide awake now, staring at the sky. My senses are as sharp as ever. Salt. Blinding sunlight. And that sickening sway.

Where am I? I want to ask, but my lips are so chapped that it hurts when I catch myself gasping. If pirates won't be my end, dehydration surely will be. I blink a few times before taking a moment to fully survey my surroundings. *A wooden lifeboat?*

If I stretched far enough, I could latch onto both the right and left. Two planks spanning the width act as terribly uncomfortable seats. The ship I had been thrown off of is nowhere to be seen, and it wasn't a vessel to sneeze at. Just how much time has passed?

"Aye, aye! Capt'n, she's awake." A boy with auburn hair tied in a ponytail sits across from me on this tiny boat, eyes glued to me, lips pulled into a smirk that bares all his teeth. He forks over a canteen, which I quickly yank the top off of and take a swig, not even considering what could be in it. Another young man, not too much older than I, is next to him, turned away. While the breeze blows through his black hair, I wonder how anyone could watch those waves without retching. I shiver.

The captain tunes out the other boy while his blue eyes take a moment to look me over before going back out to sea.

"You're welcome, by the way." The auburn-haired boy leans toward me. "We saved you." He then continues to row. I scan the horizon before sinking back down.

"You don't know who I am, do you?" I murmur.

"No thank you? Rude, much? I don't care who you are, I—"

"Thank you."

"Aww, you are so welcome, and I really don't care who you are." He shrugs.

"Even if my hands aren't," I pause to find the right word, "necessarily clean?"

He hums, that impish grin overtaking even his eyes. "I've dabbled in deadly shenanigans before. Someone pulled a knife on me and, y'know, I lost an eye. I decided to leave." He points to his right eye, which has been replaced by a gleaming red ruby.

"And join a lone captain?"

"Nah, I became a thief after that. Then I was recruited by this infamous captain!" The boy nudges his captain. Is it just the two of them? There must be more. "But me and Atlas go *waaaay* back. Ain't that right?"

He's ignored. *Captain Atlas?* The name feels familiar, but I don't know where I have heard it. Maybe in the drunken ramblings from the tavern I worked at or perhaps on one of the busy streets of port cities.

"The name's Edwin, by the way."

That's a name I have not come across. Stretching across the little rowboat, he confidently offers his hand to me. I take it. These two must have cut the rope that was tied around my wrists. I'm their captive, thankfully. Celestia, oh, thank Her Divinity for this Edwin boy, instead of some other seafaring scum.

"Alouette."

"Quite a grip for a game bird. We'll get along quite well." He gives me another toothy grin before turning to his comrade. "In'it right, Capt'n?"

I pull back and look to Atlas for an answer. I've never seen someone pay less attention to others.

"He's shy, okay?" Edwin bops from side to side. That with the swirling motion of his oars sickens me. I place a hand on my forehead in a failed attempt to steady myself. "Aye, he was the one who jumped right in to save you, though. No hesitation, he—" Atlas kicks Edwin's shin. "Geez!"

I bet the captain thought I wouldn't notice. Little does he know, I've had to pay attention to little details for my entire life. Small gestures are much more important than what they appear to be.

"He's not very nice." Edwin cackles.

"I can tell." *What better to do than play along?*

My three small words hit a nerve. Atlas turns to glare at the auburn-haired boy. I see a new side of his fair face—his tight jaw and sharp nose. Admittedly, rather refined and almost handsome for a pirate. I smile in spite of myself.

"Aww, hurt your feelings, did I, Capt'n?" Edwin fakes a smolder, exaggerating his frowned brows, one of which has a gap in it. "She agreed, what else can I say?"

"If I may ask, why did you save me?" For once, I can make eye contact with this captain.

His reluctant gaze tells me that he's holding back; he knows the answer.

"Answer her." Edwin takes one of the oars and whacks Atlas upside the head.

"Look, I don't know."

"Don't tell me, tell her!"

Atlas' eyes don't meet mine again. If I weren't perplexed by this whole ordeal and dehydrated, I'd take it as a blessing, for staring into them feels akin to peering out at the deep blue sea. And strong jaw aside, I've seen far too much of that shade of blue.

"I wasn't in the mood to see someone drown today."

I guess I wasn't in the mood to drown today, either. That doesn't stop me from giving him a quick, "Thanks."

"And I need your assistance." His posture straightens

Now that deserves my full attention. Is it the entire truth? Probably not. Will I take it? Yes.

"With what?"

"A heist!" Edwin flinches, ready to jump to his feet, but Atlas keeps him still by grabbing his upper arm. The small boat rocks. I clutch my stomach. "We're stealing something back and need another hand on deck. I dare say you owe us far more than thanks, in fact, your life!"

Really, I do. "What are we stealing, Thief?"

"Boatswain, now," he simply has to correct me, or maybe he can't help himself. "We're stealing a crown. Whose is it again?"

The captain speaks up, "It doesn't matter; we're getting it back."

"Anyway, who cares in this stupid kingdom? Not me! Oh, I can see the walls." Edwin perks up, looking over my head.

You can? I turn around, and, sure enough, a port looms on the horizon. The cream-colored masts of ships dot the coastline. Goliath walls protect the kingdom behind them.

I don't feel too great after that.

▽△▽△

"How did you end up on that ship to begin with? If I were you, I'd never set foot on another vessel ever again," Edwin pesters me as he sets the oars down in the bottom of the wooden lifeboat. Atlas reaches to tie us to the dock, which is above us, having been built for ships much bigger than our little rowboat. I'm a little embarrassed to admit that I had thought captains only knew how to boss others around rather than complete technical tasks.

"It's none of your business." I brush him off.

"Kidnapped? For your illegal dealings?" He rocks the boat from side to side. I'm not in the mood to get sick again. There's no letting this topic go, is there? "Are you running from something?"

"Aren't we all?" I shake my head and reach for the dock. My fingertips just brush the edge before a few pesky ripples pull us away. That lurching sensation comes back until a hand grabs mine. I look up to see Atlas on one knee. I grab his arm and pull myself up. Not bothering to help his boatswain, the captain rises.

I hadn't realized how tall he was until now. Compared to him, I feel like a little kid. Luckily, after Edwin claws his way onto the dock, I don't feel all that short anymore. He has two inches on me, at most.

There are posts every so often that seagulls sit on, unbothered. My first step doesn't feel any better than walking on the other ship. It's definitely what they call 'sea legs,' mixed with a terrible case of *mal de mer,* as my father called it. While Edwin prances ahead, I stagger and stumble. Atlas tries to look away, but it's like trying to turn away from a failed experiment. He uses his arm to support mine.

At least he has a little bit of courtesy now that we're off the boat. I'm guessing Edwin doesn't have any.

The captain turns to me.

I'm not sure what to expect next.

"We'll get you some ginger beer."

"Does it have alcohol?"

"It can."

Chapter 2

— The Thief —

IF THERE'S ANYTHING you need to know about the captain, it's that he can't resist a bottle of wine. Or anything for that matter.

He doesn't just *have* a drinking problem, he *is* the drinking problem. Our crew, to put it lightly, isn't very fond of him for that. He could probably go through a whole cellar in an evening. The only thing preventing me from daring him to do that is my wallet. I'd like to keep my money. Wasting it on Atlas is a terrible idea, although alcohol poisoning doesn't sound bad. Maybe I could replace him as captain! Just kidding. He's an utter fool when he's drunk, and it gets on my nerves. That's all.

I hope Alouette doesn't mind too much. She seems like she'd be a pretty tolerant person. Hopefully not a pushover, though. I hate those kinds of people. You can't let people step on your turf and walk all over you without consequences. I've let that happen one too many times. The last incident occurred in this harbor, actually. It serves me right. Never will I back down from another fight, even if it means losing my other eye. I'd just have to retire from this pirate gig. It'll get old soon, either way.

Atlas went right for a tavern, naturally. Without a doubt, he used ginger beer, a remedy for Alouette's nausea, as an excuse to get himself some hard liquor. I decided to take a stroll before dark. Maybe I'll pickpocket a wallet or two while I'm at it. The coins in my pockets jingle. Wishing fountains are so dumb. People just put money there for you to take. And when no one's looking, it's the perfect time to make bank.

The folks around here aren't the brightest. Some pirates are masterminds. The cream of the crop set sail and return successfully. The others? Eh. Not so much. I'll give Atlas some credit. We haven't lost a crew member yet; plus, we just saved a random girl's life.

I wish she would've told me why she was on that ship. Look, I'll acknowledge that sometimes I can be annoying, and that I've withheld my fair share of vital intel. I'm a thorn in Atlas' side most of the time, if not all of the time. I'm helpful, too. I promise. Or else he wouldn't have kept me. My talents are great.

A woman passes me, giggling. Her fingers are laced with another man's. She doesn't know that I just helped myself to a coin pouch in her purse. Love is distracting and dangerous. If you don't have your guard up, you'll lose. But what do I know? I steal valuables, not hearts.

Atlas, though. He's an entirely different story. I bet he's sitting at the bar with a flock of ladies around him. For some reason, they all seem to like his face. I don't understand what's wrong with them. Maybe they're jealous of my superior looks. No one can equate to me. All jokes aside, girls just swoon over him. It's crazy! Those scallywags. I could grab them by their necks, all wrapped with pearls and fake beads, and shake them. You can't pin a man like Atlas down. He's a sailor for Leviathan's sake. It'll end in ruin.

Also, knowing him, I would not recommend associating yourself with my pal, Atlas. It's a time and a half. From his harrumphs to his grumping sessions. And, aye, he's a captain, so he can just order us around at any time. Alouette better not agree to join our ranks if she knows what's best for her. He'd have her swabbing the deck in no time. Oh, no. Don't give me the but-he-helped-her nonsense. He wanted a reason to get wasted. Three sheets to the wind is what we call it.

I grab a few more wallets and antiques while I'm at it. We'll need them soon. After all, in order to steal the crown, we need to get close to it. And there's no perfect time other than two nights from now. *That's right.* They're having a gala for the ceremony or whatever they call it. A masquerade? I don't care. We need to look nice, for there's a dress code. I love my loose button up and reddish brown vest, but to my dismay my outfit is not enough. Even though the colors do suit me very well.

Speaking of colors, the day's blue begins to fade as orange reclaims the sky. There's a tavern in mind that I have a feeling he went to. He's a rather predictable guy after you've been with him for what, seven years?

There's a pep to my step even though my pockets are heavier than when we arrived. Someone is going to have to pay Atlas' tab so the three of us don't wind up in some run-down kitchen doing dishes to work off his debt.

▽△▽△

I step down into the tavern. It sits below street level, so it's not an obvious spot. Though, I've made my rounds around this place a few times, so I'm familiar with all of the nooks and crannies of this kingdom. Dare I call it my stomping ground. Just as I predicted, cheeks as red as cherries, Atlas is at the bar. I expect

Alouette to be in the stool next to him. I can't believe my eyes. She's behind the counter mixing drinks? But hadn't she asked if ginger beer had alcohol in it?

This world is full of anomalies. I roll my eyes and take my rightful place next to Atlas as his right hand man.

"Edwin." Alouette nods to me as she places a small glass in front of my captain. I can't begin to imagine what fills it.

"After this heist, she's coming on board." It's probably just one of his drunk ramblings. Our crew has never been able to make concoctions up to his standards. That doesn't mean he won't drink it, though.

"Why's that?" I lean over.

"She's a bartender. Can't you see?"

"With my one eye, yeah. I can see. Is she any good?" I turn to her. "No offense."

She laughs it off. "It's like combining elements."

"Come again?"

"Don't dwell on it too much."

Atlas takes the shot in one go. I'm not surprised, but Alouette is.

"Out of all my years in this tavern, I have never seen a man drink that much."

"Well that's because he isn't—" Atlas twitches. "Isn't one to hold himself back. Yeah, y'know. His addiction is our crew's pride and joy."

I wack him on the back. He deserves it.

Alouette plays along and turns to me, "Anything for you, chief?"

"Cider? But without the stuff he likes." I nudge Atlas. He glares. Usually, he has a pretty short fuse. Maybe he'll control himself around Alouette.

"Aye, boss!" Alouette calls. A well-dressed man—around my age—wearing all black and white emerges from nowhere. "Do you have cider?"

He replies that he'll take care of it. Great. Alouette leans down between the captain and me, resting her elbows on the table and cheeks in her hands. Her yellow eyes gleam in the light. They're a little eerie, I must admit.

"You're a little late to the party, Edwin," she jokes. "I've actually been waiting for you so we could have dinner. My father always told me that no one should eat alone."

"Whoops. I'd have come sooner if I had known." It's a lie. I needed that time for myself. I watch a young lady run her finger along Atlas' back as she walks by. The regulars probably know him by this time, and I'm very happy that I wasn't there for it.

Alouette shrugs. "A late dinner is better than no dinner at all."

"Aye, aye!" I cheer.

Her 'new boss' comes bearing my cider and an assortment of goodies for us to eat. I'm not one to refuse some nice grub. "This won't pay for itself, Alouette," he reminds her.

She goes to rise, but Atlas stops her by putting his hand on her cheek, right over hers. Here we go. I roll my eyes.

"I've got it covered, Alouette."

She brushes him off in an instant, as she should. "It's fine. I'll get you another round." Our new addition to the team gets back to work. She serves a few other customers. I help myself to the platter.

"Did you convince her to pay off your tab in advance?" Keeping my voice low, I raise a brow.

"No. She asked if she could get behind the bar and…" he trails off and reaches for the food. I slap his hand away.

"It's rude to eat with gloves on."

"I'm not taking them off." I can't stop him this time.

My brow lifts. "Fine. And what happened after that, exactly?"

"Couldn't tell you."

Of course not. I shake my head. If I had to guess, he got distracted by other drinkers. He has put a lot of other sailors to shame. As Alouette makes her rounds, she slides another glass in front of Atlas without a word. He doesn't hesitate to polish it off.

But he regretted that one. His hand clutches his throat. I take a sip of my lovely cider.

"What's wrong, Capt'n?"

"It burns," he can barely wheeze. That's a first.

"Serves you right." I snicker. "Aye! Alouette, I've got enough to cover this. We don't want you to eat alone."

Alouette looks to the other taverner who nods back at her with a smile. I expect her to sit down, but she stands across from us again.

"Like it?" A devilish spark flickers in her golden eyes.

Atlas can't tell her no.

He winces. "What was it?"

"It's called ethanol. Try something again and I'll add more vinegar to it."

I like her. I like her a lot.

And I don't even care what ethanol is.

Atlas doesn't even glare at her, opposite of my assumption. His wide eyes just stare at her. Nobody has been bold enough to make an open attack like that. He doesn't even revoke his job offer. That surprise of his eases into a grin that spreads from one pink cheek to the other.

"I like girls who can mix drinks."

He hasn't learned his lesson.

I munch as an onlooker. Atlas' saga is surely amusing. I'll be waiting for the next card Alouette has up her sleeve. She sneaks a few bites in here and there between calls from other patrons. Pinning her down seems to be impossible.

I wonder if she's afraid. Maybe she'd been kidnapped before and, even though we saved her, she believes we've taken her captive once more. Atlas is a big, scary guy. With him vulnerable like this, it's the proper time to strike. I can only hope that she doesn't let this get to her head. For someone as small as her, Atlas could easily take her out. With the addition that she can't swim, she could drown in no time at his hands. I learned my lesson long ago.

Who knows? Maybe Alouette is more than what she lets on. A lark is a game bird, but I believe she is a hunter.

It isn't too long before we retire for the night. A convenient inn sits on top of the tavern. It's an ingenious business plan if you ask me. Get wasted, go to bed. Repeat. The other bartender thanks Alouette for her service. She says that it's nothing.

▽△▽△

It's best that Alouette stays in a different room. I'm looking at Atlas, now. One full night's rest can sober him up. How? I'd have to ask what miraculous genes his parents passed down to him. I, sure as the seven seas, did not get them.

I kick off my boots and slip into bed. I sprawl out. My talent is to sleep anywhere. This inn always spoils me. King size beds. Two of them.

Atlas is about to argue with me that we could have let Alouette room with us, but I also know how to snore really loudly to make it sound like I'm sleeping. I hear him sigh. That's a win for me.

▽△▽△

The morning comes sooner than expected. I bet you didn't see that coming. My dreams were insane, and, hey, I don't remember them in the slightest. Looks like we can't discuss them. 'Tis a shame. Atlas is on the other side of the room pulling on the sleeves of his jacket. He's very meticulous, straightening out every wrinkle. Those who take extra time to fiddle with their clothes are always hiding something. It's a guarantee. He keeps his back to me as he pulls his long leather gloves on.

I have his secret, but you don't. We'll keep it at that for now.

There's a tap at the door. Atlas is still adjusting his sleeves. He takes an eternity and a half to get ready. All I have to do is slip my shoes on, which I easily complete before answering the door. It's Alouette.

"Rise and shine."

I rub my eyes. "Yeah, yeah."

"What's the plan?" She crosses her arms.

"We're paying an old friend a visit."

"I'm not," Atlas retorts. I groan. "And he's not a friend of mine."

"Then who is it?" Alouette looks past me.

"My father."

"Fine, I'll just go alone. Alouette, you keep an eye on Atlas. He knows the drill for today and can fill you in on the plan." I pat her on the shoulder before tossing a pouch of coins at him. "Find something nice for her, will ya?"

Chapter 3

— The Alchemist —

And he's gone, just like that.

Atlas, dressed in all black, tugs at his high collar. I awkwardly stand in the doorway. The world doesn't feel like it's spinning anymore. Still, I have more concerning problems to worry about. He's probably mad about the vodka and vinegar mix. I used to serve it to drunk guests at taverns if I wanted them to leave.

It worked every time.

It's a shame that I need to stay with Atlas and Edwin. This heist has piqued my interest; my curiosity will not let me leave.

"To start off, I'd like to ask if you remember anything from last night?" I say.

He pinches the bridge of his nose. "Let's forget it."

It's not the answer I'm expecting, but I couldn't ask for better. Alcohol goes right to drinkers' heads. It's a toxin. Atlas couldn't think straight. I'll give him the benefit of the doubt, for now.

"I concur. So, Captain, what is the plan?"

"We're going to a gathering at that castle tomorrow. To get inside, we need to blend in. Before the ceremony, we'll take the crown." He turns to face the window.

"And why is this crown so important again?"

"It doesn't belong to this kingdom. Or do you need a better explanation to think that we're not common criminals?"

"There's no need."

"Are you…" Atlas turns back to me with furrowed brows. My heart begins to race, for he's not the only one who's keeping secrets. "…a fugitive, too?"

"I get just as bad of a reputation." I start down the hallway.

"Then what are you?"

"Let's just find a lovely dress."

"Hey, don't go too far." Atlas catches up with me, jogging down the stairs beside me. We emerge in a busy street. The sun perches just above the city walls. "Ports bring in plenty of dangerous people."

Like I wasn't aware already.

I look up at Atlas. He's like a walking shield. There's even a scar running from his jawline to his upper cheek that can scare people away.

"I've had my fair share of dangerous encounters, Captain."

"Such as walking the plank?"

I nod. "You saw it first hand, didn't you?"

He stiffens. "Yes."

I look at the masts that peek above the bordering walls. "I do owe you and Edwin my life."

"You don't remember anything between the plank and the boat, do you?"

My eyebrows crease. I try to trace the memories back to yesterday. Nothing rises to the surface. "No, I don't. Why do you ask?"

"No particular reason."

I grin. "Fine. Keep your secrets."

▽△▽△

Most of the girls around already wear long skirts and fancy dresses. In these sorts of ports, you get the top percent and the dirt poor. It's the former that usually roam the streets while the latter stick to the alleys, as I once did.

I stare into the windows of shops. Girls around my age sit in salons together, laughing as they paint their nails with bright, artificial colors. I'd look down at mine to see if they need a manicure, but light brown gloves always cover my hands.

"I want to look better than the princess."

Either Atlas doesn't hear me or ignores me. Maybe he's distracted by everyone else having a grand old time. It's not everyday that a royal family will invite commoners to their gatherings. Open invitations are a huge risk. You get people like Edwin and Atlas, and not to forget myself.

Yet the mood seems to rise like the tides every time people get to play dress up and pretend to be wealthy for once.

The look on my face must be pretty giddy. I'm what they call a street rat, after all. These empty pleasantries are far and few between for people like me. Captain Atlas probably gets more respect than I do. He manages a crew of others. Plus, setting sail is no easy feat. I'll never set foot on a vessel again if I don't have to. Even now, I can feel the world tilting if I think too much about it.

I'm the first to step into a boutique. The bell chimes, announcing my arrival. It's also a custom in most cities to let little bells chime for guests. It's for good fortune, as I'm told.

Atlas and I must be an unusual sight, for every patron turns their head to stare. I wave to a woman with a tape measure draped over her shoulders. She looks over the lenses of her red half-moon glasses and calls my name.

Atlas raises a brow at me. Somehow I can tell he wants to ask how I know her. He doesn't know that I grew up roaming the outskirts of this kingdom, after all.

"Madame!" I greet her with my arms spread wide. She's not one for hugs, so the woman leans over and pats me on the back. It's rather odd because she spends her days taking measurements of other people. You'd think that she'd be okay with close contact.

Since I was little, she has been good friends with my father, despite his dangerous line of work. I haven't seen her much in recent years. I've taken up my father's craft. Actually, I hopped on that merchant ship in hopes of returning here, although it doesn't feel quite like home.

Atlas isn't aware yet.

"Oh, my little lark." She holds my upper arms and pushes me back. Her analytical gaze gives me a once over. "You've grown so much since you left the nest. Your father always told me you'd end up like his wife."

His wife, my mom. She never got the chance to raise me, though. That's why Rosaline has never called her my mother. Instead, the tailor has claimed that title for her own. She taught me how to sew years back, so I'll give her credit where it's due. When I was little, I saw her as family, and my father even called her Aunt Rosie, just like the flower. Beautiful, but not as beautiful as my mom, like they all say. Cliche, I know, but we all find a guilty pleasure in saying such cheesy things.

"If only I could have met her." I give her what she wants to hear.

"Dear." Her gaze softens. "If only you could have. She loved you so much, and you would have loved her even more."

Poor Atlas who has to witness this. He's a sailor, not a counselor.

"And who is this young fellow?" She lets go of me and makes her way over to Atlas. As a tailor, she's got a habit of getting a three-sixty once over of everyone she meets. That said, her craft has been mastered for years. *It's our flaws that bring out our talents.* My dad said that first, not me. He's a quotable man. When I find him, we should all meet up some time. Oh, the stories he has to tell, not just of my mother.

"Alouette?" Rosaline waits for my response. Atlas stiffens as she gives him far more than a once-over.

"This is Captain Atlas, uhm."

His eyes cut to mine. "DeLuca."

This name is even more familiar. Where from? I can't place my finger on it.

"Right. Captain Atlas DeLuca."

"And where did you pick him up?" She turns her attention to me, pulling the measuring tape off of her neck.

"It's an embarrassing story, Rosie."

"I've seen you do plenty of foolish things, little girl." Leaning down, she wraps it around my torso.

"I'm not that little."

She stands to her full height. I have to look up, still not as far up as I have to look for Atlas.

"Okay. Fine. He saved me, actually. I had been in another port and hopped on a merchant ship that I heard was coming here. Pirates raided it and found me. They took the crew hostage yet didn't feel like sparing me." Got all that out in one breath, although it's only half of the truth. I know. She's aware of my dad's profession and can infer why they decided to throw me over the edge. The tailor can put two and two together.

"So you had to walk the plank!?" Her tape tightens around my chest. I croak. "You must be more careful." A sigh slips through her lips. Although she's not my mom, she gets just as disappointed, as if I were her own daughter.

"Thank goodness Mister DeLuca was there to save you." Her words contradict the glare she shoots his way.

"It was nothing. I was on my way here with my boatswain for the gathering tomorrow." Forced humility, I presume.

"You're going with this man? How long have you known him? Don't let him take advantage of you." The fact that Atlas is standing just a few paces away doesn't bother her in the slightest. She stares him down. He avoids eye contact. "A seafarer is too flighty for you."

"I'm not a kid. I can handle myself." I hold her forearm to pull her attention away from him. "Really, it's not what it sounds like."

Her glare doesn't believe me. The narrative in her mind has already been made up. Alouette, the staple damsel in distress, falls to pirates; only then can she be saved by a bold captain, who she will sail off into the horizon with. "I'd rather you stay close." She coils up the tape and sighs. "I'll have the dress done by the morning tomorrow. You'll be the most stunning young lady."

"Prettier than the princess?"

"You really are your father's daughter, my dear. I would settle for no less."

I smile, bearing my teeth and all. She knows that she's the kingdom's best, the cream of the crop as my father described. From the gowns on display in her boutique, I have no doubt. Plus, I'm her favorite not-so-*little-girl*.

Her needle-sharp focus turns pins back on Atlas. "Run along now. Don't get in too much trouble."

I thank her one last time before exiting. Atlas follows.

"You live here?" His brows crease.

"Not quite. I lived beyond the wall—within kingdom limits—for a few years." I hop up onto a fountain's rim to walk around the perimeter. Even now, I'm still not at eye level with Atlas. He's a beast. "Plus, I traveled with my dad a lot."

"Not by boat, I'm guessing."

I shake my head. "By foot, usually. Horseback if we got lucky."

"You're lucky you're close with your father."

"He's been missing for three years." My lips threaten to tug down into a frown. It's a sore spot, a bruise we all can't help but poke at.

"I often wish mine would disappear like that."

"Is that why you're a captain? Vanish out at sea because he won't?"

His eyes rake over the horizon. "There's nothing for me here."

"At least you set sail. I'm just so trapped, and this place always calls me back."

He hasn't noticed that we've taken a couple of laps around the fountain. Something must be on his mind.

That makes the two of us.

Chapter 4

— The Thief —

I love Atlas' dad. Don't read that the wrong way. He's amusing. Just to let you know, that man never lets a wine bottle leave his sight, but it's not like he gets so drunk that he tries flirting with a random girl he picked up from the deep blue sea. That stunt replays rent free in my head.

Besides, Father DeLuca always has tall tales to tell, although I fear that they're filled with more truth than lies. Like who can make up a story about befriending a siren!? Wild, right? And coming face-to-face with Leviathan? And finding heaps and heaps and heaps of gold! Not to mention all the bounties he's cashed in from rogue fae to his own swashbuckling cousins! Although a retired captain, he's filthy rich.

It's a shame Atlas doesn't dock the ship here more often. I get a kick out of his old man. Plus, he hooks me up with doubloons. He's rolling in the dough. Once upon a time, Atlas' ship belonged to him. Satisfied with his treasures, he settled down. He raised his son on the *Aurora Borealis* until Atlas turned fifteen, maybe? My captain was given authority at a very young age. But I can't imagine what he went through, like swabbing the deck with lye, climbing the masts, growing up with liars and killers and everything in between.

I know exactly what you have on your mind. That explains a lot. It does. Trust me.

Atlas doesn't even acknowledge that some people have crappy dads and some people don't even have parents. Take me for example. My parents burned in a fire. I grew up with a mean old woman who looked like a man. Alouette looks fatherless. Come on now. Be real. What protagonists can grow to have a healthy relationship with their parents? Surely, not any of us.

And to take it a step further, some mariners dream of being captains but die a little too early, or live long enough to the point that they're too decrepit to even fathom a leadership role like his. I rest my case.

I'd never become a captain. It's too much for me. Granted, I hate getting bossed around, but taking responsibility for people sounds like a whole other nightmare. Atlas and I are acquainted enough that I can rival his orders. Plus, I'm a fine boatswain. Our crew knows what to do on the deck. My orders are brief and to the point. I know how to stock the ship and note anything that needs to be repaired. I've been doing this under Atlas for six years. We're professionals by now.

A lot of the older guys in our field raise brows as if we don't have enough wrinkles or stubble to be qualified. Atlas has probably spent more time at sea than on land. As much as I hate to admit it, he's built for this. And I've got a low center of gravity, so I am too. I'm five foot six and a half, thank you. Atlas is definitely over six feet tall, and we don't care about all those nitty gritty inches after that.

His dad isn't even *that* tall. Okay. Sure, he surpasses my height. But I don't dare imagine Atlas' mother. Because of that and one other thing.

Who cares, really? I turn my focus back to the former captain in front of me. "So, Mister DeLuca. Have you heard that we're going to the masquerade tomorrow night?"

"I have not. You convinced Atlas to go?"

I nod. "Yes, sir. We're stealing back something that belongs to Mother Dearest."

He sighs. "I did hear about that. Be safe, okay?" The man is rough around the edges, a former pirate with a five o' clock shadow and all, but he's grown into a father's mold.

"You're not going to stop us?"

"Why should this kingdom flaunt what it does not own?"

"I like the spirit." I pick up my glass and tilt it towards him. He's one to stock the good juice in his icebox. Imports from kingdoms with much better industries than this one, if it has any markets beyond the ones from overseas.

"And there's no point in trying to stop you two." He pours a glass of red wine for himself. I called it, didn't I?

"Fair point. It's us three now." I take a swig.

"Oh? A girl?"

"Your guess, not mine."

He nearly chokes. "You must kid. I wasn't serious."

"I'm a liar at heart, but this, my friend, I can't come up with."

"Hopefully he'll learn this time." DeLuca looks out the window at the bustling street. Velvet curtains flap in the midsummer breeze. "Is she anyone that I would know?"

"Does the name Alouette ring a bell?"

▽△▽△

I thanked him over and over again. I'm always as polite as I can be around him. He's the type of guy you want to impress, and if his son won't foster his relationship with him, I'll step in. Memories of my father are scarce, for the flame of Time has slowly gnawed away at them, reducing even the angles of his face to faded ashes. As I close the door behind me, I stare up at the sky. The air smells of rain. A storm is brewing on the horizon, not too far out at sea. Dark clouds sit right above the encircling walls.

These weren't here when I first came. *Yikes*. My first instinct is to look for Atlas. He's pretty easy to see. Not everyone dresses exclusively in black with a ragged cloak around his shoulders. Maybe I'm too short to see him from here, so I jog down the steps of his side porch, which sits a decent way off of the main street. My boots click against the intricate bricks that line my path. The clock strikes five.

I spent a little too much time there. As I charge through the streets, a silver coin catches my eye. I swoop down to swipe it up. I can't trust Atlas with my money. Well, it's not mine, unless you play by finders-keepers, losers-weepers. Haha, I pride myself in the phrase peepers-keepers. The rhyme is totally better. And, no, because you read it, you don't get to take it. Unless you credit me. Then it would be my pleasure. I can hear the constant patter of rain against the sea from here. The Chime of Impending Doom is what I named that noise. No one else calls it that. Nonetheless, I hate when it rains. It's a time of all hands on deck, especially when I only want to get below those floorboards. Sometimes, I'm conveniently under the weather when storms come through. Don't tell Atlas. Come on, we all know that seasickness gets the best of us from time to time. Follow that up with a double wink.

He wouldn't understand, though. His mother and father practically bred him to be a seafarer. He can hop from ship to ship like it's nothing. Sword fight on the bow. Climb the netting. Half the time, he doesn't look when he's at the helm. Plus, I hate steering the ship, so whenever it's my turn, I pass that opportunity onto the captain. Of course, a lot of that came from intense training and spending the vast majority of his life on vessels. Hey, come to think of it, I can't think of a time where he actually lived on land, aside from the occasional overnight stay at inns and slumped over bars until first light.

I turn down a street to see Alouette. That girl has insanely curly hair. The brown fades to yellow, almost golden blonde, at the tips. Her long eyelashes are colored the same. That combined with her yellow eyes, she rivals Atlas' ability to stand out. Astounding. She's kneeling to give a kid a little figurine. A few other children circle around her like ducklings.

Not too far away, with arms crossed, Atlas leans against a post. That broody scallywag. Anyway, I join him. Alouette's attention is a little too focused on the children to notice me. I pride myself in my quiet steps as I steer toward the edge of the street. Years of experience have made it so that I can sneak up on anyone. Including Atlas. I've appeared in his cabin a few too many times without making a floorboard creak.

Even now he doesn't see me. I stand next to him and follow his gaze. He's a sucker for Alouette, eh? I smirk.

If I were her, I would've snatched that little figure away from the children. Where I grew up, I had to fight for my toys. Only I know how many kids I made bets with that I could throw them off of the seesaw. It's more than my fingers and toes could count combined, to give you a point of reference. And when we played scissors on the swingset, I'd knock kids off on purpose. What's so wrong with that? I had less competition when they were crying and running back to their rooms. Kick or be kicked. That's how I played. Too rough for you? Big baby.

Alouette doesn't look like the type to have siblings. If she did, then she must be the oldest. As one kid stumbles, she reaches out to help him. If someone stumbles in my world, it's their fault, and surely not my problem.

The rain's scent grows stronger. I feel a few drops in my hair. I hold my hand out. I do take pleasure in the rain when we're not at sea. The world doesn't uncontrollably sway like a pendulum, and I don't need to worry about capsizing.

Atlas, however, does need to be concerned.

But he's too infatuated with that girl to realize it.

"*Sooooo*, Atlas."

He flinches.

"Edwin! What did I tell you abou—" His sharp tongue is muffled by a whisper, so that Alouette does not hear.

I jab him in the side. "I don't care. Are you considering dinner yet!?"

Alouette turns to look at us. Both Atlas and I gesture for her to go back to whatever she was doing. Playing with kids? Gross. In the rain? Even worse! She welcomes it with open arms, extended toward the sky. Her little followers do the same salutation.

"I haven't yet."

Tainting everything they touch, the droplets are heavier now. They pound on the roofs above and stain the bricks below. The sun has been forced to take its leave.

"We should soon. By the way, you've got something on your face." I tap my jawline so that he knows to check his. Thunder cracks. Diamond-shaped scales dot his skin. He curses, rubbing the impurities on his cheek. Through those gloves, I doubt he can feel them.

He looks over at me. "Is it bad?"

"It's…noticeable." There are matching sapphire scales on his other cheek, crawling up the side of his neck.

Alouette waves the kids off. Their parents wait under porches on the other side of the street while the rain's pitter turns into a patter.

"What do *you* recommend I do?" He arches a brow. Sarcastic bastard.

I lightly slap him on the other side of his face. "You'll be alright, buddy. It's not the end of the world." It's a gentle emotional support wack.

I think it's a common consensus that we can't tell Alouette about this just yet. It's the secret I touched on earlier.

As she walks over, I step forward. "So, tavern part two tonight?"

She nods to me. "Aye, aye."

I take the lead with Alouette. Atlas has to tag behind if he knows what's best for him.

▽△▽△

We're drenched by the time we step down that little staircase. I shiver, although it's warm inside. The bartender nods to us. He's got this adorable smile with his round cheeks and dusting of freckles.

"Another shift?"

She shakes her head. "I'll pass."

Atlas questions her decisions from behind. If he knows what's best, he'll pipe down.

"Okay, maybe." She jogs up to the bartender, exchanging a small salute with him. "Because I know how stressful it is working all alone." And back behind the counter she goes. I had wished that I could've just sat between Atlas and her. Plans spoiled.

Atlas hunches down next to me, his elbows on the table and palms planted on his cheeks. Conspicuous, nevertheless a way to hide his scales. The barkeeper and Alouette stand in front of us.

"Why don't you take off those gloves and stay a while?" he asks Atlas.

They must be soggy, I want to add.

"No. I'm fine."

"Alouette?" He turns to her.

"*Pfft*, I'm all good. I've got tattoos that'll…raise some questions."

She chose her final few words carefully, but the pause only adds to my curiosity. And possible suspicions regarding this stowaway.

Pushing no further, the barkeep raises his brows and heads to assist other patrons.

I made a greedy request of him before he fully departs. "Can we get that bread you lit on fire yesterday?"

▽ △ ▽ △

Atlas is a few drinks in already. I'm starting to get the impression that Alouette finds this addiction amusing. She hasn't mixed her signature vodka with vinegar yet. Atlas also hasn't done anything out of the ordinary, let alone pushy.

The barkeep brings out a warm loaf on a cutting board. A knife is served on the side, just as I like it. A yellow candle sits in the center of the carved bread.

"May I have the honor of lighting it?" Alouette requests. He nods and walks off. Less work for him. With her attitude, Alouette would be a nice addition to the crew. While Atlas can steer without paying attention, she crafts a ton of drinks from memory. Or she knows how to present herself confident enough to make it appear that she's experienced.

"Close your eyes," she tells us.

"What?" Atlas asks, not accustomed to being bossed around.

"Just do it."

I do.

"I'm watching," she reminds.

My eyes tighten. Waiting is so awkward. She could steal my wallet, well *wallets*, for goodness sake! I only helped myself to two today, ok!?

"Okay." Her proud smile is audible.

When I peek, she's pulling her glove back on. A small flame flickers. No flint, no steel, no matches are in sight.

"Bon appetit."

"You play with fire?" I grin.

"Oh, I *make* fire. Combustion, actually."

I glance at Atlas to catch his reaction. His eyes have only been this wide once or twice.

"Is he bad at following directions?" Alouette crosses her arms.

I shrug, pushing her question aside. Who cares, anyway? "Call me intrigued. What did you do?"

Is this what got her kicked off of that ship? Alouette puts a finger in front of her lips. Then she gets right back to work.

I reach for the knife to fiddle. Table manners are a thing of the past, from a time where I ate with my family under one roof.

It went up in flames, what else can I say? So did my civil behavior. I'm a pirate. I do as I please.

"Did you get anything to wear from my father?" Atlas asks me.

"He said he'd do some digging and let me pick up a few things tomorrow. I forgot to tell you that you should've found something for yourself. I doubt anything in his wardrobe would fit you. How tall is your mom again?"

"Don't ask me anything about her."

His sharp annunciation alone is enough to make me regret asking. Atlas hates his dad, yeah. Don't ever get him started about his mother. She's the reason he gets those scales.

Changing our topic is for the best. "Did you find anything for Alouette?"

"We went to a seamstress who seemed familiar with her. Said a dress would be ready tomorrow morning."

"Maybe she'll have something for you, too."

Atlas shrugs. His hand is practically glued to his glass. I shouldn't be surprised or disappointed by him anymore.

I grab the knife and serve myself another chunk of bread. I'm guessing the candle is butter, not wax. Good, innovative stuff. I approve.

"Are we gonna take the rowboat once we get the thingy *orrrrr*…? Seek refuge with Dad…?"

"Don't act like he's your father."

I'll ignore him again. "Grab the stuff from our rooms and leave? I'm really attached to this shirt and vest, you know."

"If we can get out without getting noticed, yes. If we're caught by anyone, we leave immediately."

▽△▽△

Nothing too chaotic happens this evening. No burning drinks, sadly. Just a mildly drunk captain. He sits down on his bed, which is closer to the window than mine. Rain beats down on the foggy panes.

"Soon, you're going to have to tell her." I walk over to him with my hands behind my back. "You got lucky when you pulled her out of the water. She was already unconscious, so she didn't see anything."

"No one else will fall in. Also, no one else on the crew knows."

"I do, Atlas. I do."

"Go to bed, Edwin."

"Listen to me. Sooner or later, she'll find out. Whether it's when you decide or out of Davy Jones' blue, the time will come."

"It's an order."

"And what did she do? Does she have fire powers?"

"I'll tell you in the morning unless you want to walk over and ask her."

"Did it have to do with the kids from earlier today?"

"She can manipulate stuff, ok?" He flops onto his back. "She shaped those little figures with her bare hands."

"You saw what she was hiding?"

"I shouldn't have told you. Get the answer from her."

I shake my head and pull the ribbon that holds my ponytail in place. It unravels, letting my hair down. With a sigh, I retire for the night.

Chapter 5

— The Alchemist —

It's Edwin who comes tapping at my door at the break of dawn. This has all been far too much excitement for me. And stress. Mostly stress. He waves. It actually took me a second to recognize him. I didn't realize that guys who tied their hair back ever took it down. For a moment, I had myself convinced that he was some random girl fresh off the streets.

"Care to explain the party trick?" He crosses his arms.

"Close the door behind you."

"Is it some kind of secret?"

"For those who knew my father, no. For those unacquainted with my arts, yes."

Edwin follows my instructions. His line of sight goes right to my hands.

"Oh. Alchemy?"

"You know?"

Edwin shrugs. "I've heard about it a time or two."

"Apparently, Atlas hasn't."

"Maybe I have closer ties to the underbelly of our operations. I will admit that I haven't seen it in action. Magic, though. I've seen that." He pauses for a moment. "Well, Atlas has, too."

As strange as it sounds, magic is far, far more common than alchemy. The ability to spellcast and channel mana, basically magical energy, is a gift granted to many by Celestia. Only a few of us, those who dare call themselves alchemists, have real ties to Her.

"Do you have a coin?" I hold my palm out. He reaches into his pockets and pulls a silver one out. My hands clasp it. Fingers shaking, I have to strain them. Edwin's eyes narrow as he stares at my hands, which are covered in circles, riddled with various symbols. Some patterns go as far as to wrap around my wrists.

I hand it back to him. It's not silver anymore.

"It's gold?"

"Not pyrite," I joke. *Pyrite*. Also known as Fool's Gold.

He tosses it around. "And this is why they wanted you dead. The power to change metals into gold. What about the lighting things on fire bit?"

"It's just combustion to spark some heat. The wick catches fire."

Simple chemistry. Modern alchemy combines that with our basis of turning base metals into gold. Any man can perform it if he has enough time to pour into studying the mechanics. By tying himself to Celestia. My father passed down all of his knowledge to me. I grew up with transmutation circles and other special runes. By now, changing elements is as simple as breathing. It just takes a bit more energy and concentration. Oh, and, we cannot forget, a big ask of Celestia. This is Her world and we need permission to alter Her creation.

"Can you make a replica of the crown? If the pedestal the royal family keeps it on is empty, attention will be drawn. But if you make a fake one, our job will be about a gazillion times easier." The way his sly lips curl tells me that this isn't his first time around the block.

"Good plan."

▽△▽△

The bell chimes again. I wave to Rosaline. Her red lips part to give me a heartfelt smile.

"Give me one moment!" she calls and rushes to one of the dressing rooms that line the back wall. Atlas stands just behind me. Edwin told me that someone like Rosaline would expect him to pay. This money isn't either of theirs, anyway. Some poor villager is searching through their purse to find their coin pouch.

She brings back a golden dress. Little crystals wrap around the silk and tulle in swirling patterns. "Your father would have enjoyed it." She glances around to make sure no one else is around. "Little alchemist." Gently, the dress is placed in my arms.

"Thank you. I-I don't know what to say." This crowned princess will be put to shame.

"And don't think I forgot about you, DeLuca." She leaves and returns again. A black suit accented with gold comes back for Atlas. "You must look just as wonderful if you're going with my lovely Alouette."

Atlas stammers, "Miss Rosaline, you didn't need to."

"Don't worry about it. This isn't for you, it's for her."

Atlas face loses what little color it has. I awkwardly smile. The moody tailor's blunt streak continues.

Because I'm a relative in her eyes, we get a discount. The price makes me jump. Tailors and designers can charge as much as they like for their craft, for towns often only have one or two. High demand? Low supply? The prices skyrocket. Atlas covers it with no problem, thankfully. I don't dare ask where he or his crew digs up their cash.

Rosaline pats me on the back, which is about as close to a hug as I can get. Without saying it, by the way her cheeks scrunch to crease new lines around her eyes, she's happy I'm back. I don't plan on staying for long. This isn't a very good time to tell her. I thank her over and over and over again. She even gives us an extra little bag with a few more accessories. What's a masquerade without bejeweled masks?

"Oh, I wish I could be there to see you." She shakes her head. "Now, I've got other gowns to tend to. Stop by soon. Okay, my lark?"

I nod. "I'll do my best." It's the truth. I promise.

"Go on." She shoos us out. There's definitely more money to be made today from last minute wardrobe repairs to impulse purchases.

Atlas carries everything for me.

Once we're out of earshot, the captain arches a brow. "She calls you lark?"

"You don't speak French, do you?"

He shakes his head.

"It's Alouette's translation."

He thinks for a moment. "Isn't there a song about alouette?"

I nod.

"And Alouette *is* your real name?"

"My father was inspired by the lullaby." I shrug. "How did you get yours?"

"Never asked."

Are his parents *that* disconnected from their son? My father made sure I never forgot the meaning of my name, nonetheless the thought he poured in behind it.

I trace the lines leading through the street's reddish bricks. Water pools in the cracks. The sky has cleared. Storms come and go quickly, like trials cast down by Celestia. I look over at the gown Atlas carries. A piece of me wants this night to last forever and a day. It'll be my first taste of the lavish lifestyle that some simply breathe day in and day out. Marble halls. Fine dresses. Rich infatuation.

Nevertheless, we're still on a mission to steal. I can't let my guard down because there's a chance to get lost in a fantasy. This heist must be our top priority.

The bells strike twelve.

We have two hours before the doors open to guests. We'll need time to find the crown, and I need a substantial amount of time to create a replica. Every detail must match the original.

Atlas' pace picks up. Mine does too.

▽△▽△

We're walking through the inn's hall when Edwin prances past.

"Toodaloo." He wiggles his fingers at us. "You know where I'll be."

At Monsieur DeLuca's place.

Atlas hands me the dress and the extra bag. Can I trust him alone? Before, we always had a mediator, like Edwin or Rosaline. We agreed to forget the first night, however a verbal agreement does not guarantee that he'll let my actions go. Something deep in my chest sputters at the thought.

I push the door to my room open. The dress gets laid out on my bed. It doesn't even feel real. I pull my gloves off again to feel the fabric. It's soft. Much more gentle than my hands.

My worry fails to exceed my bliss.

Once it's on, I spin around in front of a floor-length mirror, its muddled glass surface a little smudged from many years of use. The bottom of the dress flares out as I move around. With one hand, I have to hold the back together. It must lace up like a corset. I look over my shoulder to try and weave a silky ribbon through the little holes. Reflections are a pain. Everything is flipped. Converting base metals into gold is easier than this.

I glare at my own reflection. I'll have to ask Atlas.

Chapter 6

— The Siren —

I KNOCK ON Alouette's door. She's taking a really long time. Did she leave through the window? I call her name.

"The door is unlocked."

She's making me sound like a fool. Does that mean come in?

I grasp the doorknob and slowly turn it. She's standing in front of a mirror. Looking at her doesn't feel right. I'm used to looking at filthy men missing limbs and teeth.

Begrudgingly, she requests, "Can you lace the back for me?"

The little ribbons are a mess. She must have tried to loop them herself. Bold of her to assume that I have any more experience than she does. I walk over and kneel down to help. She pulls her hands away. I had only caught a glimpse of those tattoos yesterday. In the mirror, I watch her knead her fingers together in front of her.

As the laces draw together at the top, I tie the knot and stop. With my forearm, I lift some of the locks away from her back. My fingers trace detailed lines that match the ones I had seen under the tavern's amber light. By the time I realize I shouldn't have done so, her reflection is staring at me with wide eyes. Those circles aren't just on her hands.

"Is it obvious?" She looks over her shoulder. A weight lifts off of my tight chest. She's not mad.

I step back. She's lucky with those curls. I shake my head. "Just leave your hair down."

She lets out a sigh, but doesn't face me yet. My heart races.

"I know, I shouldn't have—" I lift my arms in surrender.

"Don't tell anyone." She turns around. Even with narrowed golden eyes and a finger pointed at me, she's gorgeous. My face gets all warm, and I can't stop it. "Okay?"

"O-okay."

For a moment, I'm convinced she's reaching for my face, but her fingers curl to adjust my collar. It must've been crooked enough for her to notice. How did I not catch it before?

"Rosaline did a great job. It's a shame Edwin won't match."

"It's better that way. He grabs the crown while we buy him time."

A smile comes back to her face. "What's with the gloves?"

I look down at my hands. "Old habits never die."

Her brows draw together.

Please don't doubt me, Alouette; we don't have time for this.

"Yeah, sure." She doesn't buy it. I hate clever people like her. Luckily, she doesn't pry any further. She pulls on long silk gloves that Rosaline had given her. "I get it, Atlas. Once, I—"

"Don't lecture me like Edwin," I snap. "There's nothing to hide."

Her light eyes prick me like needles. "Then prove it."

"Make me."

She reaches for me, but I grab her forearm. She's just a girl. She had to take her gloves off to light the wick, so with gloves on, she can't hurt me with the powers she may possess. She twists her arm down to the side, bringing mine with it. I release her and pull away.

"I'll ask Edwin."

"Do not."

Her intense gaze makes me look away. I can't face her.

"Fine. I'll find out one day."

I have a sinking feeling that she'll be triumphant. Edwin wouldn't rat me out, would he? One part of me says no. He has kept this secret under wraps for years. Aside from my parents, he's the only soul who knows.

Although, he's fair.

Maybe it comes with him being a Libra, and his urge for balance. An eye for an eye. A secret for a secret. And Alouette has exposed hers to us. In his mind, it's only right for me to share mine to stabilize the scale.

"Speaking of Edwin, when do you think he'll be back?"

"It's hard to tell with him."

If he knows what's good for him, he'll be back soon. The clock is ticking. We only have so much time to get our hands on that crown before the royal family claims it as their own for the entire kingdom to see.

"You do look handsome, by the way. I always thought pirates were peg-legged pigs."

She nudges me in the shin with her bare foot. A symbol is tattooed there as well. *Wait.* I'm usually the one who kicks Edwin. She's picking up on too much.

"Should I be offended?"

"For being the exception? No." She hooks golden chords on the buttons of my double-breasted jacket. "I can't say much about your personality, though. You're all drunken bilges."

"Landlubber," I retort.

"Aye, Bucko." She plants her knuckles in my chest. It hurts more than I anticipated.

I let a sheepish "ow" roll off of my tongue.

Edwin laughs from the doorway. Speak of the little devil who leans on the frame with his arms crossed. When did he get here? "Getting bullied by a girl? Weak, Atlas. By the way, the door was ajar."

His ramblings could go on forever if not cut short. Alouette snickers as she slips heels on. They're no glass slippers. "How much did you hear?"

"You know, just everything." He shrugs. His hair is tied to the side so it can rest over his shoulder.

"With the tailcoat, you look like a butler."

He straightens it. "Who cares? It's my favorite color." Maroon. Or burgundy. They're both close enough. I never cared for reds.

"All ready, Edwin?" Alouette walks up to him. They're eye to eye now.

He nods. "The gold fits." A wink follows.

I groan. "Stop trying to be a flirt."

"I didn't hear you give any compliments, Capt'n."

With that grin of hers, Alouette already knows just how stunning she looks.

▽△▽△

Apparently, the dress code was all that mattered. No one checked for an invitation, as long as we had masks, which Rosaline provided for us. It says a lot about those who run this kingdom. Looks mean everything. If one can pass as wealthy, then they are indeed wealthy and worthy of attending in their eyes. I act, therefore I am.

I've only been inside this castle once before. Built into the kingdom's wall, it overlooks the glittering sea. We walk along a bridge between two of the towers. The guards let us wander around. We appear to be eloquent enough. Breeze coming off of the sea blows through my hair. The hint of salt looming in the air allures me. It always has. Ever since I was a child, everything about the tides has called my name. I blame my mother. She's never stepped foot on land a day in her life.

I'm reminded of the ship, which is docked at a port far away from here. My quartermaster, Jean-Jacques Havelock, is in charge. He better not have let the storm deal too much damage. Edwin's thievery can't cover all of our repairs.

He jokes around with Alouette, who hops up on the brick wall that keeps us from falling onto the boulders below. She's a beautiful young lady, yet does not act like one.

I reach for her hand. "You're not falling today."

She stops to stare at the crashing waves. The water foams as it draws back from the rocks. It's a long, long way down.

"Why don't you go find the crown?" I look over at Edwin. It's his job. He's the expert here. I'm a captain, not a thief.

"Fine, fine. Under one condition."

"What?"

"No wine."

What kind of cruel joke is this? The royal family would be sure to have wine of much higher quality than any average tavern. For the irresistible price of *free*.

"One glass?"

He frowns.

"Okay. One."

"Two?"

"No."

"You wouldn't be able to tell if I had three."

"Atlas." He taps his foot on the ground.

"Fine."

Edwin jogs off. He's reliable once he's on a mission. That's half of the reason I've kept him around for so long. He always has a trick up his sleeve.

We reach the end of the bridge. Alouette slips her hand away from mine and hops down. Landing on slick bricks with heels, she's got some good balance.

I open the wooden door for her; it takes one good jerk to get the swollen thing to swing. She nods to me as thanks.

"Chivalry hasn't died yet." She laughs at her own comment.

"It's called being a decent person."

"Decent? You? That's a stretch."

"Wh-what?" She's already a few spiraling steps ahead of me. I rush to catch up. Little holes look out at the sea and let light pour into the stonebrick citadel. She goes faster, so I have to as well.

"I'm not that bad. I can't be worse than Edwin."

She holds her tongue.

"Right?"

"You can convince yourself."

She comes to an abrupt stop at the next landing.

Metallic steps march, echoing below us. Armor clanks. A knight? Alouette must've heard it before me, although she's a few steps higher. I slowly creep up the stairs, cautious to not make too much noise.

The guard keeps coming. It did feel unusual that they let us roam free. Or he could just be making his rounds on patrol. The space between us closes.

Okay, maybe we're not supposed to be here.

Chapter 7

— The Alchemist —

I'M PINNED TO a wall. Not by a guard but by Atlas. He's so close that I can smell last night's liquor in his breath. With one hand, he holds my wrists above my head. The other is under my chin.

The guard's steps grow closer.

My heart races. Atlas' breath grows heavy.

A man in full armor enters my peripherals. I can't breathe.

Atlas' lips are too close to mine. There's nowhere to go.

The knight then bows his head and turns away. His footsteps depart. Atlas' fingers move to cover my mouth.

"Let him leave." His hushed words are crisp in my ear.

I struggle to wiggle my wrists out of his grasp. He doesn't let me go until the footsteps completely fade. Back dragging against the wall, I slide away. That was too close. Atlas, first and foremost, and, more importantly, us almost getting caught.

"What was that?" I hiss. I need my point to get across, but the knight must not hear me.

"We don't seem like thieves that way. We look like—"

I shake my head and continue up the steps.

"I know, we're not like that. But would you rather get caught?"

"I've broken myself out of plenty of prisons before, *including* the one here."

"We don't have time for you to get locked up."

I reach the top. We enter a room full of relics. This must be what they're protecting. The two of us scan the room.

"Are any of these crowns the one?" I pick up a tiara.

Atlas shakes his head. The adjacent citadel Edwin is in has to have the one we're looking for. If not, then we can at least tell him that it's not up here. I tug off one of my gloves and place the tiara in that hand. I'll condense it into a cube so that it's not obvious that I stole a piece of jewelry. Atlas watches me.

"It's to make the replica," I explain, holding out a small silver block that had once been an accessory.

"Let's get going."

▽△▽△

Downstairs, there's a grand hall, just brimming with people like the foam of champagne. The polished tiles click under my heels. I stick by Atlas' side as we traverse this new world, unfamiliar to an alchemist and a sailor. The arched ceiling, swirled with paintings of ships and seas, almost feels sky-high above the dance floor. Across the way, the windows of the ballroom lead to another balcony. The people here love staring at water, apparently. There are fountains everywhere. What I like to call dihydrogen monoxide is a rather unique molecule, and it deserves proper credit. It was considered a whole element by my predecessors. I'm sure the nobles around fail to realize water's chemical beauty.

Atlas' arm is linked with mine. I know, it's for the best. One, so we don't get separated and lost. Two, so no one tries to mess with either of us. Slurred drunkards are opportunists, taking advantage when presented with the chance. Nonetheless, I wish the captain wouldn't get so close, especially not after the citadel situation. His attention isn't on me, thankfully. It's on the wine.

"Go on." I try to push him away. His poker face needs lots of work.

"Edwin didn't say I couldn't have a full bottle." He travels a few paces before turning back to me. "I take that back." A servant walks by. He takes a glass off of his tray. "You don't drink, do you?"

I shake my head. "Never have. Never will."

"You could." He tips his glass toward me.

"That's all you. I've seen how it taints people. It drives knives between husband and wife, son and father."

His eye twitches.

I keep a straight face. "Did your father drink?"

"Always has. Always *will*." Atlas turns his back to me.

▽△▽△

In hindsight, I probably shouldn't have asked that question. We've both lost track of how many glasses he has had, despite Edwin's request. He might as well have asked for a whole bottle. Atlas leans against a white grand piano trimmed with glimmering gold, singing along with the player. Sea shanties are never on tune, from what I've heard, but Atlas continues to defy every preconception I had about pirates. I listen from the other side of the room. Other guests are drawn to him, like magnets of opposing poles. He takes the hand of one girl and spins her around. Her date scowls. I have to smile. The little kid inside me wishes she could swoon for a handsome man like that.

I won't let her. Not for him.

No matter how his blue eyes shine under the crystal candle lit chandeliers. No matter how far his smile spreads across his face, all the way into his enchanted gaze. No matter how many times I catch glimpses of him, where I almost swear that he looks like a prince, rather than a drunken sailor.

The gold of his dark coat sparkles as he circles the piano. Why is he a captain with this talent? He exchanges short-lived dances with other ladies. And how is he not out of breath? I have so many questions about his voice and his projection. Who taught him all of this?

I find myself picking up a glass of wine. Maybe it would help me study him. I'm in the middle of the room when the end creeps near. After his last note has been drawn out, he bows. His attention lands right on me.

There's a pause before applause ensues.

Some call for another song.

Atlas walks off as if he didn't catch the entire kingdom off guard. Even myself.

"Are you going to finish that?"

I'm too dazed to see that he's right in front of me. I look down at my hand. This isn't like me.

"No." I blink a few times and pass the glass off to him. He doesn't take a sip quite yet. Perhaps he's scared. Sadly, I don't carry the ingredients for poison with me.

"I thought so."

"You could make some good money doing that. Sing a serenade, get paid in scotch if you so desire."

"What makes you say that?"

"Did you not see *them*? Even the pianist had to fight to compete with you, and he's the one leaving with padded pockets." After gesturing to everyone else in the room, I tap my thigh.

"It's nothing."

"Not everyone has talent like that. You could put it to use. Some of us aren't that lucky."

"I bet you could sing. Anyone can."

"I'd shatter window panes. Make a few ears bleed? Sounds about right."

"Alouette, if your voice is anywhere near as beautiful as you are, then—" He stops himself.

"Then?" I edge him on.

"I bet you'd steal more hearts than mine."

Chapter 8

— The Thief —

ATLAS CAN PUT on quite the performance. Just to let you know, I'm good at singing, too. Mostly lip-syncing to the rag tag bands I hear on the street. I haven't heard the captain practice once, although his voice never sounds out of tune. We blame his mom, as we do for most of his problems.

I approach Atlas and Alouette. She's dumbfounded, cheeks flushed. Beneath Atlas' dark mask of glimmering sequins that curl around his eyes, his face is red. I'm not going to bother asking how far he strayed from my wine limits. Although the king of ordering others around the ship, my captain isn't a good listener, if you haven't picked that up already.

"Did you find it?"

I nod.

Alouette smiles as I gesture for her to come with me.

"Go do your thing, Atlas. We need a diversion." He better listen to this while he departs.

Once he's gone, I inquire, "That voice is mesmerizing, isn't it?"

She nods along. "Yeah, compared to the musicals in taverns I've witnessed. Note that they weren't professionals, only drunkards pretending they're stars."

"We all have dreams." I weave through dancing couples. Partly to annoy them, partly because it's the easiest way.

"He's living that one. Besides, what are the captain's dreams?"

Atlas has everything I could imagine. A father. A mother. A talent. A crew full of fellows to follow his orders, if that counts.

"Great question. I'm trying to figure that out. I think he needs a reliable friend."

"Wouldn't that be you?"

"*Ehh.* He needs someone else he can confide in for those deep, dark, *drowned* secrets of his. The water between us is, let's say, troubled." By the way my speech breaks and voice growls, Alouette picks up the strain.

"Does it have to do with the gloves?"

Yes. Wait, he hasn't told her? That bastard! Scallywag. Scurvy dog. The next time I get him alone, I'm going to give him a piece of my mind. I've taken too long to respond. "It's messy. I would love to tell you, really, but Atlas should be the one. Okay?"

We exit the large hall. I can hear Atlas' voice again. It almost calls me back.

I turn a tight corner. The crown is on a pedestal, just as I predicted a day prior. Atlas had just wanted alone time with Alouette, so he sent me away. The gold is adorned with pearls. We both stare. It's way too conspicuous. Could this location be any worse?

"Greetings," a girls' voice says from behind. I turn around to find who I can only assume to be the princess. Her face is covered in makeup. In a society where only the rich can afford to import it, cosmetics are very noticeable. "Is that crown not delightful?" She claps her hands together.

I clear my throat. "Most certainly."

She rambles on about how in a few short hours, it'll be on her head. The real one? No. Alouette and I know that she'll flaunt a fake. I wish she'd just shut up already. No one needs a monologue about a crown that doesn't belong to her kingdom. Poor Alouette has to converse with the princess as she asks all about her dress. She's probably jealous of the alchemist. Gold suits her way better than the princess.

Once she has had enough of us, she departs. Alouette turns to the crown, pulling a silver cube out of her pocket.

"Watch my back."

"I've got it." I whistle a fun little tune. There aren't many people in the lobby anymore. Atlas is working wonders with that voice of his.

Every so often, I look back at Alouette. She's molding metal as if it were clay. Fascinating.

I turn back around to see a knight in full armor approaching us. I keep my attention locked on him while nudging Alouette to alert her. She spins around, hiding the fake behind her back. Her eyes grow wide. Does she know him? The knight stops in front of us.

"You have found your way back?"

"Yes, sir."

"And that suitor of yours?"

"Yes, sir."

"That wing is off limits. If I see you two again, we'll have no choice but to escort you out."

"Yes, sir."

He salutes and walks off.

Suitor? I grin at Alouette. "Don't tell me that after I left—"

"Hush, you." She returns to her duty. It's almost done.

"Atlas is never going to hear the end of this!" I chime. Oh, I'm never going to let this go. Yes!

She brandishes it for only me to see. I can't tell the difference. One last time, I check for other attendees. Thank goodness for Atlas' irresistible voice. No one is here to watch us. I duck below the red ropes blocking it off, slip the real crown off, and set the fake on the pedestal.

"Now how do we hide it?" Alouette snatches it from me and slips it into some kind of pocket or between the layers of her gown's tulle. Maybe girls are helpful to have around.

No man would suspect to check her outfit. She spins a little. No crown falls. It's hidden and safe. We share a celebratory high-five.

Now it's time to leave.

I make my way towards the entrance. Alouette stops me. "What about Atlas?"

I groan. "Oh, great."

A begrudging mumble comes next, "And maybe I want to stay."

Goodness grief, she wants to stay.

"Just leave with me and you can go back. Atlas needs someone to keep an eye on him. Deal?"

"Deal."

Our hands clap together.

▽△▽△

I thought that stealing a crown would be much more of a hassle. Perhaps our ease is a sign that the waters before us will churn, as they do after the eye of a storm. Bad omens are quite common and often show themselves on a daily basis. Keeps us on our toes. Tonight went swell, as smooth as a hot knife through butter. We better count our blessings before this crown becomes a curse. I set it down on the bed beside me. These coverlets used to be Atlas' when he was younger.

Fool, you thought I was going back to the inn. I did a second ago, just to gather our belongings and bring them here. Atlas' father knows the importance of this crown. After all, it belongs to his wife.

I'll leave it at that. Have fun!

Chapter 9

— The Alchemist —

EDWIN SEEMED RATHER thrilled to leave. His job here is done. My father said that some people can sense the future. Now, I have a feeling that something will go awry. I'll make the best out of this night, with Atlas or not. I don't care. A girl is more than capable of entertaining herself.

I stand on the balcony with my arms on the edge. My fingers pick at the little crystals on Rosaline's gifted mask. Lights from ships shine on the horizon while Atlas' songs resound through the night. The cool breeze brings wafts of salt. I lift my chin to the sky to trace the constellations. On clear nights like this, my father would point them out to me, and, sometimes, I tried to make up new ones. I'd name them and ramble through their lore, which I compiled on the spot. Stories always enthralled me, whether told by my father or fathomed in my head, although I wasn't always a reader. When I got my hands on books, I'd plow through them in one day. Aside from that, I'd get three pages in before staring at my father and his experiments, which I found more amusing than printed characters. I didn't just want to be like him. I wanted to *become* him.

A reliable figure.

An avid learner.

A proud alchemist.

All of that diminished three years ago. I'm nowhere near his greatness. Sure, I've been hired a time or two for my abilities. His handiwork has gone to waste. All of the knowledge he has passed down to me. Alchemy is an art. It's a chance, a risk I'm willing to take. Plenty of forebears lost their freedom or lives in pursuit of changing metals into gold.

My father's practice entailed so much more.

Understanding. The malleable metals don't need to be heated in order to be molded.

Some people—we call them the Gifted—are born with magic. I wasn't. My father wasn't. All of the other alchemists weren't. None of us could cast spells. Still, we gave ourselves a special touch.

We could have a say in the world around us.

But people don't like that power. I slam my fist down on the ledge. So we're labeled as dangerous. Creating gold out of base metals has been deemed as a crime.

I tune into the soft piano. Atlas must have found someone to dance with, or maybe he left with another suitor. A real one. His looks alone are surely enough for any girl to bury herself in his arms, deep in his embrace. My old heart would have fluttered at the thought. Instead, wasps prance around my stomach. I'm not supposed to be here. Not alone. Not with pirates. At least the captain has found another girl to amuse himself.

I feel a hand on my back. Nevermind. He's here.

"You're all alone?"

"I don't need your requiem, Atlas."

My comment goes disregarded. "About earlier, you're right. The princess offered me a gig." With a grimace, he's rubbing a lipstick stain off of his cheek.

"Well, what did you say?"

"No." He rests his arms beside mine. I scoot a few inches away. He slides closer.

"Your loss."

He rubs the back of his neck. "I know I'm going to regret this later if I don't ask now." He takes a deep breath in. I choke on my own anticipation. "Will you dance with me?"

My first instinct is to say no. The voice of my father in the back of my head would want me to take any opportunity, especially because I don't think I'll ever get this chance again with anyone else. The adventurous little girl he raised concurs. The dress I'm wearing feels as if it had been pulled out of faerie fables. In another place at another time, this would be my dream come true. Alas, Celestia is not very generous with her opportunities. I know that well. My old heart begs. Do not let this chance slip. It seems I don't have a choice.

"Just don't get mad when I step on your toes." I deliberately kick his foot as he takes his mask off and tosses it aside.

"Oh, come on." He takes my hand. And my breath. I flinch.

"Don't you have other girls to do this with?"

He tilts his head and halfway shrugs. I flick his dark bangs to the side. There's still a smudge of red on his cheek. It's the first time I've seen him with a smug smile, smeared just like the princess' lipstick. Maybe it's the wine taking over his judgment, slowly but surely consuming his rationality until he sobers up.

His arm is around my waist, mine on his shoulder. Our skin doesn't touch at all. We're too good at hiding ourselves, apparently. He knows what's underneath, whereas I haven't the slightest idea as to what he covers. He hums along with the pianist.

"The princess kissed you, Atlas. There are one-hundred percent better people to spend your time with."

"Alas, but who is the best dressed?"

I raise my brows. My own lips curl into a smirk. He knows I'm competitive. "Oh? Courtesy of Rosaline."

He guides me and spins around. For being tipsy, it's a miracle he's not dizzy. His melodies continue to come out in murmurs. I stare up at the sky. He does, too.

Words come out before I can quiet myself. "Can you name them?"

"Just Polaris. It comes with being a sailor." He looks down at me. "What about you?"

"I'd rather rename them."

He gives me a half-hearted laugh. While he's distracted, I reach for the fingers of his glove. Maybe I'll be able to reveal what he's hiding. His hand tightens around my wrist. I wasn't fast enough.

"Alouette."

"Oh, come on."

"I told you, there's nothing to see."

"Edwin told me that you need to explain."

"Explain what?" His huff and darting eyes hint at his lies. I hate people who so blatantly lie. If you can't craft a convincing fib, just tell the truth. I can't quarrel with him here. Not in front of everyone. I can feel onlookers peering through the window. He's a spectacle. Now that I'm in his arms, I'm a part of his display. As we slow dance, Atlas sways from side to side, like a rocking ship. He makes me sick.

How come I'm entranced by him?

"You haven't stepped on my toes yet." He lets go of one hand and spins me around. My dress spirals the way I always hoped it would. I fall the same way I had fallen off the plank. Backward. I hate to think into his arms. He lets me drop a little too far. My already queasy stomach lurches. His smile glints in the blue moonlight, teeth oddly as white as the gleaming star above us.

"That was close, Atlas." I claw for his arm. He tips me back onto my feet. I'm pulled closer. His forehead rests on mine. The wine he had this evening is sweeter than what he had last night. Although I shouldn't be able to tell that, I can. For a moment I fear that he'll dip down and press his lips against mine, to pull me under some kind of spellbinding enchantment.

His arm, curled around my waist, holds me captive. I reach out for his other. My heart races. I say his name. He doesn't listen.

"Let me go." I reach for his face to slap his cheek. Potentially to knock some sense into him. He doesn't respond. Instead, he pushes me away, keeping my hands in his. He spins me around so that the back of my head is against his chest. One arm is crossed in front of me and the other holds my hand above my head. I'm locked in his embrace.

"I don't want you to hate me, Alouette," he whispers in my ear.

"Maybe I won't if you let me go."

That gets him to release me.

"I heard that a ship returned to the port this morning." He keeps his voice low. I don't want to know what he's going to say. "It was covered in spikes comprised of the same wood as the thinned deck. Did that have anything to do with you?"

My eyes widen. I'm the one who locks onto his arm this time. We need to go. Trying to pull him is like attempting to drag a marble statue. Futile.

"Do you want to die?"

▽⟁▽△

Edwin had told me that he was going to pay the DeLuca household a visit. If I can help it, I'm not going to get caught by any other pirates. Atlas runs through the street with me. My heels are in my hands. Running barefoot is better than risking a sprained ankle. The bricks scrape my exposed skin, which barely beats the alternative.

"What was that all about?" Atlas yells.

"If the pirates were there, they'd know who I am." I skid to a stop. Atlas halts a few yards ahead of me. "And, excuse me, what were *you* trying before that?"

If I had the chance to stop, I'd be able to vividly recall his warm breath on my ear.

"I don't know!" His voice rasps as he looks down. He gestures to the shoes in my hands. "You're kidding me."

He storms toward me, leans in, and throws me over his shoulder. That's one solution. He knows the way to his father's house. I'm not going to fight him on this. There's no use.

The people who tried to get rid of me are still here somewhere. These two pirates don't deserve to get wrapped up in my mess, no matter how wicked they may or may not be. And I won't take my chances.

▽⟁▽△

Edwin is wide awake, but Atlas' father is sound asleep in his room. By now, it feels like midnight. We quickly get changed in preparation to make our escape. I try to catch Atlas in the act of putting his gloves on. I'm moments too late.

The crown sits on Edwin's head. He's practically screaming, "Look at me, I'm a pretty, pretty princess!"

I laugh at him.

Atlas scowls. "Quit playing around. We need to go."

Chapter 10

— The Thief —

I HIDE THE crown all the way until we get to the dock. Then I put it back on my head.

"Geez, it's kinda heavy."

"Be careful. It could compress your spine." Alouette warns.

"Oh, no." I tilt my head and let the crown fall back into my arms. Atlas shakes his head and hops down into the boat, which bobs in the black water.

"Ladies first." I gesture for Alouette to go. It's a gag. I couldn't imagine being in her shoes. A, they would be too small. B, we all know how sick she got before.

She jumps down and sits across from Atlas. Great. I get to sit with him. I will not give Alouette the chance to throw up on me. I hand Atlas the crown before jumping down. Davy Jones will reclaim it if we're not careful. Atlas unties us from the dock, and we're off!

"Is that a bottle of wine?"

Atlas has something cradled in his arm. "And if it is?"

"I've got cheese. I'm sorry I stole it from your dad." I tap my bulging pocket.

"At least we'll have something to eat."

That's right. When we took the trip here, it took around two days drifting across the sea. I got so hungry that my stomach growled louder than I could speak. Plus, Atlas has stolen from his parents before. Let the first without theft cast the first stone. He can't blame me.

Atlas pops the cork off with his thumb and takes a sip. Will he ever get enough?

▽△▽△

Slumber claims its first victim: Alouette. Atlas is dozing off, too. He's battling his eyes to stay open.

"You can sleep, you know. I'm fine with paddling."

▽△▽△

We swap shifts in the middle of the night.

▽△▽△

Screaming gulls wake me up. Atlas is rowing. I check for the crown. It's around his bottle like a horseshoe on a nail.

"It's about time," he remarks.

"Yeah, yeah." I look across the boat at Alouette, who is slumped over. She didn't wake up during my shift.

"Leave her alone. She's better asleep than seasick."

Yep. "Couldn't agree more."

I slip the crown off of his bottle and set it on Alouette's head. Not a perfect fit, for it's a little crooked. Without another word, I lean back. Atlas hands the oars off to me. By now, you would've hoped that someone would invent a small vessel more efficient than a rowboat. Canoes are basically the same. Sailboats don't count. We need a steam boat. The blisters on my palms sting. If only I wore pretty much permanent gloves like Atlas. He probably doesn't have raw palms from hours of rowing.

I whistle a sea shanty and row to the rhythm while the sun rises above the distant kingdom. Those stupid walls are still in view. I have to take pity on everyone under the monarch's rule that doesn't get to live inside. Nothing is there to protect them from pirates or raids from inland.

Thank the seven seas that I grew up inside of a different walled city. The royal courts must think that it's trendy. My parents had lived outside, but after their home burned to the ground, some old folks decided it would be safer if I lived inside those giant stone bricks rather than beyond them. A swell decision on their part.

I stop rowing for a moment to pull some cheese out of my pocket. Atlas holds his hand out for a piece. I give a small chunk to him and a larger one to myself.

Usually, I'd request that he use his words like a real person, but it's best if we stay quiet so Alouette can sleep.

Blimey! Our efforts are fruitless!

Alouette sits up and stretches. Atlas and I jump to stop her. There's a deep kerplunk.

"What was that?" She looks over the edge at the brewing ripples. After realizing, she covers her mouth.

"Oops." I turn to Atlas.

His chest heaves. I'm not sure if he's going to strangle me or jump in. Luckily, he picks the latter. He vanishes with a splash. I can only lean back and wait for this all to crumble.

▽△▽△

Alouette sucks her lips in and looks over the edge again. The ripples have faded.

"Did he…drown?"

"Nah. He can just hold his breath for a really, really, really long—" The crown is thrown back onto the boat from the other side. I shriek. Alouette jolts. I squeak, "—time."

Black hands reach over the side of the boat. Atlas gasps for breath. I hold my hand out to help him. He knocks it away.

I gawk. "A no thanks would be fine."

"When I get in there, Edwin, I swear I'm going to strangle you."

"It'll be really hard to find a replacement boatswain. We all know I'm the cream of the crop."

"Sounds like a job opening," he grunts. His gaze moves over to Alouette.

Eyes-wide, she clutches her stomach. I'll hand it to her; it's pretty unusual to dive underwater for half an hour. "I'd never work for you."

Great, now it's everyone in the boat versus Atlas.

"Get in or I'll get you with the oar." I pretend to knock him upside the head, stopping just short of his dripping wet face. His black hair clings to his cheeks, at least covering some of the scales that creep up from his neck.

"Row and I'll get out of your way."

Captain's orders. I can't decline. Atlas dips down. The boat lurches forward. He's under us. "Don't you dare capsize us! Think of the cheese! And your wine, you brainless scallywag!"

Alouette has her nearly-green face buried in her hands.

▽△▽△

With Atlas pushing and me rowing, we're on a roll. I'm rather frightened by how strong he is. And that endurance. *He's a beast.*

Alouette gnaws on the final bit of my cheese. It's truly a shame how quickly we went through it. Less for Atlas. And that meant that Alouette and I got way more.

With a mouthful, Alouette says, "Look, another ship."

I turn around to see where she's pointing. I curse. Atlas, like an echo, also curses. The mast is not of a merchant's ship. Ol' Jolly Roger gives us his crooked grin. Pirates are heading straight toward us. Atlas and I are good at being swashbucklers, but if they have a full crew, we're just about done for. I lean over the edge of our rowboat and knock on the wood twice. Once for Atlas' attention and twice for good luck. I'm superstitious; what else can I say?

"Come on, buddy. Water playtime is over."

"Edwin!"

"It'll be fine!"

No, it won't.

Atlas grabs the side of the boat and hoists himself into it. Alouette screams and pushes herself to the back of the rowboat. I guess her fear has helped her overcome her mal de mer.

Who can blame her, though? The young man next to me isn't a man anymore. There's a scaled tail where his legs should be.

▽△▽△

I think about six years ago—just to let you know it's a flashback, you son of a biscuit eater.

In the morning, the weather and sky made me feel like it would be a wonderful day to take a ferry. I had aged out of the orphanage a few months prior and was ready to see the world. I'm lying. I didn't have anything else to do, so I had stolen enough money to take a ride across some random harbor. Details don't matter when it comes to a past I wish not to dwell on.

As I boarded, I saw dark clouds roll across the horizon. It didn't bother me too much. Rainstorms passed by our town on occasion. I hopped on and ran right for the railing. I'd rather stare at the waves than at people. Atlas had the same idea. At the time, he was a stranger.

He told me a storm was coming.

"Nah, it'll be fine." I brushed his warning off.

For the first half of the trip, I was gearing up to tell this mysterious boy, "I told you so." The weather had other plans. The waves began to chop. The clouds flickered. Almost instinctively, the two of us huddled up, like helpless chickens. He grasped the wooden rail. We were just foolish teens, fresh in the fearsome world with no parents in sight. The waves began to toss the ship around. I grabbed onto Atlas for dear life. Rain came down like pellets. When the ferry tipped one way, we slid away from the railing, and when it leaned the other way, we were face to face with the waves.

My famous last words were, "We're gonna be fish food!"

We plunged into the harbor. I thrashed around to reach the surface, but every time I broke the tension, another wave crashed down. I called for the boy. He had to be in the same situation as me. After being dunked again, I saw a dark blue tail. It didn't belong to a fish. It was part of the guy I had met. His webbed fingers reached for me.

The trip back to shore became a blur; the rain must've washed my memory clean.

I do remember waking up. Atlas stared at me from above, checking my pulse by pressing his fingers on my neck. Too scared and too drenched to respond, I stayed silent for an hour or so. The lines blurred in my mind. Maybe I only kept quiet for a couple of minutes. Or even a few moments.

I owed him for that.

Yet from that day, he was the one who was forever indebted to me.

I was the only one who knew his secret. He had to explain the whole situation to me as we dried off. His father had fallen in love with a siren. In the water, you know the story. On land, he walked as a human. Mostly. He had fins on his forearms, which he covered with long sleeves. When it rained, scales popped up. We couldn't do much about that. His nails were insanely sharp, though back then he didn't cover his hands.

I tagged along his adventures after that. He stopped at a tavern in each and every town we visited. Whether big or small, it didn't matter to him. We were still just kids. I don't know what drove him to drink so young. It couldn't've been good. In his defense, sometimes liquor was cleaner than water, but that's not a real excuse. I always tried to pull him away. I hated how taverns smelled. Most of the time, his secret got leveraged against him. I probably drove him further into drinking. Most nights we spent in town, he practically drowned himself in alcohol.

I fear that if he were fully a human, he would've died by now.

▽△▽△

Between barred teeth, Alouette mutters, "Celestia so help me. Edwin! Tell me I'm hallucinating!"

I put my hands up in surrender.

She shakes her head, trying to get as far away from him as possible. She loses her balance. If it isn't for Atlas latching onto her wrist, she would've fallen in again.

This does look pretty bad on Atlas' part. That tail of his is far more eel-like than a classical mermaid one might imagine. He has to coil it up in the small rowboat that he was already too tall for.

"We have bigger problems to worry about," I warn as a shadow falls over us.

One man lands on the boat. He has an eyepatch, how tacky. Alouette shakily stands. My best guess is that she thinks she can fight him but is reminded about her ailments. As the weight shifts, she practically topples into his arms. He latches onto a rope hanging down from the ship. Netting covers Atlas next. I draw my dagger. Another man comes down.

"Hey, can't we strike a deal?" I ask, holding out the golden coin Alouette made.

Chapter 11

— The Siren —

I ALWAYS FEARED that Edwin would finally be the one to rat me out. First, it's the crown incident, and now, this. In the past, I had locked many prisoners on my father's ship. Never had I been taken prisoner before.

Alouette won't even look at me. Her knees are pulled to her chest wedged in the front corner of our cell. I'm in the back, tangled in a mess of ropes.

"Alouette."

"I don't want to hear it."

Great. Just great. "I screwed this up."

"Yes, you did."

"I can explain, I swear."

"Explain what? Your cover ups and lies? With more fibs and fables? Even faerie tales are more believable than you."

I can't explain those. In my defense, I was embarrassed. I'm still ashamed. She's not the type to buy that as a reasonable response.

"I open myself up to two people who saved my life. And this is what I get? I could've told you I was a normal, little, feeble, foolish girl. Maybe I am foolish. Atlas. If that's even who you are? Unless you're a changeling. Unless you're a s—" She grasps for breath.

"Say it," I hiss.

"No, no." She shakes her head. Her eyes grow wide under the light peeking through the floorboards, illuminating like light bulbs. "No. That explains too much."

"Alouette."

"Don't you say my name, Siren." The iron bars shake.

I press my back against the wooden wall. Very few have scared me like the alchemist has.

She takes a deep breath. "I saw the scales at the tavern."

She did?

I can't feel my stomach anymore; an empty hole gapes where it should be.

"And your voice. How you sang at the masquerade. It all pointed to this. How did I not put two and two together?"

"You were trying to survive."

She turns to look at me. My tail is awkwardly twisted in a loop and a fin flops over my face. Pitiful, I know. Don't remind me.

"You almost died. Two strangers picked you up and forced you to help steal a crown. There were greater concerns on your mind."

"Not to mention someone who forced himself on me."

"It's not like that. You know that, Alouette."

"Don't say my name, Fiend." Shaking, she stands. I want to do the same. Alas, I'm stuck. She picks up a piece of scrap metal, reaches through the bars, and jams it in the lock. She slips out of the cell.

"I can explain!"

"You had your chance." She throws the piece of debris at me.

▽△∀△

I remember one night, although I can't remember which town we were in, but, really, it doesn't matter too much. Edwin and I were in a tavern. My speech slurred. The lights blurred.

He told me that I could make any girl swoon with my looks and voice.

I replied that I could not count on anyone staying. I, myself, left.

He followed me, trailing close behind, as always. He hasn't stopped treading in my footsteps, if not by my side, since the ferry. That night, his apologies went in one ear and out my other.

"Look, I'm sorry! Don't you know how hard it is to see the friend who saved me spiral down like this? Atlas, your parents love you. I'd do anything to see mine again. Is that not enough? You won't accept their good tidings and seek out some random lady who would love you for who you are, not what you are?"

"Are you calling me a monster?" I reached for his throat.

He tried shaking his head. "No! No! *You* seem to think that!"

He was right, but I refused to admit it.

The next thing I knew, Edwin backed away from me, blood gushing out of where his eye should have been. His reddened dagger fell on the ground between us. I stood above him. I staggered only a few steps backward before my knees gave out. My cheek stung. My eyes did, too.

I had been the one to hurt him. It was me. I was still the problem.

▽ △ ▽ △

I *am* still the problem.

Chapter 12

— The Alchemist —

I USE MY hand as a visor as I emerge on the deck. Plenty of swords and other sharp trinkets all aimed right at my throat greet me. I'm used to it by now.

"Aye!" Edwin quips. They all turn to him. He shakes his head. "Nuh-uh. Leave her alone."

I clench my fists and stand my ground. It's very unsteady. I bite the inside of my cheek.

Don't feel queasy. Don't feel queasy. Don't feel queasy!

Edwin strolls over to me. The pirates seem to cower away from him. "I said I'd unleash our alchemist if they tried anything funny. Everyone heard what happened to the other ship."

"Oh, uhm." What's the right response? Surely not an expression of gratitude.

"You left Atlas in the cellar?"

"And if I did? I don't want to see his face again. Can't we just release him?" My gaze turns to the sea, where I'm guessing he initially came from. Awful things arise from those depths.

"Well, he's not quite a fish."

"He's a siren, I know."

"Half-siren."

I stand corrected.

"If I may play the devil's advocate, his parents made him this way. It wasn't his choice."

"He did have the chance to tell me. Several, actually."

"And he failed."

Failed is one way to put it. "Edwin. What's the plan from here?"

"We're heading back to retrieve Atlas' ship, good ol' *Boreas*. I'm afraid we're going to need him alive."

The thought sickens me. Or the waves. I can't tell which anymore.

"Can I have your dagger?"

"For what?"

"I'm not going to carve out his heart."

"How assuring, Alouette." Edwin chuckles, unsheathing his blade to present it to me. "Whatever makes you feel better, M'lady."

I glower at the pirate crew as I pass them. They all cower away and avoid eye contact. Pirates aren't at all what I expected, merely a scraggly bunch of chumps who reek of fish and death.

Atlas somehow draws me back. I can't seem to get enough of him. I slam the iron door open with my foot. The dagger is strangled between both of my hands. I have a better grip without gloves. He looks up with a wince. I draw a deep breath in before approaching the half-siren.

His mouth opens to speak.

"Don't say a word." I keep the dagger pointed at him. I kneel beside him. His scales shimmer in the dim light that makes its way through cracks in the floorboards above us. I pull on sections of the rope to create tension so I can saw through it with the blade. The netting is already frayed, so it doesn't take too much effort to cut him free. Atlas stalks my movements with his deep blue eyes. Instead of growing smaller, his pupils narrow into slits, similar to a serpent.

Once the last of the rope falls to the ground, I declare, "Edwin told me about your parents. I'm not even sure how it's possible. Sirens try to lure men and kill them, don't they?"

His eyes avoid contact. "Usually."

I bend down again and lift his bottom tail fin up with my borrowed dagger. I can see through the translucent blue. If I had driven the blade through it, I wonder if he would've felt it. Touching him feels taboo. With the flat of Edwin's dagger, I trace the scales from the fin to his waist, where they seem to taper off into his light skin, but his jacket covers everything else.

He stares at me in silence. "Thanks."

"For what?" I stand and spin the dagger around.

"Cutting the ropes and…sparing me."

"Edwin said we've charted a course for your ship." I leave it at that.

▽△▽△

Back on the top deck, I spot Edwin sitting on the bow.

"I've got your knife!"

My presence makes a few scurvy dogs scatter.

"And Capt'n is still alive, right!?"

"You got it!"

"He'll be up soon!"

"What!?"

Edwin marches over to me. "He won't stay like a siren forever. Once he dries off, you'll see."

"And this happens every time he's submerged?"

"Pretty much." Edwin brushes it off. They've been mates for a while now, so his condition is no striking news. "Then why does he wear those gloves?"

"Son of a—he hasn't told you!?" He stomps his foot on the wooden plank. The board creaks. His boot almost goes through.

▽△▽△

As foretold by Edwin, Atlas emerges on deck. Ignoring his disoriented expression, he appears as if nothing happened. He's got boots, breeches, and his double-breasted jacket on. Naturally, his iconic gloves, too. By some miracle, there's a bottle in his hand.

Edwin groans. He's got a right to.

Captain Atlas bosses the confused crew around. They all oblige under the assumption that an alchemist will turn their ship into a mess of wooden spears. I'm not sure if Atlas is aware of that yet.

On this vessel, our mates can rival theirs. Assuming Atlas' voice works just like his mother's, he can use that to control them.

Last night, did he use his song to control me? My father always warned me about sirens. One melody leads to a trance, and by the time you catch on, it's already too late.

The urge to ask about what he did bugs me like an itch. Is this why he did not take the princess' offer? There are so many questions that bubble to the surface of my mind. The time isn't right to ask any of them; he's busy giving commands to the people of this ship.

I sit down and lean against one of the posts supporting the masts. My fingers press into my temples, a poor excuse for a message. How in the world did I manage to get kidnapped by pirates *twice?*

Chapter 13

— The Siren —

THIS CREW IS far more willing than I had anticipated. A rapier surrendered by one of them sits in my hand.

"Who's the captain?" I call.

The mindless men quiver, pointing to the oldest of them all. He itches his graying beard. A red bandana wraps his head, under his hat. Feathers sewn into the side waver in the wind. I approach him. With each step I take closer to him, he backs away until he bumps into the side of the ship.

"You can 'ave our booty! Plunder it! Spare me crew."

"Spare you?" I rest the rapier's fine point between his eyes. My men see this as a bluff. My enemies, however, aren't aware of my mercy. "Is this a scheme of yours?"

"A-A scheme?" He shakes his head. Gold and silver fill his mouth where ivory teeth should be.

"Why surrender so easily?"

"T-The alchemist."

Alouette?

So that ship's undoing *was* her doing.

"Spare me crew!" he begs.

I pull the blade away from him. "Cooperate and we will. The course is charted for another harbor. You'll get your ship back there. Until then, don't try anything."

Edwin cheers from the crow's nest. He acts like a fool, but I'm assuming he was the one to convince them that Alouette would tear their already rotting ship to pieces. She's sitting near the bow now. I'm not bold enough to go over to her.

"And, by the way," I add one last remark, "in exchange for my rowboat, I'm taking this sword."

Once we get to shore, would it be worth risking my own ship to invite the alchemist on board? Once, *Aurora Borealis* had been my father's pride and joy. I will not let her fall into ruin, regardless of how little I respect my father. He's responsible for the monster I've become.

The breeze carries the crew's mutterings. I let out a roar as I slam the rapier into the deck. It wobbles before settling. My fingers curl around the hilt. With one tug, it comes out. The remaining hole goes right through the deck.

▽☆▽△

I sit in a captain's cabin that is not my own. A tattered map is pinned to the desk with a knife on each curling corner. Cobwebs crawl across old bookshelves, littered with scrolls and globes. Nothing is a pure shade of white; it's all yellowed to the point where the even blue of the map's sea appears golden. Everything has a tinge of gold while Alouette is on my mind.

"Your father really spoiled you with your ship, Capt'n." Edwin can't sneak up on me here. The decaying doors' hinges scream at the slightest movement.

I murmur in response, "Yeah."

"We should arrive around nightfall. But I'm no navigator. Maybe at daybreak if we're really unlucky."

"We've had enough bad luck for the day."

"She had to know, Atlas." Edwin runs his fingers along the musty map. Dust coats the tips when he retracts his hand.

I clench my jaw. "I can't believe you convinced a whole band of pirates to surrender their ship by leveraging her against them."

Edwin snickers. "They've heard the stories."

"They're just stories."

"Oh, what now, Atlas? You're coming to her defense? If I hadn't told her that we needed you alive, you'd be a filet."

He's right.

"But they're still just tall tales. She's just a girl."

"Just a girl? Tales of terrors don't just come out of the blue. You know why sailors avoid sirens. There's too much of a risk. And the fear men have of alchemists? That doesn't either. We don't know what she's capable of. The pirates we saved her from could have just taken her captive, but no. They decided to kill her. And why is that, Atlas?"

I stare.

"Tell me, Atlas!"

"She's dangerous."

"That's right. And you're still hiding secrets from her. Do you not learn?" Edwin pulls one of the knives off of the map and holds it under my chin. "You haven't even explained why we stole *this*." He throws the crown onto the desk.

"Just go."

▽△▽△

Should I not have saved her? Would it have been better to let a stranger drown, knowing that I had the chance to give someone another shot at life?

I rub my sore neck. Thinking back to the first night, my throat still burns. Vinegar and vodka. What a toxic mix. She had the chance to poison me. That night. The following. Even when she handed me that glass of wine. She had an opportunity to taint it.

Yet she didn't.

Below deck, she could have ignored Edwin's request. Instead, she cut me free. Out of pity? Only the heavens know. Sure as the sea, her actions were not out of respect. All along, I knew she would bring disaster, and this impending doom is creeping up on us. But why can't I bring myself to hate her the same as she despises me? I'm the one who saved her. She should be grateful, not resentful.

My father once warned me that love drives men to do crazy things.

Now, I can't think straight.

It's not possible. It couldn't be. Curse me. I really am the scourge of the seven seas.

▽△▽△

I walk across the ship to watch the sunset. Besides, the cabin was getting dark. All the oil lamps were laced with webs, for their fuel had been used up long ago. Alouette sits near the bow with her legs crossed. The rays of golden hour illuminate the curls of her silhouette while I stand behind her, shrouded in a shadow.

"My father spoke of two poisons that can kill a man, the first being alcohol."

She's speaking to me? I sigh. Maybe she's aware that I was thinking about my old man. As we stand, I don't know the full extent of her power, so mind-reading is not out of the question. "I know, Alouette. I've gotten this lecture more times than I can count."

Her stiff posture eases. "The other is a mix of chemicals. It's like a toxin in our own minds. It makes us beyond giddy and rather lively."

"Aren't those good?"

"You'd think so." She smiles. "You can lose your appetite and experience insomnia. But, you know, your brain doesn't do it out of the blue. *Someone* causes your mind to produce those chemicals and flood your thoughts with only them."

"The last part makes it sound like love," I murmur.

"Aye, aye, Captain." Weakly, she salutes, off to the sunset.

"How does that kill a man?"

Pulling her legs to her chest, like me, she rests her face between her knees. "It drives him mad. He'd do anything for his love. He'd sail the seven seas, go to the ends of the earth. Though, he'd wind up going around and around in circles. When my father lost my mother, it destroyed him. It's difficult to imagine what such a loss feels like. Someone you devoted your life to, gone. And there's no going back. Metals can be restored, but beings cannot. Your parents are both alive, no?"

"They weren't meant to be together."

"How come you're standing here?"

I shake my head and watch Alouette.

"And why do I feel my life falling to shambles without a taste of either?" Her tone tastes bitter.

"Disdain."

Alouette tilts her head back to look at me. Her wide eyes shimmer like the choppy waters.

"That's the poison my old man spoke of."

Her gaze mellows. Is she really the same dangerous alchemist—the same girl—I spoke with Edwin about earlier? I sit down next to her, one knee pulled to my chest. Alouette moves away.

"I know what you are," she reminds.

"But that doesn't stop you from speaking with me, Lark."

A smile tugs at her lips. "You don't listen very well, Siren."

"My name is Atlas."

"Fine, *Atlas*, you have your own narrative made up in your mind. We all have that bias, truly. Yours is just so far-fetched. Are you a man or a monster? You can't seem to figure it out, so you want someone else to do that."

"And? So what if I asked you?"

She shakes her head. "You don't want my verdict."

"I do."

I reach for her hand. She retracts it. My heart races.

"Alouette, I do. I swear."

"Take the gloves off, and I'll tell you." She holds her hand out.

Now is my chance. But if I show her, she'll think I'm a monster. I scoff and stand. She's backing me into a wall here.

As I begin to walk away, she spits, "A man."

I look back over my shoulder.

"That's what you are because monsters don't have fear."

Chapter 14

— The Alchemist —

THAT'S WHY ALCHEMISTS are monsters. We do not tremble at the world's plans for our demise. Well, Celestia's Will, really. We fret not about knowledge that seals our fates. With bare hands, we take Her creation by its horns and mold it to our liking.

In the end, we all meet the same fate. The normal folk. The Gifted. The sirens. Us alchemists. From dust to dust. We're all made of matter. Whether we make our existence matter is up to us. Whether we want to dig ourselves into debt, set sail, or blaze a path of our own lies within our hands.

Some independent variables get in the way. Like seasickness. I lay down on the musty wooden boards. My arm rests on my forehead. The stars feel like they're spinning.

Well, this is a disaster.

You can thank Celestia for that. Disaster holds roots in the Latin terms for "bad" and "star." Whether their alignment permits my suffering or not, I'll blame them.

I still don't understand why Atlas keeps coming back. I hurt him time and time again, but he's never gone for long. Is he stupid? Maybe he's always hungover. His voice travels far, unlike Edwin's, so I can hear one half of their conversation. Nevermind, I don't want to know what he has to say.

I'll take my leave once we arrive at the next harbor. I can't stand the shifting tides. In theory, the moon's gravitational pull controls them, so I know exactly who to accuse for my ailments. From there, I don't know where I'll go, or what else I'll utilize as my next scapegoat. Atlas better not follow. He's a seafarer, not my friend. Anything but my friend. I misspoke. That could include a quote-unquote "suitor," so I take the previous statement back. I shudder at the thought. Who could stand someone like him? A manipulative liar. For Celesia's sake, a siren!

He had me entranced by his song and locked me in a dance. Now I'm captive on another ship. The last thing I want is to be a prisoner on his own vessel. Oh, the shame I would bring upon my father.

I force myself to sit up. City lights near on the horizon. Oil lamps illuminate the streets. Candles flicker in windows. I hold my hand out. The stars' faint glow makes a white outline around my fingertips. Altogether I don't care much about what happens next. I have faith in Celestia and Her plan for me.

Does this all make me a monster?

Light footsteps tap on the deck, almost inaudible. It must be Edwin. Atlas' are much heavier.

"Aye, are ya ready to dock?"

I rub my eyes. "Ready to get off, yes."

"Great, me too. This scurvy ship doesn't feel safe."

"Is it because you're with an alchemist and a siren?"

"An alchemist, a siren, *and* a thief." He lightly corrects me with a nudge to my arm. His eyes stare down at the waves. It's like another sea of stars beneath us. I have to admit, it's beautiful. "Has a nice ring to it, y'know?"

"I'm not staying with you two." I shake my head no. I can't stay. I'm meant for land, not sea.

"Not gonna join the crew, eh?" His voice raises.

"Sorry to disappoint."

"Nah, you wouldn't be a good fit, ya landlubber." He laughs, sitting with his legs crossed next to me. "The men are too grimy."

"You and Atlas are well-kept."

"We have pride. Just look at the pirates here. They're covered in more barnacles than she is." He knocks on the rickety deck.

I roll my eyes. "Right."

"I think you're pretty swell. Just too swell to join. Alouette, you made moves against Capt'n." His smirk grows. "No one turns him down like that! You'd have everyone question his authority. Besides, he has a soft spot for you, Lark."

"He does not."

Edwin turns his attention back to the sea while a smirk slides across his face.

"Celestia forbid."

"How much does that explain?" He's trying to taunt me. It's so obvious.

"It explains a lot more than him being a siren."

"Half-siren."

"I stand corrected…again." I raise my arms.

"You're actually sitting."

"We don't need to take it that far."

Edwin snickers. "We'll miss you. Well, he'll miss you."

"Ew, Edwin. Don't say that." I shove him.

"No, really!"

Repulsed, I stand and stumble over to the edge of the bow. My arms rest over the edge, as they did on the balcony. Edwin joins me.

"C'mon, Alouette. You've gotta believe me."

"Dead men tell no tales." I reach over and grab the back of his collar. I could throw him overboard if I really wanted to.

"Well, if I were you, I'd hate him too." Edwin tilts his head from side to side. "I know you're not a pushover. It's a virtue, you monster. You don't fear what others think of you or even what they'll do."

I laugh, likely confirming his suspicions. "So he told you?"

"Atlas and I don't keep secrets. You reveal intel when the time is right. He's the one who hides from you."

"I know. Liars and drunkards are the worst. He happens to be both."

▽△▽△

Church bells chime eleven post meridiem when we finally step foot on land again. I look back at the dock. It's all behind us now. Thank the stars.

Of all misfortunes to whine about, Edwin complains, "Gosh, I could really go for some cheese. Shame you finished it, Lark."

I run my fingers along short stone walls that line the street for balance. I won't let Atlas help this time.

"I'll keep a seat warm at the tavern if you grab the crew. They'll be happy we're back." Edwin balances the crown on his head again. That forsaken pearl-covered circlet has brought nothing but problems.

Atlas salutes Edwin.

"Join us for one last meal, won't ya?" Edwin takes the lead, as he did before.

My gut tells me no.

"Sure," rolls off of my tongue more easily than it should.

▽△▽△

Who knew I attracted pirates like a magnet? They reek of alcohol and stenches I didn't know existed until faced with them aboard ships. Still, I'm brought back to my time as a taverner years ago. I was probably too young for the job, but still I got to witness many other heartfelt reunions, where homemade dishes combatted their wretched fragrance. I sit in the corner of the bar, my back against the wall to watch the shenanigans ensue. Some do-si-do with their mates. Edwin challenges Atlas to a sword fight with his new rapier.

"For honor!" the boatswain exclaims.

"For honor," his captain replies.

They circle around each other before lunging. Atlas' blade has more range. Edwin's dagger ends up wedged into the tavern's wooden wall.

"Who has honor now?"

His men cheer.

Not him, I say in my mind as I raise a glass to my lips. The ice cubes do make a satisfying clink, yet the water here is a little too salty for my liking. The jolly sound of mugs tapping together always brought a smile to my face that I could not suppress.

As time passes, everyone seems to settle down. Atlas sits with another girl. By her classy attire, it's safe to assume she's not part of his crew. They smile together.

"Jealous yet?" Edwin walks up to me. I guess it's cider in his cup.

I shake my head and take another sip of water. The glass slams back down on the table. "I will be if he takes off those gloves."

"Woah, there," Edwin mocks. He slides onto the barstool next to mine and rubs the back of his neck. Reddish marks stretch across his skin.

"Are those burns?"

He shrugs. "We all hide something. They're not as pivotal as everyone thinks. House fire, *yay*." He reeks of sarcasm. "You don't need to say you're sorry for my parents that burned. Yours aren't here either." He holds his hand out for some kind of pact. I grab it.

His head tilts. "No gloves today?"

I shake my head. "There's no point in trying to cover my hands if those after me already know my face."

"Fair."

"No crown tonight?"

"Atlas has it."

I look across the tavern to see it sitting next to his fresh collection of bottles. That unfortunate girl must prepare herself. Call it envy if you must, but I'd be furious if she had been wearing the crown. We worked for it, not her.

Somehow, the night passes slowly. The chatter turns into slurred sea-shanties. Atlas stays quiet for a while. I had expected him to join in like a songbird. At least he's dancing with the young woman now. I wonder if that's what we looked like yesterday. A moonstruck couple, sickened by love. At least to the guard. A lump grows in my throat just thinking about it.

Atlas doesn't take his eye off of her, which gives me the perfect chance to stare. The regulars used to call me Hawkeye at the tavern I worked at. I always reminded customers that my name was Alouette, but they all refused to listen. I'm just a watcher at heart, I guess. One drunkard told me that I stalk my prey before I strike. Maybe that's true.

I had watched pirates take over the merchant's ship I infiltrated. Many wore eyepatches. I could have easily hid in their blindspots. The plan was to stay in the shadows until they found me, for maybe they'd spare a poor, helpless little girl. As they were plundering the goods, one made eye contact with me, which sealed my fate. The rest is history.

Edwin waves his hand in front of my face.

"This isn't groundbreaking, Alouette. He's got charisma the first night."

"And the second?"

"We're out at sea by that time. Plenty of girls living in these ports wait their whole lives to make acquaintances with sailors, only for them to leave."

"Because you're so flighty?"

He nods. "You're a lucky girl."

"He's not the sailor of my dreams, Edwin. Nor are you. I'd rather be independent than tethered to a man."

"Ouch." He winces as if I had jabbed him in the gut.

"It's a matter of relying on myself rather than someone else."

"I get it. Atlas doesn't."

The captain leans in a little too close to the girl. I look away. No wonder that knight backtracked in the citadel.

"I was actually hoping that you'd knock some sense into that scallywag." His lips tug into a frown. We sit in silence for a while.

By now, a handful of Atlas' crewmates have retired for the night. The singing has faded. A bottle is back in the captain's hand. His head rests on the polished bar. The girl says her last goodbye to him, blowing him one last kiss. I could puke. Edwin points down the back of his throat. We share another laugh. As much as I hate the captain, I love making fun of him. Edwin does, too. But at least they're friends, *real* friends. One has the other's back covered, whether with a shining blade or a crafty plan, like brothers in arms.

"Well," he stands, "I'll catch ya around, Alouette."

"See you on the flipside." I salute. Now I know what he means about getting familiar with seafarers. There's no guarantee that I'll ever see him again. "Looks like it's the end for the alchemist, the siren, and the thief."

He stops. I had expected him to smile, but all he wears is a strained straight face to keep a frown at bay. "It must be. Once you get over that mal de mer of yours, there's probably a spot for you." His lips part to bear his teeth. "I gotta have someone to taunt Capt'n with me." That's my Edwin, but with a wave, he's gone.

I wait a few minutes before standing up. The barkeep nods to me.

"Thanks."

A salty breeze greets me as the door opens. The girl Atlas had been chatting with sits on a bench in the town square. Her cheeks are pink. She twirls her blonde hair around her fingers.

"You met the captain?" I lift a brow. This is a conversation I shouldn't start.

"He's a captain?" Her eyes gleam in the moonlight. Her fascination amazes me.

I nod.

"Wow."

Wow? Not the response I initially expected. She must be tipsy.

I hear my name resound through the streets. I turn to the caller.

"You know him?"

Old habits never die, do they?

The captain sprints around the corner. His face stops just inches from mine. He grabs my hands, fingers curling around mine. I stare. His blue eyes glow in the moonlight, reflecting the stars' gleam.

"Lark, just give me one more chance."

He lifts his hands, bringing my arms with his.

"I've had enough." I step back, planting my foot on the cobblestone. I'll attack if I have to. He inches closer, singing an all too familiar tune.

"*Alouette, gentille Alouette.*"

"Don't you dare!"

"*Je te plumerai.*" With the taunting lullaby, he pushes a curl behind my ear. I take the chance to twist his other arm. There's a crack. Atlas grits his teeth. The girl gasps. I draw back and get low enough to run my fingers along the ground. My palms press into the cold stones, which strike from the ground like lances. Atlas turns to avoid them. One throws him off his feet. Within moments, he has drawn the stolen rapier. A hand on the ground, he leans toward me. His attempt at a jab is blocked by another sharp rock. He spins aside before it can hit him. I tap the ground again. A spire from behind knocks him in the jaw, right where he already has a scar. As he clasps his cheek in one hand, I pace backward.

"Stay back," Atlas tells the girl, holding his arm out to protect her.

He should be worried about himself. I reach for one of the spikes and snap off the top. I trace an upside down triangle on its surface. The alchemical symbol for water. The rock begins to bubble and spill over my palm while Atlas draws near. I flick it at his face. As with the rain, glittering scales appear on his jawline.

He curses, however the trick doesn't slow him down. He slips the blade under my feet. I trip, rolling onto my back. I extended my arms and let my palms take the hit. Someone told me it helped send the force outward. Literally. Spikes extend in a circle around us. I'm the one caught off guard by my own actions. The palisade drives a wedge even further between us. *Celestia!*

Atlas bares his teeth and takes a stab at puncturing my outstretched arm. The metal tries pressing into my palm. I won't let it. My teeth grind. His blade unfurls into curls until it gets to the hilt. Synchronized footsteps surround us. The muzzles of muskets make their way through the spires. My fingers curl as I draw back. Deep, shaky breaths make my chest rise and fall. Atlas tosses the rapier's remnants aside and plants his foot on my chest.

"He was right. You are dangerous."

Chapter 15

— The Siren —

"I'll handle her."

I grab the alchemist by her wrist. She screams for me to stop. The guards keep the barrels pointed at her.

At my command, the guards, armed with muskets, draw their weapons back.

"Report back to Jayin of Vaughan," one barks. The unit departs.

"Are you okay?" I ask the girl I had met in the tavern. She nods. Great. I drag the alchemist down the street, toward the dock.

If she's to die, it's by my hand.

Cries of my name echo through the empty road. She claws at my heels. Lucky for me, I'm not Achilles. I kick her with the back of my foot. That silences her for a moment.

Raspy weeps start up. Matted hair tangles with her saliva and tears. I step down onto the docks. Edwin waits by my ship, *Aurora Borealis*, with arms crossed. A smug told-you-so smirk slides across his face.

"What next, Capt'n?"

"Get the cell ready."

A spike protrudes from the dock. I lift her off of the ground. The alchemist dangles like a ragdoll. There's no chance to attack if she can't get her hands on anything.

As I prepare to board my ship, a strange wave of guilt washes over me.

Why do I feel sorry?

Chapter 16

— The Alchemist —

He tosses me in another prison cell. This one hasn't decayed. The walls are lined with thick slabs of metal. Atlas stands in the doorway. Candlelight from behind makes his silhouette far more intimidating than it had been before. Shackles around my ankles and neck chain me to the back. His men bind my wrists with ropes.

They leave.

It's just the two of us.

Then Atlas turns his back. "You fiend."

▽△▽△

Wailing isn't the best choice, but it's all I can do. I can't see. My limbs don't want to move. Every so often, a pirate will slam his fist on the door and shout for me to shut up. I snap for him to leave. When I'm free, I can intimidate those seafarers. Under lock and key, I'm only laughing stock.

I shouldn't have gone to the tavern.

Who had betrayed me? Edwin? It had to be. We spoke behind Atlas' back, so he must've spoken behind mine. That traitor.

Should I have given Atlas another chance?

No. He didn't deserve it. He knew what he was doing. He knew damn well that he was going too far. That first night, he tested the waters.

And the song. A taunt.

The only man who had ever sung that to me was my father.

I thrash and howl with an unbridled wrath that is not concerned by the pirates' threats nor the bruises to bloom on my knuckles.

A monster may not fear, but he does feel rage.

▽△▽△

And remorse.

Maybe I was wrong. My eyes flutter open and shut. They don't stop tears from bubbling and spilling over my cheeks. This isn't entirely his fault. It's mine. Unlike me, he needed someone. I should've been that person.

He had mercy on the other sailors. He had mercy on me.

I've still got oxygen in my lungs because of him. For Celestia's sake, I would've drowned if he weren't there to pull me out.

Maybe if I had given him one more chance, we would've clarified this murky water filled with lies and deception.

Blubbering, I murmur, "Where's my requiem now?"

My head falls back on the cold metal. The thick air and scent of salt overwhelm my senses. Tears sting my eyes.

I think back to the gathering.

"I bet you'd steal more hearts than mine."

He wasn't referring to his voice when he said mine. He meant his heart. Not in a scalpel-dissection kind of way. But I had known him for barely three days, how could it be romantic?

I kept resisting because I didn't trust him. I tried my hardest to convince myself that he was an awful person. Sure, the captain falls short of many virtues. But he's not bad. It's my fault for keeping everyone else at bay, out of arm's reach.

I don't even deserve another chance.

▽△▽△

There's a click. My swollen eyes snap open. The door shuts. Bare feet slap on the ground. A dark figure leans over me. Whoever it is reeks of alcohol, but that doesn't limit who it could be.

I sink down, pressing myself against the floor. There's nothing worth fighting over. If this will be my end, then so be it. These past few days shouldn't have been seized by me, nonetheless, I squandered them.

Hands reach for my ankles. Frigid fingers wrap around my leg. The chains release. Hands reach for the restraint around my neck. They retreat. Sharp nails are at the end of each fingertip.

A grunt fills the empty air.

The final shackle is removed, but I still can't move my wrists. Fingers pry off the ropes. I slide against the wall. I still can't see who is here.

Then I hear him. "Can you shine a light?"

Atlas.

I fumble, raising my hand between us. A few symbols decide to glow. I don't remember which marked constellations glow. I only know that Polaris shines the brightest. Dark rings shadow the captain's eyes. He moves away.

"I'm dangerous. I know," my voice scratches like a chipped record.

His tired gaze rests on my hand. He raises his arm to meet mine. A blue fin protrudes from his forearm. Did he take another dive? No. This is what he has been hiding. The sleeves of his cotton dress shirt have been rolled up to show me. All of the buttons are misaligned.

He whispers my name.

I don't know what to say. I've been upset over *this*? How petty. A voice in the back of my mind reminds me that it's not just what he's been hiding that matters, it's the fact that he's been lying to me. I have so many questions for him. My mouth is dry. My lips are chapped. My words won't come out.

He lowers his arm. "You don't want me to be here. It's clear. But, you just need to know—" He shakes his head. "No, it's embarrassing."

The light flickers. With hunched shoulders, he moves away again and crosses his arms.

"You're everything I want. Confident. Cunning. You know who you are and don't try to hide it. I do. I can't bring myself to show who I really am."

The light goes out. We sit in silence. His figure stays still.

I'm everything he wants?

For Celestia's sake, he's a captain.

"Tear my ship apart, carve my heart out. I don't care anymore."

There's a glint of light in the darkness. Steel rests on my palm. A knife? My fingers curl around the grip.

"I'm just a man, after all. I'm scared of what I can't emulate."

The knife slips out of my hand. It hits the floor with an ear-piercing clang. He listened?

"Atlas."

His eyes meet mine. "Know that you've been on my mind, a lot. Every time I try to focus on something else, I relapse and fall back to you. I'm scared. I'm scared that I love you. It's a terrifying thought."

I shake my head. I don't know what's wrong with me. Well, a multitude of things. My father is gone. I wasn't raised by a mother. No one taught me these feelings.

Words don't come out. Just fragmented weeps.

Atlas apologizes. A moment of silence ensues before he begins to hum. I rub my eyes. It's the same tune he sang earlier.

"*Alouette, gentille Alouette.*

Je te plumerai."

But it's not as intimidating as when he sang it before.

"How do you know…?" I squint.

He falls silent. "My mom used to sing me lullabies."

The runes on my hands glow again.

"Did your father sing any?"

I shake my head. "Just that one."

"What's the translation, if alouette is lark?"

"Lark, kind lark. I will pluck your feathers out."

He gives me a smile. A genuine one. Not his proud grin from before or even Edwin's sly smirk. He rubs the back of his neck. The barbs on his fin catch his ear.

"Isn't that…"

"Morbid? Yeah."

With an awkward laugh, he says, "I should probably go. Edwin will get mad." He then stands and holds his pale hand out to me. I await his next words. "Unless you want to come with me."

"What for?"

"Our heist isn't over. The crown needs to go back to its rightful owner."

My world spins as I get up. I don't plan on taking his hand, but with the floor shifting below me, I have no choice.

"I'll get you some ginger beer."

"Does it have alcohol?" I raise a brow.

"It can."

Chapter 17

— The Alchemist —

THIS SHIP IS in far better condition than the other. The polished floorboards don't creak. Snores faintly linger in the air. It's kind of odd seeing Atlas in a white dress shirt. For the few days I've known him, he always looked like a shadow looming over the rest of us. I scan the hall for any movement. Atlas carries an oil lamp and leads the way. Isn't he afraid of getting caught? I guess he is the captain, after all, not to mention an experienced liar as well. Or perhaps he'd be honest.

He's walking in a straight line as I stumble from time to time as if I were the tipsy one.

As we approach a door, Atlas slides a key out of his pocket. He slowly opens the door, careful not to make too much noise. A study waits inside. Atlas sets the lamp on the cluttered desk, which faces a window. Outside, the stars and their reflections blend.

"I didn't know you got privacy," I whisper as he locks the door behind us.

"My father liked time to himself, so he got a master key." He holds it up to me.

Atlas approaches a wooden cabinet and uses the same key to open the glass doors. Racks of bottles, full and empty, occupy the top shelves while chipped china rests beneath. He pulls out a green bottle and porcelain teacups.

"That better be ginger."

I can't let my guard down just because he does.

"I'm not in the mood to test the waters tonight." The cork pops. He fills one of the cups and passes it off to me.

"Good." I sniff the porcelain teacup first. I wince. If this doesn't smell of ginger, I don't know what does. Drinking at least takes my mind off of the sea's rocking. And the strong taste is difficult to ignore. Atlas portions a hearty sum for himself and takes a seat on a velvety sofa. I sit next to him, as close to the opposite armrest as possible. "I thought you only drank liquor."

He raises his eyebrows at me. "It has beer in the name, no? Besides, it's just a *little* fermented." He takes a sip before pulling back. "Or not. It's been here a while in wait of a landlubber."

I let my attention drift off to the side. "I'm more sick of the sea than seasick."

"Then you're not going to like the next request I have."

▽△▽△

Carrying the crown, Atlas latches onto a ladder with one hand and climbs up to the top deck. In the dim light, I notice that scales dot his ankles.

I follow close behind. He had me carry a trident for him. Stolen, like the rapier, I presume. "Are you out of your mind!?"

"Lower your voice or else we'll get caught."

I throw the weapon onto the deck. "Aren't you the authority around here?" The hatch door closes behind me. The wood lands with a slam.

He rolls up his sleeve again. "If they spot me like this? No. I'll have a lot of explaining to do."

"You still owe me more of an explanation!"

"I told you. We're returning the crown to my mother."

"And she's a siren, so doesn't she live in the sea?" I point the trident at him.

"Correct."

It's the logical answer, although I don't want it anymore. Atlas reaches for his pocket again and tosses me a pearl necklace that matches his mother's crown.

"She placed a spell on it and told me to visit with a friend one day."

"How does it work?"

"It has some special enchantment. Maybe a charm from her siren song? I don't know. Do you think I listened?"

"Fair." I nod along. "But what if it doesn't work?" I clasp the necklace around my neck.

Atlas shrugs with the slight tilt of his head, looking down at the stirring waves.

"Atlas?"

Chapter 18

— The Thief —

On the prowl, I could have sworn I heard footsteps half an hour ago. I scan the sleeping quarters. My thoughts are barely louder than my crewmates' snores. Covering my ears, I storm out. Could Alouette have escaped? Even if she freed herself, only Atlas had the key to the holding cell. No one else on this ship would think to steal that from him. Besides, I don't even know what the key looks like.

Let's say she broke the restraints and managed to escape. She'd be stuck on this ship. We set sail after Atlas dragged her on board. We didn't want to get involved with law enforcement, especially if we could take care of the alchemist ourselves.

Just to be sure, I'm on my way to the cell. I descend the steps and wind through the narrow halls.

"Curses."

The iron door is wide open. Frayed ropes and broken chains scatter the ground, as well as a small blade. I pick it up and examine the edge. Blood-free, nearly in perfect condition. It must be one of Atlas' daggers. He has a habit of stealing weapons instead of using his own. That poor rapier he took as collateral could have lived a good life, but, no, he had to use it against the alchemist.

Why would he turn around and break her free? It makes no sense. Moments before, I thought I had convinced him that she was a threat. For Davy Jones' sake, if he hadn't gotten the upper hand, we might've lost our captain.

He thinks he's invincible. If he's thrown overboard, he doesn't have to fear drowning as the rest of us would. His presence alone frightens other crews. Look how that sheepish captain surrendered to him earlier today! I'm even scared of him at times.

If he's not the scourge of the seven seas, I don't know who is.

Admittedly, thanks to him, our lovely ship has not faced an opponent she could not conquer.

Mark my words.

One of these days, he's going to lose.

I was hoping it would be to Alouette. She had the chance. I know she's capable. Maybe I shouldn't have warned her on the other ship. She could've used my knife, and we could have blamed his demise on that crew. Or perhaps we'd part ways and I'd never return to the shore again. No one would come looking for me. After all, people disappear amidst the sea all the time. Whether they're dragged under or perish by another sailor's hand on a vessel, many men never see land again.

If Alouette had killed Atlas, then she could've easily taken me. We could've struck a deal, made a pact. Why didn't she?

There's no reason for her to respect me, besides the fact that I was rowing when my captain saved her. Perhaps she felt that she was indebted to him. There's a fine line between right and wrong in this world, and, more often than not, it blurs. Men preach virtue. Do what is right. But everyone forgets that one man's right is another man's wrong.

Though, in her position, could she justifiably take his life into her own hands? He ruined his relationship with his parents. He resorted to drinking each and every night. He lied to her time and time again.

I stretch my arms and yawn. Perhaps I'll never understand her. I don't really know the first lesson in alchemy. Maybe that makes up the chemistry in her mind.

Atlas was practically asking for Alouette's boiling rage when he left the tavern. She could have driven one of those spikes into his chest. But she spared him.

What went through Atlas' mind as he pulled her away from the guards? He could've gotten them both shot. Depending on whose side of the story the events were told from, he was the provoker. If you ask me, Alouette was in the right. Atlas didn't deserve another chance, no matter how much he pleaded or pouted.

His crew and even his parents have bailed him out in the past. He doesn't deserve the mercy of his father nor mother, yet they would come to his aid in a heartbeat.

I wonder what they would think of Alouette. She's his rival.

He was born with the magical gifts of a siren and the freedom of man.

Her power came from what I can only assume to be intensive studies. Just look at the symbols on her hands, for goodness sake. Someone had to learn that intricate mess of triangles, circles, and stray lines.

I storm my way back through the slim corridors and climb up the ladder. Maybe I'll find them on the deck. I check the port side, then the starboard.

They're nowhere to be found.

▽ ☿ ⍲ △

Running downstairs, I call for my crewmates.
This will all come to light.

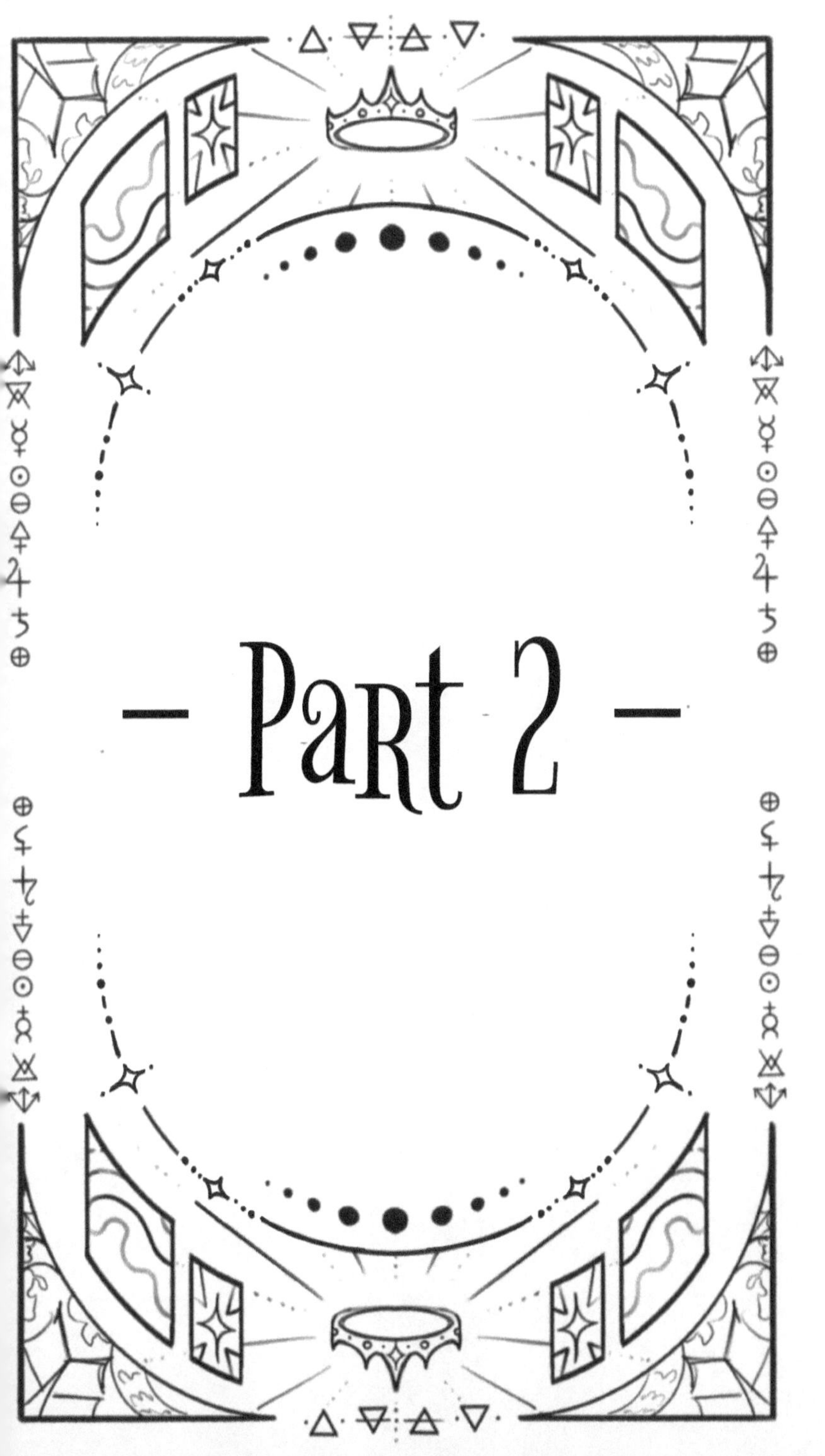

– Part 2 –

Chapter 19

— The Siren —

ONCE UPON A time, a young man made a grave mistake. He came to the castle bearing a crown and the burden of a sea of expectations. The pearls in his hands, woven together with wefts of gold, into a circlet. Meant for his mother to wear, no longer would it be; instead, the youthful fool marched through those sky-high double doors, past the guards, past all the red banners and flags that were all but begging and pleading for him to turn back. The charm he held was his key to proving that he could be whatever he pleased. No, not just a sailor. Not a captain. Not a siren. Not a man.

No, no. He would be a *king*

His boots no longer echoed through the marble hall, for the velvet carpet muffled each step. The boy's head bowed, midnight locks shadowing his eyes, while he dropped to a knee. A monarch, draped with ermine fur, silk, rhinestones, and everything a pirate could dream of plundering, looked down upon the young man. He barely had to lift a bejeweled finger to signal for the doors to slam behind him. In this vault, only the young man and a king, to whom he had never sworn loyalty, heard this deal.

In exchange for the crown, The Siren Queen's prized possession, this young man would gain the king's succession.

▽△▽△

A jest indeed, now it seems to me. I hate it. I hate it. *I hate it.*

Clearly, times have changed. If I could wind back the hands seconds, hours, minutes, years, I would without a moment of hesitation. They say you reap what you sow, and once you weave a thread into fate's tapestry, there's no unraveling it.

Chapter 20

— The Siren —

I'll admit. I didn't take it seriously when Alouette said she couldn't swim. I just assumed that everyone had the instinct.

Chapter 21

— The Alchemist —

THEY SAY ALCHEMISTS have three goals.

One, unlock the transmutation of metals.

Two, seek out the philosopher's stone.

Three, discover the Elixir of Life to attain immortality.

My father, however, initially disregarded the latter two. He believed that by utilizing the conversion of elements, he could change his place in life. According to him, my grandfather had been an indentured servant. He needed to further advance his studies yet his funds were insufficient. In return for the opportunity to conduct experiments and broaden his research, a filthy rich man wanted my grandfather to work under him. Thus he was able to dabble in his endeavors of turning base metals into gold, although he did not venture into practical uses, nor applications in combat.

When my grandfather died, my father carried his indebted service. He thought that maybe, this branch of unique science would open up his world.

▽△▽△

I've been in prison a time or two. Or three. I lost count years ago. It's difficult to detain someone who can configure the world to their liking. The toughest of substances all become like clay once you understand it as alchemists do.

We surrender ourselves to Celestia.

Whatever happens happens, as my father once put it.

Maybe that made me a monster.

I know Celestia will come to my aid when push comes to shove, and I've fallen further than before. There's nothing left to fear when I'm bound to this world's creator.

Although She has held my hand since day one, it hasn't been easy. Sure, if I make the request, She'll turn anything into gold, but I'm not always under Her protection. There's no guaranteed warm meal waiting for me at the end of every day or even a roof over my head. As many put it, my faith is a trust-the-process kind of deal.

Still, I'll never forget the first time She responded to my call. My father had always urged me to make requests of Celestia, to see if I was ready. Of course, Her Divinity would've known when I'd humbled myself enough. Yes, alchemy equates to power, but at the cost of, well, any other ambition. The day She had listened, I had been in a meadow. The puffs of wildgrass swayed in the breeze, a wave blowing across them with each gust of wind, just like the sea. My father handed me a lovely flower, a sunflower, actually. Its stem was nearly as tall as me, and its face as large as mine.

My father knelt down beside me, placing a hand on my shoulder. "Why don't you ask Her to turn the petals blue?"

Blue? But I didn't like blue. I shook my head. "I'd rather gold."

"But She told me Her favorite color is blue." He frowned. Whether that holds true or not, I am not sure. Nevertheless, I held the flower up to the sky, hands cupping the petals.

Please, please, I asked, eyes squinted shut, *turn them blue! Let this please you!*

And when I took a peek, wouldn't you know, the petals were all a lovely azure blue.

▽△▽△

We had jumped off the side of his ship. I held my breath and clamped my eyes shut. Apparently, you're not supposed to do that, or any of my following actions. I was curled up, so there was no reason for me to be surprised when I sank. Was I? Yes.

A hand grabs my wrist to keep me from delving further into the depths. He pulls it away from my face.

"Promise me you won't freak out."

I can't say anything for sure.

Alas, with my cheeks puffed out like a blowfish, I must look like the fool now.

"Just breathe."

My eyes snap open. I'm staring up at him. Soft moonlight pours through the waves lapping over us. In my head, they should be passing below us.

Just breathe? Underwater? Easier said than done. I latch onto Atlas' arm and kick off of his side to reach the surface. My face breaks the water's tension. I gasp for air during the brief second I have until I sink back under.

A hand pulls me back down.

"Atlas!" We're face to face again.

He smiles.

I open my mouth again. Seawater doesn't flood my lungs. His mother's enchantment works wonders.

"Atlas."

I don't know why he's so buoyant. I plunge like a rock, even when I kick my feet. Atlas holds my forearm as his webbed fingers cling to my cheek to stop me from looking down.

"You need to have faith in me."

By trusting him? No man has a change of heart so quickly. I try to run through the reasons why he would want to take advantage of this situation. I burned him. I backed away from our dance. I practically called him a freak. I fought with him outside the tavern. There are too many instances for me to count.

But he gave me the necklace. He had the chance to push me overboard and let me drown. But he didn't.

"Okay," is all I manage to say.

His hand peels away from my face. He picks his trident back up, which had been coiled by his tail. I resist the urge to shutter. The sea was never for me. Never had I swam in a pond, lake, nor ocean when I was a child. My father always avoided the shore. As I stare Atlas in the eye, I know exactly why.

"Follow me." He lets go of me and dives down.

No thank you. No thank you! How about no? Just no. I cross my arms and let myself slowly sink. Just how far could the bottom be? I glance down. A blue void fills my sight. A long way down it goes.

The half-siren, who looks more half-fish now, swims pretty far before looking back up. He calls my name. I don't want to listen. He comes back up.

"Alouette."

His annunciation of my name pricks my skin as would pins and needles.

"Look, I hate this as much as you." He gestures to himself. A crooked shirt. A blue webbing between each of his fingers. A pair of fins sticking out of his forearms. For Celestia's sake, a navy tail that almost blends in with the seemingly infinite sea beneath us. "And it's no curse that true love's kiss will break."

"I never planned on kissing you. And don't you remember how we met?" I squint.

"You were the damsel in distress?"

I manage to take a deep breath in. Don't you dare ask me how I can breathe underwater. It's literally magic, an enchantment woven into the pearls Atlas clasped around my neck. I'm merely an alchemist who applies Celestia's worldly principles to chemistry, not a magician nor a wizard. His spells are just beyond my grasp. I extend my arm out to him as I sink. "Give me the trident."

"Keep the crown."

I grunt and move my arms out, pushing the water to the side. It worked. I moved! I kick.

A lightbulb flickers on in Atlas' mind, which I wish would've happened later rather than sooner so I could get my hands on his weapon. He swims down. I bare my teeth, for my scheme has failed. Still, I shove myself through the resisting water toward Atlas.

Chapter 22

— The Siren —

She's a quick learner. Yet, I won't let her go faster than me. Once we get to the bottom, I stop to look down. I survey the sea floor. Colorful coral distracts me. So do the fluorescent fish. The trident tugs in my hand. I look over at Alouette. I put another hand on it. She does so as well. I frown. She grins. Her expression fades as I wrap my tail around the top of the blade.

"Oh, come on!" she cries.

Her fingers strain as she tries kicking off of me. Is this her way of flaunting the fact that she still has legs?

I dive deeper. She clings to the weapon. Alouette thinks that she's a monster, but she looks rather distraught now. I let a laugh slip, although this isn't funny to her.

Alouette takes advantage of the moment and slips the trident out of my grasp. She spins it from one hand to the other. She's bad news, although I can't seem to resent that about her. I think it makes me love her more, as crazy as that makes me sound.

She points the trident at me. "You know what these are used for, right?"

Where is this going?

Drifting closer, she pries. "Hold still."

She drives the trident into the coral. The prongs land on either side of my tail, right before it flairs out into a fin. Clever. I can't move, as long as it's in place. "They're used for spearfishing."

"Good, at least you know that much. Are you aware that each button on your shirt is misaligned by one?" She tugs at my collar. There's one button at the top that isn't aligned, proving her point.

"You could have just said so!"

"So you didn't know?"

I reach for the first button and sigh. When I was younger, all of the, what do I call them? Merfolk? I never cared. Still don't. Anyway, all of the fish people laughed at me for wearing human clothes.

"If it's bothering you this much," I gesture to the trident, "why don't you fix it?"

▽△▽△

I swear I regret that.

I can't always tell if she hates me with every ounce of her being or if she's secretly a little fond of me. Edwin would say that I'm just fooling myself with the latter idea. He has probably run back and forth across the deck a dozen times by now, cursing my name the whole process.

As Alouette grips the trident to reclaim it, another blade knocks her away.

"Human!" a voice calls. I turn to see one of my mother's guards. I think he was one of the gentry, so grew up with me in a way. I won't disclose. His green eyes shimmer as his tail does. I wince and look away. At least I know we're now in the right place. His striking gaze lands on the crown, which loops around her arm. "You stole it!"

"I stole it from the kingdom up there." She points to the sky.

His lips pull back to reveal sharp teeth, ones I'm particularly glad to not bear myself.

The alchemist's gaze sharpens as her stare pinpoints me. "We're returning it. Right, Atlas?"

Chapter 23

— The Thief —

I SLAM MY fists on the captain's door.

"If you're in there, come out! I've had enough!" My throat burns.

The quartermaster, his official right hand man, stands beside me with his sword drawn, ready to strike at my command. This guy doubles as a first-mate, too. He may outrank me in title, but the crew knows that *I'm* the captain's partner in crime.

Unless he has chosen a new one.

I ravage through my pocket until my fingertips brush a pin. I kneel down and stab it into the keyhole. The door swings open. An opened bottle sits on his desk, along with two glasses. I take a sip. The quartermaster flinches. Either Alouette or Atlas used it before. I don't mind the cooties they share. Our hands are stained with the same blood.

I lick my lip. Ginger beer.

I, myself, recoil. Who likes ginger, anyway? It's disgusting. I spit it back out and shiver.

From the captain's cabin, I move to his quarters. His gnarly blanket lays sprawled on the floor. Two empty hooks sit on his wall where one of his stolen relics should be.

"Edwin, what's wrong?" the quartermaster asks. His dirty blonde eyebrows frown. One has a piercing, which, I'll admit, is pretty gnarly in itself.

"That foul sea bass."

"Who? The captain?" He better be seeing what I'm seeing. He's one of the crewmates who stumbled back to the ship last night, just a few shades away from blackout drunk. Everyone thinks they can handle that hard stuff as well as the captain, but, dear goodness, are they so very wrong.

"You got it, matey." I turn on my heel and storm out of his room. "Call the men on deck. Unless they're a swabbie. I'm going to need more hands than theirs to clean up Capt'n's mess."

Trailing close behind, he salutes. "Where is he?"

"Far below deck." I mutter, slamming the cabin's door shut. "He's half the man you think he is."

▽△▽△

"Avast, ye!" My outcry turns all of the bobbing heads to me. Some may call summoning the entire crew to the top deck in the dead of night obnoxious, but we're all buddies by now, so they're used to my shenanigans. I may be one of the shortest, yet I have claimed my throne as the loudest.

Not to mention that I'm the newest and also the closest to the captain.

For just a moment, my heart skips a beat. What am I supposed to say? Your captain is pretty much a fish? That's a stretched truth, if I ever told one.

As if I were the man in charge, the quartermaster stands beside me, arms folded behind his back. An uneasy tug ripples across his expression.

"I know, you're all asking where the captain went. And if you have working ears, where did the prisoner go, too?"

A few heads nod. Some crewmates exchange concerned glances. Others are frozen with wide eyes. All but me have served this ship ever since she belonged to Atlas' father. DeLuca blood holds lots of value, so his return with the crown had been long-awaited. On this voyage, he had disappeared once we had already set sail. The only logical conclusion was that he fell overboard, yet even that's a bold shot in the dark. Not to mention how the alchemist vanished with him. Our fellow crewmates are no fools.

We may reek of sweat and alcohol, but we have good heads on our shoulders. At least, I know mine is pretty great.

I can't speak for the captain, though. All jokes aside, I clear my throat.

Atlas can't keep running from his past.

Chapter 24

— The Alchemist —

"IT WAS YOU!" The merman's spear turns from me to Atlas. "You traitor!" He puts the tip of his blade to the captain's neck.

Atlas can't dodge; the trident is still lodged. I reach and tug it out of the coral, which breaks off in chunks..

"You were my lady's bastard son!"

"You only wanted my place as an heir!" Atlas refutes the claim.

I ready the weapon.

The merman draws back to strike. I won't let him. Atlas will not die by this sea serpent's hand. I stop his arm with the prong of the trident.

My smirk slides from cheek to cheek. "You know this is used for fishing, right?"

He turns his attention to me, along with the spear. Picking a fight here wasn't the brightest idea, noting how Atlas had been far more agile than me. I hook his blade in between the trident's prongs and turn it to the sea floor. On land, this would be quick, although, here, the water resists my movements. Bubbles blur the attacks.

His weapon slides out of my reach, and so does my opponent's attention.

"Get out of this." A gust of water pushes me away. He can do that?

No fair! I'm at every disadvantage here.

With a lunge, the paladin's spear grazes Atlas' torso, deep enough to draw blood from his waist to the opposite shoulder. The red drifts through the water like smoke rising.

The paladin raises his weapon to strike again, yet he's unaware of my presence behind him. As Atlas raises his arms to protect the vitals he forgot to guard last time, I latch on to the spear. I pull it from behind the young merfolk. The metal presses against his neck.

My lips curl. Let's see if this works. With my fingertip, I carve the same upside down triangle as before.

His weapon vanishes, back to the water from which it came. The triton reaches out to no avail. His webbed fingers aimlessly search around.

Those green eyes of his narrow as they fall upon me.

"Don't you know what he has done?"

Chapter 25

— The Thief —

"THE CROWN WE stole belonged to his mother."

"Edwin." The quartermaster stops me. His hand hovers over my shoulder, careful not to touch, out of fear that he'd get burned, too. "But doesn't that crown belong to the Queen of..." he takes a deep breath in, "the kingdom under this sea?"

"Looks like at least one of us doesn't have seaweed for brains." I grin. "Ya hear that? Atlas' mother is a siren. If you fools put two and two together, Captain DeLuca is literally half the man you thought he was."

Thought that was a good pun, so I simply *had* to use it again.

"But how did the walled kingdom get their hands on the crown?" This young man is the quartermaster for a reason. Atlas picked a good guy to help run his ship; I'll give him that.

"Atlas stole it."

▽△▽△

Why?

You know he hates his parents. What greater act of rebellion than to steal one of Mother Dearest's treasures? Then go and turn around, handing her prized possession off to a kingdom that will only flaunt it as a sign of their riches.

Atlas isn't that stupid.

He marched up to the king, requesting his daughter's hand in marriage in return for the crown. After all, possessing the crown implies that the kingdom had the proper resources and knowledge to dive to the bottom of Davy Jones. Serves as a lesson to the Siren Queen and neighboring nations.

After all, they say no man has been able to find her underwater castle. Quite frankly, I didn't even believe those far-fetched stories until Atlas told me about his mother's lavish stronghold. And he's not the type to lie about that kind of fairytale.

The king seized this opportunity. The princess we met the other day had been unknowingly betrothed to Atlas. Sucks to be her, if you ask me.

Of course, it's been quite a few years since he stole the crown. When you're fifteen, being a king sounds like a dream. That supposed fantasy has been drawing near.

After all, they had agreed to let Atlas take her hand a month after crowning her. And why did they host that masquerade? To crown the princess.

Do you see where I'm going?

The king will expect Atlas to return soon, however, little does he know, the relic his daughter flaunts is a fake.

But why would the captain return the crown to his mother? He's a seafarer now. This betrothal of his couldn't mean less. He could set sail and, who knows, fall off the edge of our known realm, never to be seen again. And the old king would never be able to track him down, no matter how many loyal dogs he dispatched.

Aside from that, the captain could turn around and sell the crown. I would have done that. But it's not mine. It's not his. Atlas, just what in the seven seas do you think you're doing?

Returning the crown?

I don't think I understand.

Why?

▽△▽△

Now the crew knows. Did Atlas want them to? No. Did they deserve to? By all means, yes. Yes!

I stare at the sea, tracing the dark waves to where they meet the light horizon.

The quartermaster asks how I'm doing.

For the longest time, Atlas had been my only friend. Has he moved on? Maybe this random girl he saved would be a better fit for him. I'll remain a relic of his past, left behind in the hunt for love.

I don't blame him.

"Jacques. I appreciate the gesture, buddy, but I'm fine." I don't know how not to brush him off. "I've known this for…forever!"

"Edwin." If he thinks saying my name will ground me and somehow convince me he can be trusted with my thoughts, he couldn't be further from right. That's why he stands to my left.

"Atlas is your closest friend, isn't he?"

I keep quiet. Any further pursuit will get him nowhere; eventually, he'll give up.

Chapter 26

— The Siren —

I REACH THROUGH the gaping hole in my shirt to feel the wound. My whole body shudders. If only I had armor, like the triton paladin. Or even a touch of Alouette's power.

The metal dissolved into water. No. It *became* water.

"We're returning the crown, Fish." Alouette shakes her head.

"I have a name. It's Calder."

"Did I ask? We're here to see his mother. Care to take us there?"

Calder falters. "Fine. Follow me." He gestures for Alouette to follow him.

Alouette obliges and hands the crown off to me.

"I'm keeping the trident." I won't accept any trade offers.

She also kicks me in the hip. "Don't touch it."

"Touch what!?"

She saved me, and now I have to deal with this!?

"Your wound!"

The triton dives down into the cave. Yes. It's the cave, because there's only one entrance to my mother's kingdom.

Cliche, I know. Queen Farida is world-renowned for her own aquatic faerietale.

I grit my teeth. Bickering with Alouette took my mind off of the searing pain. I know it's not deep, but it stings.

"It's the salt," she tells me. "Also, I'm not going in there."

She stops at the gaping hole between the coral.

I grab her by the back of her shirt. "Alouette. You're going."

She kicks me in the side again. I let go. Still, she complies. I know she won't regret it. Floating unarmed at the bottom of the sea is equivalent to a nightcrawler bobbing on a hook. Besides, a few dozen feet down, luminous crystals grow on the walls. Light struggles to reach this place, so nature picks up where the sun leaves off.

The alchemist stops to run her hands along the unusual formations. If her eyes had gears, I have no doubt that I'd see them turning. She's not wired the same way as everyone else. She strives to understand the unknown rather than pushing it away.

I look down at my hand. If only I could do the same. Up to a point, I didn't shun her for practicing alchemy. Edwin convinced me that she was dangerous; I let his doubt become mine.

Calder watches her as I do.

The glow reflects in her golden eyes. A shadow covers them as she looks over at me. "Go on. And don't look at me like that."

I follow Calder.

"Don't fool yourself into thinking that I'm cooperating with you because I want to." He gnashes his sharm teeth at me.

I scowl at him. "My mother is the queen. Who do you think has more authority here?"

"You? A traitor?" Calder scoffs. I despise the people here. Their tempers are far worse than Alouette's. That probably explains mine. "Prince doesn't go in the same sentence as Atlas, anymore."

"What?" Alouette has to tune in now, of all times.

"It's Captain." I try to ignore her.

"A sailor? How fitting, you half-human scum."

I told you they're mean.

A finger taps my shoulder. It's Alouette's. "You've drawn enough attention."

Spearheads circle us. All of the other paladins are plated in armor, similar to Calder's.

"Alouette." I raise my hands in surrender.

Her eyes narrow.

"If anything goes wrong, can I count on you?"

Tightening around the trident, her fingers strain. *I'll take that as a yes.*

She nudges the side of my head with the prongs. "He's dramatic. We need to see his mom."

"Queen Farida," a few paladins murmur and exchange glances amongst themselves.

"Queen Farida." While she confirms, her confidence makes me feel small. I close my eyes. *At least she's here.*

Alone, I don't know if I can face my mother.

▽△▽△

"There's a whole kingdom under the sea?" Alouette catches little glowing fish that dance around like fireflies. She uses the luminous constellations on her hands to lure them in. "And no one talks about it?"

"Sailors pass around these myths."

A blade pricks my lower back. The paladins continue to surround us. They don't trust that I can make it from the cave's mouth to my mother on my own.

"Sailors spread *true* rumors." I have to correct myself.

"And you're royalty?" Alouette opens her curled fingers to release one of the fish.

I wince. I can feel the paladins' piercing stares, especially Calder's. They hurt just as much as the searing laceration on my chest.

"I was."

"You were until you stole the crown." Her eyes land on the relic in my hands.

I sigh.

What was I thinking when I took it? I don't know.

"I offered it to the princess."

"The one who kissed you?"

A nod follows.

"In exchange for what? Marrying her to become king?"

"Look, I don't want that anymore!" The spears raise with my voice. My hands are up again. I'm not interested in any more fights.

"I'm just trying to discern this situation." Her analysis astounds me. Is there anything of equal or greater value to her than understanding? "It's a lot more than what I signed myself up for."

"You didn't have to come."

"But it sounds like you need me."

I won't deny her accusation.

"Say it's for science, if you will." She pinches the tail of a poor fish. It flashes different colors. She lets go. The creature returns to normal and squirms away. "Are the people here all sirens, or…?" The alchemist leaves me to give the other options.

I look at the paladins. They're regular merfolk from what I can tell, but take my word with a grain of salt, for I try not to associate myself with these monsters.

I shake my head. Technically, sirens have more serpentine tails. My mom told me that we're more like snakes so we can strangle humans, but I really wish I hadn't remembered that. We can thank her for not strangling my father, for if she had, I wouldn't be here.

"How much longer?"

Alouette has no idea how much changing the subject means.

"Look up," I tell her. Above the grime-covered ruins around us, a Greco-Roman styled structure towers. She's been too distracted by the glowing fish to realize that it's there. The pillars have chipped and crumbled under the weight of the sea. "It depends on how much longer you drag your feet for."

She grins at me. Does she like being challenged?

"If you're all set to marry a princess, why bring me here? Shouldn't she be the one to meet your family?"

"Let's not dwell on that."

"Atlas, do you love her?"

"I wanted the crown."

"But not your mother's."

I feel my face flush.

Her knotted expression ceases. She stops to scan me, from my webbed fingers, to the tail, and finally her gaze meets mine. The alchemist only shakes her head. I don't know what for. The way she halfway whispers my name sends a shiver down my spine. Don't let her pity me.

"I won't ask why." She reaches for another fish. Pointing their spears to her neck, the paladins have had enough of her shenanigans. In return, she knocks them away with my trident.

I had stolen that weapon along with the crown. That was the last time I ventured to my mother's kingdom. The paladins only have speculations that I was the one who stole the crown.

Clearly, they're right. But the evidence was clear. One morning, the trident and crown were gone. I was, too.

Looking around, I come to find that this place hasn't changed at all. Some people are so stuck in their ways. There was no way I could have settled down here. Especially with the awful attitudes around. Perhaps the salty water acts as a catalyst for our resentment.

The gates come sooner than I anticipated. Alouette must've actually taken my comment as a challenge. The paladins open the doors for us. I don't bother to thank them. If I had opened the door, they wouldn't have thanked me. Alouette makes a point to give the door a little shove to prove that she could have handled it herself.

Pillars line the walls. Many of them stand tall, though garnished with cracks. A few reach for the gaps in the ceiling, yet fall short halfway.

Immediately, I bow down.

There's a throne across the room atop a dais. By the black blur I caught before looking at the floor, I know it's her.

Her voice echoes my name.

Atlas DeLuca.

I wince, my whole face scrunching.

"All of these years, just where have you been?"

I pull my arms to my chest. She's probably seen the gash by now and the blood that came along with it. If only I could disappear right now, I would. By alchemy or some kind of magic.

"That's your mother!?" Alouette reaches to grip my shoulder.

"And you are, girl?"

She's coming closer. Her dark tail wisps around the edges of my vision.

"Alouette, the Alchemist's daughter."

"A lark, how dear." She extends her arms and bows her head. "I am Farida to you, the Sea's Daughter. It's a pleasure."

"The feeling is mutual." Alouette nods back.

"Assure me that this rebel here has not caused you too much trouble."

She hates me, doesn't she? I stare at her crown in my trembling hands. Maybe I shouldn't have come back.

"Not too much."

"Oh, dear, don't lie. You're with him, after all."

I look up to see my mother's dark hands around the pearl necklace she had given me years ago, too close to the alchemist's neck. Alouette laughs.

"He did save my life. But I thought he was going to take it last night."

"Do tell."

I open my mouth to speak. She hushes. Her fingers pull together. I try to talk, however, with her enchantment, nothing comes out.

"Funny story, really," Alouette explains as my mother takes her by the hand to observe all of the tattoos. "Some pirates discovered me when I tried catching a ride on a merchant's ship. I walked the plank, and the next thing I knew, I was on a rowboat with your son here."

"But last night." As she pries, her fingers curl around Alouette's. Their eyes meet.

"I was fed up with his lies. So I attacked him."

"With these?" My mother presses Alouette's hand against her long, pale cheek.

Alouette confirms, "They said I'd hurt people with them. But really, the only one I've hurt is myself. Okay, and maybe Atlas. I hit him in the face with a rock."

My mother snickers. "Serves him right, doesn't it. No one likes a liar."

If only I could tell her that I changed. I still can't speak. My fingers claw at my throat.

"But, little lark, these are gorgeous. Dangerously gorgeous. Hold them dear, as dear as you are." She then turns her attention to me. Those eyes are like voids, as well as her sleek, tar-like hair. "And, you, don't you have something for me?"

Her brows crease as she raises her chin.

I hold up her crown.

I'm sorry, I wish I could say. Would an apology make the cut?

Her slender hands reach for her rightful possession. The webbing between her fingers matches mine. Though, her arms reach past the crown and rest on my chest.

"Why the sudden change of heart?" Her dark eyebrows crease.

I struggle to speak, even as the enchantment is removed.

"I don't want to marry the princess anymore."

This answer isn't enough.

"And I want to show someone that I can change."

She smiles. Her murky eyes seem to shine. My mother curls her finned arms around me. I look over at Alouette, who mouths, *hug her!*

My grip loosens around the crown. I let it drift down as I give in. If she has forgiven me, then I have no right to refuse her again.

"Know that I love you, Atlas. And it's never too late to come back."

She pulls away and reaches for the crown. "Why don't you stay a while as we put this back?"

▽△▽△

Guilt still weighed on me as we weaved through the crumbling halls I took to steal the crown. My shunned family has become my albatross.

Though, it seems that my mother could chat with Alouette for years. As the queen, she's definitely more personable than the others here, quick to welcome and connect with the alchemist.

Alouette laughs and looks back at me. "I was wondering how he got so tall. My father can't even compete."

"Are you implying that's my fault?" My mother holds her hand up to Alouette's, which is like a child's in comparison.

The alchemist's lips curve upward into a giddy smile. I'm beckoned over by the two of them, and convinced to join their activities. Alouette's palm scrapes against mine. Her eyes scan the difference. She then curls her fingers around mine and twists my arm down, per usual, until my elbow cracks.

"I have feelings, too, you know!"

Alouette isn't afraid of trying anything in front of my mom, is she?

"Can you fold it down?" The alchemist reaches for my arm again.

"Fold what?"

"Surely, it's not retractable if you cover your arms." She runs her hands along my forearm's fin to flatten it against my skin. Then, she stretches it out and skims the barbs with her fingertips. I raise a brow. There's a first time for everything.

"The daughter of an alchemist?" my mother questions. Alouette's attention drifts back to her. A fascinated smile grows on her face, too. I guess I'm used to Alouette and her strange conduct. Always quick to learn in hopes of a breakthrough.

My mother swims in a circle around me.

"You really have grown." Her hand rests on my cheek. Is she sad? She should be mad, shouldn't she? "Your tail must be longer than mine by now."

I pull away. "No—Mom, uh. Let's not talk about that."

"This is a part of who you are." Her fingers pinch my cheek. She used to do that a lot when I was a kid. A little taunting, but that's how she shows love. When she's done, her hand hovers beside my cheek with a frown. This is her first time seeing the scar. The gash might as well be carved into her face, too, for the extent that she cares for me.

"Lady—Queen Farida," Alouette stops her. "If you don't mind me asking, why *didn't* you kill Captain DeLuca?"

I've been wondering the same for years. My mother's prolonged silence makes my skin crawl as she continues on through the hall, or at least what seems to be a corridor. A small laugh slips past her black lips.

"I'm not too sure. Maybe I thought that maybe our worlds could coexist." Her eyes fall on me. "Look at Atlas."

Alouette raises a brow at me. "Are we sure he's a good example? He's still learning."

My mother merely smiles as we approach a crooked set of doors. Her fingers run along deep scratches in the marble. Those were my fault. The doors push open; they don't pull.

"Won't you do the honor?" She holds the crown out to me.

Alouette turns, golden eyes surveying my next move, though there's a good chance that she's calculated this already. My fingers curl around the cold metal, if it even *is* metal. The alchemist already knows its composition. It's my job to finish. It's my wrong to right. I press my hand against the door and push it open. The stone rumbles. I let the crown fall into the depths. I shut it as quickly as possible.

My mother applauds me. Bubbles rise as her hands collide. I look at her but quickly avert my gaze.

"You may take your leave. My people should not give you any trouble."

"And if they do?" Calder's spear flashes through my mind.

My mother bears her sharp teeth. Again, I'm reminded of the one trait I'm happy she didn't pass down. "They won't."

She pulls me in for one more hug, reaching for Alouette to join. The alchemist doesn't have a choice. "I'm happy you kept that necklace. I hope to see it again."

She winks at me and lets go. Alouette nods along. There's a bittersweet gleam in her eyes.

"Thank you for coming back, Atlas. Humans really know how to stomp on hearts. Love you."

I turn to leave. "Love you…" I pause, "…Mom."

▽⟁⩑△

As we emerge from the cave, Alouette comments, "What a mother."

I shush her.

"You're so fortunate, Atlas."

"What? Was your mother not enough?"

I shouldn't have said that.

Alouette turns away and swims toward the surface.

"I take it back." There's no response. "I take it back!"

She ignores me. I can't do anything right, can I? I rush to catch up with her, although it doesn't take much effort.

"Alouette!"

Her eyes are locked on something above us, casting a shadow among the rays of filtered sunlight. A lifeboat?

Before Alouette breaks the surface, I pull her back down.

"What if someone's on it?" she asks.

"What?"

"Isn't that what you're going to ask?" Her finger points up at the silhouette above.

"No, I–I was going to apologize."

"You can apologize by throwing any sailors overboard." Her smile strains. She's too complicated.

"Fine." As before, I grab the side of the boat and hoist myself up, over the edge. There's no one. Is this ours? I reach over the edge to help Alouette up. She isn't there. The boat tips from the other side. I fall back into the water with a splash.

She arches a brow as she looks across the lifeboat.

"Guess you didn't need to take that rapier as collateral."

"It's not like I can give it back."

Alouette awkwardly laughs. She sharply inhales and sits down next to me. Her eyes don't meet mine. She runs her fingers through her wet hair, unintentionally flinging water onto me. "About that."

With a wince, I quickly say, "Don't worry about it."

"No, no. It is, really. You needed another chance."

"As you said so yourself, I had many and did not take any of them."

"Do we have to disagree on everything?" She nudges me with her foot. I push her back.

Seems like it.

"Can't you use your magical chemistry to heal?" I reach through the hole in my shirt and touch the oozing gore. Alouette grabs my wrist and yanks my hand away.

"I wish it were that useful."

I lean back on the edge of the boat, one arm folded over my chest, the other held out in Alouette's hand.

The boat rocks. Beads of water roll down my face. Gulls call in the distance. I close my eyes to block out the morning sun.

It's over. For now.

The boat sways more than usual.

I open an eye.

Alouette has scooted closer. "Who was that someone?"

"Who?"

"The person you wanted to show that you could change."

I sit up. Well, as well as I can without legs. Alouette has hers crossed and places her hands in her lap. Her wide eyes brim with curiosity, one of her brows arched slightly above the other in wait.

"Don't make fun of me for it."

"Edwin?" She leans closer to me.

I cackle like my mother. Then I clear my throat. "No."

"Your father?"

"Guess again."

She falls silent. The gears in her eyes turn again and again. She really has no idea?

"You, Alouette. It was you."

Chapter 27

— The Alchemist —

I NEVER THOUGHT I'd spend my first kiss on a half-man-half-fish.

Embarrassing, right?

The only aspect that made this sensible was that I was drenched and his shirt had been soaked in blood diluted by saltwater. And the fact that we were stranded in the middle of the sea. That's how I roll, if you haven't learned that by now.

After the fact, we both agree not to tell Edwin about it. He already has enough to taunt us about.

In my defense, he leaned over first. And maybe he redeemed himself. Does this mean I like him? Not necessarily. He's a liar and a drinker. Both types of people I hate. There's nothing attractive about him. Sure, Edwin told me that girls fawn over him for his looks. He towers over me! Even my father wasn't that tall. Maybe I don't like feeling small. Inferior. Yet he has surrendered to me. In a way? Call it a truce if you will.

His mother forgave him, but will *I*?

My verdict is still in progress.

I look down at the water. The waves that once churned my stomach put me at ease. Strange, isn't it? How the tides change.

Sirens are supposed to lure men, aren't they? This would be the perfect chance for him to push me over the edge. Drown me or something. To our dismay, there's no plank in sight.

My focus shifts to Atlas. He has changed back to just a regular guy. He looks just as surprised as me.

His blue gaze darts to his feet. He's always had a problem looking me in the eye.

"So," I raise my brows, "what now, Captain?"

He picks up an oar and stares at it. "Atlas is fine, you know." As he stands, the boat rocks.

▽△▽△

We arrive at nightfall. As the captain clutches the wound on his chest, I help hoist him onto the dock. We had been swapped last time around, with him lending me a hand and all. After Atlas lets go and takes the lead, I look down at my palm to find that it's covered in red smudges. Should I be surprised? No. I'll just rub it off on the back of my shirt.

"Don't tell me you're going to the tavern like this."

I'm waiting for him to tell me something snotty along the lines of, *Alouette, you know me too well,* just to brush me off.

Instead, I'm confronted with a, "Don't worry, we're not."

▽△▽△

His fist slams on a wooden door. Please know that I would have never barged in on my father as Atlas is doing now. I'm crude and lawless, but not as much so as a pirate.

No one responds. I would've gotten a lecture that lasted for eons, just because my father never let all of his frustration out in one blow. Unlike him, my rage explodes up like a bomb. You've seen that already.

Crickets chip. Only sailors call in the distance. Atlas then shrugs and pulls the key out of his pocket. I'm not going to ask how it's still there. Celestia can handle that. She has my faith. The door creaks open. Only our shadows move in the moonlit parlor, shifting from the doorway to the foyer over an array of stagnant furniture, most coated in a fine layer of dust.

"Let me guess." My fingertips skim the cold kitchenette counter, only to stop at the base of a green-tinted glass bottle. "He's at the tavern?"

Atlas huffs.

"I'm starting to think you've got alcohol in your veins instead of blood." I snicker.

"Does this look like liquor to you?" He unbuttons his bloodied shirt to reveal the full gash. I guess it's not that funny; Edwin must've rubbed off on me.

I reach for a rag hanging by the sink. Running water? I reach for the knob. Quite a luxury. Just how many treasures and bounties did the original Captain DeLuca cash in during his career?

I wring the tattered cloth out before approaching Atlas. His teeth grit as I press the rag against his wound. Some people get squeamish, so I won't go through the motions of describing it. I don't care too much. Sure, the red cloth is pretty gross, but getting hurt is a part of life. My knees have been skinned far too many times to count, and I've spent a substantial amount of times stooped down in the dirt picking out tiny rocks when I used to squint and flinch. Not anymore. I've got this nasty habit of poking at bruises even though they ache when under pressure. Perhaps I'm strange for that.

I must hit a nerve when he snatches my wrist.

"Do you want it to heal?" I tug to break away. Admittedly, he's stronger than me, so my tugs are in vain. "This is your fault, after all."

"Then why are you trying to help, anyway?"

"Contrary to popular belief, I don't like to watch people suffer. Sure, I've made plenty of fun of you with Edwin, but a bystander is the last type of person I want to be. Doing nothing is just as bad as driving the blade."

His grip lets loose.

We go back to silence, which is just as familiar to me as drunken tavern ramblings. Jaw clamped shut, his head turned away from me, the captain stares at the front door. He can only hope that his old man isn't coming home any time soon. I'd be embarrassed if someone were tending to my wounds in front of my father. I should be stronger than that. Atlas is a captain, after all; he should be, too.

I run the rag under water one more time. Red taints the draining water beneath it while it swirls around and around, down the drain to who-knows-where. *That'll surely leave a stain.*

"You've got gauze?" I ask, keeping my back to him. I stare up at the moon, through the window that's just above DeLuca's sink. The rooftops and walls block out most of the stars. At least the North Star shines brightly.

Hinges squeal. Doors slam. "Found it."

As I turn around, he holds the roll out to me. I set the rag down and rub my hands off on my shorts. It's a shame the gash runs across his torso in a diagonal line. If it were just a puncture wound on his shoulder or perhaps a short slit elsewhere, it would be easier to cover up.

After an uneasy pause, his lips slightly part, as if to add another remark. Deciding against it, he turns away, yet he can't seem to help himself. "What am I to you, Alouette?"

I'm still picking to find the end of the gauze. "Does a burden count?"

"What kind of answer is that?" He lets a small laugh slip, but quickly regrets it with a wince. His fingers strain, reaching for the wound he knows he shouldn't mess with.

"An honest one." I yank the gauze and start to wrap it. I'll admit, the question rolls on repeat through my mind. What is he? A pain? A wrench in my plans? I don't really have any aims or aspirations. He did save me. Does that make him some kind of hero?

"I think that's too tight."

His comment anchors me back to his father's kitchen. I backtrack a little and redo the most recent wraparound. In theory, I could make it tighter, simply out of spite; yet, in practice, I don't.

"Look, Alouette, I know why you won't accept me as a friend."

"You're a liar."

"I haven't lied since that incident."

"Then look me in the eye and tell me why. Tell me everything, Atlas."

▽△▽△

In hindsight, I shouldn't have requested his reasoning.

Chapter 28

— The Thief —

"We're going back."

"To the walled kingdom?" the quartermaster questions. The young man in charge of navigation hesitantly salutes me.

"Yes."

A few members drop their jaws to protest.

"I'm not taking questions."

▽△▽△

I stomp my way down the narrow hall. The soft echoes of my steps can usually hide beneath the creak of our rocking ship. Not tonight. It has been a full day since I've seen the captain. I kick his door open. The surface of the ginger beer ripples in the moonlight. A slam ensues behind me.

"Come on!" I shout. My palms slam on his desk. There's no trace of him nor Alouette. Like an anchor, my stomach sinks as my mind wanders off to the thought that he could have made her walk the plank. I shake my head. No.

If he did, he could have escaped into the sea. He would never have to break the surface again. Wasn't he exiled from his mother's kingdom? I growl.

The crown is gone. Did he return it? Sell it? I shake my head. There are as many possibilities as there are fish in these deep, dark waters. The blue night can't stop reminding me of him.

That stupid, thoughtless, scallywag.

I sprawl out on his sofa, the glass of ginger beer in my jittering hand. This is worse than any case of mal de mer.

I don't know what I'll do without him.

Our mates are fine sailors. But they're not him. I hate saying it, but we're friends. He's my friend. My *only* friend.

Sure, the alchemist is pretty nice. She's easygoing and simple to get along with. But it's not like I know her as well as I know Atlas. He's like a brother, really. More so than the other smelly kids I grew up with at that joke of an orphanage.

I love him, but, boy, does he tick me off. Sure, we've had our scuffles. Our moments. None of which have been pretty on both my end and his; but at the end of the day, he's all I've got.

I down the glass, as he would. A shudder follows.

For some reason, this forsaken remedy makes my world spin even more. Crewmates call from the decks above. It's a clear night. The stars glitter in the sky, as if to taunt me with their alluring aura. I'm not here for it. My back slouches down as my lips curl back.

I can't really tell if I'm mad or sad. The bridge between my nose stings.

That bastard doesn't deserve my tears.

The glass shatters, shards scattering across the wooden floor. Crimson drops soon follow, oozing from my palms.

"I hate you, Atlas. I hate you." My boots step over the piercing pieces. "I hate you!" I back away, bumping into the door. I sink down to the ground again.

Why would he leave without telling me? That fool. Does he not know the effect his actions have on others?

When will he learn?

The window panes draw a navy grid across my face. In the blue hours of each night, is this how he felt in the captain's cabin, all by himself? Alone, afraid, and too scared to show himself to the rest of us?

Did I not fulfill my position as his closest mate, his only boatswain, as the boy who should've supported him all these years?

I had slept in the crew's quarters, surrounded by smelly, snoring men. It never bothered me. I was surrounded by other people. I didn't give a second thought as to who they were, as long as we were together. There's something scary about being alone. Every groan and creak from the masts sounds so loud. The smells call me back to better times. The past curls its threads around my neck and binds me to what should've been. Not what actually was.

You only realize the damage you've done once you reminisce in the ruins. I've been sinking ships for years. Now, my lifeboat is flooding. I'm the one being consumed by Davy Jones.

Say, if I never saw Atlas again, what would I do? Who would I become? What would become of him?

Would we lead better lives? Worse? How could it get worse than this?

A crew with a missing captain.

An exile with a hidden identity.

My gaze falls to the glittering shards. We're all broken pieces. Every one of us is like this by design.

I *will* find him. If it means scouring every corner of the seven seas, then so be it.

Standing, I lick the iron tang off of my hands. My feet plant themselves in the old wood. Our course has already been charted. If he were to seek refuge from his parents and the king he stole from, it would surely be within those foolish walls.

Well, I guess some of us are just lured in by trouble.

▽△▽△

"Edwin!" Our quartermaster salutes.

I salute back with the flick of two fingers.

"We've been looking all over. Are you sure you're doing alright?"

"Never better, chaps."

He eases closer, removing the three-pointed hat from his head to reveal his signature bandana around his forehead, which hides a scar that runs across his forehead. "Edwin."

"Oh, come on, Jean-Jacques. We're buds, no?"

"I don't like where—"

"Come on. Don't ya trust me?" I hop up on *Boreas'* taffrail. On one side of me, I have my rational crewmate, and on the other, a voice whispers for me to dive into the endless depths of Davy Jones. If I spread my arms wide enough, I'd fly like the gulls, the peckish white ones that soar among the clouds.

They can't be trusted. Neither can I.

"If it's about the captain," he begins.

I snap, "It's always about Capt'n."

Chapter 29

— The Alchemist —

I ENJOY TIME to myself. My father realized that a long time ago. He'd silently read, back against a tree, as I'd run around forests and climb branches like ladders. He'd let me stalk creatures from rabbits to foxes in the prairie's swaying grass, tufted with gold.

Let's say: once upon a time, I was traveling with my father, happy as could be. It's all too cliche. I know the story far too well; you do, too. We had been staying in a port city. The night prior, we had checked a room out of an inn. My father slept on an armchair while I had taken the bed, as I usually did on the occasion we found a welcoming place to stay. When I woke up, I looked across the room to find an empty sitting area. I remember my body feeling numb but not much else. It's like there was a hole in my stomach. My twisted gut knew something was wrong. I ran downstairs. Maybe he went to bring back breakfast. I waited in the lobby for his return. The sun reached high noon. There hadn't been a sign. I pestered the innkeeper about my father's whereabouts. He hadn't seen him leave.

The innkeeper was kind enough to let me stay another night. Then one more. A week went by. A month had passed. Downstairs, there was a tavern. If I earned my keep mixing drinks, I'd be able to stay.

I had stirred solutions for my father before, so the job offer didn't sound too bad. Besides, it would keep me busy and drag my mind away from his disappearance.

If you've connected two and two, I sought refuge behind those walls.

The barricade I'm within now.

"You don't want to suffer a loss like that again, so you make sure I'm only within arm's reach."

Atlas has moved on from standing in front of me. He lights an oil lamp, which flickers and illuminates his face with a warm amber. A faint red line runs across his eggshell-colored bandages.

A droplet draws a streak down my cheek.

"You're the sharpest person I know, Alouette. I'm sure you have realized that."

He walks past me and opens a door, which I presume leads to his room. With the light, he makes the dark disappear.

My feet trace the path to his room. Leaning on the frame, I stop at the doorway. His back to me, the captain pulls on a loose black shirt, one arm, and then the other. He sits back on an unusually small bed. This room hasn't truly been his for quite some time. Blue curtains outline the night sky; alas, the walls still stand tall to shield most stars from my view. At least white constellations dot the dark blue walls.

"Then, tell me, what are you proposing?"

His profile turns. His eyes almost glow as the moon reflects the sun's light. For a split second, I realize why that naive girl had fallen head over her dainty flats for him under the golden tavern lamps. My uncomfortably crossed arms tense in wait of his response.

That moment we shared on the lifeboat was a one-time event. If he wants more, he's not getting it. Not from me. My eye twitches. He's got to be as handsome as his mother is gorgeous. His wispy black hair falls on his forehead and curls around the back of his neck. His blue gaze always calls back to the sea. As drizzling raindrops tap on the window, his shimmering scales materialize in my mind. My skin prickles. Any other young lady would leave. She'd scream and kick and cry. Who knows to what extent she'll retaliate? Have another man make the captain walk the plank? It wouldn't get rid of him for good. I can't even shake him off, and I don't care that he's not fully human. Men are terrible creatures, whether they traverse the land or dwell beneath the sea's depths. Would I be the only suitor with this apathetic mindset? Character over genes, come on. As people, we can get over this. Sure, a pretty face is easy to look at, but what happens when their slurred speech drags you down, too?

I let out a grunt. I'm always in a tough spot when it comes to my place around Atlas.

Am I to speak now? My question isn't rhetorical. I need his answer. Is it that blatant that I don't want to associate with another creature due to my father's unexpected parting? Is Atlas leveraging this against me? Why has he grown so attached in the first place?

My father told me that I have a heart of gold, but such a nature means that it's shiny and cold. It's no place to root although easy to entangle and ensnare. After a while, any plant would wither and die.

A mutter of my name tears the veil of silence. "Let someone in." He picks and pulls at his pale fingertips. "It doesn't have to be me. Say your dad never came back, what would you do? Who would you turn to? Don't look me in the eye and assure me that you wouldn't turn to me. I know you well enough that I can guess your next comeback. It's never me. Because I'm a liar. I hide things from you. That's why. It's the reasoning you've coded into those…those cogs. The gears. The ones that turn underneath your eyes.

"Your face is like these walls. The way you have others turn away. It's a mechanism of your design, whether you intended it or not." He takes a deep breath in. "And you're right. I did lie. I drink a lot. I anger others. More often than not, I'm in the wrong, I know that and don't need to be reminded time in and time out. And time again, I swear. The way you look at me. You convince yourself not to trust me. But I trust you, Alouette. More than most. Back in the cellar. I brought the knife. Maybe I wanted to test you, or maybe I thought of defending myself. You know what I've been hiding from my crew. But you didn't hurt me. If I were you, I probably would have driven it through my chest."

I keep my lips sealed and still, yet my heart races.

"You're a good judge of character. You can analyze people. For goodness' sake, you're an alchemist. Some kind of magical chemist. You were born for this kind of evaluation. You didn't turn me away for what I am.

"I've taken off the gloves and gotten submerged in murky water with you. You know I'm doing this all for you. I returned the crown. I'm going to apologize to the king and revoke my offer tomorrow morning. Yet you keep pushing me away. This is the only plausible explanation. I just wish…" he stands and winces. "…I wish you'd tear down the walls. You don't need to surrender. Leave your heart open, that's all."

There are so many ways I could brush him off. All this for another kiss? An open heart is a broken heart. I can still feel the line that singular tear traced. My lips twitch at the edges. *Pathetic,* I know.

"Will he ever come back?" The words slip off of my tied tongue. I'm still hung up on his first point.

Atlas slowly approaches me, cautious with each step. "I can't say for sure."

That question *is* rhetorical.

He leans on the other side of the door frame with crossed arms that match mine. "What now, Captain?"

"I've asked you that before." I raise my chin. He looks down at me.

The next thing I know, his arms are wrapped around me. His soft hair brushes my cheek, contrary to his tight grip.

"My father always picked me up." The difference between our heights was far greater back then. Often, great bear hugs ended up with me thrown over his shoulder. I always laughed it off.

"Is that a challenge?"

"I don't know, Captain? Is it?" His hold on me tightens as he rises to his full height. I quickly reach around his neck to brace myself. If this were an actual challenge, Atlas would've won by nearly a foot.

He drops me at the sound of someone entering the house. The door to his room gets pulled shut. I hold my breath as I let go of the hope that I'll be able to sleep tonight.

"DeLuca?" a voice calls. "You've got a letter! Hello? Huh, I could've sworn I saw a light on. I'll just leave it…here." The door shuts.

Talk about awkward.

Atlas heads over to the window and unlocks it. He sticks his head out to survey the street. The rainstorm's wind whips his already messy hair around.

"Who does that?" He turns back to me.

I shrug and help myself to a seat on his bed. "Come in unannounced at night or talk to people who aren't there?"

Atlas shakes his head and leaves the window open. The smell of fresh rain drowns out the sea's salty scent that clings to the two of us. He sits on the other side. Scales run across his jawline.

"You've got something on your face." I reach for them with sprawled fingers. He flinches. I stop. We sit as still as statues in the night. For a moment I think he's going to push me away. He then leans into my palm.

"If you're going to ask why they appear, I don't know." He braces my wrist with his hand. His grip feels much different than the time he dragged me to his ship.

"Celestia willed it." I rub my thumb on a small, smooth patch.

"If you say so." Atlas rolls onto his back and closes his eyes. His wet hair clings to the side of his face. Droplets dot his dark lashes.

I look around his room. There's a bulletin board with pinned newspapers. Some touch on bounties for wanted men, others list potential treasure for opportunists. Some contain articles about the DeLucas. Father and son. There's another one pinned with a more recent date. Yesterday. I'm not very self-aware when it comes to my appearance, but I know it's me. Wanted. Alive or dead. My blood runs cold, like ice spikes spewing through my body.

I go to alert Atlas, but slumber has already taken hold of him. I contemplate shaking him awake. This is pretty urgent. He was right earlier, I *am* dangerous, more or less because I'm going to get him in trouble if bounty hunters put two and two together. He'll also be on thin ice with the cold blooded king once he revokes the offer he made years ago.

I flop onto my side where I can get a view of the bulletin board and Atlas. My feet hang off of the side. This is a child's bed. Yet the newspapers here are updated? Does Mister DeLuca have nothing better to do than to track what his son might be getting himself into? And if I'm on there, he must know about our association. I squint to read the warning about me. It's noted that I'm an alchemist. Clearly dangerous. Nothing new. There's testimony from the pirates and merchants from the ship I hopped onto.

Thoughts clog my mind as I try to filter them out. Will we need a disguise? Can I prance up to the king by Atlas' side if there are postings out for my arrest without consequence? My lips pull back. I want sleep, that's all. I need it now more than ever.

Admittedly, kind of like Atlas.

▽△▽△

A hand grabs me. I gasp. Another covers my mouth. The front door opens. The veteran Captain DeLuca. We slowly rise, careful not to make too much noise. Atlas reaches for a coat hanger in the shadowed corner of his room and drapes a cloak over his forearm. His eyes gravitate to a pair of gloves on his desk. The echoes of his father's pacing draw his attention back to me.

Ready? he mouths. I nod. He jumps first. I brace my hands on the windowsill and look down. The drop is further than I thought it would be. Atlas pulls up the cloak's hood and waves me down. I swallow my pride; he'll catch me if he has to. I swing my feet over the edge and let myself drop.

My landing could have been prettier. I stumble forward, having to then brace the rest of my tumble with my palms on the slippery stone street. Atlas holds his hand out to me. Not taking it would be pretty rude, so I briefly curl my fingers around his. I nestle myself under his cloak. He lifts his arm to make room.

"Should we pretend to get wasted and spend a free night at the tavern?"

"That sounds like an excuse for you to raid their cellar."

Besides, I have a better idea. One without drunkards.

▽☆▽△

The door's bell chimes as Atlas holds the door open for me, so that I may enter first. Although, I swear he had hesitated moments prior to reaching for the handle. After all, I had seen *her* silhouette prancing around from a couple of blocks down the street after all.

Not one night goes by without the tailor's floral scented candles that line her front windows. The lavender lulls me while I step into the parlor, but they're likely to regulate the pressure she faces from patrons and deadlines.

Pristine, as always, two perfectly arranged sofas comprise the sitting area, along with a little coffee table. Some scandal sheets and books are arranged in neat piles, spines aligned in perfect stacks.

"Rosaline?" I call, my fingers merely skimming the door handle as I stride away from the door.

The tailor whips around. A needle sticks out from between her teeth. On one hand, other pins prick the cushion as if it were a porcupine of the tailor's tools. While she tilts her head, her red half-moon glasses slide down the thin bridge of her nose, just so she can look over the rim at me. Those dusty red lips of hers, faded from a day's worth of chatter with townsfolk and commanding clients, part into a pearly smile. She just about throws her work aside, various ribbons, the spikeball of needles and all, to throw her arms around me. For looking so fragile in her old age, she's got quite the grip when her fingers claw at my back.

There's a fine line between endearment and condescension when it comes to her tone. "Oh, my dear, sweet lark."

She has yet to let go. This isn't like her.

"You're in one piece, right? Those pirates didn't tear you apart." Her fingers trace my shoulders, down my arms, to my fingertips, as if I were a dress of hers, eyes only buttons and tattoos merely delicate embroidery. Even as she pulls back, she keeps a hand sewn to my cheek. "I've seen what they've done to you." Her eyes narrow, peering above her lenses to glare at the captain behind me. "The posters don't do your pretty little face justice, dear."

"You've seen them?" I choke.

Rosaline shakes her head, accompanied by a disheartened sigh. "Everywhere I turn."

She then gestures for me to sit, waving her hand as she scurries off to get some refreshments, as she does for her favorite patrons. Atlas and I exchange an odd look. He frowns. I shrug in return. There may be bad blood between *them*, but I'd place a hearty sum on betting that she'd do nothing short of anything for me, including hiding a fugitive.

The tailor returns with a tray, crammed to the rims with porcelain cups, a floral teapot, pastel teacakes, tiny sandwiches, and, strangely enough, a pair of golden scissors. A string of steam wafts up from the teapot while she pours two teacups, topping them with little flower petals and dropping a few sugar cubes in each. She takes up one saucer and passes the other to me, along with a little spoon.

She takes a seat beside me and picks back up with her lecture, "You should really reconsider the company you've been keeping."

"You mean Atlas?" His name slips before I can take the time to find the right reply. "Rosaline, he's fine."

He's also right here!

She brings the golden rim of her teacup to her faded lips. "Your father would be ashamed."

The blood runs cold in my veins, spreading from my fingertips and creeping into my core. "My…" I slam the teacup down with a clang. Ripples jumble the flowers. Droplets spill. "…father?"

She nods.

"Do *not* bring him into this," I snarl.

"You know that I'm right, Lark."

My voice rasps. "You don't know the first thing about my father!"

She scoffs. "Then, tell me, what do *you* know about *him?*" Her gaze rakes across the room until it lands on Atlas.

I can't spill his secret, no. She's backing me into a corner.

"Know what? Name? Atlas DeLuca. Occupation? Captain of the ship *Aurora Borealis*—"

"And do you know what he does as a captain?"

Manages a crew? In fact, I don't know. Aside from drinking and stealing crowns, I'm not sure what he does.

"He hunts bounties," she says, flatly.

I look to the captain for confirmation. If Rosaline's accusation is true, instead of killing people, which seems impossible for him, he must turn them in for cash. That's how he sustains the *Aurora Borealis* and her crew.

He's right. You are dangerous.

My nose scrunches. "Well?"

"Fugitives and treasure, occasionally. The more of the former we turn in, the safer these ports are." He crosses his arms.

This cold blood of mine freezes.

"I had the pleasure of meeting his father, Dimitri DeLuca, yesterday morning. He said there's not a single bounty he could not turn in. There's no real reason to boast about this boy, so I'll assume that it's true." Rosaline sets the porcelain teacup down with a soft *clink*, brushes her skirt off, and stands.

Is it really?

As I sort through the last few days, I blink and I'm back at the masquerade. His arms keep my hands intertwined with his. Another blink. I have a knife pointed at him. Another. I'm turned away with my hand extended to take the blade of the rapier driving into my palm. Again. We're in the dark; his dagger sides out of my palm. Again. He pulls me back down into the ocean after I scratch the surface. Once more. He's too close to me.

Why has he fought tooth and nail to stay with me? Surely, he knows that I wouldn't have done the same for him. I'm an awful, terrible, cruel girl. The price painted on me must be enough for him to stick by my side.

Who could really love me, anyway?

Chapter 30

— The Siren —

Rosaline is a sick, sick woman.

What Alouette and I have is *not* a farce. Whatever may be tying us together, this bond is very much real.

The alchemist's analytical stare burns my skin.

"So, a bounty hunter?" She lifts her chin, so there's the allusion of her looking down on me. "Who was your next target going to be? Me?"

No. I never came after her. We all know that. The night's fog has clouded our judgment, and the rain has washed away these facades until we're faced with only our true colors. If Rosaline means to drive us apart, this was the perfect opportunity. She knows how to play off of Alouette's doubts, and, clearly, how to extort my flaws and twist them into traits far, far worse.

I shake my head. "Look, Alouette, when I pulled you out of the water, you were the last person I'd expect to be on a Wanted poster."

"You're sure?" Her ferocity wavers. She *wants* to believe me.

"Like you said, doing nothing is basically driving a blade. Letting someone drown would've felt the same as me pushing them overboard."

"I understand." The alchemist then helps herself to one of the teacakes. She looks over her shoulder, back at the tailor who has poured her efforts back into a scarlet gown. In this deadlock, the line between trusting Rosaline or me is quite fine. "Tell me who you hunt, Atlas."

"Plenty of ports put out lists with fugitives and thieves. Edwin usually decides who we go after, but recently people have been coming to us for help. I can't decline. Some hold personal grudges while others are owed a debt. No matter what, we'll track them down and turn them over to authorities, or the commissioner." I give Alouette a quick once over.

Once, I did decline.

A young man marched himself right onto the *Aurora Borealis*, demanding that we find runaway servants of his, a father and daughter. Edwin shuffled him off the ship in no time, before I could hear the young man rattle off all the details. My boatswain is a fine judge of character, so it's safe to assume that no soul should serve a man like him.

Could that have been Alouette and her father?

"And you never thought to tell me this?"

Really, it all felt trivial. With the alchemist I thought that maybe, just maybe, I could change. That, by chance, my past would mean nothing if she were in my future. My shortcomings could be washed clean, and I'd be able to write a new tale over them, one not overcome by flaws. Alas, if Rosaline had her way, I'd be scribbled out of Alouette's pages altogether.

"I was caught up with the heist." I promise it's the truth.

Alouette reaches for another teacake. "Take one. I don't want to be the only one eating."

Even as the topic has been flicked like a switch between night and day, she periodically checks on Rosaline with a cold side-eye, whereas I take one or two of the mini sandwiches. Maybe three. Look, I can't recall the last time I had a real meal.

"And just to confirm, I'm not your next target?" She's already washing a good five teacakes down with a swig of tea. Even doing so, she's not any less intimidating.

"You're innocent. There's no need."

Rosaline must not like this outcome, for she comes marching back over, measuring tape draped over her shoulders and with a fistful of pins. She cozies up next to Alouette and puts a hand on hers.

"Dear, why don't you let your friend get some rest?"

"I'm fine, madam."

"There's a spare room upstairs. Besides, we've got a few things to take care of." Her fingertips skim the golden scissors. Alouette flinches. There's no trusting Rosaline around the alchemist, with all of her twisted truths and cruel accusations. The alchemist knots her fingers together, knowing well that she cannot turn Rosaline down on my behalf.

With that, I retire for the night.

▽△▽△

The silk curtains flutter in the midnight breeze. Mist seeps through the window, the panes slightly ajar. Streaks, stains left over from the downpour distort my view of the streets below. There's only an orange blur here and there from oil lamps on other window sills, and an overpowering blue, dark as the bottom of Davy Jones. Perhaps it has been an hour. Or maybe not. The clock in the corner of the room, painted with delicate flowers and foiled with gold, exclusively sits there for decoration.

I've kicked my feet up on a sofa, propped with pillows. In the corner, a vanity with an elaborate crown engraved at the top waits under a coat of dust. My reflection barely makes it into the corner. Everything else in the room, aside from the bed against the wall next to me, is covered in white sheets.

Heavy footsteps pound up the stairs and down the hall.

Then enters Alouette.

She slams her hands down on the vanity and drags her fingers through what's left of the curls that once tumbled down her back. Now the tips of golden whisps don't make it past her shoulders. Her quiet mutterings curse Rosaline.

I say her name and swing my legs off the sofa.

She glances at me, eyes glossed over, hands still in her hair. "It's shorter than yours isn't it?"

"That's okay, Alouette. It's fine." Fine doesn't even begin to describe her. I'm no good with words when I'm around her, my speech far worse than the slurred gibberish that comes out before I black out from one too many drinks. If only she knew the way her gold eyes glitter in the silver moonlight that barely shines through the dark clouds. How even the tips of her eyelashes fade to a light blonde, whether by the sun's bleaching or by a higher power. Not to mention that when she smiles, it's with every inch of her face, from her bare teeth to the one side her grin leans toward, easing her cheeks back into those eyes. And with each smile, I think I fall back in love with her, over and over, again and again.

She paces. "It's not the same. Nothing's the same. Not since he left. Now that he's gone," and paces, "It's not...it's not...no, it's not the same." Until she perches next to me. Her fluttering eyes fight back against tears.

"We'll find him," I breathe.

She slumps onto my shoulder. "We will?"

"Of course. Alouette, we *will* find him."

Chapter 31

— The Thief —

AS I HOP off the ship, the quartermaster salutes me. I turn my attention to the misty night, for the rain had been on and off, Mother Nature unable to make up her mind. My night vision is pretty good for only having one eye. I can spot all of the cracks and weaknesses and imperfections of the planks. Stopping for a brief moment, I scan the horizon. Windows of many vessels, from skiffs to goliaths, glow like lanterns in the night. Lamps sit on posts, illuminating the wooden docks and lapping water below. A list is clenched in my hand. My job is usually to take stock of food and supplies, when I'm not looking after the captain, that is. He's a high maintenance guy, what more can I say? Luckily, my duties grant me the perfect opportunity to scour the town for Atlas. What a pain. I'll cut him some slack by admitting this is more amusing than completing the average duties of a boatswain.

There's a familiar rowboat, oars crossed between the wooden planks. The glimmer of a sea green pole rests beneath them. I jog over and slide down into the boat. How fortuitous! Atlas' trident.

The same one that had been missing when I surveyed his room earlier. Whether it was his intention to leave breadcrumbs for me to pick at or not, there's no room for me to complain. I grasp the weapon and hoist myself back up onto the dock. My determined march has a new spring in its step, despite my fatigue.

I'm coming.

▽△▽△

My first instinct is to visit Mister DeLuca. This should be Atlas' duty, not mine, but if he had a change of heart, perhaps the captain sought refuge with his father. I knock on the door. A disgruntled muffle comes from inside. Usually, I have plenty of patience for him, but the rain is creeping up on me as it patters on the stone streets. My foot incessantly taps his wooden porch.

Come on! I can't be the only person in this forsaken port that has a sense of urgency.

At last, there's a click. I welcome myself into the DeLuca household and give the man of the house a hardy pat on the back.

"Edwin?" His voice raises.

"The one and only. Did ya miss me?" I tip my head to him. Droplets run off of my auburn bangs. Sliding my fingers through my hair, I flip it back. I can't stand being wet. Don't think that just because I'm a sailor, I can handle that discomfort.

"I didn't expect you to come back so soon." DeLuca pinches the bridge of his nose. He peels his hand away and gestures to the weapon in my grasp. "And with a trident?"

"Don't dwell on it." I toss the sharp thing from one hand to the other. People get all jumpy when folks like me treat weapons like toys, because they are. Why else would we call it sword*play*?

"If you're looking for Atlas, I've got a feeling that he left about an hour ago."

Oh. Atlas must've visited, only fleeing once his father returned from his usual drinking spot, I presume.

"Shame. No heartfelt reunion?"

I couldn't be more disappointed in the response. "He took his leave as I came back from the tavern." The DeLucas can be quite predictable. The door to the captain's former room, one that he had all to himself as a young lad, sits ajar. A cold breeze blows through the window. This should've been anticipated. "Though, if you want to know, he left a bloody rag and bandages by the sink."

Shrugging, I hide my intrigue. The captain has had his fair share of quarrels, yet few of his enemies have drawn blood. This could be Alouette's doing, keeping in mind that the two of them disappeared at the same time. Though, I can't recall her ever inflicting real wounds. There must be another clue.

I point to his counter, where a letter topped with a pried-off wax seal waits to be noticed. "Who's it from?"

"The king." He picks up the envelope.

"Regarding what? A coronation for your son?" I raise my hands. "I kid, I kid."

His dark brown eyes avoid mine. My hunches have been far too accurate this evening, so my hands threaten to jitter, afraid of what may follow.

"Sit down, will you? You two are too flighty. Besides, I've heard about the girl." This is never a good sign.

"Eh? Word gets out quickly." I find my place leaning back on an armchair, perhaps sinking into the velvet is better than delving into worry. DeLuca joins me in his sitting room with a candle in one hand and an amber drink in the other. *Like father, like son.*

"She used to bartend. It's such a small world."

"It's small when you're confined by the walls."

"My years of traveling are long over. Sometimes the world is safer when you control what fraction you see."

Disappointing, really. I'm still far more intrigued by the fact that Atlas' father is already familiar with the alchemist. "Wait, so if I'm hearing this right, you know her? You *know* know Alouette? Not just know *of* her?"

He nods. "The alchemist's daughter. Doesn't drink yet is skilled with mixing for the drunkards. From my conversations with her, I'm guessing she has dealings with something similar to your line of work. Men like gold. Alchemists can provide. Not to mention the raw power she wields. She's broken up plenty of fights. The sailors who face that girl never dare to challenge her again."

That's our Alouette, beyond doubt.

"Do you happen to know her father?"

"We've briefly met in passing." That stiff tone of his tells me that he's hiding details, ones that I'll never get him to share. Instead of urging him on, I follow his eyes while his focus drifts back to the letter.

I raise my brows, hoping that he'll at least elaborate on the links between the alchemists and the king's letter.

"If he were still around, he'd be disappointed to know that there's a bounty on his daughter's head." He raises his glass and tips his head back. "*Wanted dead or alive*, that's what the poster says."

My eyes widen. What if Atlas has turned her over to the authorities, as he does to many other criminals? No. I shake my head. He'd never—not when she hasn't done anything wrong, aside from the fact that we had her partake in replicating a stolen crown for our crew. For Davy Jones' sake, Atlas *saved* her. And by sending her off to prison, or even her demise, that dive would've been a waste. If it weren't for Atlas' bleeding heart, Alouette and I would not have air in our lungs.

"Her father. Is he…dead?" My eyes narrow.

"No." His confidence and sureness surpasses mine. His fingers scrunch the envelope.

Oh? I rise from my slouch.

"This has to do with the letter, doesn't it?"

He nods. "Don't tell a soul." The candle flickers; even it trembles from his harsh tone.

I smile. "My lips are sealed."

"My son has negotiations with the king." His voice lowers. "He couldn't find a way to send a message to Atlas, so sending a messenger to me was the next best option. Tell me, Edwin. What are his dealings with the Alchemist's daughter?"

"Where do I begin?" I laugh. He cocks his head and gives me a confused snicker. "First and foremost, he's fallen head over boots for her."

"Oh?" He leans closer, either out of intoxication or infatuation. The DeLucas must have a knack for both. "Wait." He draws back. "That's no good."

I know his next words. Is she aware of…you know?

"Right you are," I say. "She's seen his true colors, or should I say scales?"

"That doesn't make this any better."

"Yeah, especially noting that after they got into a quarrel over his secrets, they both vanished. Out at sea, I must add."

He sets his glass down and raises a hand to his chin. Those dark eyes of him sink deep into thought, although the sparkly shine of crapulence veils them. He curses but keeps them quick.

I awkwardly smile. Why is it that I always need to be the bearer of bad news? "Afraid that she'll dissect him?"

His brows furrow. "Her father would."

I blink a few times.

"Knowledge is dangerous, Edwin. I'm sure you see that. Those who call themselves alchemists don't only yield physical power. They strive to depict the world around them, down to its roots. That's where it sprouts from. I know Alouette is a good kid, it's just that—" He takes a sharp breath. There's no continuation.

"It'll get her in trouble? Too late. It'll get Atlas into trouble, too? He's knee-deep in his own affairs."

"That's the problem. I don't know what to do. The king expects Atlas to step up soon."

"Because of the crown?"

"They don't know the crown's a fake. Alouette's handiwork, no?"

I suck my lips in and nod. *Those fools.*

DeLuca takes a deep breath in. "I don't know what he'll do. If he's the same lad who struck a deal years ago, he'll seize the opportunity. If he's become any better of a person, he'll rid this kingdom of its grievances with those who dwell beneath the waves." That's DeLuca's agenda. "But if he has changed, then I'm as oblivious as you."

"The real crown isn't in our crew's hands anymore. I'm guessing he returned it. Call it a change of heart, if you will."

"Then there's a chance he'll cower away. He'll have to admit the princess' current crown is a replica. If he slips and justifies his deeds, claiming that Farida is his mother..." he picks up his glass and finishes it, "...the king will pass judgment, to put it lightly."

"Well, we both know Atlas would be a terrible king." I gawk. "Plus, being the figurehead of a kingdom puts him in danger.

The common folk have their prejudices. Say, if a siren weaseled his way to the throne, questions would rise. So would a rebellion. Humans aren't inherently good. Man cannot stand monster."

"That said, how does the alchemist's daughter find him?"

Chapter 32

— The Alchemist —

I'd like to note that it's a very, very very good thing that Rosaline never became a real mother.

Inside, she's as good as the girls who prey on one another and pass around scandal sheets. As a tailor, Rosaline is surrounded by petty brats who will all sit around drinking tea and gossiping from daybreak to nightfall. Sure, her craft is nothing to overlook, but nor should her personality be pushed to the side. She's a wicked woman. I hate to say it. But she's manipulative and arrogant and everything a mother should not be. Never should I have believed her stabs at Atlas. I was a fool to believe anything she said, especially the stories she told me after she'd warded off the captain.

The story began with a cliche little, *"Mademoiselle, you cannot put your life in the hands of someone like him. I fell for the same temptation when I was a girl."*

No. She didn't. She's never known Atlas. Dare she try to see him as anything other than a bounty hunter and siren and liar; she can't; she can't; she can't.

Worst of all she claimed that Atlas was using me. No. The orchestrator has been her all along. I will stand by that until the day I die. Celestia must see through my reasoning.

▽△▽△

This morning I will leave. I will leave this tailor for good. No matter how beautiful her dresses are, no matter how she pretends to be the mother I never had. There's a reason Celestia took a mom out of my life. We all must respect that.

A hum seeps up through the polished floorboards. Pacing the span of the boutique's parlor, Rosaline is waiting downstairs, bright and early.

Atlas has his arm around me. The morning's light tints his midnight hair golden hues I haven't seen on him before. I lied. Hues I haven't seen since the masquerade. His jacket had golden buttons. That's besides the point.

He's not going to leave.

I whisper his name.

Atlas' dark lashes blink a few times before parting for his ocean blue eyes to peer through. A little drowsy, he lets out a quiet, "Hm?"

"Time to see the king?" I press my hand against his. His fingers flinch before intertwining with mine.

"And then set off to find your father?"

A smile, beyond my control, pulls at the corners of my mouth and swells my cheeks. *Please.*

Together, we trek downstairs. The tailor, to my surprise, hasn't returned to last night's work-in-progress. Her tea set is out, brimming with steam and a new scent. She raises an offering to us.

I pull in a deep breath. Funny, how difficult it is to part with what could've been. For a moment, I believed she could be a stepmother of sorts. For a moment, I was proud of her dress. For a moment, I thought she had the best in mind for me.

"Goodbye," my tone is flat, "Goodbye, Rosaline."

Her expression contorts. Never would she have expected this.

The bitter words linger on my tongue as the bell chimes, and we're back out on the street.

Atlas keeps quiet while he hands me his cloak from last night. I wrap it around my shoulders and pull up the hood.

The morning rush hits us in full swing. Merchants call to gather patrons. Commonfolk run in just about every direction. They're so caught up in their own lives that no one noticed our skirmish in Rosaline's boutique.

My steps slow as I look around. The world and people seem to blur by. Auctioned cattle. Forged swords. Fresh produce. Warm bread. Every time I move, a new waft hits me, whether sweeter or harsher than the one before it. A woman slams right into my shoulder as she passes. I stumble back in recoil. Atlas glares at her. It's meaningless. Crowds and mobs appear the same to me. I can't see more than five feet in front of me. Children whine and cry for their parents who busy themselves with stocking up on groceries and supplies. Their voices bounce off of the walls, and their footsteps amplified by the stone.

I wish I could have been the little boy sitting down in the center of the street, throwing his fists to the bricks in a fit. A tantrum doesn't solve problems, but at least it would get my mind off of facing them. I must remind myself that I am no longer a child. How come the adults no longer mind the clutter, noise, and odors?

My skin prickles like a porcupine's quills digging into my flesh. Here, we're supposed to be safe. Yet inside the walls, we're captive. There's freedom outside. Pastures. Space. Wide, open space. Room to stretch my arms out without brushing up against another wicked man. Every intersecting street has another wave in the flood of people this morning. Perhaps it's a good thing my peripheral view has been blocked by the thick fabric of Atlas' cloak. Any more than my tunnel vision and I'm not sure if I could handle it.

A few girls lock eyes with me. Their arms full of dresses and jewels, they must recognize me from the ball. I fumble to generate an excuse for being here in case they've seen the posters. Then their attention turns to Atlas.

He's the one they're really interested in. They giggle and compliment him for his recent performance. A jealous redhead expresses how she wishes she could have shared a dance with him. She twirls her fingers through her long hair as she sways her topaz-colored dress. I reach for the back of my neck, where the wisps of curls barely reach.

Curse Rosaline.

I expect Atlas to offer her a dance; yet he doesn't.

Another blonde asks for him to sing again, to which he declines. She puffs out her cheeks and pouts like a prissy prick. One comments on the bandages around his chest, which are visible under the low neck of his shirt. He doesn't have to explain himself, not to these strangers.

I tromp ahead. He better take the hint.

My shoulders brush past the bustling mindless citizens. Infatuated smiles and scornful scowls alike morph into one another. There's no place to back away. If Celestia told me I was meant for the dungeon of a ship and not the crowded street, I'd begin to believe her.

Expecting Atlas, I look to my side. I turn. And turn, and turn, until I'm back where I started. I'm aimlessly swimming in a sea of unfamiliar faces, and I might be beginning to drown. The girl's laughter fades. He's not there?

The swarm swallows me whole.

Chapter 33

— The Siren —

A HAND TUGS my wrist. I turn to find Edwin with a finger pressed to his lips. He's so quiet, yet I doubt I could single out any pair of footsteps in the town square. He tilts his head toward a vacant alley.

Before I can protest, he yanks. I take one last glance at Alouette. Roaline was a genius to chop off her curls, her most identifiable features from afar. With a hood over her head, she's already gone. I curse and join Edwin. We squeeze past barrels and cargo containers. My back scrapes against the brick wall. Once our alley is clear, Edwin turns to face me with his hands raised. It's never good when he speaks with them out.

He shushes me as I try to speak. I took too long to say anything. What could I say? What *should* I say?

"One. Why did you leave? Two. Where did you go? Three. How can we drive it through that thick skull of yours that abandoning your crew is *never* an option?" He draws his dagger and places it beneath my chin. Little does he know that Alouette has done this to me already. I leave it be.

"I returned it to her. And you can't. I'm sure everyone was in good hands with you around," I snap. Though I sounded sarcastic, I mean it. I do. I promise.

"And what do you plan to do next?" He takes a step closer. The little distance between us shrinks.

"Pay a visit to the king."

"I assumed that much. Accept your fate or defy it? That's what I want to know."

"Defy it by stepping out of my deal?"

He pulls back the blade and glides his fingertips across it. "By admitting to the heist? Apologize for hiring a wanted alchemist to replicate and replace a past offering?"

He makes me sound delusional. I hold my breath as he tugs a letter from his pocket. He smooths out the wrinkles with one hand on his thigh before raising it for me to see.

"Permission to change your mind, Capt'n?"

"You're not going to call me a scheming scallywag?" My brows crease.

His mischievous smile tells me that he has a plan already sorted out. If I reach for the letter, he'll pull it away. We're always in a stalemate of sorts.

"Oh, no. No, no. When you're king, I don't want to be on your bad side." He shakes his head.

"What makes you so certain that I'll take the crown?"

He flaps the cream-colored envelope. My father's name spirals in elegant calligraphy across the backside.

Edwin takes a shaky breath in. "He's dying."

"Who?"

"The king. He's been ill. For three or so years. We didn't see him at the masquerade because he's bedridden. It didn't make sense to me before. This man loves flaunting his power. For the past few years, he's been on borrowed time." He licks his lips before continuing. "Time granted to him by an *alchemist*."

An alchemist? Surely, not Alouette. Her father is a viable possibility. If that's really him, then this is my only shot at finding him.

"He supposedly needed the Elixir of Life. A potion for immortality. We can't rule its existence out. Not with you, a half-siren, and the amount of magic lingering in the corners of this world. Besides, aside from turning metals into gold, alchemists devote their lives to finding this potion. We happen to know one." He winks at me, contrary to his unease from moments ago.

"So what are you implying?"

"The alchemist has failed. Or maybe he has hidden the Elixir out of spite. I would have. That means the king's end is coming sooner than anticipated. He has no male heir. They say a similar illness took the queen's life a while back. Only the daughter remains. I wouldn't put power in her hands, nor will the king. You haven't forgotten the deal, have you? Betrothed to the princess, *you*," he leans closer, "are the next in line."

"But—what? We're not married." The words don't feel right coming off of my tongue.

"Your promises to the king. They're preliminary vows."

"I never took any vows."

"He sees your deal as such." Edwin spits.

I recoil.

"Don't back out because you're soft."

"I don't want the princess anymore. I wasn't interested in *her* to begin with."

"I know. You made that choice. Knowing you're here, your mother forgave you. She's your blood. The king? He is not. These are his last days and, really, his patience for dissent has run dry, assuming that it was ever there in the first place. Young Altas proposed this. Today's Atlas now must accept his fate. Don't look at me like that. Alouette doesn't want you, anyway."

The back of my neck freezes like ice whereas my cheeks grow hot enough to scorch my face.

"We'll miss ya on the crew, Capt'n. But don't let a girl stop you." He grimaces.

"She's not just a girl, Edwin. She—"

"*Do not let that get in the way of the crown. He has one shot. If he must take it in the dark, let him,*" he cuts me off, "That's what DeLuca told me. You weren't supposed to know any of this. I think you deserve to know. But this is still not the full story."

"How do I tell Alouette?" My fists clench. "If I turn my back on my plans now, I'll look like a liar again."

"We're pirates, Atlas. We lie time and time again to save our own skin!" His voice rasps.

"Alouette finally trusts me. I'm not going back to how it was before."

"You're obsessed with her, can't you see?"

My breath hitches. It's not by choice, I swear on my very own life.

"This has blinded you. You can't even see the fact that your father told me this before he told you? You're losing everyone else's trust by pursuing her! I'm the one who has to relay his intel now."

I force a smile. In truth, he's the most reliable person in all the seven seas. "Thank you, Edwin."

Edwin nods. He's a little too confident for my liking. There's no resting assured until he reveals his entire hand.

"There's also something in this for you, isn't there? That's why you've given me more than my father would have."

Edwin stares for a moment. I would've assumed that he brushed the last statement off with a shrug, as he always does. Usually, that's what he does after offending me or threatening to reveal my origins.

"I can't think of any strings attached." His eyes drift away from me. "I'm sorry you think a stranger is more reliable than I am. We're crewmates." He rolls up his sleeve and holds his forearm out to me. Burns that tried healing long ago stretch across his skin. "I swear by my life. You're our captain, Capt'n. We'll find a backdoor. He didn't say you had to stay king, nor did you have to confirm any vows with his daughter." His grin grows, easing into his mismatched eyes that return to look at mine. This smirk is for my sake.

I hold my arm up against his. "Fine."

"The wound isn't bad, is it?" He sheaths his dagger.

I shake my head. "It'll be okay. Alouette cleaned it."

"And bandaged you up, I can tell." He elbows me in the side, just beneath the ribs where he knows I'll flinch.

Edwin won't allow himself to be charitable for too long.

His voice lowers, "I really am sorry, Atlas. I-I should've done more." His misty eye quickly blinks out the brewing tears. "I was never the sailor I should've been. Not the proper boatswain, not even a decent friend. And there's no changing, uhm, you know what I mean." He crosses his arms. I start to reply, but he's already changing the topic. "The king should be waiting for you. Whatever happens, Atlas, do not refuse the crown."

▽△▽△

I'm not drunk. I just have too many thoughts to keep my head straight. The foggy drowsiness hasn't worn off, either. I bump into a few passers-by. Those who don't gawk and insult me simply ignore me, which is preferred. Now is not the time to make enemies. Especially with the people of this kingdom, and not to forget, Alouette. She knows that I planned to revoke my offer. Assuming she is not the particular alchemist I discussed with Edwin, then she has no way of knowing the king's predicament. My deal has already been revealed to her. How can I convince her that I'm not a liar while I turn my back on my own words?

If that alchemist truly is her father, this is perfect! But what if it isn't? I'd be a liar again. How cruel would it be to say I know where her father is without having solid evidence? But what if that *is* her father?

She's not that important, I try to assure myself. Edwin would say there are plenty of other girls. But she's not just a girl. She's an ally. A friend. I hold my breath. She may not see me as a friend. I kick the ground. I must not make a fool out of myself. But I already have, haven't I? With crossed arms, I keep an eye out for her.

It'll be best to explain my plans to her before making any rash decisions. Then to the crew, unless Edwin has already gotten to that. I need to trust him now, if not anyone else. There's no telling how Alouette will react. If only I had not stolen that crown as a boy, none of us would be in our current predicament. Had we not invited the alchemist to join the heist, I wouldn't have to tread lightly around a critical girl. Besides, both her life and mine would be much easier.

Nailed to a board of other parchment, a yellowed page with curled edges depicts the alchemist's profile. Her long curls, fading to gold at the tips. Sharp eyes, lined with perfect lashes. A toothy smile that spreads across her whole face. Quickly taking a glance at my hands, I remind myself that if I'm not careful, that could be me inscribed on those sheets, too. Before, I only had to worry about Edwin spilling my secret. Alouette knows it too, which on top of her skills with alchemy, make her another danger to watch out for. One wrong move and who knows what will become of us.

I push the thought to the back of my mind. I'll take care of problems as they arise. That's how I've run my crew for all these years. When a leak springs, patch it before it can deal more damage. If a floorboard appears loose, replace the wood. Enemies approaching? Attack. Don't strike unprovoked.

I've strayed off of my own code these past few days.

That won't steer me too far off course. I place a hand on my chest to ease an ache, unable to tell whether it's from the laceration or my heart itself. I wouldn't be a good king. The boy I used to be was a fool. Even now I reap the terrible actions I had sewn long ago. And, of all people, why would my father trust his homeland in my hands? I'm too afraid to face him. I'm just a man.

Perhaps my father wants me to unearth the truth of the king's illness and dealings with the alchemists in his desperate attempt to push the crown off to someone 'reliable.' With the princess' hand potentially in mine and the crown on my head, there's power for my father to regain. I doubt that would be the case, but the possibility cannot be eliminated. Too many factors from too many people are at play here. Life is not black and white, not like a game of chess with a limited checkered-board. Any player can bring pieces at their leisure.

I weave through commoners in search of Alouette. Too many people wear dark hoods like hers—well, mine. Perfect for blending in, not so great for scouting out. I tap a few people on the shoulder that are not her. Each time I apologize. This is my fault for getting sidetracked by Edwin. Looking over my shoulder walking forward, maybe I'll be able to find her face, but I bump into someone else.

"Celestia's sanction."

Thank goodness it's her.

She looks up at me with a playful smile. I have no idea how I'm going to break the news to her. "Guessing the guise works?"

"Almost too well."

She laughs. By miracle, she's not mad. *Unless she's a fine actor,* the thought crawls in my thoughts.

"To the king?" She raises a brow.

"To the king," I confirm.

She looks up at the castle, which when backlit, casts a shadow over the entire city. The hood slips down from her head. Her short brown hair still fades to gold at the tips. I wonder if the trait comes with being an alchemist. She's still pretty. I would like nothing more to be honest with her, but that time isn't now. As much as she hates my lies, I disdain myself for not being able to tell the truth.

She tilts her head with a displeased frown. "Be honest, Atlas, do I look like a boy?"

"Not at all."

She continues walking, as if she didn't ask a strange question. The tides have changed since we first met. Underneath my cloak, she wears a white button up topped with a corset and a brown skirt that comes down to her ankles. Her boots are now muddy and laced with golden chords. Sleeves come down to cuffs at her wrists and arm followed by a new set of gloves, too. I hide my hands in my pocket, although it's my forearms that are the problem, with the exception of my nails if I don't file them down. Furthermore, I'm usually the one with a cloak. For once, I'm not restrained by a high collared shirt, but it doesn't feel right. The alchemist has slowly unraveled me, one thread at a time. I cannot continue to allow this. As Edwin advised, a mere girl should not dictate my actions.

Alouette keeps quiet as we weave through the streets. Now that the morning's bustle has ceased, there's finally room to traverse the town without others breathing down our necks. I may freely speak, if I please. There are too many topics to cover with her. Why I'll look like I'm betraying her in a few minutes. How I want to sort out what happened with Rosaline. Then there's the fact that I simply cannot get over what happened yesterday. The tip of my nose to my ears go warm at the thought.

"You're blushing because of the princess?" Alouette gawks. I snap back to our saunter.

"N-no," I stammer, foundering for words that I can't place my finger on.

Alouette hisses in my ear. "Then get your act together. She's here."

More often than not, I wish I could push the sun back a few hours and wake up again. I'm then reminded that I'm Atlas, not Apollo. It's not within my power to pull celestial bodies across the sky with a chariot. If there truly is a higher power, like the Celestia Alouette calls upon, the misfortunes of my life must be for her amusement. I try my best to smile at the princess. Her oblivious smile, painted with pink lipstick, tells me that she has no idea what I just said.

"Salutations," is the only greeting I can think of. At least kick starting conversations Alouette is rather easy, granted it starts with petty bickering. As of right now, there's a daunting difference in our standings within the kingdom's social hierarchy between the princess and I. Edwin's voice rings in the back of my mind.

Whatever happens, Atlas, do not refuse the crown.

Soon we'll be on even ground. The thought doesn't sit right with me.

"What a joy it is to find you on this fine promenade." She links arms with me in complete disregard of Alouette. The way she kissed my cheek at the masquerade, I wasn't sure if her father told me that he had given her hand to me. Without a doubt, she's aware now. Lined with coal black makeup, her eyes luster with a festering infatuation as they look up to meet mine.

I glance back at Alouette.

"My father demands an audience with you. It's urgent. You must come fast, we need to chat about…" her nudge is soft, and so is her giggle, "…you know." Her cheeks turn the pink of her dress.

The princess is nothing like the alchemist.

Ignorant of Alouette's handiwork, she fiddles with her pearl necklace that matches the crown sitting on her blonde hair. The replica could've even convinced me that it once belonged to my mother.

She leads me down the street. Alouette trails like a shadow.

"How long have you known about *this*?" Her tone is sweet like tea cakes. I'm more of a wine and cheese type of captain.

"Quite a while."

Her infectious smile spreads all the way to her eyes.

"Why haven't you spoken of our betrothal? Were you scared a princess could never love a pirate?"

Not at all. I try to catch another glimpse of Alouette. She raises her brows at me in an attempt to urge me on. I guess I have to fuel this conversation on my own.

"Perhaps."

"That voice of yours is lovely. I've longed to hear you sing again, ever since the masquerade."

"Is that so?"

"Indeed it is." She stops and places a hand on my cheek. "It's almost as handsome as your face without that silly mask." Her brows crease as her thumb runs across the scar on my jaw. *There's a reason pirates keep away from nobility. I don't think I can put up with this.*

I force a laugh and peel her hand off of my face. *I can't do this.*

"Does it hurt?" She frowns.

"It kills him." This conversation is not complete with Alouette's mockery. I couldn't be more grateful for her brazen demeanor.

"And who do you think you are?" Her light tone stays airy, as if she's from cloud cuckoo land, far away from the rest of the kingdom's people and problems.

I can't say her name. We can't reveal that she's the wanted alchemist.

"His first mate," Alouette says.

What a lie. If we can find a way out of this predicament together, there's a chance I'll give her that title. I swear by my own ship, Aurora Borealis.

I quickly tack on, "She also doubles as my personal escort."

"Well, you won't need her when I'm around, will you?" Her arm tightens around mine, but note that her grip wasn't strong to begin with. Luckily, she doesn't notice anything off about my forearm. Or she doesn't say anything. It's safe to assume that she doesn't get out to interact with common people very often.

"No, we will."

"*We?*"

Her cheeks puff out along with her lower lip. "But it's just us," she squeals, all pink like swine. "You and me." She grabs the fabric of my shirt and tries to bring me to her level.

Whatever happens, Atlas, do not refuse the crown.

If Edwin and my father weren't counting on me, it would've taken her a lot more force. I lean down. As if she really had control over me, pride takes hold of her expression.

By all means, I wish I could retort, *and her.*

I will not be on this princess' leash for long. After all, the letter mentioned that I did not have to follow through with tying any knots in order to accept the crown from her father. The worst part of this all is that Alouette has to watch from behind. I steal another glimpse of the alchemist to find her giving me a thumbs up. As soon as my attention turns back to the princess, I'm faced with her lips against mine. I stand and straighten my posture, almost instinctively. She just laughs. I'm surprised not to hear a snicker from Alouette, too. The toe of her boots lands on the back of my heel instead. For her records, I'm not pleased with this, either.

The castle doors couldn't have come at a better time. A knight takes off his helmet in reverence, he raises a brow at me. Alouette's eyes widen for a moment before hiding her shock. If this is the same knight who *almost* caught us in the citadel, then this must be an unusual sight.

Yet again, I wish I could restart today. Preferably, I'd wake up in my own cabin aboard *Aurora Borealis,* the door locked, not beside Alouette with a madwoman pacing downstairs. Once we enter, an attendant rushes the princess off. Another servant bows to me and begins leading us to another room. Without the fancy guests and live music, the castle sits cold and still. The clicks of our heels are now enough to fill the space. The hallway we turn down has high, arched ceilings, covered with paintings of sirens, sailors, and the sea. Fitting for a port kingdom.

The alchemist jabs me in the side.

"What was that for?" I keep my voice low.

"You make me sick."

"Do you think this is voluntary?" I wipe my mouth on my sleeve to inevitably leave a pink stain on the dark fabric.

Her delayed laugh chimes in, worlds from amused.

The attendant opens a door and gestures for us to enter. The two of us step into a study. Glowing in the late morning light, dust dances in the air. It smells of old paper and spilled ink, a little like Alouette. With only the notice that the king will see to us soon, we're left to our own devices. I take a seat at the desk. Alouette sits *on* it.

"Can't say." She shrugs while picking up one of the notebooks strewn about the polished wood. "Tell me, Atlas, just how many girls have you kissed?"

"That's not important."

"A lot," she jumps to conclusion. "It's obvious you don't like her. Did you ever love her?"

I shake my head. "No. I should've just asked to be the throne's heir."

Her eyes narrow. "You're following through with this, aren't you?"

"I misspoke."

Her attention has already found a new fascination with the leather bound journal in her hands. The aged, golden pages flutter between her nimble fingers. The alchemist reaches for a fountain pen and dips the tip in an inkwell before bringing it to the paper. The crease in her brows and force of her etches remind me that even though she's not glaring at me, she's still boiling with frustration. This is only a distraction, crafted by her, for herself. I can't blame her. Never am I supposed to go back on my word, yet a few days into this unspoken agreement that I'll be honest, I've already broken our pact. Upon what truce can we comply with each other?

The cover is angled in a way that I cannot clearly see the page she's sketching on. It's just out of my view.

"What did Rosaline say last night?"

Alouette frowns. "*He'll drown you, Lark.*"

"Is that all?"

She sets the pen down in the crease of the book and snaps it shut with one hand. "Do you think she's a woman of few words?"

From my experience with being scolded by her, the answer is no, so I shake my head.

"She said you're only out for power and that she was once in my shoes. Then came her anecdote. There was a boy, average like any other. A young man, a sailor. Call him whatever you please. They held hands and ran around for a summer or two until he was called back to his duties. I thought that he was fine for that. He only wanted a friend, but she gave him…" she pauses as her tense face eases, "…everything? What else could I say? She pushed her business aside for him. She left her family to join him on the streets." She reminisces in someone else's story, as if her own weren't tragic enough. I silently urge her to tell me the rest of the tale by leaning forward. As a kid, I couldn't stand it when either of my parents left a story hanging. Edwin has left plots unresolved just to spite me. Alouette laughs, probably at me. "He left, clearly. Or else she wouldn't use the tale as a warning."

"And look where she is now." The insult slips. I don't want Alouette to end up old and miserable like the tailor.

The alchemist's lips pull into a tight grin, although she does not snicker again. "That's where everyone would read the story wrong. I'm not Rosaline." Her eyes finally lock with mine. "You are."

My brows crease. "How so?"

"You've ditched everything. Your crew and Edwin and the chance of attaining the power this king leaves behind. For Celestia's sake, shouldn't you be hunting bounties?"

I force a laugh. "I wouldn't be too sure about that."

"Well, I had nothing to begin with." She huffs before returning to the sketch, though still will not let me sneak a glance. I find another pen, dip it in the inkpot, and slide a piece of parchment over to me. I stare down at the blank sheet. Even Edwin is more creative than me, especially with his mockery and pranks, not to mention his purposefully unfinished tales. My hands are also used to putting brute force into turning the helm or pulling on ropes, along with occasionally gripping a sword or stolen weapon. Anything but miniscule, delicate tasks. I set the pen back down and settle for watching the alchemist at work. The desk has a slight incline, so I flick the tool and let it roll back to me. Ink splats like spilled blood on the desk.

After much time has passed, a grandfather clock alerts us of its presence when the bell chimes eleven ante meridiem, nearly lunchtime already.

She has taken long enough to process my last words. "Why?"

I take a moment to recall my last words to her. "I can still marry her," I say breathlessly. She's going to hate me either way. I might as well rip the bandage off of this aching wound than slowly pick away at the gauze.

Her eyes grow wide. The pen slides out of her hand and slips off of the notebook in her lap.

"You're kidding, Atlas."

It rattles on the ground.

"Atlas?"

The clock's pendulum swings. The spinning hands tick. I rise. My heart is racing. I take a deep breath. My mind is still out at sea on a lost hope, next to Alouette in that lifeboat. She had asked me how many girls I've kissed. Only her like *that*.

"If you will not take my hand, Alouette, I know the princess will. The king will allow it."

The words sting far more than any spear to the chest.

But, really, we both know I will hate the motions of marrying into a monarchy. All the fake smiles, spires and consorts, jewels and riches, power and abuse. The yields of my deal have grown rotten.

Her feet tap on the ground as she joins me standing. "Atlas. It's not like that. What's between us, it's…it's…" she fumbles.

"What? Nothing?"

She hesitates before vigorously nodding. "Yeah, nothing. Nothing at all. And if you feel something, I'm sorry. I really am. Without my father—"

"You're not ready. That's what it is." It pains me. "This is all about your father."

The alchemist's lips pull back. Her nose scrunches. Gloss coats her eyes.

I cross my arms, close myself off. This is indeed all about her father. "Rosaline put it plainly. I'm a bounty hunter. I extort people for money. I have two paths to gold right now. The throne and you."

"Where are you going with this?" She leans forward and braces her hands on the desk. Rage overtakes her grief. "I *can* make gold," she reminds me between bared teeth.

"It's forbidden," I snarl.

She recoils. "So is stealing. I can tell the king thief that you hired Edwin and myself to pull off this heist of yours. Don't forget that I'm the one who made the fake."

"You'd reveal yourself as the wanted alchemist. You'd get arrested, if not executed. And I'd get the price branded on you."

These possibilities make my own skin crawl. Alouette's scowl doesn't waver, reminding me that staring her demise in the face is nothing new.

The door opens. As fast as possible, I sit. Alouette fiddles with the cuffs of her sleeves as if nothing had happened between us. She's gotten good at it.

It's only the attendant. Wordlessly, he gestures for me to follow. I comply. Alouette tries to follow, but she's stopped. Her fingers twitch while her riled golden eyes stare up at me. I expected her cheeks to be reddened, but she's pale, simply flushed.

"You're free to go," I tell her. She doesn't need to stay. In fact, it would be in her best interest to leave.

Say, maybe I'd be safer if I never saw her again. Just looking at her makes me ache. Edwin always told me I had a bleeding heart. If I could apologize for breaking her, I would, for giving her a false illusion of a pirate, let alone a captain. But this farce, I need to uphold. For my father. For the king. For her, the alchemist.

Once we step into the pristine hall, we'll go our separate ways, but I have a feeling that it won't be for the last time. Or perhaps I'm fooling myself.

The attendant holds his tongue as he leads. We stop at a door plated with golden swirls that curl around the frame like vines. He holds it open for me and drops to one knee before the king's bedside once we're both inside. I slightly bow my head. Neither my mother nor my father taught me these customs, despite one's royal lineage.

My gaze falls on the king. Once, as a foolish lad, I had approached a dais with him atop the gilded throne. Now, I stare down at a lump beneath a velvet comforter that claims to be a mighty monarch. More attendants and women I assume to be nurses sit on the other side of the room. Their empty eyes peer up at me. The king groans. Hands rush to help him sit up. A crooked crown continues to rest on his brow, even in this decrepit state of his.

Whatever happens, Atlas, do not refuse the crown.

The king drops his jaw to speak.

Chapter 34

— The Thief —

I KICK BACK at a cafe's patio. Steam wafts off of my porcelain teacup. I stare up at the blue sky. Don't tell my crewmates that I like watching the clouds more than waves on the horizon. Both are unpredictable, but at least the sky is open. It's clear. You can often use them to predict what's coming, whether it's a storm rolling in from the sea or rain pattering on a tin roof across the street. The sea will change on a whim and toss a vessel whenever she pleases. So will Atlas.

I flip a coin. The king's profile with a crown is on one side, an engraving of a key on the other. I stare down at the man's face on my palm.

I grin at my luck. Though, I hope they won't put Atlas' face on currency. That would be creepy—a familiar face plated on everyday items with inflated value. I shiver at the thought before returning to my tea. I take a sip. These little crushed up leaves and herbs feel much more sophisticated than the hard liquor Atlas fancies. My gaze meets that of my rippled reflection. By chance, it was wrong to send Atlas off to fulfill a destiny he no longer desires. I must question whether letting the alchemist influence him presents itself as the better option or not. Upon further thought, she may not be trying to sway him at all. If I were in her place, I would have put as much distance between the captain and myself as possible. That said, I'm speaking from a place of experience. Nevertheless, Atlas had saved me from drowning long ago.

The more I think about it, the more guilty I seem to feel.

He does everything with someone else's best interest in mind, even if it means burning valuable bridges of his own. For instance, I have no particular attachment to the alchemist. He does. He's fond of her, and there's no denying it. By going back on any promise to her, he'll break any bonds they could have built in the last forty-eight or so hours. He'd be breaking her trust for the will of his father and under my influence. Besides, this isn't the first time he's yielded his own wellbeing. I threatened his secret for years. He's lied to our entire crew to assure the rest of his mates that he's normal, that he can be trusted. If the rest of our men knew about his lineage, we couldn't guarantee their compliance with the captain's orders. After all, men are taught to fear the seafolk. That's what my mother called them. She loved the fae and all of their tales. But not their tails.

A dark figure joins me at the table. "You put him up to this, didn't you?"

I blow on my tea to cool it off for a sip. "And if I did?"

My eyes move up to meet hers. She looks like a scout on his first day at sea. I hold back an amused smile. She lets out a heavy sigh.

"Ol' DeLuca was the one who wanted this. It's always a guessing game with his ulterior motives."

She looks down at the table's mosaic finish. I take another swig. "I believe you've met before."

"Atlas' father? I don't recall."

"He's a tavern-goer. I'm assuming you two met without realizing it, and that you knew him a couple of years before you met Atlas." I tip the teacup toward her. She raises her brows.

"The name DeLuca did sound familiar when we first met."

"So you do believe me." I grin.

"Do I trust you, though? No. You're the one that convinced the captain I was a danger to his crew," she snarls.

I laugh, a little unnerved. She's attentive and cunning. Nothing I didn't know. Just a blunt reminder.

"He knows about everything that's been happening. Father DeLuca has eyes in many places, Lark."

"I'm aware."

"You are?" That's a surprise.

"In Atlas' room, there's a bulletin with his collection of news clippings and wanted posts, one of which I am featured on."

"You were in *his* room?" My eyes widen and lips curl.

"It's not what you think." She shakes her head. By her straight face, I can tell she's not hiding anything scandalous. "Some mer-guy," she questions her own word choice, "got him with a spear. Atlas must've known his father had medical supplies. But he didn't want to stick around to see him."

"Typical of Capt'n," I scoff.

She tells me about the mysterious messenger who walked right on in. I'm guessing they delivered the letter DeLuca relayed to me about Atlas' position as the kingdom's likely heir.

Once she's done, she leans back in her chair with arms crossed over her chest. Her expression is a tangled mess of expressions, perhaps stemming from emotions that still need to be unraveled. I feel the same way, yet, unlike many people, I can hide it, especially while sipping away at tea. No one needs to read my thoughts, not even a skilled mentalist or fortune teller or psychic gypsy.

"Do you envy her?"

The alchemist's golden eyes meet mine.

With creased brows, she asks, "Who?"

"The princess, of course." I snicker.

Alouette scoffs. "Don't bring her up. I can't wrap my head around what's wrong with the captain. One day, he's fine. He's…" she pauses to narrow her gaze.

I lean in.

"Nevermind."

"Go on."

"Cover my bill and I will." She pulls up her hood and waves over a waiter.

I see how it is. She asks for a few treats for herself and the same tea I'm enjoying.

I make my comeback after the server leaves. "Only if you share."

"He told me that he was trying to change to prove himself to me."

"Virtuous." I smile.

"Yeah, right." She rolls her eyes and looks at the castle. "That was until today. He had told me that he would refuse the crown, but look where we are now. He told me that if I felt nothing for him, then he'd marry the princess. Is he some kind of player? I know he's a liar, but I never expect him to—forget it, Edwin," she huffs, "Pretend I didn't say anything."

Her eyes fall back on the mosaic.

She picks back up in a tizzy, speaking so fast that her words nearly blend together. "But how can he tell me to lend myself to others and go back on his word the moment he's faced with power?" She buries her face in her palms. "I just don't get it. Words should be worth their weight in gold, but they have no real mass."

"Can't put those on a scale." I shrug. At first, I anticipate a quick reply. The chances of one decline as time rolls on. The waiter delivers her tea, along with a porcelain plate of cookies. Painted golden leaves dot the chipped rims.

Once he departs, I add, "He's got his own reasons, and not all of those reasons are his own."

My solemn riddle catches her off guard; some kind of guilt overtakes her face. She picks up a cookie and dunks it in her tea. I'm a little disgusted but also a little jealous because I didn't think of doing that first. I reach for my promised treat.

She holds the cookie under the surface, as if to drown it. Her tone is begrudging. "Will I have to call him Your Majesty?"

I look up from the mosaic table. "I hope not. At least stay on good terms, okay?"

"And who are you to tell me this?"

She has a point. I betrayed her, in a way.

"What good is having Atlas as an enemy? He's not the selfish type. You know as well as I that he acts with someone else's best interest in mind."

She quiets. I thought as much.

"As much as you don't want to believe me—and probably won't—this is for *you*."

She scoffs, as expected.

"The king's authority can always be pushed off and granted to another. His power will not be permanent."

"But if he marries the princess, then—"

"Blimey." I pound my fist on the table. "He's just supposed to take the crown. Not her anymore."

"I knew you played a part in pulling the strings."

"I'm just a messenger boy." I raise my hands in surrender.

"You swear?"

I confirm by pulling my dagger out of its sheath. "By my very blood."

Her clenched fists rattle the table. "Then it's all between DeLuca and the king."

And her father.

She gestures for me to put it away. It's a wise move, knowing that she's on a wanted poster, and I'm, well, me; we'd attract way too much attention. Not to mention that I'm closely associated with the captain. DeLuca is no small name in this kingdom. It'll be in the chatter of every household by daybreak tomorrow if it isn't already. Besides, I hear that after DeLuca retired from the *Aurora Borealis*, he settled here and gave away rather large sums of money among the common folk here. Once they hear that this philanthropist's son has come into power, they'll be ecstatic.

"He could still say no," she whispers, mostly to herself.

Chapter 35

— The Alchemist —

EDWIN FULFILLED HIS promise. We had agreed to meet again at that cafe. I turn my face to the wind. Under the castle's shadow, the air feels cooler, more somber. It's sobering, even for someone who has only had a lick of that poison.

I don't really know if I want to see Atlas again. I kick my legs as I now sit atop the wall. It's not the same as sitting in the welcoming arms of trees, but the view from atop these stones will do for the time being.

A lump grows in my throat. The sea reminds me of the captain. I can even see the forsaken *Aurora Borealis* docked in the harbor. I don't know what's wrong with me.

It's always a problem with someone else. I pound my fists on the rock in a fit of rage.

"I'm not jealous," I must assure myself.

There are plenty of things wrong with that captain. He's a liar and drunkard and now a traitor. I don't even care that he's half-siren anymore. There's a chance that Rosaline was right. Maybe Edwin can justify Atlas' actions, in which he had a hand in aiding. I ease onto my side before rolling onto my back. I watch the clouds instead, knowing that the stars loom far beyond them. Humbled by the sun, they're too shy to come out right now. Even the cloth of Atlas' cloak smells like him.

Soon, I'll leave. Soon, I will. I swear.

Yet I can't bring myself to sit up. The last traces of my father still remain within these walls. He's so close yet still so far away. What reasons he had to leave me, to this day, I don't know. He couldn't have put too much distance between us. We were supposed to study together. To learn. To make gold. To find the Elixir of Life. To forge the Philosopher's Stone.

The future I once hoped for slips away like the clouds floating above.

I don't know where to turn. Perhaps the night sky. The stars haven't failed me thus far. But the moon. It changes. I can't stand that

Why would Atlas make me that offer only to turn a cold shoulder? This morning, we were on such different terms. Is this who he really is? But he made a means to make amends with his mother? None of this lines up.

And this is why I never allowed myself to place roots in another. The soil gets tilled and turned over far too quickly.

I rest my forearm over my eyes. My nose stings with the threat of tears.

This is no place, no time, no reason to cry.

▽△▽△

There's only one place I know to go. That's the tavern.

Not for the liquor. Not like Atlas.

I slip behind the counter and salute my fellow taverner who polishes a glass. He nods back.

"Back for more?"

I snatch a bottle. "You know it."

Nights behind the bar always passed more quickly than the ones I spent worrying about my father. I used to pretend that I was mixing special chemicals together in order to create ingenious new solutions. This evening, I can only hope that concocting these drinks will take my mind off of everything else. Atlas, in particular. However the smell of wine drags me back to the night we spent at the masquerade.

If only I could lose myself to the idle chatter and subtle melodies as the rest of them do.

▽△▽△

I spend a few days like this in the nook. The hours start to blend between last call and first light. Slumped over a table in the corner, I drift somewhere between consciousness and Neverland. Celestia must be disenchanted with me, whether by my current state or some action of mine that led Her to curse me.

There's a tap on my shoulder. The other barkeep. I had worked alongside him the first night I spent with Atlas and Edwin. Though, I don't remember his hazel eyes and chestnut brown hair from years past. The chair unleashes a wretched noise as he drags across the floor in an attempt to pull it out and sit across from me. He folds his hands and rests them on the table. His mouth, slightly ajar, waits for the right words to say.

"It's Alouette, right?"

I look up and nod.

"You've been here a lot longer than I have, from what he says." He raises his brow as a gesture to the floor above us.

"He? The innkeeper?"

"Yep. And," he pauses to wince, "you have a bounty on your head. Your father is missing. Very recently, you've had some kind of…falling out."

A fallout is one way to put it. I bop my head along.

"Um." After a moment of hesitation, he stands and rubs the back of his neck. "If you need anything. He said we're a big ol' unfortunate family here on my first day."

I watch him make his way over to the bar. A part of me wants to know where he came from, how he ended up here.

He practically knows my thoughts, or maybe he's well-acquainted with having to explain his origin. "Ran away."

"Oh," the disappointing word slips.

"Don't sweat it. They didn't like it when I read their minds. It's best to stay in a place where they don't know."

Sirens. Magic. Mind-reading. I'm not surprised. Other people are.

For Celestia's sake, the faeries and Gifted, they're the ones us alchemists initially aspired to. If it weren't for Her, I wouldn't be on even ground with them.

"But now I know." I push myself to rise.

He shrugs with a smile. "You'd understand."

I shouldn't bother to ask how he knows. No matter how this power works, he's well aware already.

"Not only are people afraid of what they don't accept, but they don't like when others have the upper hand." He straightens a row of bottles. "People crave power, but cannot stand it when it's in someone else's grasp."

He can say that again. I simply nod.

▽⟁⍒△

The fabric smells less of the sea, less like the captain as I pull up my hood. A fiery dawn streaks across the horizon, making the wall appear as if it were set ablaze by the red-hot sun. The whole city has been tinted with a tinge of scarlet. My limbs ache, for this is the first time I've been able to stretch outside in days. My eyes adjust from the dull tavern lights, them having only been fueled by oil, to Celesia's beaming star. The sun. Her favorite, as my father claimed.

The morning is too young for the crowds, who will be sure to flood the market and main streets when the time comes. Until then, I'll enjoy the streets to myself. My lips press together and resort to a hum for amusement. For a moment, I fear I'll fool myself with a melody as Atlas once captivated me. Larks call in the distance. Though we share a name, I do not speak their language, nor do I fly among them.

My feet are planted in the ground, not the sky, nor the sea.

They say we all come from dust, thus to that we will return.

I'll admit that I once believed my remnants would remain in gold. It's a stretch. Though, I should be grateful that I didn't end up as fish food beneath the waves.

My name is called from behind. I stop. The way his vowels roll into the consonants tells me it's Atlas. My pace picks up.

"Wait!"

He has no authority over me. He's not a king to me and surely no captain of mine.

"I have no dealings with a traitor."

"There's so much to explain." I pick up on his short breaths. He's distraught. Stopping once more, I turn to face him. He's closer than I expected. Arms crossed and breath held, I wait for him to speak.

"Look, I took it, okay? Only the crown." He slightly raises his hands as he eases toward me. He's sharp enough to know that he must tread lightly.

I debate whether to back away or stand my ground. Choosing the former, I put distance between us. "And you're proud of this?"

He shakes his head. "Not at all. If you gave me the chance to explain, you'd understand."

"I owe you no time for an explanation that I do not want."

Atlas stiffens. "You can love me or hate me, Alouette. I don't care." His strides grow longer. I step to the side. He pursues. "Either of the two? Both? It doesn't matter. I'm not letting you go."

His words sound planned, rehearsed, almost. He must have been anticipating this encounter from the moment we parted ways. He can't bring himself to leave me. My tongue is tied. There are so many—too many—things I need to say. Stay away from me. No. But explain. Why in the right mind are you like this? I can't seem to sort through the proper words in time.

"The coronation is tomorrow evening," he says as he pulls back. "I hope you'll come."

▽ △ ▽ △

I'm sitting at the cafe again, legs crossed beneath my brown skirt. The heavy fabric is a little too warm for the weather, but I know the sea's breeze will bring in the changing season within the next few months. Discomfort is only temporary, I must remind myself, and anything is preferable to being in Atlas' presence.

Edwin marches over, his step boasted with inflated pride. He clutches a rolled newspaper, nearly choking the poor thing.

"You've gotta get a load of this!" he calls. That smirk of his spreads from ear to ear; whether truly giddy or mockingly so, I'll never know. "Captain as king?"

I mutter, "I know."

"A captain as king," Edwin muses as he joins me at the same table as before. He slaps the newspaper down on the circular mosaic table. "*Our* captain as king."

I guess he's still letting the revelation sink in.

"*Your* captain as king." I must correct the thief. He's tickled pink.

"I'm counting you as part of the crew."

"I spent one night on that ship, and not even a full one."

He waves the server over and requests the same tea as before. Two cups. A ham and cheese croissant. I could have ordered myself. This morning, I'll take the courtesy.

"*Soo*, did you get an invitation?"

"I'm not going."

Edwin's eyebrows frown, though I don't know why he'd be disappointed in my lack of involvement. Leaning back in my chair, I fold my hands in my lap.

"Aren't you stubborn?" he asks with a snicker.

"It doesn't matter."

"You can come with me."

"I said I'm not going."

Edwin blinks. The topic is dropped. Our server brings over the tea and light breakfast. Lucky, she isn't as chatty as Ruth, my fellow bartender who could get a conversation to last for days. Perhaps this skill comes from his Gift, or simply his *Ability* as he likes to call it, for it is no welcomed present. He can tell whether a drunkard is genuinely interested in what he has to say, or if he's just going through the motions of imminent intoxication.

Edwin tears the croissant and hands one flaky half to me. He keeps the larger piece, as a pesky sibling would. I guess he deserves it; after all, he'll be the one paying.

I watch the thief gnaw on his breakfast and flip through the paper. His expression mellows, maybe to match a hint of sincerity he hides beneath his impudent facade. What an ingenious way to shield himself.

If I could rip this heart of mine off my sleeve, I would without a moment of hesitation. I'd yank the threads and feed the felt to a fire.

Perhaps his composure comes from insight, or even a sliver of control over this predicament. There's even a hint of apathy. Maybe tranquility comes from no power at all, a complete acceptance and surrender to the idea of letting Fortuna spin her wheel. I find no comfort in the act of letting waves roll over my head, only for another to come crashing down without my resistance. I'm proactive. I won't just wait. I tear shreds off of the croissant and stuff them in my mouth. I reach to wash it down with a sip of tea, but we're interrupted by another sailor, as I presume him to be.

He salutes Edwin, to which the boatswain does in return. The young man takes off his hat from his blonde head of hair and bows to me.

"The name's Jean-Jacques Havelock. Jacques is fine."

I extend my hand to shake his.

"Alouette. Alouette Le Rois."

He keeps his voice low as he addresses his crewmate. "She's the infamous alchemist?"

Edwin nods. "Yep. One of the two."

The other being my father. "And you're the other's," he pauses, "daughter?"

"Correct."

His smile extends to his bright green eyes. "I ought to step off ship more often."

"Yeah, you've missed quite a lot." Edwin goes back to enjoying his tea. His fellow sailor steals a seat from another table and the metal chair over. Edwin hands over his porcelain cup, to which his companion declines.

"I'll get my own." His polite demeanor reminds me of Ruth.

"He'll be attending the coronation with me." Edwin nudges him in the side.

"In case anything goes wrong," Jacques adds as he taps the sword at his waist. There's a sly gleam in his smile. Edwin winks at me. Jacques must *know*. Does the rest of their crew? This isn't the time nor place to ask.

"Are you sure you don't want to join in?"

I nod.

"Suit yourself."

▽△▽△

Jacques had waved me off with a smile. I never really thought sailors would be so giddy, but it's not surprising, knowing that most of my prejudices have been turned on their head by none other than that forsaken Captain Atlas DeLuca.

I slip back into the tavern. Descending the steps, I catch a whiff of hard liquor. No matter how long I spend among drunkards, the stretch never fails to bother me. It only seems to grow stronger. Ruth polishes a glass behind the counter, which seems to be his signature pass-time, or rather a nervous habit. After all, he needs to watch his tongue. If word gets out about his Gift, he'll need to run away again. From our brief discussions, he seems content with that fate, for it won't be the first, second, or even third time. This happens to be a common occurrence.

Sincerity is his enemy.

I just have a bad habit of getting others to slip.

Ruth nods to me. I do the same in response.

As I step between the bar and shelves of half-empty bottles, he remarks, "Tomorrow night will be slow."

"And?"

"Do you want to take off? You've been working around the clock."

"I just got here."

"You left a couple of hours ago, and guess who's back? I'm guessing you'll only see tomorrow's sun, if not the following." He sets the polished glass down and reaches for another. His eyes stay on me as his brows crease. "You're running from something, aren't you? Other than guards and bounty hunters."

I only shrug to avoid talking about it.

"You can take tomorrow off if you'd like. You could use a change of pace." I get back on topic.

"I'm not interested."

"That makes two of us."

He tilts his head with an unsatisfied frown.

Chapter 36

— The Thief —

I GOT A chance to catch up with Atlas earlier today. It's kind of funny how he's going to end up as the head of a kingdom that rivals the one he was born to be an heir to. If I'm not mistaken, he looked a little more pale than usual. Really, this is all happening too fast.

Did the king not know he was going to meet his end this soon? That doesn't sound reasonable, at the very least to me it doesn't. The people of this kingdom have been playing along to this little game of his.

Perhaps this is one chance to pick the next man who occupies the throne, as if it were his last will. Any person with even the smallest drop of common sense would realize that Atlas' presence is fleeting as a captain. We've never been docked at a harbor for so long, so, with that said, I'm growing sick of this port. Atlas must be feeling the same way. He's not meant to be landlocked. Quite frankly, he's beached. I find it difficult to believe that the alchemist has such a pull on him. If it weren't for her, we would've already set sail for another treasure or bounty.

Atlas always liked the latter, perhaps because it helped him feel like he could bring justice. With Alouette on a wanted poster, it's a miracle that he hasn't handed her over on behalf of our crew to earn some honest cash for the next round of supplies. He knows she's more innocent than guilty. Or he's lying to himself. Neither would come as a surprise.

I can only cross my fingers in some kind of false hope for her to forgive him. No matter what comes our way, some divine intervention drives a wedge between the captain and any kind of straightforward decision. There's always an opportunity cost or web of strings attached.

I sit with Jean-Jacques at my new favorite spot in town. He has mixed his tea with rum, as expected of any sailor, let alone the second hand man in command of the drinking problem himself, Atlas.

"I wonder, will he still be our captain?" the quartermaster muses, more melancholy than merry. He raises his brows, which have both been pierced. He's a stabby fellow. His ear is torn from a ring that got ripped out during a storm. What a bloody mess that was.

"Who would replace him?" I combat.

Jacques shrugs and takes a sip. "Surely not you." His lips curl into a small, playful smile. We both know it's true.

"But would you?"

When he goes silent, I snicker.

"No one could replace him." Jacques lowers his gaze and points his attention back at the strange concoction in his grasp.

▽△▽△

"Jean-Jacques said that?" Atlas raises his brows while he tugs at the high neck of his coat for tonight's coronation. Technically, he's a prince because his mother is a queen, and he surely looks like one, although he's been exiled from his home kingdom, or so I've been told.

He paces from one side of the study to the other, again and again and again. I slide into the chair at the desk before a notebook laying face down on the table catches my attention. My arms stretch across the polished wood to grab it. Sketches smother the page. Not just any sketches. Ones of him. Etchings of his eyes. Diagrams of his fins. Even an incomplete outline of a tail I've only seen a few times.

I call the future king over. "Get a load of this."

Once he's standing across from me, I set the journal down open-faced so that Atlas can see it. His sprawled hand immediately covers the page, then his fingers curl and pull away to reveal the sketches.

"She's got some insane memory." I laugh.

Atlas slowly nods. He reaches for the sleeve of his forearm.

"So that's…" he murmurs moments prior to snatching the notebook off of the desk.

"She doesn't want anything to do with you anymore." I cross my arms.

His brows furrow. "She's not coming, is she?"

I stay silent.

The book snaps shut in his hand. Our eyes lock as he tosses it back onto the polished wood. "No one can find this."

▽△▽△

His demeanor greatly differs in the presence of fine wine, provided by the current and soon-to-be late king. Atlas' blue eyes sparkle like the gold that adorns his pristine outfit rather than the sea at sundown.

The way his frantic gaze darts around the room is almost sobering. If he's looking for Alouette, his efforts are in vain. Or maybe he's looking for the withering monarch, who is nowhere to be found, confined to his sickbed until the real ceremony starts, as I presume. He'll be the one to hand down the crown to Atlas. The princess has already found an audience of just about every well-dressed young man. Aside from myself, of course. I stand beside Jean-Jacques in the corner of the grand room. I'll admit, compared to the ship's deck, these high ceilings feel quite confining. The quartermaster wears a solemn straight face. He's been in charge for quite some time now. I'd be surprised if he hasn't already begun to question Atlas' motives. I'm aware of them thanks to the letter DeLuca received from the monarch. This king has something worth more than its weight in gold, especially in Atlas' eyes. I won't spoil that quite yet. If it weren't for this offer on the table, he would have never agreed to this coronation. Keeping this arrangement of theirs in mind, once Atlas gets his end of the deal, he'll see no more need for the crown and pass it off. There are plenty of suitors for the king's daughter already. My captain, who wanders over to us crewmates, is not among them.

I nod his way. He nods back. His gloved fingers pick at the golden cuffs of his dark gray sleeves. Jean-Jacques smiles the captain's way and raises his glass in reverence. He had spent the last few hours getting himself prepared for this evening. He wears a combination of light blue and white borrowed from a stranger, making him nearly resemble another prince if it weren't for his excessive piercings. Funny how appearances can be deceiving.

Sailors are often regarded as low-class citizens here, or completely disregarded altogether, but with enough accessories, we're treated like the top few. I can't tell if the thought is sickening or something to be thankful for. Peasants and exiles often don't get the chance to dream about climbing up a rung in society. Neither do pirates. Atlas sure knows how to strike a convenient deal.

"Having fun?" Jacques asks while he leans over to a waiter with a tailcoat and takes another glass of bubbling champagne for himself.

Atlas takes a minute to reply. "That's one way to put it."

"Come on, Bucko." I nudge him in the gut and draw out an uneasy wince from the captain.

Jacques tips the glass back. His green eyes, illuminated with a warm glow from the candle lit chandeliers, stay on Atlas.

"Should I have gotten you a gift?"

I cackle. He's a little too considerate.

"Pirates don't give, they steal." I shrug. "Plus, he won't need anything, he'll have an entire kingdom."

"Fair."

Atlas is too busy surveying the sea of guests, all dressed in their best attire, to tune in on our conversation. A hand on his back makes him jolt. My eyes widen at the sight of *the* DeLuca. Jean-Jacques folds an arm in front of him and bows to his former captain, for this quartermaster had once been a part of the original crew. He was a skittish swabbie still decked out with piercings before the ship fell into Atlas' hands. Behind my back, I cross my fingers that DeLuca does not berate his son in front of the crowd. The chances are low but never at rock bottom. He bears his crooked teeth in a wide smile, the grin of a father that's proud of a son who has come into his own. Atlas does a phenomenal job at hiding his distress.

"Father!" His greeting remains casual. "How long has it been?"

"Too long, too long." DeLuca gives him a slap on the back. There's a glass of wine grasped in his other hand.

Their idle chatter has me on edge, along with Jean-Jacques who stares with anticipation. He's gone through quite a few sparkling glasses already. I've plucked a couple mini sandwiches from trays passing by. If I ever saw my old man again, I don't know how I'd react. This is one feat I never expected the captain to play off. The forced laughs of the DeLucas would be convincing if I wasn't aware of the strain between the two. They share a congratulatory toast, but instead of tipping the glasses back, the two stand and stare at each other. His father gives him one last pat on the back before departing. Atlas' eyes follow him. The moment he disappears, blending into the crowds of the backdrop, my captain finishes his wine in one go. His attention doesn't return to Jacques and I, though. Until now, I wouldn't have called Atlas desperate, but he's looking for something that isn't here.

We all know what Alouette's singular dress looks like, aside from Jean-Jacques. No one else is bold enough to wear the same golden gown. It's obvious that she's not here.

He doesn't want an entire kingdom.

He wants the alchemist.

I just want to get this over with. Luckily, the first part of night passes quickly when I'm in the company of Jean-Jacques, even when Atlas is dragged away by the princess. We're not fit for this line of work—or rather standing around and trying to occupy ourselves. The quartermaster nods and hums along to a tune I'm whistling. That's until the king emerges on the dais, his skin far more pale and sickly than Atlas' cheeks look now. Dark circles stoop under his eyes. He's a mess. No wonder he wanted Atlas as an heir. At least the figurehead of this kingdom would be a handsome young man and not some old, overweight eyesore. His majesty could drop dead at any moment. Okay, so does Atlas at the moment. A bead of sweat runs down his forehead. He rubs it away before anyone else can notice. Swarmed by attendants, the king stares down at the captain, who doesn't look his usual role anymore.

He approaches the dais, where the monarch is helped by a multitude of hands onto the throne. A golden cane slips from his trembling grasp, hitting the velvet with a muffled thud. This isn't the future the captain wants, nor the one his crew deserves. My fingers curl into fists. In place of the king, another man steps up to give a preliminary announcement, congratulating Atlas or whatever royal people say. I've learned to tune these people out. Next to him stands the princess, a pillow in her hands that holds a crown. Atlas' crown.

My captain yields, kneeling before the king. My ego aches for his dignity and that of this entire kingdom. This palace of phonies. Every attendee bows their heads in reverence as a servant speaks for their leader, who has grown far too frail to lead, yet has taken way too long to leave. Out of pride or greed? Possibly Gluttony? Wrath? Lust?

My nose scrunches in disgust. Beside me, Jean-Jacques grows tense. I can't really feel my limbs, on the other hand. Atlas following through with his deal with the king, even with the new amendments, always felt like a distant event. I never thought it would come so soon. Not here. Not now.

The dressed up peasant goes on with his wordy speech that doesn't mean anything. Here ye, here ye. I don't need that hornswoggling crap. Every so often, the king coughs, hacking up some disgusting mucus. The devil might as well have a hand on his shoulder, pitchfork to the monarch's bulging throat. His daughter moves closer with the golden, bejeweled circlet.

The ill man takes it and stands. His feet take short steps to the edge of the dais, which Atlas still kneels before. It's a good thing he's tall so that the king doesn't need to reach too far down.

The monarch's shaking hands place the crown on the captain's head. Wait, I got that wrong.

He's not only a captain anymore.

He's something far, far more powerful.

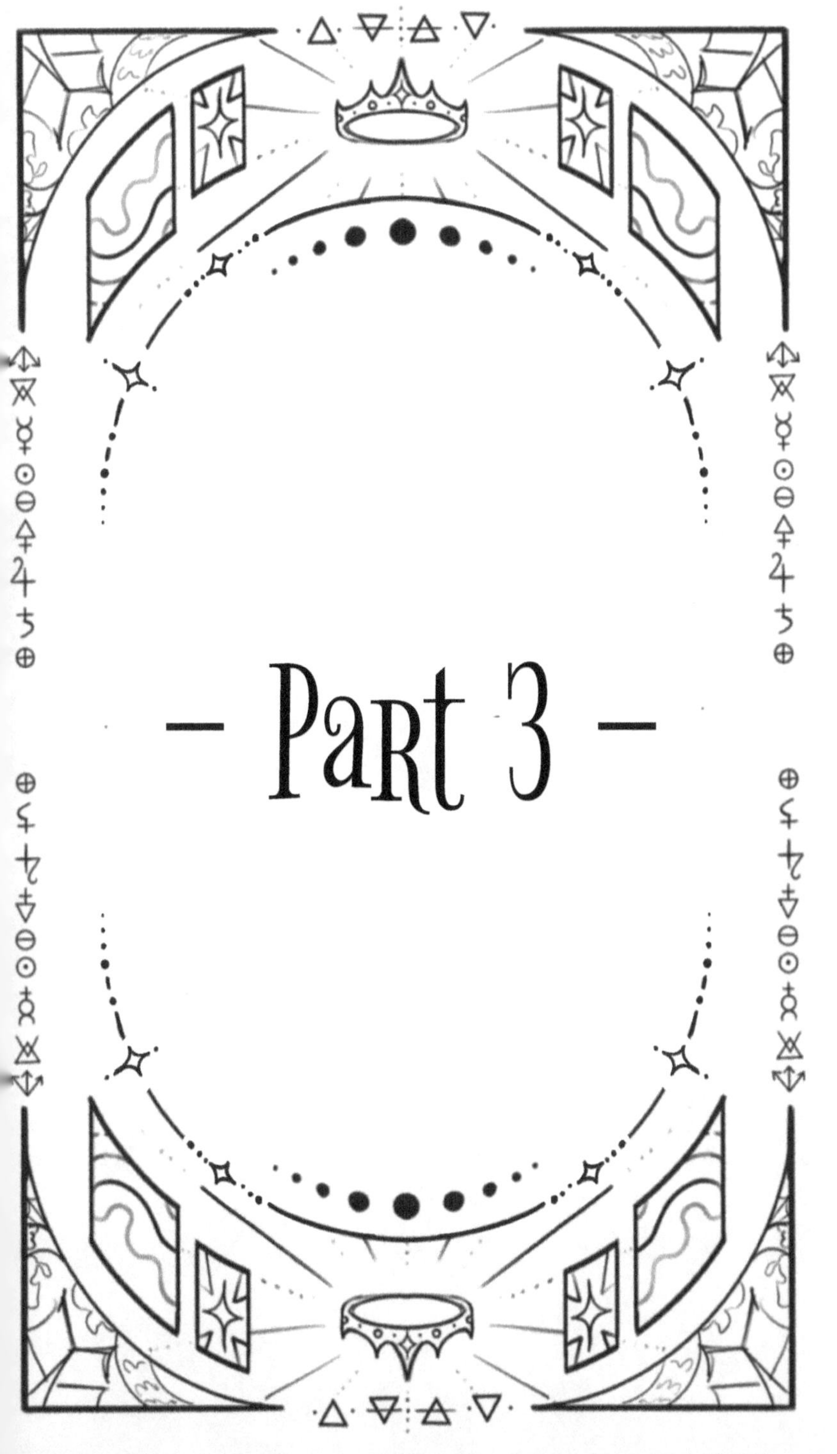
– Part 3 –

Chapter 37

— The Alchemist —

Men fear death.

That's what makes men, well, men. Besides the greed, lust, pride, and gluttony. Lethal sins. That is why they claw their way toward immortality. Their hands grapple for the Elixir of Life. No change. No age. No limits. Only consequences. Consequences upon consequences upon consequences.

My father once told me the tale of one who held the power of this Elixir. I'll share it in case he won't.

Once upon a time, there lived a man. Humble, from dirty roots planted in the farmland soil of his hometown. He left everything he knew with nothing but a red cloak and a murky dream that he would slay Gods, rather the false deities who ruled over an entire realm, one known as the Alterverse.

Okay. Far fetched, I know. When my father told me this story, I believed every last word with my entire being. From every atom to molecule to cell.

He met another dreamer. A woman with hair the color of fresh snow. She shared a dream, one of change. Maybe a nation stomped down by Gods could be ruled by the oppressed citizens. The two took up arms. Together, they fought. They gathered support. They learned to love.

But that's where their paths branched away from one another. Wedged between them were ideals. She longed for a nation run by the people, but he wanted power. The power he had spent years fighting to take out of the Gods' hands. In his mind, that belonged to the man and his wife.

My father always said alchemy was the nail in the coffin.

The Gods were only Gods because of the Elixir. Their timeless existence was a front, and people are sheep, so easy to follow others with power in hopes of taking some for themselves. Especially when it came to the Elixir of Life.

But how could these revolutionaries take down immortals?

With alchemy, it's easy.

The Philosopher's Stone. The only substance known to cut down an immortal hailing from the Elixir. Once this news had been brought to the young man, the end was in sight. Power nearly in his hands, he cut her down. His heart and hands both smeared with blood, the Gods came next.

From their spilled blood, the empire of Apthnorath arose. Czar, they called the man. The nation's head, its leader, and his people, its blade. For eternity, he would lead, the albatross of his late wife on his shoulders, her blood staining his conscience, for even an immortal tyrant cannot escape from the cold hands of guilt.

Chapter 38

— The Thief —

I GUESS IT'S my turn.

I may be a thief, but I am something far, far more adept.

My time has been split between the ship and the cafe. My time at the latter has then been quartered between spending time thinking about the DeLucas, hanging out with Jean-Jacques, treating Alouette to a meal, and, the cherry on top, earning a few honest bucks by serving. I insult more than half of the customers, but that doesn't stop them from tipping me well. I'm amusing, what else can I say? Not to mention that Alouette and I often exchanged pickpocketing skills, which speaks for itself.

Today I sit with a long piece of parchment that keeps trying to curl over my hand as I write down the ship's stock. It's been about a month since Atlas has been crowned, so, day by day, we keep breaking our record for how long we've been docked. There was a fifty-fifty chance that everything within the walls would be charred or it would take a turn for the better. The latter has really caught me by surprise. Apparently, if he can keep a crew of fifty under control, he can manage a kingdom of a whole lot more. Wild, right? I guess it makes sense.

Every so often, he'll stop by to check in on the crew, bringing rum and wine from the castle with him. Though, he hasn't had a lick of any alcohol since he took on the crown. A sober king would be best. It's difficult to fathom addressing him as Your Majesty. Stupid title, right? He's just Capt'n. Lucky for me, he's not a stickler for using titles properly.

Since the coronation, I've seen Alouette less and less often. Her hair no longer looks like a scout's now that she's given it the chance to grow out. If I were her, I wouldn't stick around. From the local tavern to the familiar streets, she's surrounded by reminders regarding her father's absence. A smile creeps up on me, knowing that I know exactly where he is. Though, as his secret was, this information is Atlas' duty to relay to her. He's taking too long. *Way* too long.

I dip my quill in an almost-dry inkpot and tap it on the side. The nib scribbles down the necessities for our next restock. I gave Atlas two months to get all of his duties done with the capabilities and resources of a king. One is almost gone.

Chair legs grind against the ground in front of me. I look up to find the alchemist.

"Speak of the devil!" I snicker.

"Me? The devil? Now that's a new one." She takes her seat. For once, she looks well-rested. Working at a cafe is far less taxing than spending hours upon hours with drunkards in the tavern, although she has better chances when it comes to slipping extra cash from guests' pockets.

"How has the crew been?" she asks, as if she hadn't come by last week to say hello to Jean-Jacques and myself. A lot can change in the span of a few days, especially with Davy Jones at play.

"We'd rather be back at sea hunting down treasures and cashing in bounties."

"Haven't you put a notice out for a new captain?"

I shake my head and tap my quill on the inkpot again.

"Couldn't you ask DeLuca to take charge and set sail with your bunch again?"

"He's a strange man, Capt'n's father." With the quill between my fingers, I lean back. The feather brushes my cheek; it's a habit I have no control over. "Doubt he'd join us."

"Wouldn't that mean he gets to see Farida again?"

"Atlas' mother? Of course. Isn't it odd?"

"That he'd decline a request to reclaim his ship?"

"In a way. Is he afraid of her?"

I shake my head. "Not in the slightest. Things don't line up."

"How so?" She lowers her voice.

"We're told to fear the folk of the water, but DeLuca came face to face with a siren. He didn't die." I shake my head with a crooked smile. "My goodness, he made friends with one. He loved her. Atlas exists, for Davy Jones' sake."

As she catches on, Alouette's brows crease. "And she isn't just any siren. She's their queen."

"Although he's the rooster of the coop on board his ship, he's at the bottom of the pecking order on land. He had a plan."

In a small voice, the alchemist murmurs, "Everything we know is wrong."

"DeLuca may have tried to prove to the rest of this kingdom that our people and theirs can coexist."

"Plenty of people, not just sailors, have been drowned by sirens." Alouette frowns.

"And men have hunted them in return."

She nods along. "From my understanding, the former king wasn't very tolerant, either."

"Perhaps it was DeLuca's intent to have Atlas take the monarch's place all along. Change the system from the top down, rather than the ground up."

"Is that Atlas' motive as well?"

I shrug.

"Guessing that's a no." Alouette stands with a stretch. The bracelets stacked around her wrist jingle. She's settling in a lot better than I am. "Thanks for your time, Edwin. Share some more next time, will you?"

"Can't make any promises if it's secrets regarding the king. You'll have to take it up with him. Personally." I wink.

She rolls her eyes with a scoff.

"Really, he wants to see you."

"I don't want to see him."

Suit yourself, I mean to say, but she's already gone, lost in this morning's crowd. Oh, well. Her loss, really. I wish she wouldn't let herself lose though. With a harumph, I pluck the quill from the inkpot and get back to scribbling our current needs. The ropes will need to be replaced soon, plus the masts have seen better days. With Atlas' new position, we'll try to sway him into utilizing some of that gold for useful purchases before he steps down. I give myself a pat on the back for such a bright idea. Really, on our crew, I'd be the most luminous star in the sky. Actually, I lied, we call that one Polaris.

As I write, I can't help but drift into the conversations of others, picking up their words from the wind. Folks have no idea how to keep their voice low, especially when it comes to steaming hot tea.

"Haven't you heard?" a young woman gossips with her waitress.

"Heard what?"

"There have been no executions under the new king's rule!" She giggles.

Next to her, an acquaintance chimes in, "Strange, they still don't challenge him."

"Isn't he a bit young?" The waitress raises a brow.

A young man laughs with the strike of his chest. "Age isn't everything. Even I could take on the role of a king!"

My smile curls at the edges. No he couldn't. The more I dwell on this matter, the more I realize that only Atlas could pull this off.

Unscathed or not? Only time will tell.

Chapter 39

— The Alchemist —

I DODGE THE chickens that run amok in the street amongst the children. Sometimes, I wish to scold kids for their inconsideration as they cut off other people, including me, but I was once one of those pesky youths—the children with scabs on their knees and crooked teeth and a knack for getting in the way.

A lot of people still see me that way. The breed in this kingdom holds a strange fascination with poultry. They're chasing the hens, as I used to do. With a quick swoop, I pick up one of the chickens and look the bird in the eye. Some say they're the closest being we have to dinosaurs. Do I really believe that? Maybe. The hen kicks and fusses to break free from my grasp, which is practically an invitation for kids to come running up to me. Their wide eyes, too big for the rest of their hungering faces, stare in baffled wonderment.

"Winner, winner! Chicken dinner," I snicker.

A pair of boys laugh. They're the ones I crafted figurines made of the streets' cobblestone for a few days back. Today, they reach their grimy hands to stroke disheveled brown feathers.

"Don't eat her!" a little girl cries with a pronounced bottom lip pushed out to pout.

A few *real* adults gawk at our rendez-vous in the middle of the bustling street. I pretend they're not even there, which is a practical tactic I picked up from Edwin. If push comes to shove, a good elbow and a sharp tongue can get any chump looking for a fight to yield. Not to mention my hands. Or my stare. Plenty of people find it difficult to look me in the eye, but I have yet to figure out why.

"I wanna pet her, I wanna pet her!" The requests come flooding in. Then the begging. "*Please?*"

I hold the hen up to my eye-level. I wish I had olive green eyes like her. They'd be so pretty. So normal. Or even brown eyes, like Edwin once had. He's only got one left, courtesy of Atlas. She bawks in retaliation, so I let the poor creature down. The kids complain and then get right back to running without skipping a beat.

A rather delicate force on my shoulder spins me around. Red lips part to speak. Rosaline?

"Look who has come into her own."

I rub the back of my neck, which at the very least is covered by shoulder-length curls now. Still not the length I'd like my hair to be, but I can't complain. Without the captain by my side anymore, or, well, me being by the captain's side, it looks like I've headed her point to a T.

"Still have that rusty blade?" I cross my arms.

She scowls. "Kept it as a reminder. Don't get tangled up in the web of people like him."

"I'll do as I please." I turn to leave. Her fingers lock around my wrist.

"This is coming from a place of love, my lark. My heart couldn't stand to see you get hurt again."

"*Hurt again?* By Atlas? No way. Celestia forbid." Lips curled, I bear my teeth to enunciate every word. Startled, she lets go. "He had no sway in the first place."

"*Talk about denial,*" Edwin once told me regarding this dilemma. Actually, it's not a dilemma. He didn't matter. He *doesn't* matter.

The only person that still matters is my father, and day by day he seems farther and farther away, along with his value. Perhaps gold is the only substance that will maintain its worth.

Okay, maybe I've grown a little attached to Ruth, Jean-Jacques, and Edwin. The rest of their crew, too. Sometimes us taverners get invited to mix drinks for them on board and to join in on their nights filled with shanties. Once or twice the captain has been there, but he's as repulsive as the same magnetic pole, so we've never reconvened. Though, because of his recent coronation, the kingdom has locked down its security, whether by the former king's or Atlas' command. My only chance at leaving these walls is through the port exit, which should be the most guarded, in my experience.

Pirates plunder. Sailors steal. Captains conspire.

They speak for themselves.

I toss a few coins at the town's baker as I snatch a roll out of a crate. Amongst the crowd, I'm already gone before he receives the chance to scold me. Besides, I paid more than enough to cover the cost. Call it a tip for cutting the small talk if you will. I'm not interested in the mindless chatter and gossip about the king that gets passed around with every transaction in the market.

Running my fingers through my hair, I pull in a deep breath. Celestia forbid that our paths align, *please.*

I stop a few yards away from the gates cut out from the towering stone-brick walls that lead to the docks. Gulls soar above, their calls screeching like the short-tempered sailors in the port. As I slip past the guards, who have cards splayed out in their hands like the feathers of a peacock, I realize that I'm stepping into what feels like another world. There's a heave-ho coming from one direction and a yo-ho from the other. What in the world "ho" means as a suffix, I have no idea. This seemingly alternate reality of theirs is far from my own. Their elements are rain and wind whereas mine are hydrogen and oxygen, along with the hundred or so others that I must not neglect.

I stretch my arm until a joint or two cracks while keeping a deliberate straight face. If no one messes with me, I'll have no problems. I could catch the next boat out of here, granted if I wanted to. Really, I do. The little girl who resides in my conscience won't lose her hope in my father. Though the flighty fire flickers in the dark, it hasn't been completely extinguished. That's Atlas' fault. It's all his fault.

My heavy steps storm across the docks. Light peers through the crevices and rotted knots in the wood to remind me just how important my footing is. Knowing me, I don't heed the warning. A loose plank nearly sends me into the lapping waves, if it wasn't for a hand around my wrists. My skin prickles at the strange sensation of webbing.

"Just let me fall in, Atlas."

"Call me that one more time and I will."

He's not the captain? I don't want to know who this is. He pulls me to my feet and off of the faulty plank. I give the boy a once-over. Calder?

"You have feet." My eyes are plastered to the odd sight.

"That traitor isn't unique. He's just more convincing."

"Riiight." I yank my arm back to my side. Green scales paint his cheeks, running down his neck and underneath armor. His ears still are finned and fingers webbed, as the Captain's were underwater. Chainmail must hide his arms' features. Okay, now I believe him. I take a deep breath in, perhaps to make sure I didn't drown and begin to hallucinate. "Why in Celestia's name are you here?"

"Listen, Lark. Queen Farida sent me to find you." In his other hand, he holds out a bottle with a coiled piece of parchment in it. How cliche.

"Not Atlas?"

"Goodness, no. She knows better than to hunt him down and assumes you're much closer than I. You're our link."

As he raises the glass, I stare down at my distorted reflection, its exaggerated frown. "I'm not the person for the job."

"It's only this once. Queen Farida does request an audience with him, for the details are in here." His sharp nails plink against the bottle. "If you pass this on, you'll never have to be our messenger again."

Silent, I gnaw on the inside of my cheek. There's nothing in this for me, other than having to face that wretched traitor.

Calder sets his shoulders back, armor adjusting with a clink and clank. "You didn't expect him to turn on you like that, I know. That's just who Atlas is."

His bitter tone brings my face to a scowl. My heart stings with grief it shouldn't bear. That's not who I wished he would be.

"That twisted liar found a new way to make himself royalty."

"Your people found out?"

"Why else would my Queen send out a formal letter requesting to see the acting king?"

My eyes go back to the bottle, thinking he cannot be serious believing that the coiled up parchment is anywhere near formal.

To each their own, that's what my father told me. He claimed that's what keeps us on our toes, so that Celestia makes sure there's never a dull moment. It's nice and sentimental and all, but I could use a longer break from these shenanigans.

I shrug and snatch the bottle. "I'll do it under one condition."

His eyes narrow. "That being?"

"You'll tell me why you lost faith in him, other than the lies." My nose scrunches.

"He stole my Queen's crown. What more reasoning do you need?"

I take a shot in the dark. "You're afraid of him, no? You weren't merely defending yourself down there. Farida would never request such an attack, making it personal, tailored to your spite. Why is that?"

The hit lands.

"He may be the ruler here, but my Queen's kingdom cannot fall into his hands. Not if I can help it."

"And by pushing him away from his mother what exactly are you securing?"

His eyes narrow into thin slits, almost like a cat's, but just like Atlas. My fingers tighten around the bottle. Maybe he'll be reminded that this bottle could be turned into dust or perhaps even gold to erase the note forever.

"My throne." His words are dry, breathless, even.

Not what I was expecting, but it's something.

"After his exile, I was chosen to replace him as the next in line to inherit Queen Farida's throne. I will not let this opportunity slip."

▽△▽△

I don't know how this information is going to be useful. *Yet*, my father would add, though he's not here. Believing in the possibility of yet makes me look like a fool without him around. He always reminded me that Celestia has a plan. I can't help but wonder what Her plan is with Farida, Calder, and Atlas?

I lift the bottle to stare at the yellowed scroll inside. Little salt crystals around the edges glitter in the late morning light. My steps hit the ground, heavier than usual. I let my feet trace the way back to the tavern so I can pay Ruth a visit. Surely, he has insight.

The door swings open, and I descend the steps. Ruth, as expected, polishes glasses behind the wooden counter. Under the amber lights, the tavern has never been so clean. I never had the patience to polish every bottle, neither the ones that would drain in one night nor the others that sat on the shelf for years, as if they were only decor. His smile is warmer than the flickering fixtures.

"All good? You're later than usual." He then raises his brows at the bottle. "The captain? Again? I thought you were done dealing with pirates." He winces. "Oh, or the sea in general."

"Same here." I shake my head and set the bottle down on the bar, rattling all of the others.

"I don't think you're going to like my advice." He straightens the misaligned glasses.

"I'll hear you out." I take my place at a barstool. Ruth's eyebrows lift, his iconic sign of disbelief.

"Make amends."

I cross my arms and swallow my esteem in an attempt to restrain myself from refuting his advice.

"Make…amends," I fail, "with…him? Ruth, do you really expect—"

He laughs. "Told you." After giving his chestnut-colored vest a quick straighten, he leans on the polished counter in front of me. Despite being a mind-reader, he has a rather kind nature. Thoughtful and truthful. He almost blushes, but he looks at an approaching patron moments before I can confirm my observations.

Ruth snaps into his taverner role with an, "Aye, welcome!" followed by his infamous, "What can I getcha?"

The man orders a glass of wine. If I'm not mistaken, it's the same kind Atlas went for on his first night drinking here. I can't stand myself for remembering such trivial details. I stare at the familiar man, who takes his place a few stools from mine. He must've been a regular from when I first sought work here.

He salutes me. A former sailor? I sheepishly gesture back.

"It's been a while, hasn't it?"

I nod along. "Yeah, it has."

"Edwin has told me plenty of stories of you tagging along with the crew." He lets out a chuckle, which is soon drowned by a sip of wine.

I raise a brow. "You know him, too?"

"I know nearly everyone who traverses these docks, Jolly ol' Roger to Blackbeard. They sing shanties of my past valor." His raised glass glows in the golden light, mahogany wine turned a deep amber. "Do you remember me?" /

I shake my head. "Not well."

"Honesty is a virtue." He takes it far more lightly than how I would have responded. With an extended arm, he introduces himself. "Does Captain DeLuca ring any bells?"

I pause, frozen in some sort of shock. "DeLuca as in *the* DeLuca?"

He nods.

"*The*," I continue to pry, "*DeLuca.*"

"As in the king's father? Yes."

"Why don't you pass this on to your son?"

Ruth speaks my name between bared teeth as my fingertips slide the bottle over to Monsieur DeLuca, who stops it just short of clinking with his glass. The gleam in his eyes mixed with his pensive expression tell me he knows that it's from his wife. Crystalized notes may bring back memories, as certain formulas continue to conjure up past images of my father.

DeLuca's smile even reminds me of my Dad. "I believe you are far more than capable of such a small task."

"But you were the one who put him up to this, am I wrong?" I stand. Ruth flinches, as if I'll regret my next decisions. He can only read minds; he has no premonition.

"Atlas said yes of his own accord. I cannot force that boy to do anything." His weathered face does not crease with disdain, instead his lips part into a toothy, almost amused, smile. He picks the bottle up by the neck and hands it to me. I grasp it and pull. His grip refuses to let up. "But you, Alchemist, move tides like the moon. Your sway may rock the boat."

▽△▽△

My fingers fiddle with the cork, which is more secure than I had let on initially. No matter how hard I pull, it won't let loose. I wonder if it's enchanted as I inspect it further.

Two guards stop me by crossing their spears in front of the castle's towering front doors.

"State your business."

I frown and display the bottle by holding it out for the pair to see. Together, they lean over to examine it, synchronized from years of practice, I can only assume.

"Queen Farida sent this."

Jittering, pale faces with wide eyes crane their necks to look at me.

"The former king wouldn't dare correspond with the Siren Queen," one croaks.

"Let me in or I'll demand that she raises the sea so that this kingdom may keep its place on maps." I hold up the bottle, which repulses the two men. The note may as well be a severed head atop a bloody platter based on their expressions.

The doors swing open for me. I nod to them with a straight face. Once I'm shut into the palace, I suck in a deep breath, holding it for more time than I should. Nobles and their servants bustle. Two curved staircases lead to a second floor, with a little balcony overlooking the foyer, velvet running along the marble steps. I march toward the next set of double doors, which I presume leads to a throne room, if not another lobby. A wrinkled man in a pristine tailcoat stops me from traversing further, fingers curled around my forearm. I yank my arm away.

"Get off," I snarl.

His cold glare does not yield. "You do not belong here, Plebeian."

A well-dressed lady, not too much older than me, frowns. "Go back to the streets, Gypsy."

"I'm here to see Atlas." I raise the bottle. "Queen Farida has a message."

"His Majesty, to you." Another young man, arm linked with the girl, draws his own blade. A silly weapon, really. It's practically a thin rod, and I'm willing to bet he hasn't faced off in real battle.

"No, it's just Atlas to me," I correct. I'll stand my ground. If this gets messy, it'll be Calder's fault for not putting those sea legs of his to good use.

The young man lunges at me. I grab the blade and jerk the hilt out of his grasp and into mine. My teeth grit as I fight the urge to check my lacerated palm. His jaw hangs agape as I press the tip to his Adam's apple. No blood of his spills. Only droplets from my hand trickle down the grip and onto the floor.

Two knights draw their swords. I drop the bottle and rub my wrist against my side to roll the glove off.

"Stand down."

My focus turns from the courageous noble to my new armored opponents. One brings their weapon down at me, aiming for the stolen armament. I slip out of the way, literally, and roll across the cold floor in an attempt to cover up my miscalculation. My weapon spins across the floor. Splaying my fingers, I reach for the bottle, which by some miracle—or enchantment—has not shattered into a million splintering pieces. The second knight aims to pierce me while I'm on the ground. Little do they know, the floor is my greatest ally. I press my unscathed palm against the polished marble. A spike knocks the sword out of his gauntlet. More metallic footsteps echo as doors to another hidden hallway spring open. The last time I fought, it was only against a singular captain. Now I'm against the entirety of the royal guard.

"Celestia," I beckon as I peel my bloodied glove off.

One knight makes an attempt to slice my head, clean off my shoulders. Kneeling, I bend back to flatten my back against the floor. He stumbles over.

"Celestia," I repeat, leaning forward like a fool to press both hands against the floor. "Come on, come on." She has to hear me. The marble beneath my palm begins to glow. From it, a circular rune expands to spread across the entire floor.

Lords and ladies gasp and back away, as if the ground beneath them were lava. It's just to scare these folk. Celestia knows that even the guards back away from unprecedented forces. Except for one. I take a blunt force from behind. My cheek hits the marble. Iron and salt taint my tongue. I scutter away from the attacker, hacking up beads of blood that dribble down my chin. I wipe them with my sleeve as I push myself to my feet. The edges of my vision darken. Celestia's stars dance around while I utter Her name again. I'm not done. I hold my hand out, fingers flared once again, palm raised toward the chandelier. Another glowing rune appears. My strained fingertips twitch.

This power isn't mine. It's Celestia's.

By now, the rest of the knights have realized that the transmutation circle on the floor is harmless. Air quotes on that last word. The guard who had landed the last hit readies his sword like I'm a real threat. His toothy smile makes my lips curl into a grin as well. Eyes on him, I draw near. He approaches, weary of the glowing rune emanating off of my hand. As his blade swings up, I dip down to press my hand against his chestplate. That metal armor is no match for alchemy. It oozes and melts. After all, mercury is a liquid at room temperature. The newly synthesized metal returns to its original alloy as the globs settle on the rune below.

That doesn't stop this attacker. The edge of his sword grazes my shoulder. His allies rush to aid the armorless knight, now his vitals only guarded by a mail shirt.

"Celestia," I murmur. Their boots turn to marble, plastered to the matching floor. Although not unarmed, they're immobile. Wide eyes turn to me again. I sputter, hacking up another round of blood. The floor's glowing rune flickers. The one on my hand fades. I'm running out of borrowed power.

In desperation, a few knights take shots at me with their swords. Something whizzes past my ear. This isn't good. Traced along the staircases, archers are positioned all the way up to the second floor's balcony, overlooking the open space.

I take another slash, this time to the heel. My knees fail me as I fall back to the ground. I cover the back of my neck with my hands, head tucked down. An arrow pierces my shoulder blade and draws a wretched scream from somewhere deep in my chest.

The throne room's doors burst open. More knights rush out, sights set on no one other than me. I reach for the bottle and hold it out. Maybe I can use it to defend myself; I don't know! It's enchanted, and I don't often play with magic. A blur of silver approaches. I hold my breath.

"Stop!" a muffled voice shouts. "Stop!"

Before another sword can draw blood, a blade knocks it out of the way. The back of black boots stand in front of my vision.

"Stop."

My ringing ears tune in and out on the scattered screams and commotion. Fingers rubbing against my face, wrists digging into my eye sockets, I can't seem to pull myself together. These threads have come unraveled one too many times. Between the blur, I catch glimpses of a shadowy fighter dressed in black pushing away my opponents.

A command from him makes the whole room fall silent.

I tear my hands away from my face as my eyes narrow to focus. A golden circlet sits on the man's head. The floor's rune fades. My body slumps over.

As he returns his sword to its scabbard, my defender strides over. Using his foot, Atlas nudges me. I don't. and won't budge. Once he realizes this, he rolls me onto my back to plant a foot on my chest as he did before. His actions and eyes tell very different stories. He must distance himself from someone like me, a fiend, a savage. But his eyes gloss over, as sea foam coats the crests of waves. The arrow snaps under my back. I let out a quick weep.

If I'm not mistaken, he winces for me.

"What do you think you're doing?" he demands. Even in a hushed voice, the whole room can hear even the slightest waver.

I grit my teeth. With the last of my energy, I curl my fingers around the unscathed bottle and hurl it at him. He catches it against his chest. "Your mom sent you a message."

His blue eyes, pupils narrowed to thin slits, rake across the room. Bile bubbles in the back of my throat. Atlas removes his foot and reaches to help me up.

A few of the knights protest.

"Your Majesty, be careful."

"Let us handle *it*, Your Highness."

My lips curl. I am not an *it*, I want to spit at them.

"Clean up this mess. Everyone goes to their scheduled post."

"Take extra guards with you."

"There is no need." The acting king shakes his head. The gold crown glints under the chandelier. I could've crushed everyone with that fixture. They should be grateful I didn't. Instead of waiting for me to take his hand, which I never would have, he grabs the collar of my shirt and hoists me up so that I'm on my feet, his hand around my upper arm keeps me upright.

"Who started it?" 'His Majesty' inquires. Everyone avoids eye contact. How convenient. Then they all point at me. Though, Atlas knows me more than any of these fools. Their gesture will not suffice.

"If you come out now, no one will be put on trial."

The young man, who I had taken the sword from, steps up.

"Guards, take him." His words slice like daggers.

"But, Your Majesty. He was just protecting—"

"I will speak with him later." As Atlas walks, the crowd parts. Aside from the knights who I had adhered to the floor, of course. A few sharp ones had stepped out of their boots. The remainder awkwardly salute. I stumble beside him. I might as well be the court jester.

Atlas has a knight lock and secure the door behind us.

"Alouette, what am I going to do with you?" His grip tightens. I flinch. He removes his hand to realize it's my wounded shoulder. My weak body slumps over. He catches me again.

"Send me to prison," I ramble, "execute me, perhaps feed me to your scaled enemies."

"No. How are we going to fix," he pauses, "this?" He lets the bottle fall on the ground as he pulls the fabric of his cloak off of the broken arrow on my back.

"Be cautious of the barbs?" I sarcastically suggest, speech slurred.

"Alouette." Atlas sighs. I rub the blood off of my jaw. "You could've died."

"Nothing new. You can just kick me out the back door like we do after last call. I'll be fine."

He squeezes my arm in an attempt to get me to follow once more. "Let me help you."

I won't budge. "Read the letter," I spit, "then maybe I'll comply, Your *Highness*."

His eyes flash with a gleam somewhere between sympathy and guilt. "This is really from my…" He doesn't finish.

I nod and wiggle myself out of his grasp so I can sink down on the floor, legs crossed. He takes a knee and picks up the bottle. It only takes the push of his thumb to pop the cork off. Enchanted, for sure.

His poker face hasn't improved at all. Good thing he's not a gambler.

"A peace treaty?" I ask. "Oh, better yet, a declaration of war."

"The former," he states.

I blink a few times. The world has to come back into focus.

"It's what my father wanted."

I raise a weak brow. "Isn't that a good thing?"

"I'll have to take it up with the king." He folds the crystalized paper and tucks it into his black and gold tunic before rising. I run my non-bloody hand along the velvet carpet.

Making my voice unnaturally deep, I mock him "I'll have to *blah blah*."

"What did you do to get," he gestures to my wounds, "this? Did you mock a lord or something?"

"I offended your subjects by calling you Atlas. Should've thrown captain in there, really."

"You do have permissio—"

"They didn't think so. I'm a gypsy. A plebeian."

"Alouette, you're not—"

"I *am*, Atlas, and you're a king. There's a greater difference between us now. I swore to myself I'd never see you again, but, thanks to Calder, I'm here now."

"He could've taken it up with me himself."

"Right!?" I force a hysterical laugh. "When I'm not a threat, they see me as a tool. When I'm not a tool, they see me as a threat. Just like you use me." I weakly stand, wobbling.

"That's not true." His dark brows frown while his voice lowers, "Alouette, this is all for you."

"The gold, authority, and glory? Yeah, definitely."

"There's something else," he whispers, leaning close enough that his cheek brushes mine. His eyes fall on the guards around. "Let me return the favor and at least help you clean the wounds."

"You have half an hour. I work this evening."

▽△▽△

I take off the cloak that once belonged to Atlas and throw it into his arms. He sets it on what I guess he claimed as his bed in one of the castle's royal rooms. A pair of gloves sit on the desk, so I'm guessing it's his living quarters.

"Worst first?" I ask and turn my back to him. He grits his teeth and pulls off his gloves. His fingers curl around the remainder of the arrow.

"You might want to sit down for this."

Those are the last words I want to hear. I totter my way across the room and sit on a tuffet of coverlets. Atlas takes a seat behind me.

"Just this once." I can't tell if he's speaking to me or himself.

He whispers quietly. Fingertips dig into my back, around the arrowhead. His breathless murmurs morph into hums. I can't quite fathom what he's doing. Each time he repeats, his words grow more clear.

"Cure sometimes, treat often, comfort always."

I let out an awful whimper when he dislodges the arrow. It doesn't hurt. Nothing does. I look down at my palm. The gaping line along my hand narrows.

"Cure sometimes, treat often, comfort always."

His fingertips run over my back. Where there should be a divot from the arrowhead, it's smoothed over. That doesn't fix the bloodsoaked hole in my shirt.

"Your voice can heal people?" I wheeze and look back over my shoulder. "Why didn't you heal yourself?"

"It wasn't necessary."

I lean back into his arms, into his embrace. My eyes look up to meet his wide pupils, irises like the ocean. A siren's voice cannot be trusted. Neither can I under an enchantment.

"And one other thing." He pushes me away, as he should.

"What? You'd fall in love with yourself?" I snicker, a little delirious.

"Not interested in risking it."

"But you're okay with risking me fa—"

"It would be mutual."

I force another laugh. "Hilarious." My feet kick over the edge, and I stand. Atlas keeps his hands folded in his lap. "You look stupid in a crown, by the way."

From there I take my leave.

Chapter 40

— The Siren —

I wash my hands off and find myself staring at the cloak I lent her. In truth, it has no more use to me. Tattered and bloodstained and riddled with holes, it belongs to the alchemist now. I turn the sink on and wash off my face, as if that would erase her from my recent memory. She's right. I do look foolish with a crown, so I set it aside. Until the scales on my cheeks dissipate, I'm left glaring at my reflection.

A figure appears in the corner of my eye.

"P-princess," I stammer. "How did you get in here?"

She looks back at the open door. Naive and innocent.

"She isn't your first mate?"

My fingers curl as I shake my head. "It was a fib."

The princess crosses her arms. "I never believed her. She doesn't look like a first mate."

Okay?

"Then what does she look like?"

This gets the princess to quiet and think for a while.

"A mistress?" Her wavering answer is unsure.

I hold my tongue. An old friend, I could say. Or perhaps she's just a girl. An alchemist I got a little too close with. Though, I wish she wasn't. If anything, I want her as an acquaintance, an ally, a *friend*.

This crown has cost me far, far more than it should have.

"She said that the message was from your mom, right?"

I nod.

"But she said that it was also from Farida. Isn't she the Queen of…?"

She pauses, as if speaking of what's under the sea is taboo. My hand presses against my jaw to feel the remaining scales. There's no point in denying it.

"She's the Siren Queen," I confirm.

"So that's why you're a good singer." She giggles and twirls around in her pink dress. I can't tell if her matching cheeks are from blush or blushing. Only recently did I learn there's a difference. Thank the princess for that. Her painted lips part into a charmed smile. "You love her, don't you?"

In her mind, it makes for a pretty entertaining fable. The half-siren king falls for the rebellious commoner; they both end in ruin and live happily never after. Sounds about right, doesn't it?

"I don't want her to leave me."

▽ △ ▽ △

Though, Edwin has told me that it's already too late. I may be a fool for believing this, but I feel like I still have a chance. Admittedly, the last card I store up my sleeve came with the crown. It's neither riches nor glory. It's something everyone values.

Well, except for me.

I've forfeited my own long ago.

Servants bow to me as I walk down the hall. I resist the urge to salute, but every so often I'll nod back to them. The king told me I am not supposed to pay much attention to them. Still, that doesn't change the fact that disregarding them is rude. My standards may be low, but they're present nonetheless.

The king's chamber practically sneaks up on me. I'm not ready to face him, especially if it means mentioning that Farida is my mother. If her letter reads, *dear son*, I might as well resign. I pull out the paper and unfold it. My position as king doesn't feel real. To start off, I forgot the crown back in the bathroom, so I look like some well-dressed, foolish princeling striding down the halls. Then we can't disregard the fact that nearly every one of my decisions must go through the former king. I hope that Alouette does not tell a soul about the enchantment I used on her. He could wrap me further around his decrepit finger if he knew I could keep his symptoms at bay. Death comes to all, eventually. He's putting his fate off as long as possible, even if it means dragging those around him down.

I knock on the door, which opens right away. Attendants bow. I slightly bow back to them. The king shakes his head.

"Queen Farida sent a correspondence," I announce.

"Burn it."

"No. Read it."

"Burn it."

There's no hesitation before his replies.

"I will read it out loud." I clear my throat. "Dear King Atlas,

"It is with high regards that I congratulate you on your coronation. I look forward to the bettering of our two kingdoms. As you are aware, the late king refused to maintain peaceful relations. On behalf of my people, I extend a chance to work toward a—"

"Boy!"

My next words come out with a snarl. "Better world for the subjects of both land and sea. If you desire to start your rule on a good foot, prepare for my arrival on the next full moon. Best regards, Queen Farida." I crease the paper and tuck it away again. "If we decline, she will raise the tide to your neck and mine. I will handle everything. Let me play king. Your turn is over, and it has been for a month now."

"I know why you're doing this." He coughs. "Your father wishes for peace, and you're chasing the alchemist's fickle daughter."

"You're resentful because I am not interested in yours. Besides, you still haven't taken me to *him*. That was our deal."

"I suppose it is time, Boy." He snaps his weak fingers to make a disappointing noise. A knight picks up the cue.

▽⍓▽△

After nearly five minutes of silence, the knight strikes up a conversation. "So that's who you were with." A twisted smirk wrinkles his face. "Affairs are no good."

"It's not an affair."

"To the rest of the kingdom, she's a threat." He stops and turns to face me. His long blonde hair has been tied up to keep it off of his polished armor. A white cape hangs off of one shoulder. He must've been the one in the citadel. Why can't I get rid of him? "I won't let your meddlings with her risk my standing among the knights. This kingdom must be protected, and I will not lose my position because of your foolish fondness for this girl."

I keep my jaw clamped shut so he can continue.

"I saw what you did at the masquerade."

"It's not what you think."

"Let me guess. The captain betrothed to the princess only wants her hand to win over the approval of the alchemist for…who knows what kind of malevolent plan a siren would have?"

"You don't know the terms of the king's agreement with the alchemist, do you?" I cross my arms.

"Which entailed?" As I expected, he's clueless.

I keep my voice low. "I'm sure it's above your pay grade."

I know the terms of the deal well. In exchange for a secure place to experiment here in the castle and Alouette's safety, her father—the alchemist—would live under the castle and perform experiments for the king. That was violated when he created the wanted posters, in addition to today's fiasco. In essence, by taking Alouette out of that situation, I was upholding the former king's obligation.

The knight scoffs, dissatisfied with my response, as he should be. He then pulls down on a light fixture attached to the wall. The panel swings open to present a dark passageway. I gesture for the knight to go first, guessing that he has done this a time or two. Maybe it's a shot in the dark, but I don't care. I've taken my fair share.

We wind down a spiral staircase that goes deeper and deeper underground. I run my fingers along the wall until the stone bricks grow damp. The air reeks of metal and wet rock, two distinct smells I'm well acquainted with. The knight then pulls out his scabbard and rattles the bars at the bottom of the stairs.

Chapter 41

— The Thief —

Rise and shine, scallywags.

That's what I call to my crew nearly every morning. To this day, some hate me for it while others have learned to tune me out. A few mates slump out of their hammocks or roll over on the floor. Most of us have gotten accustomed to sleeping in due to our lax schedule at the docks. Once we set sail again, they'll be in for a rude awakening.

Jacques hasn't slacked off one bit. That's why he's Atlas' favorite to work with, and why he was chosen as a quartermaster over me. Besides, we all know I'm brutal. The captain isn't like that. He isn't like the others. He only strikes in defense, and, nine times out of ten, the person he's defending isn't even himself. I find that it gets under my skin, so, half the time, I start fights just for the sake of it. At least the captain has got a good bluff going for him. His empty threats send other captains and their crews running away, tails between their legs and treasure trailing behind for the rest of us to plunder. You've seen it yourself. He'd make a terrifying duo with the alchemist.

I tap my fingertips against the ship's side as I stroll through the hall. *Boreas*, that's what I call her. God of the North Wind. Just a fable, though. I even carved that name by my bunk. *Aurora Borealis* is her true title, though. Apparently, DeLuca takes a liking to Greek names.

Once I reach the main deck, I greet the dawn with a good stretch and yawn. My fingers rub the crust out of my eyes before tying my hair back with a cream-colored ribbon.

Jacques greets me from the helm. Sometimes, I wonder if he pretends to set sail again. It's an itch we have as seafarers, one that only Davy Jones can scratch. The sea's breeze must suffice for now. I jog up the steps to meet him and overlook the port. Under any other ruler, we would've overstayed our welcome. This kingdom charges taxes per transaction made. In the eyes of a governor, our ship is depleting the king of his rightful dues by taking up space reserved for a merchant's vessel.

I'll let you in on a little secret. We never paid those to begin with. Don't forget, we're pirates, here to cash in bounties, plunder, and get three sheets to the wind. The last one applies to the captain in particular. Speaking of him, as I look over *Boreas'* edge, I see his head bobbing down the docks.

"Aye, Capt'n!" I salute. His blue eyes peer up. These narrowed pupils of his freak me out to this day. I know he can't help it because the sea folk are all the same.

He salutes back, halfway shielding his eyes from the sun, halfway to me.

While he boards, I pester, "You missed Alouette by a day, y'know."

"Oh, really?" He has to restrain himself from asking anything more.

"I'm sure it's been a while." My footsteps fall into line with his as he surveys *Boreas*. She's his secret pride and joy. A gorgeous ship, really. We could call her *Notre Dame* for all she's worth. That name's claimed across the harbor, though.

"Saw her yesterday."

"She didn't tell me about that." I cross my arms. "Anyway, she took one of your shirts, 'cause, y'know, hers was covered in blood and riddled with holes. I won't ask what happened."

"It's not like her to hide anything from you."

"She didn't say much. Bad mood, I'm guessing."

"Surprising." His grumble brims with sarcasm.

"Oh, you're stuck-up too?" I roll my eyes and press my weight against the ships' taffrail. Atlas leans beside me, raising his chin to watch the gulls soar above us.

"I am not."

"Am too!"

"Am not."

Jacques' laughter breaks our bickering. "You only come back when you have important intel to relay."

I knew that!

"So, Capt'n. Any grand revelations?"

"The king wasn't lying about the alchemist. They made a deal. In exchange for Alouette's protection and a secure place for him to work, the alchemist would work on a project to find the Elixir of Life."

"Which is?"

"A potion that grants immortality."

"Sounds like a tall tale if you ask me, taller than you, Capt'n. Living forever is for the fae. Wait, Atlas, is your mother immortal?"

Regrettably, my false siblings at the orphanage had told me that sirens never aged. Though, timelessness and eternity do not always equate, as confusing as it may be. Besides, I've pretty much grown up alongside a half-siren.

"Both the alchemist and king believe in it. His Majesty was convinced it would heal him of his ailments. If I were Alouette's father, I would've turned it down. She's fully capable of defending herself. She doesn't need a king's protection, especially when it has failed her."

"Ah, the wanted poster," I nod along. "Oh, and the plank thing."

That king never upheld his end of the bargain. Still, I must play the Devil's advocate, the voice on Atlas' left shoulder. "Haven't you wondered if the alchemist sought protection for himself? Anyone aware of his powers would lust after that seemingly infinite wealth. If not that, then think of what Alouette has gone through. Even pirates want her dead. Imagine what they would do to someone more experienced."

"What would drive someone to seek refuge provided by that man?" Atlas' face contorts. The captain does not often disdain people. His Majesty must be an utterly filthy creature.

"Someone after him—that's the motive."

Atlas' frustration digs into unease. If it's safe to assume that Alouette's father has failed to craft the Elixir of Life, then the king must have pushed the alchemist's threat onto Atlas' shoulders. Great, another roadblock.

"Don't pout, Edwin."

"I'm not pouting." I plant my hands on my hips. "You're pouting."

"He's just eager, Atlas." Jean-Jacques makes his return. Our captain's gaze lowers. He is, too.

Chapter 42

— The Alchemist —

WHEN I GOT back to the tavern, Ruth had asked me what happened. Well, sometimes he's blunt, so naturally after he told me that I looked like a wreck. Before I could finish assuring him that I was fine, I passed out at the bar.

Magic has its limits. So does alchemy.

I spent an entire day sleeping. I got up at dusk just to fall back asleep. Edwin had left Atlas' cloak at my doorstep, though I couldn't bring myself to thank either of them.

Today is a new day, but I've already burnt up most of it like kindling.

Pulling my hood over my eyes, I pass by the guards at the gates. I haven't seen any wanted posters picturing my face as of late. No one stops me from leaving, contrary to what other civilians had told me about the kingdom gates. The stone brick road tapers off into a dirt path as I stray further away from the walls. Children raised within the kingdom's confines fear what waits within the meadows. Not me, I've tumbled down the hills of the rolling grasslands many times before. Merchants with wagons drawn by horses and mules pass by. They often raise a brow. They must think I'm a fool for exiting the walls of my own volition, which isn't quite wrong. I could trace the winding paths through fields of wildflowers and weaving trails through thick forests like the runes on my palms, but they wouldn't know that.

I hold my hand up to the bright sun. I've still got a few hours until sundown. The plan was to leave at daybreak to allow myself to go on a few side quests here and there, whether to visit observation towers or to catch tadpoles in the creek. Now that I'm older, I don't have the time to dally. My morning had a rather late start. For once, I treated myself to breakfast from the market. I splurged on a few goodies and accessories for myself. Edwin helped pay with his stolen pocket change. If he hadn't gotten punished under the former king's rule, I don't see Atlas ever passing judgment on him for his thievery.

New earrings dangle beside my cheek. Beads circle my wrists. I enjoy handing myself over to secular desires every now and then. I tie a bandana around my head to keep my hair out of my face. Though, I do let a few bangs slip through. I think it's cute. Rosaline says it looks messy. Who cares? I'm not trying to impress anyone.

My new boots take the blunt of the dust and mud. I scan the green horizon for all of the little cottages. The hay roofs call me back to the Three Little Pigs. The predators beyond the wall are far more vicious than the huffing, puffing Big Bad Wolf. Most kingdoms stick to the shore, so there's little protection inland. During our travels, my father always carried a double-edged ax, just in case we faced hostile travelers. Some raiders attack for riches, using empty threats to steal jewels and commodities for reselling. I remember biting a man who tried to take a stitched creation of mine. I hope he got infected.

My focus wanders off to the bushy tips of wild grass, to the daisies that bob up and down in the breeze. Sure, no one is here to guard me, but at least I'm free. I look back to glare at the walls. The spires only appear as tall as my fingers while the glittering sea feels like a mirage in the distance.

The destination ahead will give me a better view of both. I stray from the path and pluck a few flowers. They'll whither soon enough, so I'm sure Celestia won't mind if I take a few of Her creations for myself. When I was younger, I had wanted to preserve them forever. My father had sat me down to teach me the art of not just turning metals into gold. He let me turn a daisy into precious metal. A looter stole it years later.

That's probably why I don't have many nice things anymore.

I've learned to let go. If Celestia deems that I can no longer have something, I'll put it into Her hands to take. I wonder what in the world She had in mind while placing a crown on Atlas' brow. Nothing has felt quite right since his coronation.

I pull my hood down. Today isn't for him nor about him. I'm tired of thinking about that captain and the way my chest tightened when he let the princess kiss his cheek. In frustration, I knot the stems of wildflowers together. I fill my pockets with daisies and poppies and violets and cornflowers. I pass up the blue forget me nots.

I nod to a few merchants who stare as I diverge off of the beaten path.

"Is she crazy?" one mutters. Oftentimes, people don't realize their voices travel on the breeze, especially if Celestia wants you to hear them. In terms of how others perceive me, I'm already well aware. That doesn't stop me from running my fingers along the long grass. A line of trees stands before me. The sun tells me I still have time, even if I dally a teeny tiny bit.

I let the twisted branches welcome me. The trail may not be obvious, but I've taken this route plenty of times alongside my father. Never have I trekked this course alone.

Galloping hooves beat down a few yards behind me. I look over my shoulder to peek through the bramble. A crown glints.

Perhaps Celestia refuses to let me venture on my own.

I groan and turn my back on the young man. My pace quickens. He calls my name. It'll be best to pretend that he's not here.

I stomp my way through the briar, crunching the fallen leaves. Atlas' steps fall into line with mine. I stare at the ground. His black shoes kick beside my boots.

What business does he have here? Sure, the land beyond the walled city belongs to the king, but he could always send others to spread news or give orders in his stead.

Forget it, Alouette; I must remind myself.

My feet trace the path on their own as I pour my focus into knitting these flowers together. So far, I have a loose circlet. I reach into my pockets to fill the little gaps in between petals.

"Your craftsmanship is spectacular."

Pretend he's not there, I remind myself to do.

He waits. "Who's it for?"

Another pause ensues.

"Are you meeting someone?"

I'm sick of this. "If I said yes, would that make you leave?"

I set the flowers on my head as I use roots to scale a steep incline. A gloved hand reaches down to help me up. He reached the top before me? I knock it away so I can get a grip on my own.

"No."

"I can only appreciate your honesty." I push past him. "But I'm a danger to the kingdom, aren't I? You should've just exiled me."

"I feared you took that upon yourself."

"Then why follow me?" I push a low-hanging branch out of my way in hopes that when it rebounds, it'll hit him.

"Keep your friends close and your enemies *closer*."

"Good one. Now get lost." I wave him off. "You're a king. You have more important duties."

"I'm a king. I may do as I please."

I scoff. He's gotten better at banter. Using the trunk of a tree to push off of, I climb up the next bank. No one waits for me at the top. Still, I haven't been able to shake him off.

"So, *are* you seeing someone?" he calls up.

"Is that coming from you as a captain, king, or man?"

"A king."

"Shame I never swore an oath to serve you." I brush prickers out of my way.

He says my name. I twitch.

"And I'll never make vows for you."

"Then we'll always be enemies." I can hear a pout.

"You sound disappointed."

He then falls silent. Rustling leaves fill the air where our voices once resounded. The gnarled trees feel smaller than before. The branches hang lower than they did back then. I'm no longer a child tagging alongside her father. I'm a girl who should have been exiled, pursued by the young man who should have banished her. My stomps crunch the loose foliage. His steps are constant, steady, without malice. Unlike mine.

I hold my arm out to brush the bark of the last few trees before I reach the clearing. Some have tally marks that my father had carved for each trip we took here. I grab the pocket knife that I now keep tucked away in my boot to carve my next scar.

Atlas' eyes trace my movements, his attention pointed at the tip of my blade. He doesn't deserve the pleasure of leaving a mark here. Not on the tree that my father claimed for his family—no one else—just him and me. He reaches from behind, his pale hand gloveless, and etches a line with his sharp nail. Jealous, much?

I retract the knife to slip it back into my boot. Regard returning to the sun, I close my eyes and welcome its golden warmth on my cheeks. Far beneath us, the waves crash against the shore. Leaves rustle behind. Celestia's works astound me until Her breeze slaps my hair against my face. And this is why I don't get to experience nice things. The last time I used Her power, I pushed myself to the brink of death, only to fall back on a certain siren's song for mending.

I scout around the perimeter of the woods for twigs and kindling, any small foliage that'll catch fire, really. Once I'm satisfied, I settle a few feet away from the cliff. I scoot little rocks in a circle with my foot. Not many people venture here, so they haven't been moved too much from their position the last time I visited, which must be far over three years ago by now. The twigs lean against one another to create a cone of sorts. Not a pyramid, those have four sides that come to a point. I brush off the thought with the shake of my head. Building campfires is not geometry.

Before sitting, I kick my boots off, which is a custom many families in this kingdom do at home. Atlas hunkers down beside me. I scoot to the other side of the fire. At the very least he can take a hint. He sets down a few logs, too big for the start of a fire. I snap my fingers for a spark. The twigs combust. A flame sprouts. The fire will grow on its own. A little time and oxygen are all it needs.

In the meantime, I'll lean back with my back flat on the grass, rather than the ratty scraps we had sewn into quilts that my father used to bring. As dusk falls on the shore, fireflies rise from the wildgrass. The cream masts speckling the sea turn blue. Dancing bugs turn my hand green as they bump against my fingertips. As a kid, I would pretend to communicate with them by using the constellations on my hands, all so I could trick them into landing on my palms.

Atlas hums to himself, blue eyes illuminated amber by the fire, which has grown large enough to gnaw at his logs.

"How are your wounds?" He catches me picking at the scab on my palm.

I stop and bring my arm down, across my chest. "Better."

Out of the corner of my eye, I watch him poke at the fire and rearrange it with a twig. Embers dot the tip as if it were a sparkling wand.

"Why don't you use enchantments?"

"Oh, now you get to ask me questions." He lifts his eyebrows at me with a frown.

"That's not a real answer."

He takes a moment to respond. "I want everything to be genuine."

I roll onto my side, toward him to my own surprise. "Magic is pretty genuine if you ask me."

"But not a siren's." He feeds the twig to the fire, which flares up, as if on command by Celestia. Atlas jerks his head back, wide eyes blinking. "You're going to think I'm a fool for saying this, but sometimes I regret kissing you. It made me believe that maybe I— maybe you…"

He swallows the thought.

"That what? I loved you?" As I look up at him, he turns his attention back to the fire. My stomach knots at itself. I can no longer feel the grass between my fingertips. It's all numb. I only lay there within a silent void in wait of his reply.

"Look, that's the problem. I don't know."

With a frown, I add, "I wonder the same thing too."

"Really?" Our eyes meet again.

I dig up the dirt around a stone and sling it at him. His crown takes the blunt, then falls to the ground inches from the fire. If I had it my way, it would've fallen into the blaze, as many other reigns meet their end. He's not an authoritarian nor is he submissive. From afar, the captain merely occupies the throne, with no real sway over the courts or his subjects.

"Of course not. Who am I, a commoner, to harbor any feelings but resent toward her ruler?"

Atlas makes no move to pick up the crown. Besides, he mentioned bringing his mother's notes to the king, not the former king or even the old man's first name. Say, the captain is bridled like a steed, only for the king to rule from behind the reins with no choice to defy the monarch's orders.

"I'm doing all of this for you, Alouette."

"How so?"

"I can't tell you now."

"Why not?"

"It's not the right time."

"You're tying the knot?" My eyes grow large; my pulse grows fast.

"No, never."

I pry. "Wasn't the deal to marry the princess?"

"Look, the king is dying. He needed an heir. Because of that mistake years ago, I-I happened to be that person. The Queen died a long time ago, anyway." He picks up another stick to poke at the fire with. Agitated, the flames flare up again. "I didn't know the full truth back then, so I—well. I was frustrated. I've hated every minute of this."

I pipe down and return to laying on my back.

Between us, the fire crackles and spits. A few embers fall on my cloak, but it's not worth panicking to brush them off. If Celestia wishes for me to burn, let it be. She has already burdened me enough with the captain here. I raise my arm to the sky and pretend he's not here, that I'm alone as I planned this morning. My mind takes over to match the glowing symbols on my hand with the real stars across Celestia's vast atmosphere. The light fades after a while. I stretch my fingers to see if a little energy will revive the glow, but to no avail, I fail. My father would've deemed it as a sign from Celestia to refocus.

I eye Atlas. Legs crossed, he rests his hand on his cheek and holds a stick in the other. His pensive stare reflects the flames. He doesn't smile. I must remind myself that association with him is not worth it.

I'll lose no matter what. Safety. Dignity. Even a friend.

I break, momentarily. "Why are you doing this? Here. With me. Now."

His eyes peer over at me as his head lifts a little. The response he gives is a little mumbly. "*Doing nothing feels just as bad as driving the blade.* You said it yourself. It's hard to see you like this. Alone when you could have allies." He lifts his head and gestures to me.

"And?" I edge him on.

"You know it already. I'm here for you. Why do you keep fighting back?"

Chapter 43

— The Siren —

SHE TURNS AWAY from me and sits up. Her gaze glazes over. "Just look where that got my father. He loved my mom. He gave her everything. He put aside his work. His aspirations. All other desires to be with her. He thought it would last forever. And look where that got him." She draws her knees to her chest, hugging them with her arms. "She took him to the grave—a part of him, at the very least. My mother's absence drove a great alchemist into ruin. He probably left because I'm a reminder of everything he lost." She recoils. "I don't want friends—I don't want to love because I know what happens. I've seen it. I've lived it."

"Alouette, but then you'll never know."

Her eyes roll and land on me. "Oh, please. Know what?"

"What it's like for someone to give you everything in return."

Her glossy golden eyes lock with mine.

"You'll never know if you don't take risks." I go back to picking at the fire.

Branches snap behind us. I push myself off of the ground. Alouette only looks over her shoulder, expression more mundane than panicked. Arrows spring out of the ferns. One clips my ear, followed by a drop of blood. I draw the sword from the scabbard at my waist. The alchemist plucks the knife from her boots before jamming them back onto her feet.

A second arrow comes right for her forehead. If she hadn't ducked down, she would've been taken out. I hate archers. She picks my crown up and hurls it at my chest, which I catch it against. Why bother? It has no value to her, but perhaps to someone else. Without taking another glance at me, she charges into the foliage. I follow. We'd be sitting ducks on the cliff. A dark silhouette moves amongst the trees. Alouette stands with her back against mine. Another assailant catches my eye. Then one more. The odds aren't in our favor. Really, they never are. My grip tightens around the hilt of a sword I took from the castle before coming here. The slim blade reflects the moonlight, making us a target. One attacker lunges out of the bramble. I deflect her dagger with my sword and turn her toward the ground. The leaves crunch below. A woman groans.

Blades scratch behind me. Alouette grabs my arm and pulls me around, so that we swap places.

"I'm not fighting at your side because I like you," she has to snarl at me.

She pins my attacker to the ground with her foot as I take on her opponent. He swings his sword at my feet. I block his blade with mine.

I won't let her words slip under my skin. "A shame, really."

Another arrow splinters the air between us. A tree takes the blunt. Teeth glint in the moonlight, grinning at me. Was it a warning shot? My foe takes the moment to swing at my face. I turn my cheek so that my jaw takes the hit. A scabbed gash and blooming bruise will be all it brings tomorrow.

Another arrow spirals toward us. Alouette blocks it, the tip digging itself into the cloak I lent her instead of my side. A strange liquid oozes off of the tip. Venom?

"I knocked him out," she mutters.

I deflect another swift attack.

"Find the archer," I tell her.

She glares and disappears into the foliage.

I exchange hits with the swordsman. Overhead. Down. To the side. I'm on the defense.

That's until he trips. With my boot, I take the chance to kick him in the stomach. He crashes onto his back. I wedge the sword in the prickers beside his ear. Inches over, I could've taken his life.

In the bushes behind him, yellow eyes peer up at me. With a blink, they're gone.

Another arrow reaches for the sky. Shouts resound, muffled by the rustling leaves.

"*Stay,*" I command the fallen swordsman as I yank my blade out of the ground.

While I weave through the trees, he won't be able to follow with an enchantment restraining him.

I knock branches out of my way as I follow the scuffling sounds of skirmish. Alouette's mutterings of her deity's name grow closer and closer. Their silhouettes tumble through the trees, into a clearing. I stay within the foliage, waiting for the right time to strike. The branches sway in an unsettling way. With a curse, I raise my hand to my ear. Poisoned twice in barely over a month? My jaw tightens. I've fought during storms before. A little rocking won't throw me off.

Spiraling silver sparkles in the moonlight. Alouette's knife. As the archer draws his own blade, I jump from the thorns and slash at the back of her knees. The last enemy falls. Or not. A blade presses against my throat. Yellow eyes stare into mine.

A sword in one hand, I raise my arms. "You don't need to go that far, Lark."

Though, her attention isn't on me.

"He's mine," the alchemist barks. At whom?

There's no time to ask. The alchemist is pulled to the ground by the archer. Her knife drags down my shirt. The blade doesn't drive into my skin, by some deity's power. Maybe hers. Stepping away, I back into my initial opponent. Her hand reaches for the crown on my head.

I dip my head down. Let her have it. The circlet falls into her hands. Her weapon drops to the ground as she takes it.

"It should be gold," her whisper hisses.

A hand grabs my wrist. "Come on!" Alouette shouts.

The crown isn't gold?

Her grip lets loose; she doesn't stop for me. I'm frozen, watching as my opponent trades the crown for her knife.

"It's evidence," another grunts.

Come on.

It's time to go. I know!

I sprint after Alouette, stumbling to avoid arrows soaring past me, abundant as sea spray. Ahead, the alchemist tugs to untie my mare's lead from the tree where I left her. The trio pursuing us exchanges shouts and squabbles about the crown. Three voices. The enchantment has worn off. I shouldn't have expected it to stay.

Alouette throws herself onto the horse. My boots stomp over flowers as I run after her. I make out her frown in the darkness. The mare turns away from me.

I curse again. Arrows strike at my heels. My pace quickens.

Once I'm close enough, I grab the rein and pull myself up behind Alouette. The mare rises to her hind legs, kicking up into the air. I can feel myself free falling. My hands claw at Alouette to find a grip. The next moment, we're slamming back on the ground. As the mare gallops, I'm pressed against Alouette, arms curled around her.

The alchemist snickers. "You can't ride horseback?"

My teeth grinding, I respond, "Not well. I'm a seafarer. This isn't my turf."

"You're a king. It is now."

I tear my head off of her shoulder to look behind us. Three dark figures stand in the distance.

"I don't want it to be."

Alouette shakes her head. "You're so confusing, Atlas. You don't want to be king, but you took the crown anyway. You say it's for me, but what have you done but…" She sighs and leaves the sentence unfinished, like a half-written letter crumpled up, thrown to the side.

"I'll tell you tomorrow."

She scoffs.

"Really, I promise. I swear. Please. I'll show you everything. You won't regret it. Then everything can go back to normal."

"There is no normal," she spits. "It hasn't been normal in years, not without my father."

"It will be normal, I promise. You have my word."

"Your words have meant nothing so far."

"Does my heart count?"

She contemplates her next words.

A laugh follows. "Sure, Atlas. And you promise everything will be back to *my* normal?"

"Yes." I speak a little too fast. "Well, kind of. Mostly. Yes. Alouette, yes."

Her sharp gaze mellows, drifting off to the midnight meadows. Frazzled flowers loosely sit in her hair, having survived the skirmish. Her fingers splay out to run through the mare's ebony mane. They're unsteady, almost trembling. She's no monster. Not in my eyes.

"If you're lying, I get to drive a stake through your heart. I'll show it to your crew and your mother and your father and everyone who cares about you." Or, maybe she's a little bit of one. She adds, "While it's still beating. So, you still promise?"

"More than anything."

She slowly nods along, bringing the horse to a trot. There must be a lot on her mind, more thoughts than wrecked ships at the bottom of Davy Jones. Normal is her father. *The* alchemist. In her world, she's just his daughter. In mine, she's my alchemist. The feisty, stubborn one that will sprout spikes from any surface. The one that no matter what bramble she gets tangled up in, she adapts to the briar. The alchemist that brings a new lens to every little thing she sees, who does not stop until she understands. Perhaps that is why she has not left me.

Maybe she's mean and blunt and cruel at times. With no family and very few friends, if any at all, someone like her is just going through the motions of surviving. Besides, take our assassins and those wanted posters for example. The world wants her dead. Somehow, she has defied fate, going against the odds stacked like cargo crates against her.

"An arrow got you, didn't it?" She's not amused.

I lift my head, realizing that I had drifted off.

"*Grazed* me," I correct her.

"Fine, one *grazed* you. That crown on your head is a target. Cover it up or learn how to protect yourself."

I disregard her demand. I'm well-aware. "Who were they, Alouette? You knew what the bandits were after."

"It doesn't take much to realize that a king's golden circlet is worth more than most thieves out here. They're land pirates for your purposes. Jumping from trees. Crawling out of shadows."

"They come after you, too, don't they?" My eyes narrow. She shrugs, which, usually, I don't take as a proper response, especially from Edwin. Somehow I can always make exceptions for her, unapologetically. Besides, her gesture is enough of an answer.

"One said the crown was evidence." I keep my voice low.

She stills.

"Then they think you're a decoy…" her words fall short. I have a good idea as to what the alternative is.

I place a hand on her shoulder. To my surprise, she doesn't knock me away. "…or they know it's you."

The walls come back into view, citadels lit with fires and all. If I got the chance to leave this port forever, I'd snatch it in an instant. Perhaps I'd leave my father behind. Would it be right? No. He could set sail on his own. But at least now I understand how Alouette sees this place. There's nothing here that we couldn't seek out somewhere else. Wine. Tea. Gold. Helping hands for the deck.

I'll admit it, the salty breeze at sea can't compare to the way the midnight wind blows through my hair on the back of a galloping horse. Alouette pulls up her hood as she slows the mare down to a trot. Guards sit on crates at the entrance, playing with dusty cards on the dirt path below. One has a pile of rocks, presumably from a bet. Once they look up to meet my stare, they spring to their feet and their salute. I narrow my eyes. The guilty rarely have enough guts to cast the first stone.

The alchemist avoids any attention.

"Where do we go from here?" she whispers once we're through the gates.

"Do you want to keep her?" I reach around the alchemist to stroke the mare's mane, now laced with some of the leftover wildflowers.

Alouette turns over her shoulder, lips curled to bear her grin, which nearly glows in the moonlight. "Really?"

"If you go on any other excursions, promise me you'll come back."

As much as I long to leave this place behind in my wake, I can't. I'm tied here, wrapped around the posts of these docks. My blood has spread through these waters as they run through my veins.

"Why's that?" Alouette tilts her head.

I try sliding off of the horse. Instead, I slip, only to have Alouette catch me by the wrist. Once my feet hit the ground, I put my hand over hers. "It's not worth letting go of you."

What follows is between a laugh and a scoff. "Maybe I'd agree."

Then there's a crack. From my elbow. I mutter off a string of curses. "Why do you keep doing that?"

She shrugs and leads the horse away.

"Wait." I hold my hand out. It's silly, petty, foolish of me. Her yellow eyes peer through the night. "Tomorrow. In front of the throne. I'll show you."

Hooves clack against the cobblestone street to an unfamiliar rhythm.

"Please?"

Chapter 44

— The Alchemist —

"I LOVE HIM, I love him not." One by one, flower petals fall to the ground. A whole bouquet must've been used by now.

"Edwin, is this really necessary?" I knot the stems together in frustration.

He plucks the delicate petals off with a pinch of his nimble fingertips. "I love him, I love him not." He drops the poor, stripped plant onto the mosaic table. "This is for your sake, y'know."

"Isn't it a bit…*cliche*?" Sitting across from him at our usual spot, I pick up his fallen flower and add the stem to my tangled collection.

He goes for his next victim. "Atlas is a strange guy. You either love him or you hate him. Our crew loves Capt'n. Perhaps they see his ol' man DeLuca in the way he holds himself, even in the authority his voice has over our mates. You wouldn't know, really, Alouette. Capt'n melts away when he's around you." A snicker follows while another handful of petals flop down in one swell tug. "You're just frustrated because you can't decide how he makes you feel." His smile eases into his eyes, his ruby fake and the gap in his left brow. "Like, I used to think you were cool, but weird. You're still weird, and basically a walking knot of prickers. Dangerous, but aren't we all, really? Some people take a liking to that."

I pick at my crepe, rubbing strawberry jam off my fingers and onto a wax wrapping. It's sweet. Sweeter than the bitter decision I'm faced with, at least. "If you know so much, what do you think?"

His laughs, a little embarrassed if I could tag it with an emotion. "Follow your heart? It's cheesy." The boatswain reaches for his tea. I reach to stop him, but it's no use. He's going to do whatever he pleases either way. "You'd know if this was the wrong move if you weren't compelled to see him, plus," he pauses with a sip, "I believe he has something for you—something you want."

With a wink, he'll tell no more.

▽ ☖ ▽ △

I took the wax to go, although I had polished off the crepe. My tongue laps every last bit of remaining jam and cream. If I paid for all of it, I'm going to eat every last crumb.

A tinge in my chest pierces as my eyes catch on the guards. Last time I came here—I'd rather not recall. My scabbed palm shows enough of the story. The guards let me in without question. Atlas knows who to expect now. Servants run around the lobby, per usual, carrying baskets and rolling carts. One of which has half of an extravagant cake. They say that's how the other half lives, with luxuries, but I believe it is only a select few. Another hole digs at my chest when my eyes slide across the marble floor. Flawless, fixed. Unlike magic, alchemy does not release after spells wear off. Chemical changes cannot be undone unless transmuted or synthesized again. Who else would know this?

The young man who took the first jab yelps once he realizes who I am. He doesn't apologize, though that shouldn't be expected. The knights' armor clinks and clanks as they ready themselves for my potential next moves.

"Atlas. I am here to see *him*, upon his request," I announce myself, although, really, no one should have to. People best keep their actions and motives to themselves. Guards bow to me. Maybe Atlas warned them about trying to cross an alchemist again. Common knowledge should be that my path is riddled with false riches and spilled blood. The double doors part for me to enter.

Never had I ever thought there was a wrong way to sit on a throne, until now. Chin tipped to the sky, Atlas leans his back on one of the golden armrests, his legs kicked over the other. A mostly-eaten slice of that cake rests in his hands. A new circlet rests crooked on his brow. There's no shortage of treasures in this kingdom.

"Alouette." He swings his legs over the side and stands.

"Really? Cake?" The captain has gotten accustomed to the life of the top few, hasn't he?

"Would've been rude to decline." Or maybe not. He holds the white porcelain plate out to me. I shake my head.

"I'm only here to see you hold up your end of what you said last night. If you don't follow through, I hope you'll remember what I told you."

"Drive a blade through my heart and flaunt it in front of everyone who loves me? You got the point across." He hands the plate off to a servant, telling her that she could finish it. She scarfs it down. No hesitation.

His fingers reach for mine as we march down the hall. Two guards trail close behind. My mind cannot begin to imagine what he has to show me, but, by the look on his face, he thinks it'll be groundbreaking, earth-shattering, realm-collapsing. My chest tightens while my throat threatens to close up on me. He's trustworthy, right? The halls feel like a labyrinth to me, a wanderer of open grasslands, but this royal maze is nothing to a navigator like Atlas.

He pauses in the middle of one corridor and reaches for a light fixture. After the lamp is pulled down like a lever, the wall opens to reveal a dark passage. Atlas takes the lead.

A spiraling staircase takes us underneath the ground floor, like Alice down the rabbit hole. What lies beneath is no Wonderland. Atlas takes a flaming torch off of the wall that flickers to light up the crumbling steps. A dungeon?

We reach the final landing at the bottom, which happens to be a musty dirt floor. A door crafted of iron bars stands between us and another cell that lies around the corner. Atlas pulls a key from his pocket—the same one he used on the ship. I raise my brows.

"It's enchanted," he whispers as he clicks it into the lock. That explains why it's called the *master* key.

He sets the torch aside and pushes the squeaking gate open with held breath.

"Who goes there?" a rough voice asks.

No, it can't be. Not who I have in mind.

My eyes snap open as they shoot to Atlas. He gestures for me to enter. More torches flare up as we trudge deeper into the cell, as if to light the way and reveal the path before us.

Lab equipment litters the place. Glowing liquids fill glass beakers. Machinery covers the walls. Chains string the walls like garland. A man stands in the center. Not just any man.

My father.

He's alive.

I can't feel my legs as I run up to him. *He's alive.*

His arms embrace me. I think, but I'm too numb and overcome by thoughts. Tears burn my eyes as I press the side of my head against his chest, almost to check for a heartbeat. He's alive.

His hands pull me away so that our eyes can meet. He's the only one with the same yellow irises he once claimed were a gift from Celestia. Ones that only the alchemist and his daughter bear. My father leans down, a trembling hand on my cheek. The glossy sheen on his eyes, I've only seen once before at his wife's grave. Celestia has drawn many new lines across his face, like an old scrap of parchment folded over and over again. White and silver lines streak across his untamed hair, which colors once matched mine.

"You're alive," I blubber, as if that is all I can say. There's too much to cover, so much he's missed, a lot to catch up on.

"You are too. Never doubted it." He hugs me again. I don't want to let go, even when he does. I guess he's had to do it a multitude of times. A hand on either of my shoulders, he grounds me. With a thumb, he rubs the tears off of my cheeks. "Look how much you've grown. Learned a lot, hm?" He raises his brows as eyes fall on the captain behind me.

Atlas blinks a few times, surprised that I've turned to see him. This was his plan all along, the one that I fought so hard against, wasn't it? Why wouldn't I accept that?

And we're going through these motions all over again.

Was this the kind of love he described? Unconditional. A little sacrificial.

I haven't experimented enough to observe, so how would I know?

I rub my own tears with my forearm as I stride over to the crowned captain. He gestures for me to go back to my father. I grab onto his hand and yank him over with a stumble. Atlas is the next to get the wrath of my embrace, which could be compared to abdominal strangulation. He looks to my dad before wrapping one arm around me and placing the other on my father's shoulder.

"I'll have a meal prepared. We'll all dine together." He nods and pulls away. Admittedly, I'm a little sad to see him go. My father watches his departure with a weathered smile.

"Who is he? Your knight in shining armor? Or perhaps clad in black?"

"Far from." I pick at the tears and disheveled lashes from my eyes.

He laughs and pats me on the back. "Bold kid. DeLuca's, is he not?"

"Your words, not mine."

"You've got to tell me all about him."

"Not until you show me all of this." I gesture to one of his many, many workbenches in the dungeon. Notebooks piled on scattered etchings, leather-bound and shredded paper and crumpled up around the corners. Glass bottles plink when I tap them with my nails. Glowing solutions bubble inside, breaking the surface like the child inside of me I've repressed for so long. I flip through his journals, adorned with his etched handwriting, jotting down Celestia's creation.

He stops me by placing his hand on mine. That's when I realize it isn't his. No, not anymore. It's a mechanical gauntlet. Wires run up a metal arm, tucked beneath his rolled-up sleeve.

"Father," my breath stops short. Shaking my head, I raise my gaze to pinpoint his. "What did they do to you?"

"Nothing you need to worry about." He places his other hand for me to see. It matches mine with constellations and runes for transmutations all over. Except for one thing. They're burnt into his skin. A seared, faded red. They're branded scars. Mine are only tattoos. A reminder of how my studies could have been much more painful and far more tedious. His father, my grandfather, had an even harder time, chained to a man he was indentured to serve for a seemingly infinite debt. My father told me stories of grandfathers' own scars, whittled carvings in his own skin. "Just remember that Celestia won't replace a limb, no matter how much you beg."

I slowly nod. "Of course, Father."

"Well!" His golden eyes brighten as he swings his arms to march across the room, leading me to a wall of papers plastered onto the stone bricks. "Do I have exciting news for you."

His lips pull to reveal his crooked smile, full of misaligned and stained teeth. Still, not as bad as a pirate's.

"And I thought Atlas' news was exciting." I pursue him, jogging back to his side, where I once lived, where I belong.

"You remember the Elixir, right?"

I nod, a little jittery with anticipation.

"And Czar?"

"Do you even have to ask?" I roll my eyes. That story raised me. "He's like a *great* grandfather."

"That's my girl." He presses his mechanical hand on the wall of cream-colored papers. "These—they're all from him."

Words flee, escaping me. I skim the wall with my fingertips. My hands stop to see his name signed in swirling curls at the bottom of every page. *Czar.* These cannot be fabricated. My father only knows print.

"He—I—You—Czar—Uh." My jagged words don't come out as they should.

"Crazy, right? The tyrant of Apthnorath is indeed my penpal."

"He's still alive." My breathless words make me sound foolish. Really, it's a miracle he hasn't been impaled by a rod of Philosopher's Stone. The restlessness and resent of war torn countries rip totalitarians apart. Remember what he did to his own Gods.

My father pulls down a letter and hands it to me. My unsteady hands do not deserve this. The fable, the knowledge, the power.

Dear Thierry Le Rois.

My father's name in the script of a man from legends. I swallow the lump in my throat as I push on to read the rest. His handwriting, although cursive, is quick and scribbled and quite frankly a mess.

I read one note aloud. "Strange interest you have, my friend. Does my hair grow? No. Nothing changes. Between us, I'm too scared to shave the stubble that remains." My anxieties fade into snickers. This is the man I always wanted to learn more about? And he calls my father a friend?

"Fascinating, no?"

My father tugs more yellowed papers from his wall and hands them off to me by the fistfull. A smile intoxicated by dopamine and the thrill of wisdom overtakes my face. I'm very greedy when it comes to learning, especially leeching off of my father's works.

He drags over a wooden stool for me to sit. His seat gets taken on the floor as he looks up at me, as eager as a school boy. A little like Atlas. I scan the letters.

"Ophiuchus? Is that her? His wife?" I pry. "And he has a son now?"

"Adopted son." My father shrugs and urges me to read on.

I press my lips together and blink to fight back tears. Atlas promised me normal, but my father has presented me with so much more. Everything I've ever dreamed.

Czar felt the same way, years and years and years ago. A nation of his own. An iron fist. A loyal following. But he was missing something. Love, he admitted. Love. Friends. Trust.

As of last year, he locked the doors to his fortress, his residence, his room. Supposedly, he has a son, but they're separate, similar to my father and myself. Sometimes the tyrant would cry but never shed a drop of blood. Alone for years. His most loyal military generals died left and right, for their lives were the price of expanding such an empire. He would not bat an eye; he could not bat an eye. Weakness was not to be shown, not to his subjects, not to anyone.

Although we're realms apart, he's a little like me.

He's no alchemist, but he makes requests of Celestia all the time. I wonder if she ever gets annoyed. Between the three of us, that is. Czar, my father and I.

"He wrote you a letter, too." He pulls down an envelope, still sealed with red wax. It's the same shade of red I imagined his cloak to be. A little like rose red but not far from fresh blood. *Alouette* swirls in delicate letters on the front. He must've taken his time with this one. My nails dig to pry it open.

▽△▽△

This is everything.

Once I'm finished reading, I hold it close to my chest.

The last words cling to me like magnets.

Man fears death because he loves living. Only when his life loses glamor and gold does he make peace with death.

So, live. Live, Lark. Live. Love a little.

▽△▽△

I lead my father up the staircase, up toward the ground floor. A chopped shackle drags from his ankle, scraping against every stone step. Our snickers and exchanged words echo. Once we reach the top, the light from the many windows nearly blinds me.

Back against the wall, Atlas is waiting for us. With a leather glove tucked under his arm and by the way he's examining his own nails, I'm guessing that he's been here a while.

"Retractable?" my father asks.

Atlas curls his fingers. Sharp talons extend. The captain blinks a few times. "Apparently so." With an appalled shake of his hand, his nails return to their usual state, and he slips his glove back on.

"Sirens are dangerous creatures," my father comments as Atlas takes the lead. I walk in line with my kin.

"Alouette is, too," Atlas affirms.

"A dangerous creature? Me?"

"Says the girl who threatened to carve my heart out on multiple occasions, and on one you warned you'd show it to everyone I loved. Still beating."

I look away, anywhere but at him. He has spent the past month trying to prove himself trustworthy.

"You kept your word, so I won't have to."

My father stares at me. I'm not the girl he remembers. I'm greedy and cold and brutal. Graceless, to say the least. With him here, I wonder if I'll go back to the girl I once was. The child who embraced kindness and curiosity and fondness for all of Celestia's creation.

"My family and crew will be forever grateful." His sarcasm gets an amused smirk to tug at my lips. If he's trying to look good in front of my father, he's surely going about it in an odd way. Calling me dangerous and then hinting at his values. Rosaline had been right to a point. He's a schemer, without a doubt. I trot ahead to land a spot beside Atlas.

Czar's words echo in my mind with the low, gruff voice I always imagined he'd have.

▽△▽△

Edwin waits, legs kicked up on the longest dinner table I've ever seen. Obviously, he has taken his seat at one end, marking his position at the head.

"The alchemist?" His brown eye brightens while his ruby one glitters under the intricate chandeliers that line the dining hall. Crystalline gravy boats might as well be hanging from the ceiling.

My father nods and pats the brown apron tied around his waist, which is filled by plenty of test tubes and small tools.

Edwin points to his face. "Your complexions match."

My father pulls a chair for himself and takes a seat beside Edwin. "She has her mother's face. It would be a shame if she took after me." The two clink glasses of water, acquaintances already. I sit on the boatswain's other side.

"The light hits your eyes the same." Atlas crosses his arms and puts his weight against the back of Edwin's ornate spruce chair. His crewmate pays no mind and reaches for one of the little sandwiches in the center of the table, stacked in pyramids on plates. Fresh fruit of various colors rests beside in bowls. This kingdom sure knows how to trade for delicacies. I heard they tax each and every transaction in this port—not to mention the farmers and a few feudal lords that live right outside the wall who must pay to maintain control over their fief. Atlas probably doesn't get a cut of that. With his stance, it'll go right past him to the dying former king and nobles.

▽☖▽△

After lunch, Edwin takes off with my father to give him a tour of the castle, for Atlas has been showing his closest crewmates around for the last few weeks. I decide to stay back. After this, I'll have the rest of my life to spend time with my family. Edwin won't. He'll be back at sea soon, along with Atlas and Jacques and the rest of the crew. I feel so small, so minuscule in this hall with its high ceilings and windows that tower at least a dozen feet above us.

"Guessing you don't want a tour?" Atlas gives me a crooked smile. He's either forcing one or trying his best to hold one back, but it isn't clear which one. The captain catches himself and charts a new course for the conversation. "You don't need to say anything. You don't have to like me, Alouette." His fingers push off the chair as he approaches the window. Golden swirls on his tunic remind me of the way waves curl before crashing down on the shore.

"Perhaps I'm selfish. I wouldn't let go of you for the world. Technically, I seized an entire kingdom just to bring your father back to you.

"I chose to take the crown against my better judgment, knowing that it could drive me into ruin just as it did to the king. But I'd be bringing a family back together, and to overlook that would be wrong. Choices don't come easy. Not to you, not to me. But this, this was the first time what I want and what is right align like the stars."

I slowly shove my chair out, which screeches against the floor under my weight. My feet tap over to him, only stopping once they're beside his.

"They're always out there, you know. We just can't see the rest because of the sun. It's too bright." I press my hand against the window.

"The stars? Well, there's another I can see all the time."

"Which one?"

"Polaris."

"Really?" I scan the sky. Weightless clouds drift above the churning sea. The sun overtakes the rest of his friends. Perhaps our dear Soleil is the one he means. His hand reaches for mine. I let him take it.

"You are my Polaris."

The way he says it with a straight face, he doesn't even bat an eye. I giggle a little, still delirious with an unfamiliar kind of delight from earlier.

He quickly adds in his defense, "Well, you remind me as to why I followed through with the king's offer, so I don't lose sight of myself with all the cake and riches. Gold is rather suffocating you know."

"Oh? Gold? Then do I take your breath away?"

"Yes. Yes you do."

His sincerity silences us for a minute. Then laughter follows. I don't quite know what to say.

"Is thank you enough?"

He arches a brow. "I said you don't need to say anything."

"That doesn't answer my question."

Atlas grants me a smile, which eases all the way into the dull scar on his cheek. "Thank you does cover it." He lifts his arms and tugs at the fingers of his gloves, pulling them away from the tips before adjusting. Combined with his narrowed eyes in the late-summer afternoon's light, I'm reminded of cats kneading biscuits with their paws. "Your life can go back to normal now, Alouette."

Normal. I'd love to take up his offer, but I'm not sure if that's what I want anymore. The letters from Czar, my father's mechanical arm. Too much has changed to go back. "If I recall, there's a spot on your crew for me. First mate or *not*," I set the stage for him to pick up the next line.

"If I recall, someone gets quite seasick."

I shrug. "Nothing a little ginger beer can't fix. Besides, I'm no longer sick of you."

"Sick of me?" He lets out an awkward, almost embarrassed laugh.

I nudge him before resting my head against his shoulder. "Don't think too much about it."

Almost instinctively, he wraps an arm around me in return. If I had the chance, I'd stay by his side, just like this. Preferably forever.

Embarrassingly so, I proceed to ask, "Atlas?" He tilts his head toward me, accompanied by a faint hum. "Why did you love me?"

Lashes low, his eyes linger on my face. "I thought I told you. Well, not the part that I envied you a little at first—"

I'm breathless. "*Really?*"

"Yeah, I know. But I thought that maybe if I got closer to you, I could be more like you." His fingertips barely brush mine. His gaze "You don't hide; you don't run. You know what's yours and stand your ground." As his gaze meets me once more, a smile plays across his face, rounding the jagged scar on his cheek. "And, don't you forget, I still *do* love you."

I yank a sharp inhale. "And what if I loved you, too?"

While a rosy shade of red swallows his cheeks, swelling his blue eyes, my own skin prickles with thorns and briars of the thought that perhaps I do, I *really* do.

"First, I'd be surprised." He shrugs off his bashful demeanor "Then, perhaps the happiest captain to ever dock his ship in this port."

"I bet you'd be even happier to set sail." I nudge him, playfully, rather than in the gut where it hurts.

He squeezes back, bringing me to his side. "Only with you."

Chapter 45

— The Thief —

I KICK THE kitchen doors open. What? My hands are full. Atlas told me about this phenomenal cake, and, boy, was he right about it. I scraped all of the frosting off first, so it's in a glob on the side of my plate. Don't worry too much, I'm not wasting it. Saving the best for last, that's all.

Thierry, Monsieur Le Rois, whatever you want to call the alchemist, trails behind. He's also got a slice. Though, he must've taken a serving of weariness after being locked away for years. His eyes squint, brows furrowed. Not to mention his face is covered in soot. His vest, too, mixed with loose stitching and patches.

"Did they feed you?"

"Do I look like I can perform photosynthesis to you?"

His remark turns the heads of a few cooks.

"Photo-what-now?" I lean against the center counter and slip one of the chopped carrots onto my plate, next to the cake.

"Yes. The king gave me rations. You can't starve workers."

"With those living arrangements, I dare say you were a prisoner." I stab my treat and drag the prongs to make an awful screech. The poor bakers and cooks wince. The alchemist has no response. Instead, he stands beside me and wolfs his portion down. The man eats like a rabid dog. I'm willing to bet my own rations from the ship that he was given scraps and stale leftovers to live off of.

Voices shout from the other end of the kitchen.

"One of you must know where your ruler is."

I look over my shoulder. Wouldn't you know? By the bejeweled circlet on his brow, it's another king or entitled brat. The two blend, really.

"It is I, Jayin of Vaughan."

He approaches one servant. She quickly bows, clearly unsure of what to do. "You. You must know where he is."

"H-he handed me a lovely slice of cake in the main hall."

"He's not there! Useless—"

"Aye!" I call.

The moment he turns to us, the alchemist drops to his knee, head bowed so that it cannot be seen over the counter.

I point my fork right at him. "He's in the dining hall."

"Take me there!"

"No." I gesture to my cake. Such a rude man will not interrupt my mid-afternoon snack. Instead, I provide him with instructions for the long way around. It'll give him a nice tour of the castle. Take 'em past all of the statues and fine art on display. Rich people like that.

He scoffs and takes his leave.

Once he departs, I toss my fork aside and pluck the frosting up with my fingers. It's time to find Atlas before this Jayin of Vaughan does, especially if this entitled young man poses a threat to the alchemist. Before now, I didn't realize that was possible.

Alouette's pretty fearless. She didn't even resist when those pirates threw her off the plank. The plate gets tossed aside.

The alchemist stands. He knows there's a shorter route. We took it here. I take the lead, sprinting. He huffs behind me.

"Who was that?" I press.

"Find the boy king first. I'll explain then."

I slide around a slick corner and nearly slam into the wall. Whoops. These marble floors have less resistance than wooden planks. I throw myself against double doors leading to the hall. The alchemist catches them behind me.

I shout, "Jayin of Vaughan!?"

Atlas whips around to look at me. "Why is he here?"

I look over at the elder alchemist, the two of us out of breath.

"My father was indentured to him."

Two ends meet. Now serving the king here, he had escaped a debt to Jayin.

"How does he know you're here?" Atlas marches over.

Alouette's brows frown. "He knows I'm here. The soldiers must have relayed the incident back at the other port after putting their muskets away."

Her father draws a deep breath in. "Alouette."

"I know. I should've stayed away."

"We have to go. Now." The alchemist turns and opens the doors.

Alouette raises her hand to stop him.

"Do you want to die?" The way his lips pull to bare his teeth remind me of his daughter.

She plants her feet, beside my captain. "I'm not leaving. We're not running."

"We'll be safe when we're gone. Your Majesty, thank you, but you must forget us. You know nothing of this deal when Jayin of Vaughan asks."

"If you are indentured, there must be a price we can pay."

"For my father's debt and three generations running away? It's something you cannot cover, not in your lifetime." Le Rois shakes his head.

"Furious fancy pants will be here soon," I grumble. People love to debate, don't they? Or, whether realized or not, they like to hear the rasp of their own raised voice.

Atlas makes eye contact with Alouette's father, his gaze as cold as the northern seas. Although crooked, his crown serves as a reminder of his authority, no matter how little regard the alchemist holds for it.

"Wait on my ship."

Alouette goes to protest.

"We'll sort this out from there. Take your father."

The captain's orders are final.

Alouette's heavy steps trek toward her father. The two exit side by side, as if their synchronized footsteps and similar set-back shoulders had been rehearsed.

Jayin throws the far doors open. I clap my hands together. It's showtime.

He points at me. "You."

"Me," I reply, dramatically, running my fingers through my hair to flip my bangs back. I've got to show him the dash through my brow, which many equate with ruffians.

"How did you get here? You tricked me, didn't you?" His stare pivots from me to Atlas. "And where's the king?"

"You're looking right at him." I lift an arm as a gesture to my captain, or, rather, His Highness. Jayin's reaction is beyond satisfactory. He's holding back a scoff, choking on an insult.

"So that's what they meant by DeLuca."

"Son of the legendary *Aurora Borealis'* captain." If I can't brag about the legacy my father failed to leave behind, I'll drain Atlas' ancestry for all it's worth. Besides, Jayin's wicked expression is worth every moment of adding honor to the DeLuca name, even if it's not backed by the gold standard.

Meanwhile, Atlas has approached this vile man, so that they stand toe-to-toe, not quite eye-to-eye due to their height difference. Surely a six-foot-something half-siren is intimidating enough to strike some sense, and possibly respect, into this young man. He's not too much older than Atlas, mid-to-late-twenties at most. He lifts his chin and straightens his pristine deep blue jacket, attempting to get the same effect as a pirate sharpening his cutlass. A failed attempt, really. The captain is far more intimidating, especially as a king, no matter how young or inexperienced he may be.

Anyway, I'm here, by his side, armed with a dagger. This princeling wields a silver tongue, if anything at all.

"The king providing sanctuary for the alchemist has been brought to my attention."

Atlas keeps a straight face. He's not going to reply until Jayin continues.

The young man takes a deep breath in and presses his finger tips together. "In case the late king has not informed you, the Le Rois family belongs to mine, for they are descendants of a man who once served my father."

"*Three generations running away,*" I recite the alchemist's words under my breath.

Atlas holds his tongue. His narrow stare is enough to bead sweat on his rival's forehead.

"I ask for you to hand them over."

My captain's tone cuts like a blade. "I refuse."

"You know his daughter made a mess of my street. That quarrel of yours did not go undocumented."

"And you believe I continue to associate myself with her?" Atlas pulls out a chair and sits, crossing his legs, leaning back, almost relaxed. He pours two glasses of wine. One stays in his hand while the other is pushed to Jayin. "Do inform me why."

Jayin blubbers. To fill the empty space between them, he reaches for a glass and tips it back. I find my place beside Atlas' chair. This princeling has made the first mistake, so now it's up to the captain to not slip up.

"I have evidence."

"Is that so?" Atlas' straight face remains flat, unamused. I find it almost enchanting how he can hold himself when Alouette is not around.

Jayin nods.

"Let me guess. You sent three assassins to follow the two of us."

He nearly chokes on the remainder of his wine. "What makes you so sure of that?"

Atlas slides his hand to the side of his head, lifting his hair to reveal a scab. "An archer said that my altered crown was evidence. Evidence for what, Jayin?"

The young man presses himself against the velvety back of his chair, his eyes plastered on the tiny wound. He's got the helpless stare of guilt I know too well.

I clap my hands together. "Shame, harming the king is quite the crime."

"Look, I-I didn't mean to—"

"Gottem." I hold my fist out to Atlas. He only gives me the pleasure of a smirk. Better than nothing. Jayin shouldn't realize that we're a tag-team. He then holds up a gloved hand to silence me.

"He's right, Jayin of Vaughan. We can either press charges or drop this to let you walk away a free man under the condition that you leave the Le Rois alchemists alone."

Jayin refuses. "No. The alchemist and his daughter are worth much more than an arrow clipping your ear."

"Sure, the Elixir of Life is."

"Then you understand why I will not leave this kingdom without the alchemist. I have a family back home. And the ill. Ill kin."

From his blubbering, I can't tell if he's bluffing by making excuses up on the spot or actually letting his real concerns spill out.

Atlas raises his glass, stopping short of his lips. Does he not know what to say?

"Rather, I understand why he left."

His hushed voice rings through the hall. He might as well have lit a bomb's fuse with Jayin's face growing red-hot.

"I wish to speak with *the* king. He made this deal. You know not the motives nor the terms." Jayin's fingers strain around his glass as he stands. Atlas' eyes follow, cold under the shadow cast by his dark bangs.

His silence equates to refusal.

"Fine. Bring me to the alchemist."

Atlas keeps quiet.

Neither of us know to where Alouette and Le Rois have run off, if they have even left castle grounds. His icy glare hides our shared frustration.

"As I said, you may accept punishment for the attack or receive innocence in exchange for the Le Rois' freedom." Atlas rises to his full height; Jayin should surely be humbled.

"Press charges if you so desire. I am not leaving without the alchemist and his daughter."

He reaches into his back pocket, slipping something out from under his tailcoat. Not a knife. It's something far, far more deadly.

A lone shot fires.

Chapter 46

— The Alchemist —

I SIT NEXT to *Aurora Borealis*, legs kicked off of the dock, feet in the water. Her shadow protects us from the late summer's sun. Masts flutter in the breeze. Ropes sway. Her crew bustles around to protect my father. Jean-Jacques had invited me on board. I don't know why I didn't accept his offer nor follow Atlas' instructions. Usually, I'd seek refuge with Ruth at the tavern. He can't get pulled into this. If the man after us covets my father's power, then what would become of a Gifted like him?

Another unlikely companion rests his finned forearms on the wooden board beside me. Every so often, the tip of an emerald-color tail will break the waves' surface.

"You do know what that port is known for, right?" Similar to a feline, nearly akin to a serpent, Calder's eyes narrow in the same way Atlas' do as he peers up at me.

"Doubloons? Wait, no. Alcohol? Indentured servants? How about underpaid workers?"

"Gunpowder."

I think back to the circlet of muskets around me back at the port. "Oh. Alchemists invented that, you know."

"Which is why they want you. The power you wield is dangerous. Whoever your father served will unleash the handiwork of your studies. Queen Farida doesn't dare rival them. Too many of her people come home with bullet holes." His tail fin lifts out of the water. A circular gap cuts through the translucent green.

"Is it new?"

He shakes his head.

"Why doesn't it heal?"

"We're not all sirens like Atlas and my Queen," he mutters and hoists himself onto the dock to sit beside me. Water runs off of his armor in shimmering beads, almost like jewels. "Not all of us can use enchantments. Folk of the sea are not very different from you humans."

"So Atlas would be Gifted like Ruth…" I murmur.

He doesn't let my ramblings confuse him. "Watch out, Alouette." His dripping wet hand presses against mine. "Do not overestimate that traitor's abilities. He may be king, but this kingdom is at the mercy of what other merchants will trade. Its arms come nowhere close to the muskets and pistols that your enemies wield."

I pull my legs out of the water and push myself to my feet.

"He's not a traitor." *Anymore.*

Calder scoffs. "See if he works against his mother again tomorrow."

"Tomorrow?"

"*She's* coming."

▽△▽△

I climb on board *Aurora Borealis*. Calder won't follow. Whether he has rock bottom respect for the captain or fears his motley crew, I didn't bother to ask. The sea must be the safest place for him, beneath the feuding kingdoms and their naval warfare.

I should have realized this sooner. Why my father had refrained from going over the details about that port. Why he had heeded me not to go there but stopped short of providing a proper reason. Why they have gunpowder and muskets and weaponry the other kingdoms fail to obtain.

My father is conversing with Jean-Jacques, the two of them leaning against a cannon. The gritty, onyx-black surface almost sparkles under the sun. Easing all the way into his squinted eyes, the alchemist's grin only grows wider as he converses with the quartermaster. There are new wrinkles alongside his dimples that remind me of the years that have passed since I had last seen him. I'm surely not the same person. With a mechanical arm and an array of new scars, is he the same father I used to know?

See, I had once wished that looking at him would be like staring into a mirror. In a way, that has come true. The same brunette hair and golden tips. Matching eyes. Transmutation circles and alchemical runes and maps of the stars.

But do we share the same values?

He had told me the story of the Le Rois' downfall countless times. I should have feared Jayin of Vaughan. If only I had known. With a deep breath, I look up to the sky, where Celestia may reside. I can often feel Her near, yet to find Her face, I never know where to search.

"Alouette!" he calls.

I want to run over. The girl who missed him so much wants no less than to jump into his arms once more. But I hesitate, frozen by an unfamiliar shock, one that the summer's heat won't melt. Over the years, this is all I had asked for, all I had dreamed of, yet why won't I allow myself to accept, to appreciate that?

My strides are slow, steps creaking across the deck's wooden floorboards. "Why didn't you tell me more about Vaughan? Or Jayin?"

The quartermaster looks to my father. I do, too.

"Some time alone, please?" My father keeps his voice low. Jacques nods, taps his fist on the cannon, which sounds like a gong, and takes his leave. His smile fades a little as he turns to me. "Pirates have much better manners than I had anticipated."

"Yeah, yeah. Some of them do. Hiding information isn't polite."

"It was in your best interest." He shakes his head and lets his gaze fall on the sea, which I thought he had once resented. I once believed that I knew many things, if not most, so that maybe I understood every little aspect of Celestia's creation. Naive. I know. No one needs to remind me. "You are aware as well as I am that knowledge is power, and that power can be dangerous."

"And?" I step toward him.

"I wouldn't want it to bring you harm. Sometimes not knowing is better, especially in this case."

No, ignorance is *not* bliss. Instead of my blood boiling, I find that it freezes, like a million little needles of ice piercing me from the inside out.

"If Jayin had found you, there would've been no need to lie." His metal hand splays its lifeless fingers to run along the cannon. "If this secret had ended with me—" he catches himself.

"Then what?" I nearly spit. He's my father. I know. I know. I know. But we're allowed to get frustrated with each other. We're family.

His warm hand reaches for my shoulder. "You know I love you, Alouette. More than anything else. Your safety comes first and foremost."

"And so you left me?" My question comes out as a whine, the sour pout of a child.

His words remain stern and steady as he presses a hand against his own chest. "I was the biggest danger in your life."

My head shakes, slow jerks to stuttering sways. "A lot has changed."

His hand slides down from my shoulder. There's no more smile. Only a sigh passes through his thin lips before his teeth are bared. "There was no right decision."

Chapter 47

— The Siren —

"You messed that up, big time."

"I know, Edwin! I know!" I lift my hands and throw them back down to the side. He follows close behind me as I tread through the halls, red velvet carpet muffling my footsteps.

If he hadn't missed, no, I can't dwell on that. His bullet went right through the window, shattering a pane, not my friend, not me.

He could have taken my life yesterday, along with Alouette's. He could have barged in, threatening the king at gunpoint to lead him to the alchemist's dungeon. Why didn't he? Why attack with a crossbow, blades, and venom? Maybe I wasn't supposed to put two and two together. After all, I'm a seafarer. An uneducated captain trained only to fight unruly crewmates and unbridled waves. A foolish young man who took up the crown. If that is the way the world sees me, then so be it. The other option would be to burn me at the stake for being a monster, a shame to man for having the sea's blood in his veins. See me as an atrocity, a barbarian, a beast.

It is best for enemies to underestimate me than overestimate my abilities, better if they come ill-prepared.

As strange as it feels for me to note this, Celestia must have shuffled the cards in our favor.

I curse beneath my breath. The former king needs to know.

We come to a halt. My fingers stop short of the doorknob. Knights on either side eye me. Their gauntlets' grip tightens around silver weaponry. Unarmed, I can't help but worry while I swallow my dread.

I grip the doorknob and jerk the door open. Edwin keeps behind me.

The room smells of smoke and burnt wax. The curtains have been drawn open to let the window's light flood the room, yet melted candles scatter every surface. If he's trying some sort of ritual to stay alive, I promise it won't work. Thierry Le Rois made it clear that only the Elixir of Life grants immortality, so that there's no other way to evade mankind's fatality.

I speak first. "Jayin of Vaughan. The deal with Le Rois was to evade his family, no? Seek the Elixir for yourself, not him? Great." I clap my hands together. We'll do this Edwin's way. "We've got an enemy who seeks war."

A grunt responds. "Where's the alchemist?"

"You're not concerned with impending war?"

"Where's the alchemist?"

He should be on *Aurora Borealis*. Is he? There's no way to know. He could have taken Alouette and run away, far, far, far away from this rotten kingdom.

"I…don't know."

"Bring him back."

"I cannot."

"*Now.*"

"No."

"You defied me!"

"I realized that. Know, old man, I am king, and you are no longer. Your time has passed."

Edwin, in a hushed voice, warns, "*Atlas.*"

"I can revoke that entitled privilege of yours. This kingdom will not answer your call. These selfish beckonings of yours are futile—"

"My good sir, it is popular belief that Atlas has been a good king," Edwin interjects, cutting the decrepit man off. "No executions, less hostility among the guards. A scuffle here and there but not bad."

I raise a brow. Really? Commonfolk have noticed? I wouldn't have.

"If you ask me, the people would respond to his command." Edwin's smile beams, glowing with a confident, mischievous aura.

The king sits up. Blankets slide off of him. Attendants rush over to aid him again. His sunken, nearly lifeless eyes stare. "Will they stay once they know what you are?"

I exchanged a rather forced, confused glance with Edwin.

"Don't you mean *who* he is? Tall isn't his only personality trait." And this is why my boatswain is not a salesman.

"Get this thing out of my sight." The king points a jittering finger to Edwin. I step in front of him.

"Kidding, kidding. Do I see a court jester opening? I'm the guy for the job."

I shush him so that he suppresses whatever comes next with another one of his imprudent smiles.

The king's attention lands back on me. "I know what you are, fiend. It is only a matter of time before the whole kingdom knows."

Edwin's face strains, eyes widening. This isn't new. Alouette got to know, so did my crew.

I'll use the alchemist's tactic. I'll be oblivious.

"What do you mean?"

"I know what you are, Fiend."

"I am the king? Dimitri DeLuca's son? Captain of *Aurora Borealis*?"

"The spawn of Farida."

I hold my breath. The attendants all turn to me, face as pale as the castle's marble floors.

"Several have confirmed. My daughter first. Then your father. Tell me, boy. Is this why you took the crown? Did you aim to claim my land in her name?" On the other hand, he's boiling, face the shade of red-hot embers.

"No. That was never my plan. I wanted the alchemist. No family should have been torn apart under the guise of protection."

"Says the foolish boy who left his own," the king sneers before calling upon his guards. "Seize him!"

Chapter 48

— The Thief —

I DON'T CURSE very often, but, surely, this is the occasion.

They threw me out of the room. A jester I appear to be. A fool. Atlas' mother comes tomorrow. Will the dying king pulling the strings have him put to death? Jayin is still out there, his plight unresolved. The stupid crown is a shining target on my captain's head.

This half-siren friend of mine must hold his own. I stomp through the halls. The servants all yield to me. After all, whenever I make an appearance here, it's with the acting king. That makes me look important, like someone who must be respected. I hate that about these people. Appearances are deceiving. I have the nature of a common thief, not some noble or member of the court. The kingdom's folk don't dare look beyond the surface. Very few wish to seek anything beyond their initial perception. I, on the contrary, would love nothing more than to unveil everyone's deepest, darkest, most degrading secrets. Disgraceful? I don't care.

Queen Farida's son has opened my eyes to just how many layers people hide.

A young king. But he's a captain. Son of Dimitri DeLuca. He's got a dark demeanor, but he yields a soft spot for the alchemist's daughter. He loves her, yet, at first, not enough to share his secret with him. If we go further into that, he's a siren. Half-siren, actually. People see him as seductive and dangerous. Yet he will risk his secret to save others. His mother is a queen, tying him back to royalty, but not to the crown he wears.

Though no one will ever catch all of that at first sight.

The king saw him as a puppet, a valuable tool to control. Now, Atlas is a threat. I fear for what will follow.

Especially regarding this Jayin of Vaughan.

Someone calls for me. It's him, isn't it?

"You tricked me, you devil. You must be hiding the alchemist."

I nestle my hands in my pockets, slump my shoulders, and prepare my worst to face him.

"Who? Me? Really?"

He approaches. I look up at him. Just a tiny bit. I wish I could look down on Jayin as Atlas once did. My *slightly*-beneath-average stature doesn't help others find me as intimidating. This princeling is sure to find out how wrong he is about me.

"Yes, you. You scheming liar. That ploy of yours bought enough time for the alchemist to escape with whomever else you're hiding."

"And?" I cock my head to the side.

"There is no *and*," he spits back.

"So, just name calling? Okay then." I pivot on my heel to turn away.

"Wait!"

"Hm?" I glance over my shoulder.

"You can't just leave."

Moving a few paces, I chime. "Yes, I can! Look at me, I'm a free man."

A hand grabs my shoulder and yanks me back. His furrowed brows knot in fury.

"What is your name, lad?"

"Wouldn't you like to know?" I spit.

"I would indeed. Besides, you have no right to decline, pirate."

"Boatswain, actually. It's my official title." I give him my toothiest grin. At least he's intuitive enough to know that a former pirate captain's right hand man would surely not be some silly noble or member of the gentry. "If you really, really want to know, the name's Edwin Winters. Remember it, will ya? Jayin of Vaughan."

"Of course, Edwin." He strains to say my name. "Why don't we make a deal?" In an attempt to look sly, his lips curl into a smirk to rival mine. Shame, I'm a lot better at this. He can't see my concern. Not one bit of it slips through the gleam in my eyes nor the tone of my speech.

I look down the hallway. Precaution is what they call it. I'm just saving my own skin. Good. It's just us. Even if someone happens to catch wind of his offer, I'm innocent until I respond.

"A selfish captain you have, no?"

Wrong.

"He took the crown and ditched your crew, didn't he?"

Half true, mostly wrong.

"Don't you want riches? For a smaller price than your life on the line every time you set sail?"

I see the rhetorical appeal he's trying to make. But he's got me all wrong. I love the thrill of thievery and treason. That'll come out with my counter offer. Let's hear him out first, shall we?

"And if I did?"

"I'd give you anything in my possession for that alchemist. Both of the remaining Le Rois kin. Thierry and Alouette."

I arch a brow. A sign of my intrigue. Fake, of course. "And why do you want the alchemists? Power? Discovery? Unique, aren't they?"

"In short, everything you just covered. You're sharp, Edwin."

He's soothing my ego for the sake of the deal, not because he actually respects me or my ideas.

"Then let me make you an offer." I keep my words clean cut and sharp. "You may have my captain instead. The only son of the siren Queen Farida and the living legend Dimitri DeLuca. Atlas' voice is laced with enchantments and power far beyond changing metals into gold. Want your people to submit? Just use him. Worried about how you'd gain control over him? My captain, I dare say, is in love with the alchemist's daughter. He'd bend a knee to you in order to keep her out of harm's way."

Jayin keeps a straight face.

"Say, if you did want to negotiate, perhaps the Le Rois alchemists would trade places with him. After all, they're supposed to have hearts of gold."

That brings back his grin and holds his hand out to me. Maybe he plans to use Atlas' siren song to bring the alchemists back so he can have it all. Ingenious plan, really, though I'm in no position to theorize his plans in awe. I stare for a moment. It'll be fine. At worst, we'll tick this guy off in the process, making a lethal enemy in the end. Nothing new. I unsheath my dagger and pierce my palm. A dribble of blood skims my skin, drawing a red line that looks far worse than it really is.

With a grimace from him and a smile from me, we shake on it.

"Where is your captain now?"

I laugh. That's the good part. "In the former king's captivity."

Jayin glares at his hand, which has been smeared with my blood. Gross, but a pact through and true. A proud young man like him must respect that.

"Dangerous, that old man claims. But I say he's useful. The siren song, for starters. Knows how to navigate as well as his father did, won't drown like any other hand on deck. He's worth whatever you put on the table for him. That king may even discard my captain for all he cares." All true. Truths not even Atlas wants to admit.

"Fine, Edwin Winters. We hold another negotiation tomorrow, just off-shore. I'll have your captain captive by then. Bring his crew. Bring the alchemists."

I salute. He turns to take his leave. Once he's out of sight, I let out an unholy wheeze. My hand grabs my vest, pulling at the fabric just over my pounding heart.

▽△▽△

Curse this all! I run through the busy streets, dodging people and their senseless gossip. Pirate. King. Scandal. Secrets. Alchemist. Siren. Thief. I swear I hear them all. Before I know it, I'm at DeLuca's porch again, my fist against the door. Pounding. He opens. The stubble on his chin and cheeks make for a darker five o' clock shadow than usual.

"Come to *Boreas*, now."

"Edwin, what is it?" He looks out to the wall. The sun has dipped beneath the towering stacked stones.

"Grab your weapons, quick." I shove past him. His arm grips my shoulder, as Atlas used to before I'd make rash decisions or stop him from going for another bottle.

"I made a deal. Your son's life is on the line."

His grip draws a squeak out of me. That ring of his digs into my skin. I must not squirm. I must not show my fear. Pain. Anguish.

"The king has him. I don't think he wants Atlas to speak with Farida. I don't know what he plans to do. There's this princeling guy—Jayin of Vaughan. I'm sure you've heard of him before. He thinks he's a pretty big deal," I ramble as fast as I can. DeLuca's gaze grows more intense by the second. Atlas, aside from DeLuca's filthy fortune, is the only thing he has left. He has poured his prospects, his crew, and even *Aurora Borealis* into this boy. I'm nothing of value to the former captain. "So I told him to take Atlas instead of the alchemist and Alouette."

"Thierry Le Rois," he utters. "You exchanged *my* son for his family?"

If he were anyone else, I would have drawn my dagger again and sliced his hand clean off his wrist. I can barely get out a mere, "Yes."

"You sick weasel, scurvy dog. Get lost!" DeLuca shoves me to the door, snatching a cutlass on the way.

I'm the only one on Atlas' crew that wasn't a hand-me-down from Dimitri DeLuca. His old man has no real reason to care for me.

"I'm not done!" I cry.

"I am."

The door slams. I throw myself against the wood.

"Listen! Jayin will be the one to get Atlas out of the king's grasp. Go see if you can meet with Farida tomorrow! Put a wedge between them!" I sink to the ground, like an anchored fool. "If we fail and Jayin gets his hands on Capt'n, I-I have a negotiation with him. The alchemist can take his place or we fight. I'm counting on fighting. I need you. Dimitri. Atlas needs you."

The door swings open. My face falls flat on his foyer.

The next thing I know, DeLuca is loading me up with weaponry. He tosses me a mostly-used roll of gauze, which I wrap around my lacerated hand. The man's tight jaw keeps locked shut. There's an unsettling silence between us. I know it's time to leave when he's waiting for me by the door, brand new wine bottle in-hand. The grape never strays too far from the vine.

▽△▽△

Back on *Aurora Borealis*, all of the crewmates salute or remove their hats, for their former captain has made his long-awaited return. Jean-Jacques goes as far as to get on one knee, which is over the top if you ask me.

DeLuca doesn't have time to chew the fat of idle chatter, nor does he want to, for the former captain marches up to Le Rois.

"Happy to see you're catching some rays, Thierry."

The alchemist turns, his golden eyes wide with shining surprise. Alouette does as well. Their postures stiffen.

"My son has been through quite a bit of trouble for you." DeLuca, as Atlas told me, was once known for his offers and dealings between pirate crews. His negotiation skills far exceed mine, and I'd say I'm rather talented when it comes to transactions that serve me well.

"I am indeed indebted to his selfless acts." Le Rois bows his head.

"I must wonder if your daughter would have done the same." DeLuca grips the alchemist's shoulder. "If you truly are birds of a feather, that is."

Meanwhile, Alouette's eyes trace the deck from DeLuca to myself. She disregards the former captain and marches over to me, latching onto my upper arm in the same place the orphanage director used to grab when he dragged me for punishment. Her grip is still strong for a game bird. She yanks me aside as her father quarrels with DeLuca.

"Atlas. Where is he now?" Her teeth gnash.

I raise my brows. "Woah, attached to the captain, are we?"

"Now is not the time nor place for your theatrics."

I swallow hard. "They took him."

"Who?"

"The king's personal guard."

"We need to get him back."

"No. Jayin. Jayin is going to take him in place of you and your father. He'll be able to escape. We can help. He's Farida's son after all. She could aid us, too."

She frowns, not in the disappointed way DeLuca did. She's almost saddened with a tinge of guilt.

Chapter 49

— The Alchemist —

A FEW DAYS ago, I would have cursed his name. Swore to never see him again. If I had gotten my hands on a blade, I would've driven it into his chest.

Not today.

I make my way down the docks again. Calder roams among the sailors and merchants that traverse the rickety old boards. I wonder if Farida has stationed him here. Like me, he wraps himself in a cloak, hood over his head to cover his finned ears and draw attention away from his eyes.

I approach him. "That traitor is rather virtuous, you know. Edwin says he is now held captive by the old king for my sake."

"He'll squirm his way out. He always does." Calder sighs.

I don't feel the same way. A sixth sense of mine, almost like Celestia whispering in my ear, warns me of the impending dangers.

Out of the blue, the dock's crowd parts. A few bow. Some drop to a knee. In a glittering pink dress, the princess stands in the gap, her attention pointed at me. I exchanged a worried glance with Calder. He urges me forward.

"Your Highness." I'm bad with official titles and honorifics.

"He took him!" She runs and throws her arms around me. I stagger back, a little too close to the edge of the dock. Makeup runs down her face like pink and black blood.

"I know, I know." What should be a shaky voice sounds calm. Maybe my subconscious realizes that we cannot have another person panicking, especially her, the young woman to which the captain should've been betrothed.

"Shouldn't you be rejoicing?" Calder arches a brow my way.

The princess steps back. Her eyes flutter to hold back tears. Strange. I've only cried out of rage for Atlas.

"He never hurt me." She raises a handkerchief to her cheeks. "Even though he's a…a…"

"Siren," Calder and I practically say in unison, unphased. At first, the concept is a rather strange one to grasp, but I should've given up questioning Celestia long ago.

"He's not bad. I-I don't want him to die." Her voice falters as she fumbles over each word. I pat the girl on her shoulder. She takes a sharp inhale at the up-close sight of my hand.

"He stole his mother's crown for your hand to get the king's crown." Calder tries to leverage an argument. A complicated one indeed. He gestures to the pearl crown on her head. "He stole it back. Look, you've got the alchemist's replacement."

Instead of recoiling, she gently removes the crown and inspects it before giving me a very, very slow once-over. "You made this?" Her dainty fingers raise the crown to the sky so she can admire the entire accessory.

After a twitch of hesitation, I nod. I'm a criminal anyway, my face formerly on an army of wanted posters.

"It's beautiful." She pauses. "You're beautiful. No wonder he likes you so much."

Tongue-tied, I look to Calder, as if he could offer me the proper response. Really. *As if.* Insults are far easier to combat than compliments. He shrugs me off. Thanks, useless paladin.

"He often spoke of you."

"Oh?" And to think I couldn't be caught any more off guard.

"I was jealous at first. I dreamed of a man like him, only with sights for me." She relishes in her little fantasy with the flutter of her eyelashes, decked out in makeup. "But, oh dear, as you said, he's a siren. Atlas can be all yours, if he isn't already."

Calder leans toward me, using a hand as a shield to keep his words protected from the princess. "And we're sure he never placed an enchantment on her?"

I shrug.

"He said he'd only sing for Alouette."

The paladin frowns at me. That's the answer to his question. No siren songs, no brainwashing enchantments.

I raise my hands in partial surrender. "I'll admit, the last time he sang for me, he did it to heal an arrow I took to the back."

"Don't get indebted to him." Calder throws up his arms.

"He was repaying a favor."

"He's a pirate. He doesn't repay anything."

"Let me see. He saved me from drowning. He paid for a place for me to stay. I almost killed him. Then we fought. Then he kept me from drowning *again.* Then he took the crown to free my father. Now Celestia only knows what kind of mess he's in now." I'm nearly out of breath by the end of rattling off all of his deeds.

Calder's wide eyes blink.

"Not the Atlas you swore to hate? I've been there, Calder. Why don't you play catchup?" The snap comes out with more bite than bark.

He pauses, most definitely wounded. Considering the offer? If we're to make an enemy out of Jayin, Calder is an ally we want on our side, especially when he is filling in as Queen Farida's heir.

"Fine." Begrudging, yet we're taking a step in the right direction.

I gesture to the princess. "Why don't you fill him in, M'lady?"

Calder twitches. Her glittering, gloss-stained smile grows wide.

"What? I thought you—"

"You've got a testimony. I have more pressing business than your petty grudge."

I loosely salute. Without another word, I turn and start my return to *Aurora Borealis*. If I'm not mistaken, Calder and the princess already have the kindling of a conversation started. The cold in my veins feels a little warmer than usual today.

▽△▽△

"So, you refused to tell me about Jayin. I'm not mad." Anymore. "Let's open the closet doors to find all of the skeletons."

I hoist myself onto the side of the ship. I'll sit while he stands.

"I've been communicating with Klaus Czar, as you already know."

I nod. "Yes."

"He also sent me this." My father reaches into his patched vest, fingers slipping into a hidden pocket. He reveals a vile of a strange substance. A viscous liquid. As it slowly moves, the dark surface glimmers, as the night's sky does. Blue, violet, and pink hues appear when the sun hits it right. "The Elixir."

"*The* Elixir?" I press.

"The Elixir of Life."

Chapter 50

— The Siren —

My head still throbs from where they knocked me out with a cutlass' scabbard. Specks of dust and debris dance through the dim light, as if to taunt me. Floating and free. Far from me. Iron chains shackle my wrists to the wall behind me. My arms feel heavy from the strain. I've only been held captive once. That was with Alouette. Now, I'm alone.

There's no calling for help.

Metallic steps approach. The king didn't even bother putting me in a cell. He might as well keep me on display for any passing guard to ridicule and laugh and spit at.

That same knight is back. Apparently, we can't get enough of each other. This dreadful evening, he has let his hair down.

"Have you come to pass judgment?"

His strained straight face resists a grin, twitching slightly at the edges. If I had to guess, he's dreamed of nothing else. He went from turning away, I dare say retreating, from Alouette and I to submitting as one of my subjects. In theory, as the alchemist would say, but not in practice. There's always dissent. No matter what.

"You must think rather highly of me." I force a smile. "Chaining me up like this."

"You're a prisoner."

"And I am far more capable than your entire guard." I hate the words rolling off of my tongue. But they're true. And I'm fed up.

I'm sure Edwin has warned you. I've got this nasty high alcohol tolerance and very, very low tolerance for fools.

"Then sing for me, Sire. Show me what you can do."

"Is that not why you restrain me?" I lean forward as far as the metal allows. The collar around my neck digs into my skin. He steps back. His fingers splay, tips brushing the hilt of his sword. "So you're safe from me, Goldielocks?"

Within seconds, his sword is unsheathed and pressed under my chin. I lift my head. The crown slides to the side. Impossible to wear straight, the fickle thing.

"Do *not* call me that."

Edwin would've sang his name over and over again until it rang in his ears. I could if I wanted. I refrain.

"I should've known something was *fishy* with you, DeLuca. The deal with my king. Your performance. That girl, rather the alchemist's untamed daughter. The one you freed. What else were you planning to do as king?"

"Nothing. I only wanted her father to be returned."

His narrow eyes don't believe me.

"What? Not the answer you hoped for? Did you believe I planned to take over in my mother's name? The king expected that much. I don't want anything else this kingdom has to offer."

"You're not the monster you think you are."

I curl my lips into another smile. Though I do not share the same sharp fangs with my Mother, my smirk never fails to make others flinch and squirm, this knight being no exception. "Your actions beg to differ."

He scoffs.

"If I'm not a monster, let me walk free. Show me you're not scared."

Petrified, this knight pretends to stand his ground, convinced that he has the upper hand when it comes to his sword against my jaw. There's a waver in his taught expression. He *is* scared, but he can't show it. No, if the monarch deemed him a coward, unfit for the job, he'd let the young man go. There are plenty of aspiring warriors waiting to fill his place.

"The king wants your power." The knight's metal plated fists clench. His blade returns to its scabbard. "We cannot let you leave."

"I assumed that much."

"Your silver tongue will get you nowhere no matter how powerful you believe yourself to be, Siren."

▽△▽△

Daybreak or not, the cellar does not brighten. There is no first light. Though, more footsteps bustle above, and I ward off a few visitors, who take their leave as soon as I address them. I'll assume that this wretched day has already begun.

I'm guessing the king had more than enough confidence in my restraints, so I did not have the company of guards after that ridiculous knight departed for the evening. Or he knew that breaking out and leaving would put me in a rough position of treason and trial. Witch hunts are not on my agenda, nor will they ever be, no matter how much I wish to leave. The sea calls me. The shoreline. The waves. I never found my place on land. With this string of unfortunate events, I've unraveled my chance. The more I'm stuck, the more I understand Alouette. Her desire to leave. I know what's waiting beyond the castle walls, out at sea where we pirates set sail. The rhythm of the waves sings a familiar tune, almost like my mother's lullabies, which I had sworn to forget, but, alas, they're carved deep into my heart, as far as the sunken ships beneath the sea. In the dim dungeon, surrounded by the patter of foreign footsteps, I'm grateful her voice hasn't left me yet.

Though, I fear for what she has to say today.

This would be the perfect opportunity to snag revenge. To Calder, I'm a traitor. My mother could have proposed a peace treaty to cover up the possibility of starting a war. With Jayin on our backs, there's no chance I can fight my family's battle alongside the Le Rois'. I can only hope that the stars align for my mother to look beyond the crown on my head, if the late king allows for me to keep it through today, that is.

The knight returns, brandishing a pail that weighs his arms down. Water, my best guess is.

If my father had a hand in revealing my cards to the king, he surely told him about the fins and scales. As I pull my head back, the knight smirks.

"When you fail to comply, we dunk you."

"That should be my line." I spit.

Without hesitation, he hurls the pail my way. He then calls for another. There's no reaching to cover my face. At the very least, my point comes across, clear-cut. The knight takes in a few deep, shaking breaths before tossing the empty pail to the side. Scaled. Finned. I'm a monster.

▽△▽△

Shackles bind my wrists together, connected to a metal clamp around my neck. *Fit for a king,* I had told the knight. He ignored me. Several other guards accompany us as I'm led out of the dungeon. I find it difficult to imagine how many secret cellars this castle hides and how many others must be locked away. The alchemist had his own dwelling for goodness's sake.

Voices chatter above.

"Where is she?"

Idle footsteps patter.

"Has the Siren Queen arrived yet?"

They'd know if she were here. She's not a quiet visitor. Besides, as the sea's quote-unquote Siren Queen, my mother is not one to be overlooked. Her presence is enough to make the landlubbers of this kingdom tremble in their shined boots. My golden knight's eyes dart from me to the others around us and back to me. Even as a captive, and possibly a hostage, I'm another threat to be feared. I'll play that to my advantage. Still, their stares are difficult to shake. I'm not one of them. We all know it well. Alouette would say the same.

A few unintelligible shouts follow from above. Then everything falls silent, aside from our shuffling footsteps.

Queen Farida must be here.

Chapter 51

— The Alchemist —

Once, I had looked forward to the whimsicality of this world, all of the curses and charms and enchantments. Simply everything that Celestia had set out for us, her people, the mere commonfolk of realms. We all dream of spellcasting and faeries when we're young. I know I did. This is the Mirror Realm after all, a charming land where we may hope to find our happily ever after. Befriend a prince, take his hand. Spin through the halls of a castle, hold on tight. Raised by fairytales that are more true than not.

Sorting through the letters of the immortal tyrant Czar, the tales of my childhood have been unraveled to reveal an ugly tapestry bearing the face of reality. Not Celestia's face, though. I'd always imagine that she'd be the most beautiful girl any other entity has ever laid eyes upon. Perhaps hair of gold. Eyes, too. My father said we have taken on Her traits. In more ways than one.

To Her, magic is nothing. It's normal. In a way, it's science.

The Elixir of Life has no effect on Her. After all, Celestia is forever. We alchemists are mortal; our lives are fleeting, quick to slip through hands of the eternal like sand through an hourglass. Our time is short. A clock ticks behind me. The hands spin, never to stop. Would Celestia pause her continuum for me? For Atlas? For anyone?

I shake my head. My hands tense, nearly crumpling the delicate parchment, gifted to my father by the tyrant. Life immortal only appears to be a fleeting dream. He had roughly written that dozens upon dozens of times. There is nothing more taxing than watching the endless cycle of life and death. Some of his papers still had tear stains, which confirmed that he could still feel, although multiple accounts from others describe him as a ruthless leader, never breaking his straight face.

Under any circumstances, we cannot let Jayin of Vaughan get his hands on the Elixir. Celestia forbid.

Alas, how will we get Atlas back?

I slide my hands across the strewn papers, pulling them into a frayed pile of golden parchment and ink. *Aurora Borealis* has quite the beautiful desk in her captain's cabin. She's a lovely vessel, really. Much nicer than the merchant ship and that of the barnacle-covered pirate crew's. Oil lamps flicker to illuminate the dark, polished wood. A few candles burn, golden plates collecting the dripping wax. From the cabinet of bottles to the map pinned onto the wall, this place reeks of Atlas, although he is not here.

My hand rests on my forehead, as if I could pull out tangible thoughts with my fingertips. Celestia has yet to allow that.

"Don't forget he's a captain," someone advises. I peer up from the desk and my half-scattered mess.

My limbs go stiff. "DeLuca."

He leans on the doorframe, arms crossed, one foot planted on the wood beside him. Though, I'm surprised not to find a scowl smothering his face. He's rather thoughtful instead. "Dimitri is fine. I'm sure my son would call your father Thierry."

His eyes survey the room before he moves over to the desk. I lean back. I'm the reason his son is in the hands of Jayin.

"Finding something to leverage against Jayin, are you?" He picks up one of the letters. My whole body is stiff; there's no flinching to stop him. I might as well turn myself into a golden statue.

My nod feels more like a twitch, an uncomfortable, unwanted one at best.

"A young man like Jayin will not surrender without a suitable fight. I'm sure he plans to use Atlas against you."

DeLuca makes his rounds. He opens every drawer and cabinet, each nook and cranny. Still, my eyes trace his movements across the cabin. What could he possibly be looking for? I'll admit I'm too afraid to ask. If Dimitri DeLuca is anything like his son, he's a well versed question-dodger. I roll open one of the desk's drawers, careful not to make any noises to draw his attention. Pens. Pens? Quills, fountain, charcoal. They're sorted into different compartments. Little porcelain ink pots decorated with blue strokes are tucked away in the back, arranged in a straight line. The next drawer has maps and diagrams of all kinds, even worn blueprints of *Aurora Borealis*. Yet again, the items are flawlessly organized. A compass on each stack of papers holds them down, compressing the tawny pages.

The mutterings of Atlas' father drift through the air like a note in a bottle bobbing through the waves. His son had reorganized everything. A smirk creeps across my face, so I turn to hide it from DeLuca. Edwin had told me that the captain, and I quote, *melts* when he's around me, so I find a strange pleasure in learning about the other aspects of his life when I'm not around. Call these bits and pieces scraps of the tapestry we call Atlas DeLuca, woven from bits of aquamarine sea glass and golden threads and now trims of ermine fur.

"I believe there are other paths to immortality than your Elixir." The former captain opens Atlas' cabinet and pulls out a bottle, accompanied by one glass. He knows I don't drink. I raise my brows for him to continue. "The DeLuca name is not going away any time soon. In my youth, my name was on the tongue of every sailor across the seven seas." He pops the cork, and the bottle glugs while he drains it. "Atlas is something else. Sailors will pass down the story of a captain turned king for generations."

My attention moves from his hands to his eyes. "Are you going to propose that to Jayin? So that he becomes an epic instead of a living relic?"

"A relic, you say?"

"Like Czar of Apthnorath. He's history in the flesh."

"Let me guess. A man who took your Elixir."

I nod while my eyes trace to the stack of his letters. "Perhaps his testimony will turn Jayin away."

DeLuca shakes his head. "Words will not make him back down—not when Man is blinded by power."

"His eyes are opened once tormented by its influence," I mutter in return. Poor Czar. He had to figure that out the difficult way. One that tore away his humanity.

"Does that come from him or you?"

Him? Czar? My father? Or me?

A confused almost-laugh, slips. "Me?" I go to deny the claim. I can't. I can't? I can't. My jaw hangs, swaying somewhere in the gallows where they could've killed me. On that rickety plank where I should've died.

For what reason? Power.

I stare down at my hands, the tattoos crawling across my skin. Light pouring from the window behind, my shadow darkens the years of knowledge and calluses and bloodshed. A life I spent hiding, running, fighting for another breath.

DeLuca lifts a little jewelry box. "If you had the chance, would you change anything? Would you be happier without those marks? Would you forsake power for…"

He leaves it open ended. Peace? Happiness? Safety? A real home?

Without alchemy, I could've just been a common girl. One who dreamed of faeries like any other, lost in the pages of storybooks. Delusional. Longing for something more. One who looked out at the sea and imagined mermaids, unaware of their nasty demeanor. Shut in the dark so she cannot fear what is revealed when light comes flooding in. A smile on her face. Father to her side. Perhaps she'd hold a regular boy's hand with no reason to hide herself. Her face wouldn't be on Wanted posters; no bounty would burden her shoulders. There'd be no walking planks or heists. No thievery. There wouldn't be a boy who'd push his life aside for her. No one like Atlas.

No one like me.

The alchemist's daughter would be no one at all. Another face in the crowd. These runes, the scars and scabs and star-charts, they're all a part of who I am. Elements in a compound.

Do I regret my actions? More often than not. But they've all led me here. And I'm okay with that. Celestia knows what she's doing.

With the shake of my head, I give him a delayed verdict. "I would never."

"Spoken like your father." DeLuca opens the box and pulls out a ring. "Now," he turns to me, "remember all you have to lose when you face Jayin."

I nod. "R-right."

He sets the pearl ring, crowned with gold, on the desk in front of me. "You might want this."

"Is it like the necklace?" I reach for my neck, fingers pressing against the medallions against my collarbone. I kept the necklace Atlas had given me the last time we were in his cabin.

"As in enchanted? Yes. Farida aimed for this to resist a siren's song."

I pick up the ring and slide it onto my finger. It loosely circles my index, a little big. DeLuca flinches. With my other hand, I press against the metal. His narrow eyes watch as I mold the solid material, as if it were soft clay. "Is it yours?"

"Long ago, it was." He muses, a little enchanted spark gleams in his eyes. Funny, how he must love Farida. "She gifted me many things."

He returns to scavenging about his old cabin. His quiet hums are enough to fill the salty air between us. His rough voice, worn down from years of shouts and commands, has rusted.

> *"Dimitri, Dimitri,*
> *sailor of the sea.*
> *To fall in love with a siren,*
> *filled with much glee.*
> *Don't let his story,*
> *don't let his story*
> *happen to me."*

Chapter 52

— The Siren —

THE UPTIGHT KNIGHT is as stiff as his scabbard. I let myself relax. My mother liked Alouette. She'll understand. Besides, while I'm the one chained, her real enemy will be as clear as a ship's Jolly Roger. It's the king. The ones unwilling to bend, out of fear that they may break. Now it's their intent to push until I reach my breaking point. I won't give them that pleasure.

The blades of their spears pierce my back, jabbing into my shoulder blades to inch me forward. When I glance over my shoulder, the guards all advert their gazes or recoil, as if I were a hostile beast planning to turn on them and eat them alive. It's a shame they did not react the same way to the former king. For none of them know true hostility, raw savagery. Unyielding pirates who push innocents off of planks. The dozens of men, cutlasses piercing their hearts in a fruitless battle. The many lives lost out at sea, under the false promise of Neverland and wealth. The plunder is never worth the cost, not if it's life.

Another guard, clad in shimmering armor carved with swirling waves, brandishes another set of chains, which she uses to rebind my wrists. A new silver collar clamps around my neck. A chain links them. She unshealths a dagger, which had been hidden between the intricate plates and mail, and runs it along the scales on my jaw, careful not to draw blood. Her fiery gaze meets mine.

"Shame how such a good face had to go to waste." She rests the tip of her blade on my throat.

"Your words, not mine, Mademoiselle."

She scoffs. Her dagger lowers and returns to its hiding place. A golden bullet replaces it in her palm. "When I give you the sign, you come with me, Siren."

My jaw tightens. She's one of Jayin's. What dealings does he have with the king? I mask my concern with a silent glare. As she turns to leave, the royal guards return to proding.

I quicken my pace. There's a good chance we're going to face the wrath or disappointment of the Siren Queen. Neither are pretty coming from my mother.

▽△▽△

I'm shoved onto the throne, atop a dais as if I were a display. My mother is standing in the doorway, which looks to be miles across the grand hall, between the bobbing heads of civilians, up on their toes to see either of us. She's the monstress of legends—the Siren Queen. Here, she stands in a dress as white as the pearls that encircle her neck. Her hair tumbles down to her waist, black as tar. The golden-haired knight readies his sword. In case I stand? Who knows? Who cares, really?

My mother lifts her head, that dark gaze of hers rising to the dais. Should she make peace or threaten to decapitate one of us, the choice is all hers, and I have no idea which path she'll take. Pop the cork on all of this? Release the ship, bobbing in this glass bottle on display? One crack and all the pent-up water will come gushing out.

That's until someone rasps, "What are you doing!?"

A ripple slides through the people. Guards' shining helmets move to restrain a young man. He looks like the tavern's barkeep boy.

"Ruth?" I flinch forward.

The knight puts his blade to my throat. Again? If his attention were where it should be, he'd be faced with my mother's piercing stare. Instead he meets mine.

The taverner shoves armored knights away, and even his fellow civilians, to clear a path. "He's not a bad guy! Let him go!"

A few join his shouts.

The guards march.

I push onto my feet. "Wait! Stop!" I reach for Ruth. The knight at my side pursues.

With a quick turn, I give him a boot to the gut. He stumbles back a few paces, off the dais.

"Stop!" I'm stepping down.

They're not obeying?

"Listen!"

I push off of shoulders and trembling bodies.

Ruth's eyes meet mine. His bloodied lips pull at the edges. Some shout my name while others cry to attack. No. Stop.

"*Stop!*"

Not even a blade rattles on the ground. Stuck in time, they all stare. Not a drop of blood rolls down the bartender's face. But his eyes are so wide. They all are. I back away, weaving through the room of civilians, still as statues. Not even my mother has moved. There's no telling how long this enchantment will hold them.

A blur in the doorway draws me back to reality. The female knight, presumably one of Jayin's, waits for me, hands over her ears as she seems to pull little plugs out. Jayin must have prepared her, knowing that a siren's spell only works if others can hear the command. She nods. The signal? Over my shoulder, I take one last look at the people I should have protected, the ones I was never meant to lead.

If I said that I were sorry, would it even reach their ears?

Besides, it doesn't matter anymore.

There's no returning now. I will defend my crew, and if it means dishonoring both the crown and myself, then so be it.

Chapter 53

— The Thief —

I PACE.

And pace.

And pace.

Look, some of us need to walk it off when we're stressed. But on a ship there's not much space. Can you blame me!? I sure wouldn't. Thanks for the consideration or lack thereof.

Jayin should be here any minute now.

I puff out my chest with a deep inhale. I'm not ready to let go. Not yet, that is. My gaze finds itself on the horizon. Scanning, always. First watch was mine. So was second. And third.

The sun is setting. Where is he? If Jayin wants the alchemist, this is his only shot. That man has buckets of bullets, but I've got the Le Rois family.

"Avast ye!" Jean-Jacques calls from the helm. I run up to meet him.

He points to a merchant ship approaching ours. It must be Jayin. That scum. Dimitri joins us as well and finds a place right behind me. His hand grips my shoulder. He has to be at least a little scared. I'm the son he never had. Nor the one he wanted. It's fine. It's all going to be alright.

Swallowing my pride, I know what he expects, for if one of us is to die, me it must be. My life should be the one on the line. Not the captain's. Not even Alouette's. Sliding away from DeLuca's grasp, I inch over to the rail and look along the side of *Boreas* to find the alchemist's daughter, fingers kneaded together. Dots on her fingers glow in twilight's misty glow. Her lips are pulled in, brows frowned.

"I won't let you down," are my last infamous words.

▽△▽△

A plank slams.

There's one board connecting our ships acting as an unsecure bridge. My crewmates light oil candles among the port and starboard. I'd rather be in the dark, unable to see their expressions—from that gnarly greenish queasy to knotted in frustration. The folks on Jayin's ship call. A lone gunshot fired into the abyssal night sky silences the dozens of men running around. A figure appears on the plank. Then follows a glittering silver muzzle that stares me down.

Great!

"Jayin!" I extend my arms wide to greet him. He returns a sly smile, teeth bared in the moonlight. Somewhere on his ship looms my captain, either in control of Jayin's crew or held at gunpoint for him to comply. Blue eyes flash. That's him! It has to be.

Thierry steps up beside me. I nudge him as a signal to get back, after all, I was the one who made this deal in the first place. He won't budge. Oh, come on! I mutter his name.

Jayin steps down from the wooden plank. My crew takes a collective pace back. Of course, Alouette isn't an official part of the team, so she stands her ground. Pirates are cowards!

I approach Jayin with my arms held high in surrender. Atlas' blood must be boiling. "So, you've got me Capt'n?"

"I want the girl."

Straight to the point, what a demand from Jayin. I take a sharp breath in. The evening air is crisp and bitter. Just how I like it.

And then Thierry makes his move. "You will *not* take her." He marches up to Jayin and displaces me in the process, forcing me to take a few stumbling steps back. Jacques frowns my way. With a crooked smile is all I can reply.

Jayin crosses his arms while his attention slides back to his ship, but, more precisely, Atlas DeLuca. With a scowl, he embraces his mother's dramatic flair. The oil lamps really illuminate the gnarly scar on his face.

Jayin's personal guard is on his back. Atlas quickly turns his head and snaps at them. I can't begin to imagine the threats he's been holding over their heads.

Alongside the reflection of flickering wicks, there's a weakness in his eyes when he turns back to Jayin. With a blink, it's gone.

"Alouette," Atlas says.

Alouette recoils, gritting her teeth. She knows what's next.

"*Alouette*," Atlas *sings*. His gaze traces the plank, the deck, the crew, all the way to the alchemist's daughter. This isn't good. No. Not at all.

Thierry's jaw tightens. Within seconds of his fists clenching, he throws a punch Jayin's way. That weasel dodges. Lucky bastard. If the alchemist had gotten him with his mechanical gauntlet, maybe we would've gotten out of this. Jayin grabs the alchemist's forearm and twists it behind his back. He pushes Thierry to the edge of the ship. The pendant around his neck—the Elixir—sways off of the railing. With him restrained, Jayin points his gun back at me. Shouts resound.

Then Alouette yells, "Stop!"

If I'm not mistaken, all of the small amber flames lining our ships falter with her outcry.

Jayin calls for Atlas. His guards inch closer to my captain.

"*Alouette.*"

She turns to his beckon.

"No!" I reach out to her, but my fingertips don't even come close to grabbing her wrist.

"Resist any further and I will not hesitate." Jayin's pistol clicks. The safety? He was bluffing before. Now this young man means business.

Alouette is already walking the plank between our ships. No. Her golden eyes peer down at the black waves below. She hesitates, her fingers curling back, balling into strained fists.

"*Gentille Alouette.*"

Atlas extends his hand to help her down, for a brief moment, looking like a fine gentleman instead of a pirate captain. Her splayed fingers tremble as they press against his.

No enchantment masks her fear.

She's not under his trance, is she?

Chapter 54

— The Alchemist —

"Je te plumerai."

His hand braces the back of my head as the other pulls me into his arms. I press my palms against the buttons of his jacket. We can't stay like this forever, no not in this cowering way; I need to push away.

His voice fades to a whisper, sharp in my ear. "Does Edwin have a plan?"

"You don't?"

"Do you?"

I hold my tongue.

He shakes his head. "You have to go."

"No."

I lift my hand so he can see Dimitri's ring. Atlas holds my wrist. He can sing as much as he'd like without his siren song influencing me.

"We pretend Jayin's plan is playing out?" He keeps his voice low. Occasionally, his eyes dart to Jayin, who "He's going to come back over once he gets Edwin and your father to surrender. And if they don't…"

"And?"

"He'll bargain for the Elixir of Life. Which makes him invincible, doesn't it?"

"Immortal."

"All the same. If we can't kill him, the blood of all my men will taint this sea."

"So we kill him before he can kill us?"

"Not yet." He draws me closer and leans down, just as he did at the masquerade. I don't like how full-circle this is coming. His narrow eyes watch Edwin draw his dagger to face Jayin. My father calls upon Celestia. A palisade of spires protrude from *Aurora Borealis'* deck. Atlas twitches. She's his jewel. Jayin is pushed back to her plank. He scrambles to retreat. We'll get him once he steps foot on this ship!

"Wait." Atlas bares his teeth.

Even if he were to use magic to command me, it wouldn't work.

"Now is our chance." I squirm in an attempt to release myself from his grasp. His brows furrow. He doesn't think this is a good idea, but this is an opening! And only Celestia knows if it'll be our only one.

Jayin flees. Arms extended, his guards help him down from the plank. He calls for Atlas, a new gravel in his voice, burnt by the salt of the sea. Too bad I've got other plans. I break free from Atlas. My fingers skim the deck. Spikes shoot toward him. I'll end this wretched man! Let him meet Celestia, for he cannot face Her by himself. Bullet holes riddle the deck around me. Some guards break off and run for Atlas.

"*Stand down*!" All stop. A few collapse. Atlas slides over and places a hand on my back. He reminds, "I can't hold them forever."

The captain only has a limited extent of control over his siren song.

Footsteps pound toward us. "I can!" Edwin brandishes his dagger. My father readies a wooden rod he crafted out of the ship's deck. Together, they knock aside a few of Jayin's crew. Granted they're enchanted, the men go down without a fight.

Atlas rips a cutlass from one of the fallen fighters. Jayin's jacket flutters in the breeze as I approach. That wretched man aims the pistol at me, bloodshot eyes pinned on mine.

"Join me or your father dies."

The captain calls my name. His voice is drowned by the blood pulsing through my ears, my limbs, my whole body. My father was forced into hiding because of him, and I've made a fool of myself running from bad men who thirst for power.

"I won't miss again!" His gaze goes to Edwin and Atlas. Just what happened between them!?

Jayin's finger trembles, right on the trigger. One twitch and—

Atlas has pushed on my shoulder, sending me back as he faces Jayin, before a shot resounds through the night.

Chapter 55

— The Thief —

IT SHOULD HAVE been me!

It should have been me!

It should have been me!

"Captain!" The words burn my throat. Sear my heart. Tear me apart.

Chapter 56

— The Alchemist —

As I SAID, pirates are nasty fellows. People die by their hands every day! But the captain! He's the last person I expected to—Celestia damn it all!

I ran in too early. I should've listened to him. We should've waited for Jayin to let his guard down.

Now it's Atlas! He—*he's*—

I trip and tumble, onto my knees. I reach for his face, splattered with blood. His lashes twitch, clinging to the hanging threads of his life, torn apart by no one other than me. I hoist him up and prop his head on my forearm. His lips pull back, fingers clutching his soaked jacket.

"The Elixir of Life!" I wail. My father is frozen. He must have the same ice splicing his veins. This is our fault. Not his. And he's going to die because of it. "*Please!*"

My voice doesn't even sound like mine anymore. It cracks and scratches and breaks until there's nothing left but incoherent sobs.

My father clutches the vial. Jayin's eyes flash. My father sends an elbow into his gut. Dimitri shoves him over the bow. A deep kerplunk drowns out his resounding scream.

Upon turning back to me, the alchemist I've always looked up to stares into the dead of night, his hand clasped around the Elixir of Life, his life's work. Our future studies and prospects flash before his eyes, reflected in his gaze like Celestia's stars above. With a quick tug, he breaks the chain around his neck and hurls it my way.

I extend my arm to catch it. The vial slips between my fingertips. It hits the deck. The glass shatters. So do I.

"No!"

I drag my fingers through the spilling, pooling elixir. With my stained fingers. I rub what little is left on Atlas' wound. This has to work. If it can grant immortality, maybe it can heal, too. *Please.*

Celesia, if you're there—

Have mercy.

Edwin kneels beside me and does the same. We lap up the Elixir and lather it on Atlas.

No. His face is losing color.

"Don't die on me." Everything trembles. Except for him. No, he's too still. Slowly, Atlas reaches for my cheek. I lean into his bloody palm.

His eyes threaten to shut. His lips part. "I knew you weren't a monster, Alouette."

"Shut up!" Edwin stumbles over to hush him. "Save it for later!" He lands with a dull thud.

There may not be a later. I can't say that. I can't say anything. I'm choking on my own tears, rasping to snag a breath.

"You're afraid…" Atlas half-smiles at the two of us.

Edwin scrapes up the remainder of the elixir, mixed with blood and stained with tears, he slaps his captain on the chest.

The captain's head lulls. "...of losing."

Edwin riles, rubbing his glossy eyes. "We're not losing you. Ever!"

His hands ball into fists. I lay Atlas back down. Edwin grabs Atlas' shoulder and shakes. And shakes. And shakes.

Then stops.

Edwin's chest heaves. He blinks, unable to hold back the flood of dammed, damned tears. He drags a hand across his face, smearing his fear with his beloved captain's blood. No. He was more than a captain. A friend. A brother. Family. For a moment, that's what we felt like. Family.

And we're losing again.

A soft glow illuminates his face. And then my hands. Where is it coming from? Edwin and I look to Atlas. His face twitches. His wound is...glowing?

"The Elixir," Edwin gasps.

"It can heal!" I cry.

Chapter 57

— The Thief —

I TOLD YOU we weren't going to lose him! I had no doubt, I swear! I swear, but not on my captain's very life. Not the time? Okay.

Atlas braces himself and sits up. He winces as he reaches for the bullet wound, right in the center of his chest, knowing well that he should be dead.

"Jayin," is his first word. Rather, name.

I cock my head to the side. *Really?* "Jayin?"

"Where is he?" My captain turns to me.

"In the sea."

"Lower a lifeboat."

"What?"

"You heard me. Lower one of his lifeboats."

"Aye!" I call for our crew to follow his orders. Atlas stands. I don't quite know how. If I ever get shot, you can just leave me on the ground, alright?

Alouette reaches for him, placing a hand on his arm. "Atlas, are you sure? You, well—" She's all choked up on her own words, and even I wouldn't know what to say if I were in her place.

"I need to remind him as to why you don't mess with the DeLuca's crew." He looks from Alouette to me. His lips pull into a crooked, bloodied smile.

"Ya hear that, Game Bird? You're one of us now."

Jean-Jacques calls from across the deck, an oil lamp raised to illuminate his face and that of the crewmates around him. The lifeboat is ready.

I unsheath my dagger and present it to Captain Atlas. He stares for a moment, as still as the night. It's the same blade I've kept all these years, the one that gave him his defining scar. His gloved hand reaches for the worn grip. His eyes meet mine, for some kind of last-minute confirmation. "I won't lose it."

"I'd be more concerned if we lost you." I laugh it off with an inappropriate snicker. "Go show him who's boss around here, Capt'n."

Alouette nods, followed by a two-fingered salute.

We pull one last toothy smile out of Atlas before he turns away. The captain straightens his jacket and brushes loose strands of hair from his eyes. He and the quartermaster share a quick nod before preparing the rowboat.

Chapter 58

— The Siren —

Off the side of the ship, there are pulleys and ropes. In these waters, it's better to be safe than sorry, better to have a lifeboat than not. Jacques salutes me before I'm lowered into the water.

Jayin couldn't have made it too far. If he's a seafarer, he's prepared to tread water until rescued or until he meets his demise. Man will cling to every last second of his life if there's a glimmer of hope, an alluring thought that, maybe, he'd be saved. I set Jaque's lantern down and brace myself. The small boat creaks as the waves rock the vessel. Shouts and calls from above fade into the misty night. Picking up an oar, I call for Jayin. The rowboat drifts on its own.

"Jayin!"

There's a splash. Amidst the creeping fog, I see a head bobbing on the surface not too far away. I push the vessel toward him.

"Thank goodness!" his drowned voice exclaims. He doesn't realize it's me, does he? "Did you secure the Elixir?"

I hold my tongue until he approaches. Hands grab onto the side and offset the vessel's balance. His head pops up over the side, drenched hair flopping across his face. The moment we lock eyes, he dips back into the water. I lean over the side and grab his wrist. He thrashes. I don't let go. Out of breath and energy, he settles.

"Y-you're—" His eyes dart across me, from my face to where there was once a bullet.

"Alive?"

His frantic nods follow.

"The Elixir," is my short explanation.

"And after that," his brows furrow, creasing down on his glassy eyes, that intense gaze of his watered down by guilt, "you're saving me?"

"No man deserves to drown at sea." I shake my head while I help hoist Jayin into the lifeboat. He coughs and wheezes. Water must've gotten in his lungs. A long and painful death, drowning is. And in vain, too. Jayin doesn't look too much older than me, so he's still got time to turn his life around.

"Th-thank—"

"There's no need for gratitude. You have two options."

He jerks his head back. His stare falls on Edwin's dagger, which I lift to point at my enemy.

"W-what?" He sinks into the wood, almost knocking over the lantern. I stand above the deflated Jayin.

"You have attempted to kill me not once, but twice. A bold move. Not a wise one. You may come back to my kingdom anytime, but I'll have a warrant out for your arrest, along with a generous bounty."

"No…" he shakes his head, eyes wide in disbelief. A young man with such pride would've never planned for his downfall. I had once been the same way.

I get down beside him and press Edwin's dagger against his throat, careful not to apply enough pressure to draw blood, but just enough to remind him that I could if I wanted. "Keep your distance and keep your freedom." I lean to whisper in his ear, sure to make my words crisp and clear. "You will never lay hands on Alouette or her father *ever* again. They're part of my crew, under my protection. The Le Rois alchemists will be a distant memory to you."

"B-but if I go home empty handed," he blubbers. Tears bubble around his eyes, mixed with saltwater and sorrow. The rest of his statement dissolves out at sea to be taken away by the currents.

I lean in closer. "Then drift where no one will find you."

Jittery, he nods. I pull back. He gasps for breath and brings his hand to his neck. His fingertips drag against where the blade one was.

"As I said, no one deserves to drown at sea, but not everyone deserves to keep their life, either."

I pick up the oars, sit back, and ease the lifeboat toward the ship.

"I'll let your crew know to sail back home. For all they know, you were thrown overboard and met your demise," I hum. Jayin rights himself and sits back up.

He skeptically pulls his head back a little. "Why are you doing this?"

"Take this as your second chance. A blank slate to fix anything you please."

▽△▽△

With Edwin's dagger I sever the ropes, making sure the ends are nice and frayed, beyond repair. Not my ship. Not my problem. I reach up for one of the loose ends and hoist myself up onto Jayin's ship. He looks up, eyes wide and jaw agape.

"This never happened," I mutter. In a little frenzy, he nods back. I trace the side of the ship, up to the blurred lights above. The fog is too thick for them to see me.

"Aye, Jacques!" I call.

"Shouldn't you be calling on me!?" Edwin shouts. I should've expected nothing less from him. I plant my feet on the side of the ship and use the rope to climb up.

"Pull the rope!"

My crew obliges. Once I've reached the top, Edwin grabs my arms and yanks me over the rail. Alouette nudges him as I push myself onto my feet.

Jayin's crew turns to me. Some have straight faces, others have their brows frowned. "Chart a course for your homeland. I wish never to see the likes of your bunch again."

Thierry and my father, bottle-in-hand, wait on *Aurora Borealis*. He offers me the presumably celebratory wine. Or perhaps he wouldn't be able to face my death sober. Either way, I shake my head no. After the last of my men, Edwin and Jean-Jacques, have rejoined us, we remove the plank.

Edwin sticks a tongue out at the crew as they sail away. Alouette snickers at him before walking my way. Her lips pull back before her eyes burst with tears.

"I'm so sorry. Y-you almost died." She buries her head in her hands, emotions drowned by her heart.

"I know." I approach her. "But you—and Edwin—saved me, didn't you?"

She parts her fingers and stares at me from beneath those tattooed symbols of hers. I brush a few curls out of her face.

"Yeah, you owe us big time for saving you!" Edwin tromps over, as usual.

"Thank Celestia." Alouette shakes her head, lowering her arms and folding them in front of her chest.

Edwin meets my gaze and tilts his head toward her, urging me to make a move. That fool.

"No, Alouette. Thank *you*."

Chapter 59

— The Alchemist —

THE MISTY MORNING fit like a glove, as they say. Like, really, the townsfolk would not stop alluding to that. I kid you not. The ballads and poems of late have rubbed off on them, not to mention the over-romanticized newspapers following Atlas DeLuca the new heir's trail. Oh! Not to forget the striking headline that their former king, supposedly, had a heart attack and passed away. I'm guessing that Celestia planned on only keeping him alive to protect my father, so he would not be lost to time in that dungeon. Back to my point, as soon as we reached this awful port, Atlas had nearly jumped off the ship and scurried across the docks, followed by Edwin with a crown and myself, of course. We're now a trinity of sorts, bound by amended lies and spilled blood, and *lots* of each. I was the one to spot them first, Calder and the princess sitting on the ledge of a wishing fountain. Black lines that sparkled with pink glitter ran down the poor girl's face. There was a tinge of sadness in my heart, for I had known how she felt. The ache of knowing you'll never be by a father's side again. The king would never be able to pass down all of his stories or even be there to watch her grow as a young lady. Calder, despite his oddly dismissive demeanor, had an arm wrapped tight around her, and the princess even leaned her head on his shoulder. Edwin, as anyone would expect, gave Atlas and I a smug look.

That's until the crowd came pouring through the streets, rushing in from every crevice like a flash flood. Many bowed their heads; a few took a knee. This captain was their king, after all. Without the former one pulling hidden strings, Atlas was free to do with the kingdom as he pleased. Edwin handed him a crown, although his captain never figured out how to wear that stupid heap of gold without it being crooked. Some of us were never meant to be shrouded in jewels. And that's okay.

Atlas stared down at the gold circlet with a flinch of hesitation. His attention went right to Calder. His emerald green eyes swelled with mostly surprise and a hint of delight.

The acting king sank to one knee before the fountain, crown held high.

And just like that, the walled city found its new leader.

Was it a good choice on Atlas' part? Only time will tell. But the princess had no opposition, so I'm going to say more good than not.

▽△▽△

Luckily, that was all this morning's shenanigans. The fog has packed all its dread and left. Now my father stands to my right, his arm around my shoulder. The sunset gleams gold, as it should. The waves sparkle and reflect the orange clouds. I barely even notice how thick and salty the sea's breeze is anymore. Even as it scrapes against my skin, rushing inland, I keep my feet planted on the dock. *Aurora Borealis'* crew scrambles around her captain and his father. Shouting out supplies and taking stock with a feather quill, Edwin drags a list that rivals his height. He calls everyone a scallywag, if not a scurvy dog, at least once in the process.

I never thought I'd hear my father ask, "So, you'll be going?"

Not once did my younger self ever consider the thought of leaving the nest. Perhaps it's time to spread my wings and take flight.

I take in the sea one more time, giving Celestia the chance to tell me if this is the right choice. My *mal de mer* is no more, and I'd miss my new friends, my newfound family, if I stayed back.

"Would you come?" I press my hand against his. If I squeeze tight enough, maybe I'll be able to hold on to it all. My father. Atlas and his crew.

He shakes his head. *No.*

"But I'll be here for you. Celestia will be with you. She always has been." His fingers rub against my shoulder.

My lips tug at the edges, and the bridge of my nose begins to sting. "I-I'll send letters." My voice cracks, so do my dammed tears. I think of Czar. If he can pass on messages from another realm, surely, I'll be able to get a paper across the sea.

"Looking forward to them." He gives me a pat on the back. I look over at him in case it is the last time we're together. His leather jacket, covered in patchwork, flaps in the breeze. Wrinkles crease, molded to his bittersweet smile. Silver and gold streak his brown hair. One day, I know it'll turn to gray and white. That goes for us all.

I nestle myself into his arms for one last goodbye hug. He holds me tight and lifts my feet off the ground as he did when I was a kid.

"Okay, okay, that's enough."

We share a quick, bittersweet laugh.

Meanwhile, Atlas and Edwin shuffle the rest of their crew onto the ship with the aid of Jean-Jacques. Some cheer with bottles-in-hand. I'd be celebrating too if I had been a pirate stuck in a harbor for far too long. Eventually, the captain and boatswain make their way over.

"Aye, Game Bird! Ya comin'?" Edwin calls with a salute.

Atlas, without a word, holds his hand out to me. I reach to take it.

We both look to my father, whose smile is the final seal of approval.

The captain's grin creeps through his usual serious facade. His grip is firm. We're not letting go. *Ever.*

"Well, here's your official welcome to the *Aurora Borealis.*"

Epilogue

— The Alchemist —

SITTING ALONG A polished bar, once again. How do we end up circling back to this place every time? Can't pirates find a new hangout spot? Myself included. Yet there's something alluring about the rows of comrades and bronze bottles under an array of amber lights, flames flickering in the hazy night. Not to mention the bard and occasional bar fight. These ballads and stories have been getting out of hand around the ports lately. Regarding the former king, the *former* former king, and the new one, of course. The thought of mermaids and sirens and enchantments sounds like nothing less than a far-fetched fairytale, but, really, it's our reality.

For decades they'll tell tales of the captain who befriended a siren, a ruby-eyed thief who could pickpocket any passerby, the immortal tyrant's penpal, and the girl who used a spectacular elixir to save a pirate's life. Then, again, we can't forget the pirate who became a king, but not *the* pirate king.

I look over at my companions. From Atlas' slightly slurred speech to Edwin's mocking smile, I don't really think we're all that they chalk us up to be.

For now, you can call us the alchemist, the siren, and the thief.

ANOTHER ADVENTURE! WELL, this isn't quite the end for the alchemist, the siren, and the thief! A sequel, you're asking. Not quite. But, but, but you'll catch them in my next few books!

Anyway, thanks for sticking with these gremlins until the very end of their messy adventure…and flipping the page to find these often skipped-over acknowledgements. As the kids say, it's been a long time comin' and sometimes three-hundred pages can be rather intimidating, granted many of us have classes, work, and general human duties. Shame we can't run around, jumping from ship to ship as they do in fantasy novels.

First, we'll thank Edwin. This book would not be the same without our dearest boatswain and his lack of restraint. I'm sorry if he called you a baby. You likely deserved it. Just kidding!

Shoutout to the circulation staff and all the lovely folks at Lewes Public Library. Thank you for putting up with me and whatever rants stemmed from TATS&TT. Ama, I'm looking at you. You're the best.

Also, a round of applause for my mom. *I don't hear you clapping.* She's my champion and cheerleader rolled into one. Also the best.

Another thank you to all of the people whose hands touched this book, from telling me I spelled a word awfully wrong, or advising me to rewrite an equally terrible scene. (Boy, did you get spared as readers.) Damian, you're a real one for all your commentary. This sounds so cheesy, but this book would not be where it is without your feedback!

Sadly, I have to pull this back to my highschool, from which I have been recently released. I probably won't ever understand teenagers, and we won't come close to comprehending what vicious monsters we are. Fearless, fierce. But it's all a farce. We're a little bit broken, beaten down, whether by ourselves or others. Players, we are and always will be. To all the phonies out there, I see you, and Holden Caulfield does, too.

And to the folks who wouldn't let a quiet art girl stand in their spotlight, my name is on a 300-page book and yours is not.

All snarky comments aside, the emotions in this book wouldn't be running so high without betrayals and senior year crushes. A wild ride I wouldn't recommend, really.

And thank you, Black Sheep Literary Management for holding my hand through the trenches of marketing and publicity. It's a miracle to think this book is in someone's hand right now!

Goodwin, Ogre, benjj\, Peach Jam/Dustin Bates, and anyone else I missed your support never wavers and I can't thank you enough. To the cast of *Fight Pub*, you'll always be my muse. Shoutout to my brother for being my personal—granted begrudging—photographer, and to the rest of my family for always sticking with me.

And, I know, you're wondering. Where's my shoutout as a reader?

Here it is: Thank you, reader!

About the Author

Mia Dorsch is an artistic author. Dreaming of whimsical lands, she brings out-of-this-world ideas to life. You can find her spending her days with earbuds plugged in and lost to lyrics as she navigates fantastical realms. When she's not daydreaming with music, you can find her behind the circulation desk at Lewes Public Library or curled up somewhere, pen or book in-hand. Here, she's playing hooky with her brother, A.K.A. her awesome photographer! *The Alchemist, the Siren, and the Thief* is her third novel, and she'd much rather spend her time aboard the *Aurora Borealis* than sit in class.

More by Mia

Out Now!

Matthew Eversen and the Wild Space Goose Chase

▽⟁⩑△

Threads of Amends

▽⟁⩑△

Czar: Testimony No. 1

Stay Tuned For...

Apthnorath

▽⟁⩑△

Wayfinder

▽⟁⩑△

Trailblazer